Easier Said Than Done

a novel by Nikki Woods

BROWN GIRLS PUBLISHING

Houston, Texas * Washington, D.C.

D0238369

This book is a work of fiction. Names, characters, places and incidents are products of the author's imagination or are used fictitiously. Any resemblance to actual events or locales or persons, living, dead, or somewhere in between, is entirely coincidental

Brown Girls Publishing, LLC
www.browngirlspublishing.com

Easier Said Than Done © 2014 by Nikki Woods
ISBN: 978-0-9915322-4-7

First Brown Girls Publishing LLC trade printing March 2014

Cover designed by: J. L. Woodson www.jlwoodson.com
Interior design by: Lissa Woodson www.macrompg.com

Manufactured and Printed in the United States of America

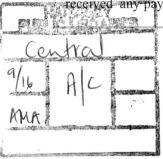

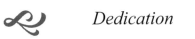 *Dedication*

For Mama Mae

Acknowledgements

I send abounding love to my mother, my father, my sister and my two amazing sons—Tyler and Willis. You make everything worth it.

Many thanks to Victoria Christopher Murray, ReShonda Tate Billingsley and Lissa Woodson (Naleighna Kai) for the gift of a second chance.

It would be impossible to name everyone but I am surrounded by a group of strong, talented, prayerful women who alternate as teachers, supporters and drinking buddies— not necessarily in that order. The lessons I have learned are priceless.

A special fist-bump to Mary Boyce—who constantly has her head down on my behalf.

I am grateful.

Chapter 1

Nothing would be the same again. That I knew for sure, though the uncertainty of what exactly that meant sloshed inside of me as I unlocked the door to my office and quietly asked my mother for guidance.

Instantaneously, a peace settled in my soul, just as I knew it would; but the question marks still pricked at my brain.

Three hours later, my secretary alerted me via the intercom that I had a phone call and the feelings of unrest surged again. I pushed the Talk button.

"Kingston speaking," I said.

"Job well done, Kingston." The booming voice filled the room, seeping like honey from the gray and black state-of-the-art speakerphone. It slowly spread to each corner in my small office and coated the dreary olive-green walls with its rich bass.

"Thanks, Mr. Mansini." I relaxed, picking up the receiver to welcome the good news from my boss. Adjusting my nylon-clad leg, I leaned further over my solid oak desk. I didn't want to miss a word. The phone cord didn't stretch enough to allow me to sit comfortably in the chair and still be heard above the rumble of the twenty-year-old furnace. That, combined with the squeaky whirl of the ceiling fan, was causing me to come dangerously close to losing my mind.

So, I jotted a note for the receptionist, Jonetta, to write up yet another work order for the maintenance man/janitor, Mr. Carter, to replace the current phone cord with a longer one and apply some WD-40 to the fan. Of course, the chances of this request not joining the ten previous requests—crumpled and forgotten in the round metal garbage can within minutes of receipt—were slim to none.

Since he was inherited when the building lease was signed, I had resigned myself to working with Carter—'Just Carter, Ma'am; no Mister,' as he had reminded me more than once—and all that came with him no matter how many times I had to re-clean the office the next morning. But, Carter always managed to show up on time. Drudging through the door at five o'clock on the dot, pushing an ancient wooden broom with matted bristles, his torn knit cap pulled down low on his furrowed forehead, a wad of tobacco shoved messily into the side of his mouth, and a perpetual smirk slashed across an otherwise handsome face.

I looked longingly at my misplaced Shrimp Caesar salad with garlic croutons. One didn't make the head of the company one worked for leave a message, so I pushed my half-empty plate and Diet Coke to the less-cluttered side of my desk and settled in to hear what he had to say.

"I couldn't have landed a better deal myself," Mr. Mansini continued, not needing much input from me. He was what my grandfather would have called an inflated windbag. He didn't have conversations, just dialogues—blowing out enough hot air to send any size balloon floating across the Pacific and back.

But at this point, dialogue was just fine because though I may have appeared calm and composed, I was giddy, my insides twirling around like a five-year-old girl—arms outstretched, frantically trying to capture the sun.

"Apparently this rapper person, Scooby, had several offers on the table that his team was considering, but you were able to charm him over to our side. I'm impressed, Kingston. You've proven yourself to be extremely sharp and a savvy negotiator. Even though, I'm quite sure the fact that you're a beautiful woman didn't hurt our case at all." He chuckled before clearing his throat.

"We're just waiting for his lawyers to approve the contract and send it back. We put together a nice financial package so I'm anticipating receiving it any minute now. When they sign on the dotted line, you'll be able to say you've locked in your first major recording artist. And he'll be the first rap star to come under the urban division umbrella of this record label. That's quite an accomplishment for a newcomer and precedent-setting for the Mansini Music Group."

The reference to the lily-white company Mr. Mansini founded more than forty years ago made me smile. After a year-long, hair-pulling fight, the board of directors of the heritage Rock n' Roll station finally had to acknowledge the huge revenues that could flow from African-American pockets into theirs. One PowerPoint presentation, three project-management breakdowns, and six positive-cash-flow projections later—the board could no longer argue with the obvious. Hip-Hop had proven itself to be a cash cow.

"You're going to help us make quite a splash in the urban music arena. Other record label heads are starting to sit up and take notice, too. Bad Boy, Cash Money, Roc Nation—they're going to be calling, trying to get you on their team. I'm not mentioning this to imply that I question your loyalty, Kingston. I don't. I gave you a chance when they wouldn't and I know you won't forget that. We're going to make big money on this one. Sweetheart, you're going to be my golden girl."

I looked out the small window as snowflakes fell. Ironic how white and innocent they appeared, until they hit the ground and turned into nasty gray slush. The scenario reminded me of Mr. Mansini.

His voice took on a more personal tone. "I would really like to celebrate to seal the deal. Maybe fly you up to New York for an evening of dinner and dancing so I can show you why I love this town so much." The rest went without saying. He'd already made it clear the other things he'd also like to show me—things that definitely didn't include the Statue of Liberty.

I could see him pacing the length of his palatial office suite—spoiled, balding, and fat, an earpiece shoved in his ear, and spittle flying from his too-wide mouth. A shiver tripped up and down my spine. Mr. Mansini was a dirty old white man—reminiscent of the plantation owner tipping past the cornfields to the slave quarters under the cloak of darkness while the Mistress sleeps in the Big House.

A night of dinner and dancing with the master would not be happening. Mr. Mansini glossed right over my murmured excuse—something about my impossible schedule. Why let something like a little "no" stand in your way?

"I'll have my secretary check my schedule and call you to arrange something." He cleared his throat again then transitioned back to business. "We'll talk soon though. I want to get this project underway as soon as possible. We also need to get Scooby some media exposure while he's recording his album. So draft a proposal as to how you'd like it to go, your timeline, budget, etcetera's, and we'll get things going. I want you to take the ball and run with it, subject only to approval from me. You won't have to worry about the board of directors on this one."

Mr. Mansini paused for effect. Papers rumpled and a voice came in the background. Looking at my calendar, I thankfully realized today was the bi-weekly board meeting. "I have some other matters that I must attend to, plus I have to give the board the good news and I'm sure you're trying to get things wrapped up for the day. You're much too pretty to be cooped up. Go out and have yourself a good time."

The rumbling in the background got louder. The natives were getting restless. Mr. Mansini covered the microphone and mumbled something I couldn't make out before signing off. "Congratulations again, Kingston."

I pushed the off button on my receiver and settled more comfortably into my overstuffed chair. Tapping my pencil gently on the armrest, I basked in the glory of my shining moment until I couldn't sit anymore. My butt was wriggling with joy.

So even though my door was open and Jonetta could see and hear everything in my office, I kicked off my red patent leather pumps, flexed my toes, and started doing a furious victory shimmy dance that hiked my short A-line skirt all the way up my thighs. Tina Turner be damned.

Only nine months had passed since I quit my job as a sales and marking executive at a local radio station and pitched the proposal of a lifetime to the Mansini Music Group, or MMG for short. Early on a

Monday morning, I had sashayed in there and laid it out like an Easter Sunday dinner spread. Not only did they need to start an urban music division, but they needed me to head it and operate it from Chicago, my hometown. One week later, Mr. Mansini called and said we had a deal.

A month later, I moved into a suite on South Michigan Avenue in Downtown Chicago. In contrast to Mr. Mansini's luxury eleventh-floor accommodations, my office was just four rooms, including the reception area and the bathroom. Nowhere near Park Avenue, but it could be worse. I could still be working for the man at the man's radio station. With this new job title, at least I had carved out a piece of the pie for myself.

Jonetta rapped on the door before poking her afroed-head in the room. I fell back in the chair, my heart racing, and motioned her in, but she still hovered near the doorjamb. Her posturing indicative of our relationship—not wanting the lines of employer and employee to be blurred—she was determined to stay on a strictly professional level.

Despite my frequent invitations, there would be no male bashing over mugs of coffee; no lamenting about the extra pinch of fat discovered in inappropriate places while putting on pantyhose; no family horror stories shared while deciding what to order for lunch; no conversations tossed between office and reception area, and certainly no laughter. Just business.

She leaned against the door with an amused grin that she quickly checked before clearing her throat. "I'm gon' be leaving in a few minutes. Next month's supplies have been ordered, the work request has been submitted, and I've confirmed two of your three appointments for the next couple of days. I'll take care of the third on Monday. Anything else you need me to handle?"

I patted my perspiring face with a Kleenex and tried to smooth my unruly curls back into some kind of order. "Can you set up a conference call with Keela O'Neal and Essence Heathrow?" I asked.

She nodded and started to leave before turning back. "Way to go, girl." She gave me the thumbs up, briefly relaxing her guard of professionalism.

"Thanks, Jonetta. Have a good weekend." I smiled before turning back to the computer screen. I called Scooby's manager to congratulate him on the good news while deleting unwanted e-mail correspondence with a swoop of my finger. No one answered, but that didn't surprise me. Scooby and his entourage were probably already somewhere celebrating—pants sagging, diamonds blinging, and a joint in every hand. I left a quick message.

Jonetta knocked on the door again. "Ms. O'Neal and Ms. Heathrow are holding on line five. And this just came in for you." She laid a neatly organized stack of papers on my desk. The cover sheet read: "Deal's done. Congrats."

I thumbed through the finalized copy of the contract that made Scooby the newest member of MMG. "Thank you, Jesus!" I said, breathing a sigh of relief. Jonetta coughed softly waiting patiently for the clear to go.

I waved her out the door before punching the red flashing line.

Essence's sarcasm cut through the phone line. "To what do we owe this pleasure?"

"Don't start with me, Essence," I replied and Keela giggled in the background. "I just got some good news—no, fabulous news—and the first people I wanted to share it with are my two best friends in the whole wide world. Can you guys meet at my place in about thirty minutes? I think we're in need of a champagne toast."

"You aren't going to tell us what this is about?" Keela asked.

"Of course. In thirty minutes."

She exhaled loudly before grudgingly agreeing. "You know I hate to wait."

"Make it forty-five and I'll see you there," Essence added.

The next call was to my boyfriend, but his secretary sneered, "Randy's in a meeting and can't be disturbed."

Likely story, but I left my name anyway.

Shutting down my computer and tidying up my desk took less than five minutes; another two, and my black mink coat was buttoned tight, my Louis Vuitton briefcase was clutched tightly in my hand. I dashed out the door headfirst into the fierce Chicago wind, not so fondly nicknamed, "Da Hawk."

I settled in for the twenty-minute drive from my office to my home in Kenwoods's historic district. My house was just a stone's throw away from the luxurious mansions—including that of Louis Farrakhan—which marked this south-side community.

The skin of the city shed as the high-rises diminished to tiny specks in the rearview mirror. Traffic was light for this time of day; and as I negotiated my car into my parking space, I realized that I hadn't cussed anyone out.

The sun was setting to the west of the neatly landscaped courtyard. Dotted with just the right mixture of large oak trees and small flowery bushes, it was designed to evoke feelings of peace and serenity.

Irregular footprint patterns were stamped in the snow, left over from a child's snowball fight. Christmas decorations were up in full force. But the holiday spirit hadn't touched me yet. I hadn't started shopping and Christmas was just a week away.

A neighbor from two doors down waved a gloved hand as I strolled up the walk. "Hey, girl!"

"Hey, Henry! What's up?"

Proline Hair Sheen and Drakkar cologne tickled my nose as he enfolded me in a hug. "Child, please, it was a horrendously busy day at the shop, do you hear me? Busy, busy, busy! My feet are positively screaming. All I wanna do is soak these dogs in some Epsom salt, maybe make my baby rub them for me. Anything to make them feel better." The wind whistled between us and Henry shrugged deeper into his high-collared wool coat, his neatly groomed goatee now barely visible.

"Sounds like a good deal."

"Yeah, having a live-in lover has its good points at times. Though those may be few and far between," he chuckled, his body jiggling with laughter. "Hey, did you hear about that body they found in Robbins?"

"Nah, I haven't had a chance to check out the news today."

"They're finding bodies all over Chicago. The paper said five, but I think there may be more. They say it's some kind of a drug conspiracy. You don't want to fool with them drug boys nowadays. Cheat them out of money and see what happens. You'll end up worse than dead."

"It's a damn shame. And so close to the holidays. People don't care anymore." I sniffed as another wind whipped through the courtyard.

Pulling the paper from his bag, he showed me the front page. "Here, read it for yourself." He stuck the folded up newspaper under my arm. "Oh, and they're trying to have one last association meeting before the New Year. Something about new storm doors. I guess they'll be sending out a memo."

"Figures. They always want to have these meetings, but then nothing gets done."

"You know some people just like to hear themselves talk." Henry's eyes narrowed, then his mouth widened into a grin. "Your hair is off the chain."

I touched my wool hat rimmed with fur. "How can you …"

Henry burst into laughter before I could finish. "Oh, you're just saying that because you did it." I smiled, amused.

He snapped his fingers then blew me a kiss. "I know that's why it looks so good." His laughter trailed behind me long after his door closed.

The sun's orange glow cast elegant shadows across the marble-tiled floor of my townhouse's foyer. It was almost beautiful enough to make you forget that it was the middle of winter in Chicago and cold enough to freeze the blood in your veins.

Cocoa, my chocolate Labrador Retriever, bounded down the stairs and practically pinned me against the wall.

I pulled the door back open. "All right, down girl! Go on." Barking anxiously, Cocoa dashed outside and took care of business before scampering back to warmth. I dropped my keys on the hook by the closet and hung my coat before sitting on the bottom step of the staircase. I ducked and dodged Cocoa's wet kisses while trying to slide off my pumps and slip my feet into fuzzy houseshoes before trotting upstairs with her on my heels.

According to the silver plated clock hanging on my kitchen wall,

Keela would be ringing my doorbell in less than ten minutes. I stuck a bottle of Dom Perignon in the freezer to chill, then called a local pizza joint and placed an order for delivery. Checking the Caller ID came next—Randy had yet to respond to my messages. As I changed into my pink jogging suit, I decided that I was not going to call him again. Two can play that game.

The front gate slammed. Trotting downstairs, I flung the door open just as Keela was about to ring the doorbell.

"Get in here!" I yelled, startling her.

She pulled me into a tight bear hug. "Hey, sweetie! I know it's only been a day, but I missed ya'!"

"Girl, puhleeze, let me inside. It's freezing out here!" I laughed, wiggling out of her embrace then yanked her into the house. She tugged off her red cashmere hat and shook her hair out, each ringlet falling in perfect alignment, framing her round dimpled face. Cocoa danced around our legs.

"Hi, Cocoa." Keela said, patting her on the head. "Essence is right behind me. I saw her pulling into the parking lot."

"Wow! She's early." The snow was now falling in earnest, picturesque oversized flakes fighting each other to reach the ground first.

Essence opened an umbrella before climbing out of the white BMW 745i Sedan that her parents bought her for her thirtieth birthday. She laughed when she spotted us standing in the doorway. "Don't start talking smack!" She teetered on stiletto heels, stepping carefully around ice patches.

"Don't fall! I ain't got homeowner's insurance."

Her high-pitched laughter followed me as I went upstairs to check on the champagne. The front gate squeaked and slammed again.

"That's the pizza. Take care of it, will you, Essence? I'll pay you back later." I leaned over the banister, drying a glass with a paper towel. I couldn't quite hear Essence's response but I did decipher a few expletives mingled with the flirty banter she exchanged with the deliveryman. The aroma of spicy pepperoni wafted slowly through the house, my mouth watering before Essence and Keela even made it up to the second floor.

"Will you get your dog?" Essence yelled as she crossed the room and pecked me on the cheek. "If he scratches a hole in these stockings, you're buying me a new pair." She placed the greasy pizza box on the kitchen countertop, opened it, and fanned her hand grandly in invitation.

A snap of my fingers sent Cocoa scurrying to what I had dubbed her "basement apartment."

I flipped the switch to the black accented gas fireplace and flames sparked in mixtures of blue, red, and yellow. They painted a pretty picture on my matted cream walls and then stretched in ominous shadows across the ceiling.

"Paper towels, Keela," I yelled. The grease was already starting to seep from the box onto the countertop's newly polished surface.

"Ooooh, Lordy! It's been one …" Essence declared as she propped her narrow behind on the armrest of my earth brown leather sectional.

"Bad day?" Keela asked, heading back to the kitchen, returning with a box of orange juice and a handful of paper towels.

"Another day with my nose to the grindstone." She sighed before sliding down into couch.

I threw my head back and laughed. "Essence, you manage a day spa. It can't be too grueling with the smell of sea salts and that motivational music playing all day."

"Look, I deal with broke-down women looking for a miracle. Trust me, it's high-pressure. You know black women will snap if they don't walk out of the salon looking like they belong on the pages of a beauty magazine and that is not reality for ninety-eight percent of them." She paused in the middle of her tirade. "What's the orange juice for?"

"I'm going to drink it instead of champagne." Keela smiled with wide-eyed innocence as Essence rolled her eyes.

"Can't you suck it up and drink just this once?"

"You know I don't like champagne." She read the label on the bottle, "even if it is Dom Perignon."

I shook my head. "You're such the kindergarten teacher." Her current job as a substitute teacher was the latest in a long string of jobs, including pastry chef and buyer for an adult bookstore.

Essence stood up, poised to pop the cork to the bottle. "Are you ready to do this?" I nodded and she poured the two of us a glass.

"Let's toast to dreams coming true." I raised my glass and clinked it with theirs; first one, then the other.

"I'll toast to that," Keela murmured before taking a sip of juice.

"Hmmmm. Nice and dry." Essence downed her entire glass, then poured herself another one. While refilling mine, she raised one eyebrow, crinkled her smooth forehead, and a half smile danced across her delicate face. The shadowy light from the flames only accentuated her beauty; from her luminescent skin to the deep almond eyes set under the flawlessly arched eyebrows and bowed lips. "Well?"

"Ladies," I paused to add even more drama to the moment. "You are looking at an entertainment executive who within a year of creating a position and a department with a major, albeit-outdated record label, has signed her first major recording artist."

"No, you didn't, Kingston!" Keela shouted, hitting me in the arm.

"Of course, I did." I crossed my arms in front of me and pursed my lips.

"You got Scooby!" Essence screamed.

"I got Scooby!" I reached into my briefcase, pulled out the signed contract and waved it in front of them. I watched their expressions as the magnitude of my accomplishment sunk in. What happened to me, happened to them—good and bad. Their excitement was genuine. I threw the entire contract up in the air and danced as the sheets of paper fell around us.

We drank more champagne and orange juice, toasting to everything from fat paychecks to good sex. We never got to the pizza. Keela and Essence scooped up a slice on the way out.

"Your mother would be so proud," Essence said at the door, pulling us into a group hug before leaving.

I smiled sadly and leaned against the closed door. Yes, my mom would be proud. I only wished she had lived so I could see that pride for her little girl shining in her eyes.

The salty taste of bittersweet tears mixed with champagne, then with the contract in hand, I fell across my bed and slipped into a restless sleep.

Chapter 2

*I couldn't breathe. No matter how hard I tried, I just could not lure
air into my tightly squeezed lungs. My chest was compressed as if two
tons of bricks sat on it, weighing it down. And it was so dark - a thick,
dark, murky black mass that threatened to swallow me.*

*The jagged rocks snuggled on the river bottom pierced the pads of
my toes as I shifted from one foot to the other, trying to balance my
weight. The images spinning before my eyes were too fast and furious
for me to distinguish. But they felt familiar. Ahh! the scenes were from
my childhood. How old was I? Five, maybe? No, six. Funny, you always
hear that when it's your time to go, your whole life flashes before you;
but I always thought it would be like viewing a movie on one of those old
film reels: sitting in a plush seat watching places and people magnified
on a big screen, popping alternate handfuls of popcorn and licorice
candy, waiting for the happy ending. But this was not the end, and it
certainly wasn't a love story. I was trapped in a horror movie that was
careening out of control.*

*I tried to breathe again. Wasn't it Toni that sang that song? Breathe
again. Breathe again. "I'm trying!" I screamed violently to myself.
Then something floated by. I squinted and strained, but still couldn't
distinguish what it was. My heart pounded in my ears with the ancient*

rhythm of African tribal drums, growing louder and faster by the second. Then a voice joined the dance in my head. It was faint; I turned. I searched. Me? I waved in annoyance as if swatting away a mosquito looking to fatten itself on my blood. I didn't have time for this. "Cha na man. Me soon come." I recognized the sound of my voice, but who was I talking to? I spoke again and my Jamaican patois is at the same time familiar and unfamiliar. The irregular cadence of the rhythmic language tried to connect me to a memory tired of being ignored.

Sinking further and further toward some unknown pit, I'm supposed to be doing something, but I don't know what. Then I saw her. She was floating. Peaceful. And she was so very still. She almost looked as if she were sleeping and the river was her bed, the soft waves, her pillow. I stretched out my hand and waited to feel her familiar grasp. The gentle current tugged at her as if trying to coax a shy child into joining a schoolyard game. Everyone was running to the edge of the river in a mixture of arms and legs and the film that was moving too fast before was now in slow motion—each detail in excruciating clarity. If I couldn't breathe before, now way too much air gushed into my lungs. Screams came at me from all directions, ringing loudly in my ears. Despite the noise, I could still hear feet pounding on the sandy bank.

Everyone else seemed to be in motion, but fear and disbelief would not allow me to move. No amount of coaxing could draw me any closer. I am already close enough, close enough to see the pink, yellow, and green bathing suit that I had convinced her to put on earlier that day. Close enough to see that her chest was painfully still. Close enough to know that the vision of her slight motionless frame would forever be branded in my heart and soul.

I bolted straight up in the bed, terrified; my spine ramrod stiff. Eyes wide, mouth dry, and my pulse raced—but at least I was awake. My nightgown was attached in circles to my body, stuck by the sweat that also created a small wading pool in the small of my back. And with each chill bump that sprang up along my arms, my breathing slowed and I prayerfully realized that the terrible images from just seconds ago were gone.

The mocha-colored window blinds swayed angrily against the windowpane, trying to withstand the force of Chicago's winter wind. I must have fallen asleep on top of the covers after Essence and Keela left. The scattered pieces of the contract that I had tossed triumphantly in the air were strewn along the side of my bed, peppering the tan, blue, and maroon area rug. Then I remembered: I had placed them there, meaning to read through them again before I fell asleep.

Sometime during the night, I had yanked my heavy homemade patchwork quilt from its folded position to further buffer against the icy night air and I gathered it closer to me now. I strained to remember the ending of the recurring nightmare, but it always stopped at the same point. Cocoa slept soundly, curled in her corner of my room. I smoothed my lace eyelet sheets beneath me as if a neatly made bed would provide security, but the haze refused to clear.

The phone shrilled, slicing though the silence and my thoughts scattered even further. Something was wrong. Why else would someone call this late at night? It had to be two, maybe three o'clock in the morning. I rubbed my eyes and squinted, but still couldn't quite make out the numbers on the caller ID. Again, the phone rang. Deep down, I knew. Of course, I knew. I knew, but my breath still caught in anticipation as if willing, alone, had the power to change the outcome of this call. I picked up the phone in the middle of the fourth ring. The receiver was barely to my ear when I heard the voice, soft but urgent, heavily accented and harboring a lifetime of secrets.

"Kingston." The voice belonged to my great-aunt Beatrice, my grandmother's youngest sister, calling from Jamaica. The line crackled and I pressed the phone harder against my ear. Aunt Bea's voice was steady, but the pain hidden beneath her whiney, alto tone would be embedded in my mind forever. "It's time, Pickney, time for you to come home. We just found Mama Grace." She paused before the dreaded words, "She's dead" left her lips.

Chapter 3

I hadn't been to sleep since my Aunt Bea's early morning phone call. In only three hours, I had packed, booked a flight, and called Jonetta to let her know I would not be coming into the office. I even arranged luxury accommodations for Cocoa at the Paws House Hotel. Pretty good in my estimation, considering I was totally numb—numb and disconnected like a balloon that had slipped from a toddler's hands. My grandmother's passing had not become my truth yet. The scenario belonged to someone else. Death can do that though, make you reflect on what's really important, which was exactly my target of deep thought as I glanced over at Randy.

Despite yesterday's conviction, I had dialed Randy's number and roused him from a deep sleep so I wouldn't have to catch a taxi to O'Hare.

He was blinking the sleep from his eyes and trying to smother a yawn while he negotiated his Mercedes Sedan through the pre-morning rush traffic that could be a nightmare along this stretch of the Dan Ryan Expressway.

Despite being dressed in a sweat suit, he was still quite fashionable, the latest Nike Air Jordan gym shoes completing the ensemble. His hair was cut low and shone from this morning's application of Dax Wax that had been worked in by his stiff bristle brush. Randy's thin mustache and goatee were just as neatly groomed, a toothbrush dipped in gel brushed downward to keep every hair in place.

The muscles in his triceps bunched as he absently wiped some residue from the control panel of his car that looked like it belonged in a fighter jet. Not an ounce of fat draped his body as if Michelangelo were brought back from the dead, dropped in the middle of the ghetto and forced to make a black woman's version of David. His hands lightly gripped the steering wheel in standard driving format. Sparse black hair covered his knuckles, and his long fingers tapered into tidy square nails. His hands were well taken care of as he visited my nail technician for manicures more often than I did. Finally, I slid a lingering glance over the fullness of his lips and my memory sparked faintly. Each time I was just about ready to walk out the proverbial relationship door, memories of those lips whispering hotly in my ear, and deliciously exploring all the secret conclaves of my body would keep me right where I was—in a dead-end relationship.

I would be the first to admit that our relationship started out as one centered on an almost animal kind of lust. We had incredible sex, nasty sex—sex so good it stank. But what started out as an electric connection had withered into merely a mutually satisfying relationship. He used to play the role of the perfect boyfriend to a tee, but now all we'd become is a textbook case of one hand washing the other. A stockbroker who modeled on the side and aspired to be an actor, Randy needed connections. Because of my new foray into the entertainment business with the Mansini Music Group, I was constantly attending fund-raisers, benefits, and political soirees. This put me in a position to meet people who could possibly further his career. I needed a man on my arm who was not only debonair, but also an intelligent conversationalist with the capability to conform to any situation. It used to work very nicely. But it was getting harder and harder to remember why we'd ever hooked up.

Randy already had his Bose stereo set to a popular Hip-Hop station, volume blaring at a deafening level from the ridiculously expensive surround-sound speakers, his low cut fade bobbing lazily to the upbeat tempo. The morning-show personalities were hamming it up. The current target of their humor, the Chicago Police Department, which once again found themselves on the cover of the leading local paper thanks to yet another police screw-up. I lowered the volume and flipped the knob to a news/talk station to get the real story behind the accidental shooting without busting an eardrum.

Randy sighed and clamped his lips together. He viewed my changing the station as an invasion of his personal space, but he must've decided it wasn't a battle worth fighting and busied himself switching lanes. Then, the news segued into commercials and I adjusted the volume even more for either conversation or silence. I opted for conversation. Though things had been strained between us for quite some time, we were still a couple; the least we could do was talk.

Adjusting the vent, I looked over at Randy again. "You look so cute when you're sleepy. I can just imagine what you looked like waking up early on a Saturday morning excited about watching cartoons and eating Captain Crunch."

"I didn't get much sleep last night."

"Well, thanks for getting up and taking me to the airport. I really appreciate it—just one more thing I didn't have to figure out. I already think I left something behind and it's driving me nuts. You know how it is when you're packing in a hurry. I hate to forget anything when I'm going to Jamaica. Things are so expensive there. Even the little things— soap, toothpaste—you know what I mean? I checked everything twice, though, so I should be okay." I wasn't okay, though. I looked around and couldn't believe that I actually was thinking about asking Randy to pull over so I could go rumble through my bags and check for the twenty-eighth time when suddenly he did another lane change to avoid something in the road. This put us solidly in the middle lane sandwiched by other testy commuters. Pulling over was out of the question; we were pretty much at a standstill.

"So this was a big load off my mind," I continued. "I know you had a late night with the Reebok photo shoot, but Essence is leaving to go out of town herself this morning and Keela is, well, Keela or I would have gotten one of them out of bed."

Randy grunted in response. All right. Humble appreciation was not working. Not a morning person even after a full night's sleep, he perked up only after a Grande Vanilla Latte and a cinnamon roll slathered with icing. But pile a lack of sleep on top of that and it wreaked havoc on his home training. Unfortunately, we didn't have enough time to swing by a Starbucks so we both had to do without the daily shot of caffeine to smooth our rough edges. I closed my eyes, settled into the leather seat, absently fingering the one-carat diamond stud in my ear and continued undaunted.

"Essence should be back when I return, so you don't have to worry about picking me up from the airport. Either she or Keela'll do it."

Randy grimaced and I rolled my eyes. Keela and Randy couldn't stand each other. She disliked him because she spotted his more-than-obvious game from Jump Street. He despised her because she constantly tried to hip me to it. Keela was just looking out for a sistah. In the reverse situation, I would do the same. But I understood Randy's game, too, and decided to play with him anyway. I'm a big girl. What they both failed to realize was that I really never cared that much and it has just gone downhill from there. Two years of indifferent convenience and only moderately good sex can be hell on one's self esteem.

Randy sent me a sideways glance, his nostrils flared. "I don't know why you still hang out with her, Essence either for that matter."

"They're my best friends."

"They're nosy and they're sneaky."

"How can you say something like that? They've never done anything to give you a reason to even think something like that." I shoved a frustrated hand through my hair. My defense sounded weak to my own ears.

"All they do is ride your coattails, Kingston. That's not a friend. That's a user."

"So what do you do, Randy? I mean if you really think about it, they could say the same thing about you and have quite often, I might add. But last time I checked, I was a grown woman who could form her own opinions about who she dated and who she hangs out with."

Randy laughed dryly and honked his horn at a car in front of him. "Mark my words, some day you'll wish you'd listened. As the old saying goes, 'with friends like that, who needs enemies'?"

I waved a tired hand in his face to make him mad. It angered him to be dismissed like a child.

As expected, Randy growled, "I'm not a little boy, Kingston."

I pursed my lips smugly at his loss of control. "Then don't act like one. You're entitled to your opinion, Randy; I just don't want to hear it right now, especially if you have nothing to back it up with. I mean really, do you have to start a fight just before I leave the country for my grandmother's funeral?"

The conversation came to a dead stop just as the traffic picked up. We snaked under the viaducts and various exit ramps that made up the loopy intersection of Chicago's expressways before we broke into open ground. Drizzle started to fall as the gray in the sky deepened to a foreboding charcoal.

Whipping out my cell phone, I angrily punched in the number to Scooby's manager while counting to ten. This was the third time I'd tried to call him and still no answer. They were probably passed out from partying. I hung up without leaving a message.

I wanted to fume in silence, but I also didn't want to leave on such ugly terms. So wanting to be the bigger person, I tried again. "Please run by and check on Cocoa before you go to work. I left her food and water, but you know how she can get. I don't want her tearing up something because she's lonely. Last time I went out of town, she got into my sock drawer and I don't think I have two pairs that match anymore." I ignored the frown that flashed across Randy's face. "Don't worry, that's all you need to do. My neighbor, Henry, will come over after he gets off work and check on her. And Keela will take her to the kennel tomorrow.

"And I left your Christmas present underneath your bed. Don't open it until Christmas, Randy, or at the very earliest, Christmas Eve." I delivered these instructions knowing full well green foil wrapping paper would be strewn all over his beige two-ply Berber carpet by ten o'clock tonight. The latest model HD video camera —searched for and purchased on the Internet—was going to disappoint him. He would much prefer jewelry or clothing, but I was no longer, motivated to engage in that kind of personal shopping. Besides, Randy really did need to get organized and according to the advertisement this new-age gadget was better than a real-life, note-taking, Danish-bringing, secretary. There you have it, rationalization at its best.

I continued adjusting my seat into a reclining position but couldn't get comfortable, then it dawned on me. Randy's silence was making me uncomfortable, not the seat; so I flopped into a final position and stayed put.

"I hate that I'm gonna' miss your annual Christmas party. I bought a new dress and everything, red, tight, and slinky, just the way you like 'em."

Randy responded with effort, his deep voice pushing the words forward, "Well, then we'll have to find an occasion for you to wear it when you get back." He patted my leg, a nervous attempt to mask the insincerity in his last statement.

"You're not too disappointed that you're not going to make this one, are you?" I asked.

He raised an eyebrow at my assumption and threw back casually, "Who said I wasn't going?"

Never lifting my head from the leather headrest, I turned and looked at him. "Well, I just thought …"

The cold glance on his face stopped me mid-sentence. It clearly said, 'That's what you get for thinking.' The iciness in his sleep hooded eyes caught me off guard.

"So, who do you plan on taking?" I tried to be as nonchalant as possible. Even though our relationship did not fall into the "happily ever after" category, might not even fit into the three-more-months slot, still some rules and regulations applied. As of right now, Randy was still my property. I was not going to be disrespected—thus my line of questioning. I needed to know who was tap dancing on my territory.

"What are you talking about, Kingston?" Randy's half-hearted attempt at feigned innocence only fueled the fire.

"Did I stutter? I meant just what I said. Who are you taking to your company's Christmas party?"

The name 'Cynthia' had to fight its way from between tensely gritted teeth. It sounded like it hurt. He switched on his turn signal, looked over his shoulder to make sure the coast was clear and merged to the right, the exit ramp for the airport blessedly less than a mile away.

"Your ex-girlfriend, Cynthia?"

"Yes, Kingston. My ex-girlfriend, Cynthia." He paused, then exhaled, air rushing from his nostrils like a bull. "Is there a problem, Sweetheart?" he drawled. "If so, I really don't see what it is. You obviously can't go to the ball and Cynthia fits the bill."

My blood boiled. "First of all, don't call me Sweetheart. And actually, Randy, there are a couple of problems. The first one being that Cynthia wants to get back with you so badly, she literally shakes each time she sees us together. She's been sweatin' you ever since we hooked up and you know this, but yet you're still gonna flaunt her in front of all your colleagues. That's just disrespectful."

I paused slightly for effect. "And secondly, you must have already asked Miss Cynthia to go if she's already accepted. I mean, I didn't even know I was leaving until three hours ago." The third problem went unsaid. Cynthia just happened to be a blue-eyed, blonde-haired, very white debutante who had never once stepped foot on the South side, not even to visit Randy. And if that wasn't bad enough, she was an heiress to a billion-dollar tobacco fortune. Randy was her "doing good in the hood" project for almost two years.

My words were low and steady. "What's the deal, Randy?" Bullets sat on my tongue, aimed to pierce the jugular should I have detected even the tiniest bit of bull. One look at his face and I might as well have tattooed "busted" on his forehead.

"You know this isn't working, Kingston." He blinked rapidly, sweat beading on his forehead. O'Hare International Airport loomed right in front of us, poking out through the early morning fog like a giant phallic symbol.

"I do know this isn't working. But correct me if I'm wrong, shouldn't you quit one job before moving on to a new one; or in this case, I should say going back to an old one?"

"I was going to tell you, Kingston."

I locked and loaded. "When, Randy? I've already bought the dress and shoes, scheduled the hair appointment, everything. Your nail appointment is the same day as mine! So, when exactly were you going to tell me? When Cynthia and I both showed up at the same party because you weren't man enough to tell me the truth?"

Randy maneuvered alongside the curb directly in front of the terminal and threw the car into park. He sat back in his seat as if trying to think of an answer that wouldn't totally set me off. Two minutes later, he was still quiet. He knew when a black woman was about to snap past mad to "way out of control." He popped the trunk, then slid from his seat to the back of the car and in one fluid motion, began to pull my luggage out. I stomped from my side of the car, waved him off, and did it myself, signaling a skycap in a spiffy red jacket to load it up on a dolly. I started to walk away, then that womanly instinct hit me like a brick. I turned back and faced Randy as he was about to fold himself back into his Benz. The Bastard.

"Are you sleeping with her?"

He stared at me blankly, his jaw slack. He opened his mouth, then closed it just as quickly. Nothing else needed to be said—by him or me. Besides, I had more important things to worry about. And lying, cheating, broke men barely fell into the top ten. Chalk this one up to a lesson already learned by a million women the world over. I shook my head sorrowfully. I didn't even get to share my news about Scooby with him.

But as quickly as the thought came it left. I had more important things than Randy to focus on. Worrying about this was just a waste of my time.

Chapter 4

My nonstop Air Jamaica flight scheduled to take off more than forty-five minutes earlier still sat idling on the runway, delayed so the wings could be defrosted. It was expected, so I bypassed the irritable and pissed-off phase and settled decidedly in the resigned stage. The lady sitting in the seat on my right hand side—her hair overly teased and dyed an unimaginative shade of red—was fidgeting and fussing, trying to memorize the safety instructions on the air mask as the flight attendant whined another update over the loudspeaker. The complaining that seeped through her falsely-full lips, stained Bubble Gum Pink, amazed me. I would much rather arrive at my destination late and safe as opposed to the other option—not making it at all.

The ruddy-faced man seated to my left had already requested a complimentary bottle of scotch and a can of orange juice. "Flying makes me nervous," he said, gratefully accepting his medicinal mixture from the flight attendant while ogling her more than generous breasts.

"Hi, my name is Jim," he added as an afterthought and it took all I had to bite back a comment about his last name being Beam.

Instead, I shook his beefy hand. "Kingston," I replied shortly and flipped open an airline magazine.

Jim was not discouraged. "Business or pleasure?"

"Neither." I solidly met his gaze. "My grandmother just died. I'm going to the funeral."

"Oh, I'm sorry to hear that. So your grandmother was Jamaican?"

I nodded simply.

"I thought you looked exotic." He memorized my facial features, then snapping his fingers, he came up with an answer. "Sort of like that model, Iman."

"Iman is from Somalia."

"Yeah, right," he said as if it was all the same thing to him. Jim swirled the light brown liquor in the tiny plastic cup before thrusting it toward me. "You mind?"

I shrugged and held the cup while he shifted his cumbersome body in the undersized seat, sticking his elbow in my side as he struggled to fasten his seat belt, then reclaim the prized cup. He tipped the plastic cup to his lips as I reached up and adjusted the vent. The cool breeze blew lightly on my face and I felt better. How I longed for the day when first-class flying with its additional elbowroom, leather seats, free top-shelf drinks, and food that tastes like something other than cardboard would be my reality. For now, I shrunk into my seat to avoid any additional contact from either side, pulled out the latest whodunit from James Patterson, sighed, and awaited departure.

After another fifty-eight minutes and minimal turbulence, we were gliding through the air. Jim—as I learned was short for James—snored, his breath catching every other time he sucked in oxygen. Spittle congealed in the corner of his mouth. Barbie Doll Sue had skipped off to an empty seat closer to the back of the plane. "To join my tanning buddies," she explained as she crushed my toes while reaching into the overhead compartment. It wasn't long before a disgruntled Asian man shuffled up the aisle and plopped in the seat next to me. Obviously not happy at trading seats, he stuck his nose in a book and sulked.

The silence was welcomed, but at the same time it was overwhelming. My thoughts continually floated back to Mama Grace. Her passing was no surprise, she was well over ninety years old and pretty sickly toward the end. The doctor had advised me that most of her ailments just came with the territory. Even with that said, I could have done more for her. It certainly didn't help that Mama Grace was in Jamaica and I in Chicago. I sent money; I called and wrote, but would my presence have meant more to Mama Grace? Shouldas, wouldas, couldas were designed to send one on a guilt-tripped ride. And if that wasn't enough, Randy kept shouldering his way into my head. No doubt we would have broken up eventually, but it irritated me that it wasn't on my terms. My heart wasn't hurt, but my pride sure was.

"Not worth my time," I swore again softly and Jim choked himself awake before resettling with his head on my shoulder. No amount of nudging moved him. A long two and a half-hours passed before the flight attendant called for seatbelts to be fastened and chairs to be returned to an upright position. I elbowed Jim sharply in his side and he shot straight up. I repacked my small carry-on bag, made sure my papers were in order, and wiped a tear from the corner of my eye before it had a chance to travel too far. This was not about Randy. I knew that another one like him would come skipping along in no time. No, this was about the dream. The dreams that daddies tell their little girls as they tuck them into bed, dreams of Prince Charmings on white horses who whisper of that special, poetic, forever kind of love.

As the plane made its final approach, I knew that as sure as I had left one country to be in another, I had just left another piece of that dream behind.

Chapter 5

The plane dipped dangerously close to the sea before righting itself and touching down on the narrow landing strip of the Norman Manley International Airport located right off the Kingston Harbor. A slight haze covered the Blue Mountains as they rose majestically in the background and the long finger of the Palisades curled enticingly out into the sea.

My legs tingled as I twisted in my seat, slowly rolling one foot, then the other, before my toes came to life.

Jim polished off a final plastic bottle of scotch, then breathed heavily in my face before scooting into the aisle. "Enjoy your stay." He frowned, then added thickly, "Well, as much as you can."

I fought against the urge to flip him the finger and waited until the other passengers had finished hustling though the exit doors, jostling luggage and elbowing people with hurried sorries and apologetic looks. Didn't they know they had just arrived in the one place where time really did stand still? Where the phrase, "soon come" could mean five minutes, two days or a lifetime.

A feeling of peace washed in with the salty dampness of the ocean. The pungent smell of the rubber trees combined with the persistent heat, vibrant sounds, and glorious colors all meshed to weave a fabric that cloaked me, protected me. I was home.

The sun beamed overhead and a humid breeze gently rolled across my back. Finally, I slipped on my tortoiseshell Liz Claiborne shades and looked on top of the airport at the hundreds of family and friends, in a sea of color, cheering and waving; the majority anxious for a glimpse of their loved ones, the rest have nothing better to do with their time.

I scanned the throng of waiting relatives, but already knew that no one would be standing up top waiting for me. My Uncle Winston—who for the last thirty-five years had been designated as the airport pick-up person —would be in the parking lot leaning against his truck, one leg kicked lazily across the other.

"Cha na man! Why fight the crowd when you have to meet me in the parking lot anyway?" he always asked with a shrug.

Thick brown-skinned women attired in the colors of the Jamaican flag—yellow, green, and black—greeted each passenger, while carefully balancing baskets of fruit on their heads. They grandly swayed their hips in wide circles and sang the Jamaican National Anthem: *"From riverside to mountain, From cane field to the sea, Our hearts salute Jamaica, Triumphant, proud and free."*

A sign, "Welcome to Jamaica" hung above their heads, featuring a skinny ass white woman with a hunky overly tanned white man in speedos, drinking a margarita served by a plain, round-faced brown Jamaican woman with a mammy rag on her head.

A handsome, smartly dressed customs officer detained me for a few minutes, even though my papers were in order. He gave me the once-over with sparkling brown eyes, his teeth white and straight. His smile was marred only by the gap between the two front ones—the left yellow, the right gold. He moved aside my stash of books and fondled my Victoria's Secret lingerie with a sneer. My lacy purple bra twirled on the same finger that sported a dull gold wedding band.

The stifling heat and humidity had already caused my stiffly-ironed white linen suit to go limp and maneuvering a large suitcase, one overnight bag and a briefcase while balancing on strappy gold sandals that were made for style and not comfort was no easy feat. Thankfully, I spotted Uncle Winston quickly, and yep, he was propped against his 1977 sky blue Toyota pickup, sporting what looked like the same navy blue polyester pants and white button-up shirt he wore last time he came to pick me up. A blue baseball cap fit snugly on his head. Uncle Winston had always had a thing for blue. He still smelled of the same cheap, spicy cologne, but his hair was peppered with a bit more gray. Other than that he didn't look as if he'd aged a bit. West Indian blood preserves very well. I counted on that as I grew older.

After a brief hug and peck on the cheek, I hopped into the left side passenger seat. It still felt strange to sit on the opposite side of the car and drive on the opposite side of the street than we do in the states. I buckled my seat belt, then checked it twice to make sure it would hold my weight and prevent me from flying through the windshield. It's not that I didn't trust my uncle's driving. I did—sort of. Who I didn't trust was everyone else out there on the roads. Jamaicans drove as if they were at an Indy 500 on streets that are better suited for Matchbox Cars.

"You look good," I said as my uncle readjusted his mirrors and seat for probably the fifth time since morning. The habit had been a long time in the making.

"Thanks." He then proceeded to give me a laundry list of his aches and pains, ending with, "But I'm hanging in there."

I waited for him to inquire about my health, but he didn't. "And how is everybody?"

"Oh, just fine." He smiled weakly then ran down a second list of aches and pains, this one belonging to his worrisome wife, Auntie Dawn.

"I'm sure everything'll be all right, Uncle Winston."

He "uh-huhmed" as if he'd heard that line before and fiddled for the pack of Kools in his front pocket. He grabbed the weathered box, tapped it, and when one crumpled cigarette popped out, stuck it between his lips, now black after forty years of smoking. "Yeah, Mon. And you know, dealing with Mama Grace has been difficult for her; difficult for everyone."

Dealing with Mama Grace? I knew what he meant. But the phrase "dealing with" didn't sit well with me. You deal with clogged pipes. You deal with unruly pets. You don't deal with your dying stepmother. But then, one would have to know Uncle Winston for the "dealing with" phrase to make perfect sense.

Uncle Winston was my grandfather's child—the product of a relationship my grandfather had prior to meeting my grandmother and continued for a short while after they married. Winston's mother had left him on my grandparent's doorstep when he was one month old and Mama Grace was nine months pregnant. Pa-pa never said who Uncle Winston's birth mother was and I don't think Mama Grace ever asked. She just did what she had to do. Uncle Winston was a living, breathing reminder of Pa-pa's infidelity—an automatic strike against him. He was a lazy bum by most people's standards. That was the second strike. The third strike—we were forbidden to talk about in public. When you don't feel accepted in your own family, it's hard to feel accepted anywhere else. But I guess that could be said about all of my aunts and uncles.

My grandparents had a total of five children together. Only two were still living. The oldest son lived in the states and couldn't find his way out a paper bag with a flashlight in one hand and a map in the other. Uncle Paul had only returned to Jamaica once in the past twenty-five years and that was for his father's funeral. Doubt existed as to whether he would return to bury his mother, citing work and family reasons that, when added up, wouldn't amount to much.

My Aunt Lonnie, the baby girl of the family, remained on the island and seemed to have it all—beauty, a loving husband and daughter, and all the success anyone could ever want; she and her husband owned a grocery store in Ocho Rios. But appearances could be deceiving. She also had paperbag issues; or more specifically, the bottle contained in the paper bag.

Two of Mama Grace's children died before they reached their teen years: one from scarlet fever and one from a bullet, both boys. My mother was the third child who died before my grandmother, thirteen years ago.

My uncle continued to drone on, filling me in on the family gossip and scandal: who was pregnant without benefit of marriage; who done "tiefed" whose husband; who done turned Rastafari; and who had narrowly escaped jail for selling ganja, which in Bob Marley country, despite what the law books say, is not really seen as a crime, just an act of stupidity for getting caught. He added exaggerated colorful sidebars more for his amusement than mine. He did this as he negotiated his way out of the parking lot, honking and cursing, causing sweat to prickle the back of my neck. The windows were rolled down because no air conditioning existed and I had to fight to keep long strands of hair from blinding me permanently. Finally, I gave up and fished though my purse for an elastic band, pulled my hair back into a ponytail, tucking stray hairs behind my ears. I was listening with only one ear and half a heart. I had come back to Jamaica for only one reason.

I sighed and pressed my forehead to the window. Even a year was too long to have been gone from a place so firmly embedded in my spirit, but the pressures of working and paying bills tended to cut into one's vacation time.

Kingston, the island's capital, was quite different from the Jamaica depicted in those seductive TV advertisements with their bikini-clad populated beaches, lush landscapes and refreshing waters. Steeped rich in culture and history, Kingston was no longer in the business of scenic splendor. Where once palm tree after palm tree lined the streets, now one-hour cleaners, express patty shops, and gas stations complete with slurpee machines had taken over. A barefoot woman walked down the street, carrying a baby. A small child was clinging to her hand, his belly distended from lack of food. You wouldn't see that on any postcard.

My uncle calling my name yanked me back into the conversation. "I'm sorry, you were saying?" I twisted a bit and faced him.

He sucked spit through his teeth good-naturedly. "Lawd a mercy, chile! You woulda' thought you were my age de' way you hard of hearing so! I was saying that you would understand everything when you read the letter."

My forehead pulled together in a puzzled frown. "What letter?"

"Aunt Bea didn't tell you about the letter?"

"No."

Uncle Winston's lips formed a perfect "O" and he slid into the role of the innocent. "I thought she woulda' mentioned the letter."

"Dammit, what letter, Uncle Winston?" I was tired, hot, and my patience had been stretched thin.

He hesitated and stroked his chin.

"You might as well tell me, Uncle Winston." He hesitated again and I was fed up. No backbone. "You know, that's why this family is so jacked up. Too many secrets! I'm gonna find out anyway so you might as well tell me what's going on!"

Uncle Winston had the nerve to harrumph and I shot him a look designed to pierce not only flesh, but bone.

"Tell me."

"All right. All right." His hands gripped the steering wheel. "Mama Grace wrote this letter addressed to you. Aunt Bea found it while they were readying Mama Grace's body for the funeral home."

"What did the letter say?"

Uncle Winston shook his head and his lips flattened into a grim line. "Now that, I don't know. You know Aunt Bea ain't going to tell me something really important. She mentioned she found it, but then just as quickly shut her trap and we haven't been able to pry anything else outta' her since. I thought maybe she brought it up when she called."

"You know good and well that if she didn't say anything to you, she wasn't going to say anything to me."

"I can't really speak to what people do or don't do." He took a long drag on his cigarette and shrugged. "No sense in raising your blood pressure over it."

I fumed silently but he had a point. Finally, I said, "You're right." I let it go for now.

Relieved, Uncle Winston nodded, then cut me a sideways glance. "Bianca's gonna arrive at de' house later tonight. She said she wants to spend some time and catch up."

Bianca was Aunt Lonnie's daughter and my favorite cousin. We were born on the same day, in the same month, in the same year, only in different places; she in the islands and me in the states. Bianca was absolutely gorgeous with long black hair, slanted doe eyes and exotic coloring that her father's Chinese ancestry brought. When she was nineteen, she was crowned as first runner up to Miss Jamaica. She was hoping for a Vanessa Williams' type scandal to occur so that the title would pass to her but it didn't happen. She still had the crown hanging on one of the posts to her bed and the dried bouquet pressed between the pages of her diary.

Bianca was beautiful, rich and extremely confused. In her early twenties, she was constantly on the hunt for true love. As she got closer to thirty, she started settling for whatever happened along. She became a member of the Baskin Robbin's flavor-of-the-month club. Now she was content to spend her daddy's money, breed horses, and talk shit. Bianca made most family members nervous. Whereas they – including Uncle Winston– were content to gossip about family behind their backs, Bianca spoke the truth about everyone to their face, no matter how painful that truth might be.

Having her as company would certainly be interesting.

"She can help you get Mama's things in order. You know, Mama, didn't believe in throwing anything out. There are piles of newspapers, old letters, and photographs all over the house. I was going to do it myself, but just couldn't find the time." I almost smiled at how easily the lie slipped from his lips. He wasn't about to clean up anything. "I was just speaking to Bianca on how helpful your little friend's brother had been to Mama in the end. The girl you spent the summer with, her brother. His grandfather was the doctor at the health center. What was his name? Him take mighty good care with her." Uncle Winston chuckled softly as if he had shared a joke. Surely, he hadn't realized what he'd just said. "You remember him, Kingston. What's his name again?" He scrunched his face up and scratched his head. His perplexed look almost made me sick. How can you not know the name of the man that took care of your dying stepmother?

"Damon," I said, my back teeth clenched, almost choking on the name. A long time had passed since I'd uttered it. And an even longer time since I'd felt good about doing so. Damon. I repeated the name to myself, but it still didn't make sense. Why would Damon be involved?

"Yeah. That's him." Uncle Winston popped his fingers and pointed at me with a slick smile. "Damon." He chuckled a little more than necessary and slid me a sideways glance. I wanted to tell him to keep his damn eyes on the road. His comments seemed too coincidental. I stared straight ahead and focused on the street signs flying back. No wonder Mama Grace never liked him.

"I think her and him will make a good couple." Shock slammed against my chest and almost knocked the breath out of me. "Who would make a good couple?"

"Bianca and that doctor fellow. It's about time for her to settle down, anyway. I must tell her to go check him when she gets in town." I had nothing to say that would have been even remotely pleasant. The name Damon was enough to bring back a flood of painful memories and Uncle Winston was not helping. I folded my arms and hunkered down in my seat. Tense silence accompanied us the rest of the way home.

Mama Grace, Randy, and now Damon; what else could possibly happen?

Chapter 6

The old mango tree still stood prominently in my grandmother's front yard; the years gone by evident in the gnarled and weathered bark. I wrapped my arms around the trunk, pressed my cheek into its roughness, and closed my eyes. If you need guidance, hug a tree and gain some strength from the ancestors; the roots stretch deep. That's what my mama told me. I held on now for dear life.

Lush tropical plants danced along the iron-rod fence and bordered the sidewalk leading to the verandah: hyacinth, roses, and lilies intertwined, making a living collage. No longer healthy and vibrant, but slightly limp, the plants strained with the little strength they had left to catch a few leftover raindrops that were falling from the roof. The limestone wall that separated Mama Grace's house from next door was overgrown with moss and thick vines mingled with the low branches that hung from the orange trees that lined the edge of the property. Blossoms were scattered throughout the yard like splatters of paint dropped from a careless painter's brush.

Mama Grace's four guard dogs yapped from the backyard, straining to be released from their cages. Toy, her poodle, jumped, twisting as I tried to pet her. Each jump causing me to dance to prevent her from marking her territory on my white linen pants. Her coat was dirty and matted. Many a summer day was spent as a child sitting on the verandah with cousins combing her fur for ticks. We would pick them, squash them, and watch the blood splatter on the steps. Sometimes we would bet bananas on who could spray blood the farthest. In Jamaica, dogs were a necessity to keep people from "tiefing'" you out of house and home. They were not pets. Cocoa was spending her vacation time tucked away in a doggy hotel, groomed and spoiled. My grandmother would tease me mercilessly about that. I would tease her back and tell her that I planned on letting Toy sleep in my bed while I was here. She would twist up her nose in disgust and click-clack her false teeth. But Toy had outlived her.

My luggage sat on the sweeping, red-brick verandah between the two wicker rocking chairs that still sat in the same place by the front door. The one on the left had been empty now for almost two decades since my grandfather, Pa-pa, passed away when I was ten. The chair on the right appeared to be rocking slowly, singing a soft lullaby of days gone by. Between the two chairs, used to sit a small square that proudly held my grandfather's most prized possession: an ivory chessboard that had been carved by hand. My grandfather won it in a card game while in the army stationed in Cuba. Mama Grace was his *second* love, he would always say. Chess was his first. Pa-pa could have played chess all day long and half the night, even play by himself, if he had to—if Mama Grace had let him, which most times she didn't.

"Cha na man, Stewart, you stay glued to that chair any longer, your backside's gonna take root!" She'd suck her teeth lovingly before shoving a rake in his hand and sending him off to pick ackee.

The double doors that led from the verandah to the front room were thrown open; the sun gleaming through the antique stained-glass windows in the doors. The woodwork framing them had been done by hand. Uncle Winston disappeared through them heading to the kitchen for "something to cool down my throat," he explained over his shoulder.

He didn't offer me a thing. So I stood there, looking up. The house still overwhelmed me; architecturally magnificent from the wide sweeping verandah made up of red tile, to the high arched doors trimmed in light yellow. The body of the house itself was made of white limestone. A carport extended from the left side and held decades of junk but had never actually sheltered a car.

Inside, the ceilings stretched more than fifteen feet high, peaking to almost eighteen in the center of each room, creating a dramatic diamond effect. In the front sitting room and living room, ornate chandeliers hung, reminiscent of the 20's. Drapes yellowed from the constant humidity of the island cascaded in ripples from windows just as tall that lined three of the walls in the front room. The hardwood-planked floor still shined with polish and was covered in spots with fluffy oriental rugs tossed every which way. The interior decoration had been done haphazardly; each year new pictures, souvenirs and handmade drawings were added. No two things matched; and so my godmother, Aunt Jelly, had dubbed Mama Grace as the queen of bric-a-brac. Aunt Jelly was my mom's best friend and second only to Mama Grace in the knick-knack department.

I walked slowly into my favorite room—the room where I slept, the room where Mama Grace birthed my mother with the help of a next-door neighbor. I used to hold my ears and scream, "Yuck!" whenever my mom would tell the story—all that blood and gook. Now that I was thirty and wanted babies, being in that room made my uterus jump with longing.

"It's only one step." This was what I told myself. "One little bitty step." But it was a big step, and I knew it. One step would take me inside that room and reality would kick me right in the butt. Until then, I could still pretend that my grandmother was sitting on my bed—smelling like lilac and ginger—waiting to enfold me in her arms. My mouth watered thinking of the freshly baked coconut tarts and hand-squeezed limeade sweetened with brown sugar that Mama Grace would then thrust into my hand before sitting me down. I stepped over the threshold. Nothing. No kisses, no tarts, no catching up. Nothing but dust and silence.

I cradled my face in my hands and wept.

Chapter 7

After throwing my suitcases on the bed, I changed into shorts and a tank top, pinned my hair up, then tied it down with a scarf. The first thing on my agenda: cleaning. My grandmother kept a meticulous house and would be mortified at the way they had let her home go. Mama Grace employed a woman from down the way to come in daily to cook, wash clothes, and clean. It was typical with most middle-class Jamaican families being that labor was much cheaper on the island than in the states. Just the same, every day just like clockwork, one would find my grandmother scrubbing, washing, and disinfecting. If inventing "something else to do" were an art, my grandmother would be Picasso. She always said, "A nasty house is owned by a person wid' a nastier backside!"

I looked first in the kitchen, then in the dining room. Nothing was there. Nothing. Word traveled fast on this island when someone died. I couldn't help but wonder why the stream of family members who would normally visit when a loved one passed was drier than the parted Red Sea. No steaming home-cooked dishes sat on the dining room table. No Tupperware dishes filled with peppered rice and peas or steaming pots of curried goat. No fragrant pies covered in foil. Friends and neighbors would be by after the funeral. They always waited a respectable amount of time before converging upon the bereaved. Family was supposed to come first. They should be here now.

Uncle Winston had fallen asleep on the chaise in the back room; empty Red Stripe bottle sitting on the floor, mouth slack, and strange noises wafting from his nose. Toy was asleep as well, content in the knowledge that this nap would go uninterrupted. Mama Grace was no longer here to swat her outside with the broom.

Cleaning only took an hour and that included watering the plants. My grandmother certainly didn't pass on her meticulous genes to me. For the most part, I just dusted, scrubbed, or mopped dirt visible to the eye.

Mama Grace's room was last. Everything was exactly as it was when she was living—as if she had just run across the street to the neighbor to borrow some cho cho and would soon be back.

The steel-frame twin beds were neatly made, her many French perfumes and scented powders arranged in alphabetical order on the oak dresser. One lonely dress was flung carelessly over the door as if my grandmother had returned late from a cocktail party and was too tired or too tipsy to hang the floral creation in the closet. I spun and looked in the opposite direction. The armoire consumed an entire wall. I ran my hand over the intricate detail of the dark stained wood, and peeked inside at the impossibly small space where I played hide and seek as a child. My Uncle Peter built and fashioned it inside the bedroom as his final project for carpentry school two weeks before he was shot and killed in a robbery gone wrong.

Even years later, Mama Grace's chest would puff with pride when telling the story. It was his most inspired and only finished piece. The armoire now belonged to me, but I'd have to take it apart piece by piece to get it out of the house. I guess like me, Uncle Peter, thought Mama Grace would be around forever and there would be no need to remove the armoire from her space.

Finally, I made it to the desk. Pa-pa spent much of his days and nights sitting at this desk reviewing invoices, scratching off number after number, and adding them up again until the totals were correct. Some of the grooves and indentations, reminders of his frustration, were fat enough to hold my ring finger. A cubbyhole was added later and each compartment held a myriad of office necessities: paperclips, rubber bands, and erasers.

An old quill pen rested next to a dried pot of black ink faded to a dark gray. My grandfather wrote his first letter with that pen. My mom said it took him two days to get one paragraph on paper and frustrated him so much he never wrote another letter. I opened the top desk drawer and then slammed it shut. Guiltily, I glanced over my shoulder, feeling like a five-year-old in danger of being caught stealing.

It was too damn quiet, almost eerie; so I turned on the old radio that had kept my grandfather company every day. It was still propped up on three yellowing Perry Mason novels. He must have gotten it at the turn of the nineteenth century. It was still set to the same news station.

As expected, all of my grandmother's papers were in order: bills, receipts, tax information, all filed according to the date. A manila envelope lay on top of the desk and with shaky fingers, I pulled out the letter and unfolded it carefully as if it might disintegrate if handled too roughly. The familiar scrawl tugged at my heart.

Did she use Pa-pa's quill pen or just grab a regular, everyday ballpoint? I really wanted to believe she used the quill pen. The letter was dated more than a year earlier.

November 1, 2010

My Dearest Kingston, First let me apologize if this letter is hard to read. The worse thing about getting old is you don't have control over things anymore. My hands are shaking. I can't get my eyes to focus, but I'm not complaining. I've lived a good life.

Kingston, I know that I'm dying. The doctor says it's cancer. I'm not sure how long I have to live so I want to start taking care of my affairs now.

I have chosen you; and though I know that you don't quite understand why as yet, I hope as you look through my papers and read my instructions, it all will be made clear. Know that I have every faith that you will execute my wishes fairly, wisely, and with love.

My attorney has my Last Will and Testament and is to contact you immediately following my burial. Many of my closest friends and family, including my children will be vexed with me at first. But then, Kingston, they will be vexed with you because you will have the power. They're just looking for a handout and I'm not going to be the one to give it to them. They have done nothing to deserve it. They're going to feel slighted. It's human nature, I guess; and you will have to be strong. Ya' hear me, girl! If they try to fight it, fight back. Stand your ground, Kingston. I remember when you were three. You were such a stubborn little thing, following your Pa-pa everywhere and for the life of you, just could not understand why he wouldn't let you drink out his favorite cup. You asked once and he told you no. So you watched and waited. The first time he turned his back – there you were. I have never seen a three-year-old so drunk up before. You got so sick and then you never looked at the cup again. Kingston, I need you to be that stubborn now.

I did the best I could, Kingston, but my family has not turned out quite the way I thought they would. I had high hopes for each of my children. Your mother is the only one that didn't disappoint me. I think God was punishing me by taking her away so early. I think he was vexed because I did not do as well with my other children. In turn, they did a poor job with their own children. I love all my children dearly, Kingston, despite their faults, but I don't like them very much. If I could do it all over again, I would be much sterner, try to give them some backbone. But I guess that is just the foolish wish of an old woman. I can only try to make my wrongs right in the best way I know how.

Also, you're going to hear many stories. Some of them will be true, but most of them will be lies. It'll be hard for you, but remember who you are. What people say can never change that. You have strong blood running through your veins, Pickney. There is one thing though that I want you to hear from me. All the whispers you've heard about your

Pa-pa's other women and illegitimate children are true. It's true, but it's okay. I loved your Pa-pa with all my heart and he loved me. I have no doubt about that. He was a good man that took care of his family. And Kingston, he loved you more than anything in this world. Don't let the mistakes of a simple man change how you feel about him. He was a man of integrity.

I am going to close this letter. Thank you for indulging an old woman's ramblings. Kingston, I will always be with you. If you need me, just look to the sky.

My love always,
Mama Grace

I was absolutely still. I re-read the letter, waited, then read it again, my shoulders sagging at the thought of what lay ahead. If I didn't love my grandmother as much as I did, I would have left right then, gone back to Chicago. If the trouble to come was only half of what my grandmother predicted, things were gonna get ugly.

Uncle Winston snored loud enough this time to wake himself up. He stood up and stretched, then walked in the kitchen and rumbled through the refrigerator, Toy skipping at his heels. I stuffed most of the papers still scattered on top of the desk back into the drawer and tucked the letter in the back pocket of my shorts.

"I'll have to send Queenie to the store. Nothing in here to eat attall'." What Uncle Winston really meant was that all the Red Stripe was gone.

"Don't worry about me. I'll manage," I said with more gusto than I actually felt.

"I'll still have her pick up some things. We can't have you starving, now can we?" Uncle Winston shoved on his baseball cap and hiked up his pants. "You sure you and Bianca going to be okay here by yourselves? Maybe Queenie can sleep over 'till after de' burial just to keep you company."

"No, really, we'll be fine." I followed him to the front door.

"All right then. Queenie'll be here in the morning and will still come every day to take care of things until we figure out what's gonna happen to the house. If ya' need anything else just let her know. We'll settle up with her when you leave." Just like him to put someone off—to not even consider that Queenie might need her money now.

"Have all the arrangements been made for Mama Grace's funeral?" I asked suddenly.

"Yah. Mama had taken care of everything long before she got sick, y'know. Paid for it and everything. They just followed her instructions at the funeral parlor. The burial is the day after tomorrow." Uncle Winston jiggled his keys in his pocket and started down the steps. "All right then, Kingston, I'll check on you tomorrow; going to head up the hill now, don't wanna vex your auntie by being late for dinner." And with that, he was gone.

I turned and went inside the house, never feeling more alone.

Chapter 8

After I unpacked my bags, not much was left to do but wait for Bianca. I left a message for Mama Grace's attorney before plugging up my laptop and making sure my cell phone was on the charger. Sitting on the verandah, I prayed for a cool breeze and tried to concentrate on reading my book again, but even James Patterson couldn't capture my attention. Too many thoughts parlayed back and forth inside my head. I checked on the dogs, then wandered aimlessly around the garden. After a few minutes I gave in and headed back inside with purposeful strides, Toy right on my heels. Work was the only thing that could possibly help.

Phone calls to Scooby and his manager proved fruitless, so I powered on my laptop, and still amazed that my grandmother had ventured into the 20ᵗʰ century – logged on to the wireless internet connection. I plopped onto the floor and soon Toy was curled up against my leg, her butt propped up against my thigh. I rubbed her belly as I opened up my email account. As expected, it was full but at least I had something constructive to do that didn't require too much brain-power. Five emails from Jonetta were marked "URGENT" so I opened those first.

"Yes, please schedule all of my appointments for the following week." I mouthed the words as I punched them out on the keyboard. "Yes, please let Mr. Mansini know that I had to leave town for a family emergency and if he needs to contact me he can do so by email. Yes, it is important that I talk to Scooby. Have his manager email me with a good time to call later today. No, I'm not sure when I will be back in the office so direct all urgent matters to Mr. Mansini." I typed in my grandmother's phone number before clicking the send button. I quickly deleted all of the junk e-mails before sending messages to Essence and Keela just to let them know that I made it safely. I almost e-mailed a "Dear John" letter to Randy, but what would be the point? After a few more quick replies, I was done. I grabbed a pillow off the couch, lay down on the floor and smiling brown eyes danced into focus.

Damon: just one more thing to figure out. Too proud to get the scoop from Uncle Winston, I had to work things out on my own. But with nothing to go on, my imagination was running wild. With Damon in such close proximity, I was bound to bump into him. We might have to be in the same room, maybe even talk. Was I ready for that? A blinding flash of red burst through my brain at just the thought of our eyes meeting and I swore with frustration. Even with a lifetime of preparation, I wouldn't be ready for that. Not after what he did.

The phone rang and I jumped off the floor, dragging my laptop with me. The familiar voice sent a surge of warmth through me.

"Keela! How are you? I just sent you an e-mail." I sat down at the small desk and cradled the mustard yellow phone with my shoulder.

"I know, I just got it. That's why I'm calling, silly. I had to send the kids out to recess before I could call you back."

"You're calling from work?"

"Where else would I be calling from, Kingston?"

"I guess my point, Keela," I said, "is that this is a pretty expensive call. Your principal might not appreciate your making it on their dime." I wrapped the phone cord around my finger and opened up a game of solitaire on my laptop.

"If they figure out it's me, I'll just pay for it. No big deal." Keela paused. "So how's everything?"

I clicked on the deck of cards and sighed. "Pretty much as I expected. There's not one person here to pay their respects and that blows my mind. I thought a few of the closer family members would show up. But then this is my family we're talking about. So it's quiet, I'm bored, and ready to get back to my life."

"If you need me to come out there, I will. My thong's already packed. I'm sure the school can get a substitute for the substitute." She giggled.

"You in a thong? I'll pass." Chuckling, I dragged the ace of spades to the top of the screen. "Don't worry, I'll be back before you know it. One of my cousins is going to stay with me and kind of go through some of Mama Grace's things." I looked at the small pictures that lined the desk. One was of my mother in pigtails climbing a tree. Another of me, also in pigtails, at about the same age. It took my breath away how much I looked like her.

"What else is wrong, Kingston? I know you're sad because of your grandmother, but it seems like there is something else." Her gentle prodding was all I needed. The barrier broke and I sobbed out the tale of Mama Grace's letter making me the executor of her will, the animosity from the family, and Randy's betrayal in one long breath. Keela listened, inserting comforting sounds at appropriate intervals.

"Poor baby," she said when I was done. The tears had gradually dried up and I felt better, cleared. I appreciated Keela's friendship in times of crisis. Whereas Essence tended to approach situations like a volcano spewing lava, Keela was calming. But when she was sure I was properly subdued, she got mad.

"I can't believe that trifling jerk would do this to you. And with that white girl," she spat with venom. "I always knew something wasn't right with him."

I grabbed a tissue from the Kleenex box on the antique curio cabinet and blew loudly.

"His loss. He doesn't deserve you." It was the typical best friend answer, but I was glad she said it. I didn't realize that I needed to hear I wasn't to blame until she uttered the words.

"I know, I know." I wiped my nose again. "It's just been a lot all at once, you know?" When tears threatened again to blur my vision, I attempted to lighten the conversation. "So, what's going on at home? I know it's only been four hours since I left but I miss you guys already!"

Keela sucked in her breath and I could practically hear her hopping around in her seat. "Girl, you missed it. Henry and Darryl had to throw this ghetto chick out of the salon while I was getting my hair highlighted. You didn't tell me they got down like that? I felt like I was on some Jerry Springer type show."

"All this time, Henry's been my neighbor and doing my hair, I've never even seen him raise his voice."

"Well, he certainly did this morning. Apparently the girl thought Darryl had been looking at her boyfriend the wrong way when he dropped her off for her appointment. She was fussing about it the whole time until Henry called her out and then it was on. She got to hollering and cussing and calling Darryl all out of his name. All I heard was Darryl, HIV and young black men and that was all she wrote. If she thought Darryl was a soft, she doesn't think so now because he picked her up about fifteen feet off the ground and tossed her out the shop."

"You are lying!"

"Kingston, if I'm lying then may lightening strike me right now. I've never seen anything like it. And you know she called the police. But everyone vouched for Darryl so they took a complaint and left it at that."

"Never a dull moment."

"And, girl, Essence is tripping. She called from Ohio or wherever the hell she is and I could tell from her voice that she's up to something. She says she's on a buying trip for the salon, but do you really need to go out of town for scented oil and nail polish remover?"

"I haven't heard from her, but she's been particularly sneaky lately."

"It's a man!" we said at the same time. "It's gotta be," I added. "It's just like Essence to take the dick on a road trip. Any idea who it is?"

"Not a clue. She hasn't said a word about anyone new."

"Well, she's going through quite a bit of trouble to keep this one undercover." I could hear the faint ringing of a school bell.

"Uh oh. That's the five-minute warning bell. I don't have much time left so enough about her, what about you? Have you gotten your pipes oiled yet?"

"I'm not here for that, Keela," I replied almost too quickly."

"That don't mean you can't get some while you there. Girl, you in Jamaica. You betta find you a Dexter!"

"Keela, I've been here exactly four hours. You think men just walk around with their penises slung over their shoulders looking for women to service? Besides, I've had more than enough Dexters in my life; thank you very much!" I grinned. I knew what was coming next.

"You can never, and I mean never, have too many Dexters!"

I refocused my attention on the solitaire game, moving the queen of hearts to the king of clubs. "You are not going to worry me, Keela. You're starting to sound more like Essence everyday!"

"Well, Essence ain't sleeping alone every night either. And for the record, if I recall correctly, it's been almost one year since you last got you some good stuff and two years since you had your last orgasm! Randy has been hell on your sex life." Keela continued through my protests. "Look, I'm your best friend. Who knows you better than me? I'm trying to help you out. You go without good sex for too long, not only will your stress level shoot way up, but your skin will break out! And a diva can't have bad skin."

I glanced at the clock. "Girl, this is going to be the most expensive therapy session you've ever conducted. They're burying Mama Grace the day after tomorrow and I figure a few days after that, I'll be ready to come home."

"Aiiiiight! Let a sistah know and she may come get you from the airport."

"You got it." Then, my voice dropped to a level just a notch above a whisper, even though I was alone in the house. "Keela?"

"Yeah, girl?"

"Damon's here. He helped take care of Mama Grace before she died." I closed my eyes as Keela drew in a breath out of surprise. "What? Are you sure?"

"My uncle told me when he picked me up from the airport, but I didn't have the guts to ask him any questions."

"You're such a chicken." She paused and let the news sink in. "Well, I'll be damned." She, too, lowered her voice to a whisper. "I got news, too, but it can wait."

"You sure?" I asked but was already betting money in my head that this was just going to be another installment of "The Keela and Dwayne Saga – Ghetto Love". "I have plenty of time."

"Later's better. The kids are gonna' be traipsing in here any minute." As if on cue, the piercing school bell rang. "See," Keela griped. "You could lose your hearing working here. I better go. Watch yourself, Kingston." The tenderness in her voice almost made the tears flow again.

"Don't worry about me." I stood and tried to end the conversation with enthusiasm I didn't feel. "Be good."

"And you be better," she answered, then hung up. In the twelve years we'd known each other, she had never once said good-bye. She didn't believe in goodbyes—said they were bad luck.

Keela, Essence, and I met our freshman year at Howard University. Keela and I were roommates – occupying space on the third floor of Crandall Hall – the freshmen women's dorm. Essence lived above us on the fourth floor.

The first night, Essence was so loud that Keela and I stayed up half the night debating what to do. We were finally so upset from having no sleep that we marched upstairs in our pajamas intending to deal with the problem. We banged on the door and this girl, with enough weave to put at least ten horses to shame, opened the door butt-naked! I don't know whose mouth dropped to the floor quicker, Keela's or mine.

"Are you going to join in or just enjoy the view?" she asked, causing some guy—who we later found out was the quarterback for the football team—to laugh in the background.

Our faces turned even brighter red.

"I can handle all y'all," he drawled in an accent straight from Mississippi. His real name was Bernard, but his nickname was Slick.

We didn't stick around to join in or watch, but took our new-to-the-big-city butts back downstairs.

"They don't know nothing about breakin' in a new place," Essence said as she closed the door. When we returned to our room, the noise had resumed—it was her way of laughing at us. And she was still laughing the next day in the cafeteria when she glided by us on the arm of yet another fine dude. She had shut us up and won our admiration at the same time. After that day, we became inseparable.

I sat quietly for a few minutes. It was getting late and I expected Bianca to be here by now. Even though the sun had set, the humidity still hung in the air. A moist film had covered my body for most of the day and was starting to wreak havoc on my hygiene. So I gathered the necessities for my nightly ceremony: herbal shampoo, conditioner, and body scrub, a loofah sponge, salt sea oil, almond body cream, and the vanilla-scented candle I always packed in case of an emergency. I slipped my neatly manicured toes into bright yellow flip-flops, hung a right at the kitchen and headed east in search of heaven—the outdoor shower.

Being a Cancer, I connect very deeply with water. At least that's what the psychic told me when I called. And for a hundred bucks, I had to believe she was right.

Mom told me that around 1962, Papa broke down and installed a shower inside. She said he just got so sick of Mama Grace bitchin' every time she had to haul one of the kids out back to scrub them down. Now I'm figuring around 1962, most of them kids should have been damn near grown so weren't they old enough to wash their own behinds?

Standing outside, gazing up at the sky, the sweet tang of hyacinth in the air with warm water running down your body could be a very spiritual thing. It also could be a very sexy thing under different circumstances, of course. I sighed as I felt a familiar stir in my belly, knowing if I squeezed my eyes tight and pretended really hard, I wouldn't be alone in that shower.

"Now is not the time, Miss Kingston." I forced the knob until the water sputtered, then blasted full force from the showerhead. The temperature of the water was not as hot as I liked it, but the water caressed me as it cascaded down my body. Bending my head back under the stream of water, my scalp began to tingle. I massaged the silky lather into my skin, beginning at the base of my neck. By the time I reached my stomach, my legs were clenched together tightly. Keela was right. It had been too long since I had felt appreciated by a man. The kind of man whose appreciation keeps a smile on your face all day long and makes your soul jump in anticipation with the thought of seeing him. It had been way too long. I quickly washed my hair and rinsed off before wrapping myself in a fluffy brown towel.

There was a bit of bun and cheese in the fridge and that sufficed for dinner. I munched while pecking on my laptop—the two-finger tango— the faint noise of kids playing in the street mixed with horns honking and wheels screeching as neighbors rushed home from work. While I tried to drum up ideas for the proposal for Scooby's debut album, I also worked on losing my eighth straight game of Solitaire.

A car engine cut off and Toy's tail shot straight out, sniffing the air and barking in earnest, knowing good and well she wasn't gonna do anything should it be an intruder. I smoothed her slightly arched back reassuringly – thanking her for her loyalty.

A door slammed and a lilting high-pitched voice floated across the verandah into the front room. "Kiiiiiinnnnnggggston!" Bianca always managed to draw out my name and then end it on a sing-songy note. Too bad she was tone deaf.

I unfolded my legs, flung off my grandmother's afghan, and set the computer aside. I'd always felt a little inadequate next to Bianca—my features considered a little too black, my hair a little too nappy. I checked my appearance in the hallway mirror, tucking a few stray strands of hair behind my ear and wiping some crud from the side of my mouth just as Bianca entered the house amidst a cloud of expensive perfume and stale ganja smoke.

"Bianca. It's so good to see you, sweetie," I said and meant it. She was by far the most genuine person I knew; and I needed genuine right now.

She put her bag down and rushed to embrace me. Her body was warm, her hug comforting, and for the first time since my arrival, I felt somewhat at ease.

"How ya do?" she asked and spun me around with one hand. "Go on girl, witcha bad self. You looking damn good. You must have given up the sweets."

I struck a pose and we both dissolved into laughter. It didn't matter how long ago I lost my baby fat, family members still saw me as Mama Grace's chunky granddaughter.

"Had to. And I have to give up more and more every year to stay this way."

Bianca frowned, her light brown eyes assessing me. "I hope you aren't doing anything crazy—not eating, throwing up, taking pills and everything! You know you Americans always take things to a whole 'nother level."

"You look good, too," I responded, pulling her long ponytail. "And you've grown." I poked her left breast and my finger hit a silicone wall. Bianca dissolved into laughter. Growing up, we would compare our bodies, standing naked in the bathroom, inspecting each other's newly acquired assets. We would dissect like physicians and evaluate like men. "When did you get these?"

Bianca cupped both of her breasts and squeezed them together. "Last year. My birthday present to myself. Well, actually, Daddy paid for them, but he doesn't know that yet. Remember when I went to New York? Well, shopping was only part of the reason. I came back with these and Daddy almost had a fit. He calmed down only after I told him some boyfriend had footed the bill."

I nodded and smiled, imagining Uncle Lee's expression—his rugged face somber, his fists clenched, but anger controlled. A prime candidate for a stroke, absolutely nothing made Uncle Lee happy and absolutely everything pissed him off. Breast implants could only fall into the second category. It may be status quo in the United States, but was still a bit taboo to older Jamaicans. "You like?"

I nodded again. "What size cup are you now?"

"I went from a B cup to a perfect size D."

In my nonprofessional opinion, I thought a D might be a conservative estimate. Double D was more like it. They looked to be quite a bit bigger than my generous C cup.

"Are you happy with them?"

She giggled and shimmied her shoulders like Marilyn Monroe. "Don't I look happy?"

"Perky is more like it." I poked the right one this time. No give, no softness, no squeezability. The nipples popped out even through her shirt. Cuddling with Bianca could now be dangerous. Move the wrong way and you risked losing an eye. "You're not worried?"

"Worried about what?"

"Worried that your boobs could explode! Don't you watch TV? They just aired a special report on *Dateline* detailing the monstrosities that happen when silicone leaks into your system."

Bianca crossed her eyes and stuck out her tongue. "Nah. You can't worry over every little thing. You know us women, anything to look good. Besides, I went to a really good doctor. He does a lot of models and movie stars in the states."

When I realized that we were still standing in the doorway, I grabbed one of her bags. "Let's put your stuff in the back room. Did you eat? There's not much in the ice box, but I'm sure I can scrape something together."

"I'm not hungry, more thirsty than anything and I brought my own beverages. Let me change first, then we can catch up."

As I picked up everything off the floor in the front room, I heard Bianca moving around and I imagined the room looked as if hit by a Saks Fifth Avenue tornado —clothes and shoes everywhere.

Bianca returned in a tank top and thong. Glasses clinked in her hand and she swung a bottle of wine. I spread a quilt in the middle of the floor.

"Oh, wait a minute!" I yelled and trotted back to my room. Bianca plopped down on the floor, already popping the cork.

I yanked my suitcases from underneath my bed and combed through the largest one until I found the stash of goodies I smuggled in from the states: potato chips, candy bars, pretzels, and cheddar-cheese popcorn. I swung by the kitchen and grabbed a bottle of hot sauce.

"All right." I sat beside Bianca, stretching out on the quilt. I accepted a glass of white wine and laid my bounty between us. The glass was cool to my lips, the wine refreshing as I took a hefty swallow.

"Yeah, man!" Bianca broke open a bag of Frito Lay's and shook some hot sauce right in the bag. "Let the pig-out fest begin."

Two glasses of wine later, I was so relaxed I could no longer tell the difference between the floor and my body. Bianca had shared way too much information about her horse farm and the horse-breeding process. I never knew how much was involved in artificially inseminating a horse. I didn't think it was the kind of knowledge that I would need anytime soon and the visual that I had now was not the most pleasant one. But to hear Bianca tell it, inseminating horses was the next best thing to playing God.

"I'm creating life!" She gestured with her hands, her brow wrinkled."

It all sounded gross, but I had to give it to her, she seemed to know her stuff. Which was good because Bianca was known for never finishing anything she started.

I stuck a potato chip in my mouth, wiping the excess grease on my leg.

"What about the family?" I asked Bianca before she could start talking about horse sperm again.

"What do you mean, what about the family? What about them?" Her eyes narrowed and she freed her hair from the ponytail, mussing it with her hand.

"Anything new going on?"

"Nope. Them still crazy." She flipped onto her stomach and picked a piece of lint off the blanket. I figured one more glass of wine was what she needed to loosen her tongue so I filled it to the brim and watched her take a healthy swig before adding, "Even crazier now that they know about Mama Grace's letter."

"You've heard about that already?"

"Who hasn't?" She shrugged. I waited, but Bianca wasn't giving up any information easily.

"I can't believe how nosey Aunt Bea is. I just found out about it, and it's my letter."

Bianca finished her third glass of wine and poured a fourth. The first bottle of wine now bone dry, she bounced up and stumbled to the back, giggling stupidly when she stubbed her toe. "Everyone's vexed!" she yelled. A few minutes later she reappeared, a fresh bottle of wine in her hand. Her brown eyes were foggy from wine, but she took in my hurt expression. "Oh really Kingston, you can't possibly be surprised? You had to know they would be pissed off! Has anyone stopped by to pay their condolences? Don't families usually band together during a time like this? They're not here because they feel that they've been cheated out of something. But mark my words, they'll be at the funeral, showing a good face to the public – all done up in their mourning black, playing the role of the bereaved and they'll definitely be here for the reading of the will. You better believe that! But I'll be damned if they're going to support you in private."

Eyes shimmering with passion, Bianca took a deep breath and her words slowed. "All of Mama Grace's children have a million and one reasons why she should have picked them to distribute her estate, even though none of them are qualified, not even Mommy. She's sloshed ninety-eight percent of the time, but still thinks she's capable of handling her mother's business affairs. And why would she pick Uncle Paul? He wasn't even talking to her when she died. He didn't visit her while she was sick. He may not even come to the funeral.

"Nobody took care of Mama Grace like they should have, not even me. And now everyone is standing around with their hands out, mad because Mama Grace saw right through them. It would serve all of them right if she did leave everything to you. They don't deserve a thing." Silent tears dripped down Bianca's face.

I pushed a stray piece of hair from her wet cheek. "Is that what they think, Bianca? That Mama Grace left everything to me? It's not true! I'm just the executor of her estate. I just make sure her wishes are carried out. That's all! None of us will know what the deal is until after the funeral."

"Even if she did leave everything to you," she began again and when I started to object, she raised her hand to stop me. "Even if she did leave everything to you, it would be right. For whatever reason, Mama Grace ended up with a messed-up bunch of spoiled children and grandchildren. Most of us are idiots and the rest are damn fools. But not you, Kingston, and certainly not your mother. You two were the sparkle in Mama Grace's eyes. She was too kindhearted, her spirit too gentle to ever say something like that. But then, she really didn't have to. We all knew and it still didn't change the way we acted." She sniffed and raked her arm under her nose, leaving a trail of snot that I dabbed at with a greasy napkin.

"Kingston," she continued, her voice now small. "I live two hours away and I only saw her one time while she was sick. Rumor has it that some neighbor down the street cared more for her than her own children." Bianca was sobbing now, and with her thin shoulders shaking, she looked so small. Her hair fell forward creating a veil around her face. She paused, wrapping her arms around her middle, trying to collect herself. "How many grandchildren does she have? Why are we the only two here? Where are her sisters? Mama Grace never did nothing but good to all of us."

I took her in my arms. My tears mixed with hers and I tasted the saltiness of them as we consoled each other.

"Shhhhh!" I rocked her back and forth, her whole body shook with the force of her pain. "It's okay, Bianca. We do the best we can at any given moment. Mama Grace knows that."

Suddenly, the sorrow turned to rage and Bianca rolled her eyes upward before looking square into mine. "That's bull and you know it. Letting down the ones that love you when they need you the most is not the best you can do. I should have been here, Bumble Bee." She hadn't called me by my nickname since we were little and she refused to call me Kingston because according to a five-year-old Bianca, no one is named after a city.

Guilt could be cruel and as much as I wanted to alleviate Bianca's anguish, it was not for me to do. I agreed with everything she said; but not wanting to add to Bianca's pain, I kept my thoughts to myself. Besides, I had my own pile of grief and regret to deal with. She should have been here. We all should have. I could have visited more, or made sure she had someone there at all times. Mama Grace deserved better than a bunch of no-good insensitive children and grandchildren. And regardless of what anyone else may think, I felt as if I had earned a spot in that group, too.

Americans flocked in droves to psychiatrists, therapists, counselors, and as a free last resort—talk shows—to share their problems with strangers across the world. But as dysfunctional as my family was, in Jamaica you didn't talk about such issues. To my family, if you didn't talk about it, well then, it did not exist.

My arms started to feel numb; Bianca had fallen asleep and was fast becoming dead weight. I jostled her and she stirred briefly before her head rolled back down. I laid her gently on the quilt, careful to avoid the debris of chips and popcorn.

The wine was causing an enormous amount of pressure on my bladder and I dashed to the bathroom, narrowly missing Mama Grace's china cabinet.

When I returned, Bianca was sitting up, shoving popcorn into her mouth, scavenged from what was spread out on the quilt. There were little pieces of lint clinging to a few of the kernels.

I laughed and sat opposite her, legs crossed Indian style. Music blasted from a house down the street, horns and loud voices competed with the dance hall beats. "Your drunk up!"

"Not me. I can drink a lot more than this." A hiccup punctuated her statement.

"I can see that." I laughed and tussled her already-messed-up hair, feeling an overwhelming sense of tenderness for Bianca. "All right, now tell me the gossip in your life. A new boyfriend, perhaps?"

Bianca tried for another sip of wine and came close to hitting her nose. She frowned. "Please, my horses are getting more action than me and I am not too sure that I care anymore."

I wrinkled my nose. "How can you not care? Aren't there times when you just need some?"

"I was lying when I said I didn't care, okay? I care and of course there are times when I just need some. But when you start to think on all the trouble that goes along with it, it's not worth it. And then when you do find a man that has things right in his life, he's lacking elsewhere if you know what I mean." She started putting the crumbs in a neat pile on one corner of the blanket.

"Wow! That's a terrible campaign slogan for a Jamaican Man."

"Is it different in the states?" she asked pointedly; and that shut me up. "Check it out, Kingston. When a man first looks at a woman, he has enough niceness and lyrics and promises to give her the world." Lazily, she slipped back into the island slang of patois. "No amount of 'me love is deepa dan the deepest sea and higha dan the airplane can fly' and he means every word. But even di' softest skin gets rough after six months, then the romance starts to flap."

"Bianca," I said, my brain too tired to translate.

She sucked her teeth and gave it to me in English, her hands dancing with every word. "All I'm saying is when a man is courting a woman, in the beginning he's very gentleman-like, with lots of promises of eternal love. But even the softest skin becomes rough after a time—that same passion waxes and wanes after months pass. The sunshine fades away. It always happens. In the first week of dating, he opens the door for her, pulls out her chair, picks her up from work and drops her off. He would take her to the hairdresser and return to pick her up. By week three, she has to open her own car door, draw up her own chair and take taxis to and from work. 'Honey, I would pick you up, but the work pressure is holding me.' It's just funny to me, Kingston. The work pressure wasn't there before, only the pressure between his legs." The bitterness wafted from her pores. Too many love situations gone sour could leave a nauseating stench that was hard to wash off.

"Come on, Bianca, it works both ways. It's not only men who seem to work on this six-month schedule. When a woman first meets a man, she's well groomed, she buys new outfits and shoes, her hair is done, she smells good, make up is fierce. All his boys are jealous. At the beginning, she cooks for him, sets the table with candles and fine china. She greets him at the door in a thong and high heels. Then after the first few months, she greets him with curlers in her hair, a torn housedress, slippers on her feet, and a frown. If he dares asks her about the warm meal, the reply would be, 'Something wrong with your hands? It's in the fridge, just take it out and put it in the microwave. I worked just as hard as you today.'

"Whatever happened to the well-groomed woman he met, who greeted him with a warm meal and a smile? The six-month calendar catches her, too. The same way you got him is the same way you keep him. Men need to be loved and cared for just like a woman."

Bianca drew her legs into her chest and wrapped her arms around them, resting her chin on her knees. "So if men are all that great, where's your man?"

I readied my laundry list of reasons why this was not a good time, my hectic schedule, wanting to just enjoy me, etc., etc., etc. But even to my own ears, my reasons sounded like pitiful excuses. And to tell her the story of Randy seemed too much like admitting failure. So once again, I sucked up the pain and humiliation and didn't answer.

Sometime later, we both tumbled into the back room and fell asleep on the small twin bed in my room—conversation unfinished. Sometime during the night, Bianca returned to her own room. I didn't even stir when she left, but I knew she was gone and I missed her presence.

Chapter 9

The stirring sounds of people preparing for their day and the bright sun refused to be ignored. I looked at the clock. Seven was late for me. I usually got up earlier than this on Saturdays. I stretched long and lazily like a cat, flipped over and pushed my face deeper into the pillow. But I knew I wasn't going to be able to go back to sleep. I had been twisting and turning for the past half hour anyway. The buzz from the wine had long worn off and all the thoughts that had been absent for a few fleeting moments were once again racing around in my head.

Insomnia had been a problem for me ever since I was little. My mama used to say that I was the only five-year-old who walked the floors when the only thing I had to worry about was which Ken doll was going to ride in Barbie's Corvette. I just worried. I'd gotten better with age, but would still zoom into the panic mode at the first sign of trouble, then have to work myself out of it.

I reached for the shorts that I'd worn yesterday. I pulled Mama Grace's letter out of the back pocket and skimmed the contents again. I had no idea how to handle this situation. Having been surrounded by strong women since birth, I didn't know what to do except carry on. I had strong blood running through my veins. There was no need for Mama Grace to tell me that. My mother—the master of "carrying on"—taught me the fine art of "Making it on the broken pieces" as she called it. "Everybody got hard times, baby. You just mix it all together and either make something sour or something sweet. It's up to you."

I wanted to make something sweet from my grandmother's passing, but there were two big situations that I had to face. This whole business of my grandmother's will and how Damon figured into the equation. He was back in Jamaica, I knew that, but why in this city and why was he hanging around my family? It had to be a ploy just to get next to me. He's too arrogant to do anything without an ulterior motive. He may have fooled me once but, I wasn't about to let it happen again.

"All right, Kingston, get yo' lazy behind up," I said, but didn't move. Only an image of squeezing my impending large posterior in a bikini forced me out of the bed and in search of my running shoes. Running would clear my mind.

I knocked out a few jumping jacks and like Rocky Balboa, imagined myself dancing in victory atop the steps facing the Liberty Bell in Philadelphia. I thought briefly about waking Bianca to see if she wanted to run, but then remembered, Bianca's allergic to sweat. I stretched again, snapped my sports bra into place and when shrugging into my Howard University Homecoming T-shirt, started to feel something come alive. My limbs shed that early-morning molasses feeling; so encouraged, I went through a half-hearted routine of Tae-bo.

The beaming sun was already smoldering hot as Toy escorted me to the gate, then, barked pitifully when she realized she was not going to tag along.

The first fifteen minutes I concentrated on settling in, getting the feel of the road, perfecting my form and working the remaining kinks out of my joints.

Running had been both a foe and a friend. I hated it, always had; but running has helped me out physically, making my legs my best feature, especially when I threw them in some black three-inch spiked heels. They were long, well-defined, and strong enough to wrap around a man and keep him just where he was supposed to be.

My stomach was toned, but it retained a pudge of softness. Men may stare at the women in those *Abs of Steel* videos, crunching their lives away to maintain their six-pack tummies, but they preferred to curl up next to women like me and lay their heads on my belly like a pillow. My breasts are just the right size; shape and I love the weight of them in my hands. They have dropped a notch since I was twenty, but still enter the room before me even without a bra. My god-sister, Amber, said they are pre-baby stage, but she was just being spiteful. With three kids and working on the fourth, she needed a harness to hold her puppies up.

Most intriguing about my anatomy though is my face—like an artist took a mixture of features from various ethnic groups and blended them together. My almond-brown eyes are fringed by thick black lashes and sit above high cheekbones that called to mind my Arawak Indian ancestry. My head is full of thick, wild and curly hair—the in-between kind of hair that is testimony of the master dipping in the slave shack when he thought people weren't looking. It wasn't quite that good kind of white people hair. Mine begged to be tamed, but I refused to put any chemicals in it. The haphazard crinkles: waves and occasional naps soothed me and drove men crazy.

One hour later, I jogged up to my grandmother's gate and headed straight to the shower. I turned the heat all the way up to insure against any muscle tightness and I massaged some Ben Gay into my calves and the back of my thighs. Securing my wet hair with a clip, I checked on Bianca; but she was still asleep, curled in the fetal position, humming softly through her nose.

I walked into the open kitchen that used to be a back porch. Pa-pa had enclosed it to make more space. The ceiling was made up of slated wood and the floor was a maroon marblesque swirl, which was typical of a lot of Jamaican houses. Two ceiling-length metal gates made up the outer wall. A bit of morning fog still lingered and birds hummed in the distance as I fixed myself a cup of Starbuck's Dark Blend that I had brought from home and settled in Pa-Pa's easy chair. But even the shot of caffeine wasn't enough to keep me going because the next thing

I knew, Queenie was calling my name. I hadn't even heard her arrive. When I looked at the clock, almost two hours had passed.

"Kingston! Hello! Kingston! You have any clothes you want me to wash for you? Kingston! Oh, there you are!" she exclaimed as she rattled the metal gate door. All of this said in a slow cadence while she swept at the leaves with a rusty rake. "Come chile, ya still sleep as hard as when you were a little bitty pickney. Did you get something to eat? I know there isn't much to choose from, so Ima go to de' store in a bit to fetch more groceries. Let me know if you want something special."

When I didn't respond, Queenie poked her head back around the corner. A brown-patched threadbare dress—worn in spots from too much washing—draped her slight frame. My grandmother had probably passed it on to her so it wouldn't get thrown away. She wore no bra. Thin shoes, patched together with duct tape, sans socks, pinched her swollen ankles. A combination of white tufts and tiny plaits peeked from beneath the blue scarf on her head. She had worked for my grandmother since she was sixteen years old. Her hands told the tale of a hard life and all this together made Queenie look much older than her forty-four years.

"I'm okay for now, Queenie. How is everyone?"

"Everyone's fine, thanks." She leaned the rake against the house.

"Glad to hear it. I brought you some Baby Ruth Candy Bars and some books for your grandkids. Don't make me forget them."

"No, Miss Kingston, thanks for thinking of me."

"Is Bianca up?"

"Up and gone, Miss. I passed her on my way in. She said she had to take care of some business in town. Shopping, I'm sure. She said she didn't want to wake you, that she would meet you back here for dinner."

"Okay." I said with a slight pout. "I don't want to go through my grandmother's stuff alone. I didn't realize I was sleeping so soundly."

"You know how she is. Sneaky at best is what I say." Queenie shook her head causing one end of her scarf to flap like a wounded bird. "I'll be out back if you need me."

"I'll be fine." I smiled at her awkwardly. In her eyes, there was hesitation. I had assumed the role of her employer. While growing up, Queenie had assigned me chores that I had to complete under her watchful eye. She had spent as much time raising me as Mama Grace when I spent the summers here. Now things were reversed and I wasn't too sure how comfortable I was with that.

Queenie just accepted it as life. People marched to a different drummer here. Where in the United States you had the rich, the poor, and the people that fell somewhere in between; in Jamaica, you were either at the top or at the bottom. Most of the people who had risen to the top had done so not by their merit alone, but with the help of their family's name. Those on the bottom, tended to stay on the bottom. It felt awkward watching others clean my house, cook my food, and wash my undies.

Once when I was about eight or nine, my great-aunt, Aunt Bea, was having some work done on her house. It was a particularly hot day and one of the workers had knocked on the back door where I was playing.

"Miss Kingston, I was wondering if I could bother you for a cool drink." A grown man addressing me as Miss impressed me, and I went into full hostess mode. I might have even put some delicate soda crackers on the fine china if Aunt Bea hadn't caught me. She chastised me for serving the worker a drink in the good glasses. Now she was going to have to sterilize it. Didn't I know that the plastic, chipped, dented glasses were for the workers? I could still hear her ranting.

I had quite a long moral discussion with my dolls later that night. I knew in America that sometimes white people didn't like black people, but that some guy named Martin had made things a bit easier. Never had I heard of black people not liking other black people. When I posed the question to Mama, she said that if you hated someone else who looked like you, that meant you hated yourself. I would ask the same question at the late-night tea parties. My blonde-hair, blue-eyed Baby Alive would just stare at me in silence.

I stood up, pushed my chair back and took my dirty dishes to the sink. Queenie fed the dogs and then started to sort the clothes. After washing the small cup and plate and setting them in the dish rack to dry, I headed to the front to check my e-mail. Two were from Jonetta. The first was to let me know that Scooby's manager had tried to return my phone call. Apparently, the celebration had been even bigger than I thought and was in no danger of stopping anytime soon. They wanted to schedule a meeting for early next week. The other was to let me know that Mr. Mansini wanted me to come to New York as soon as I returned and that he had sent a huge bouquet of roses in honor of my grandmother.

When I called my grandmother's attorney again, I was informed by the secretary that he would be busy all day, but that the reading of the will had been scheduled for the day after the funeral—two days away. I couldn't help feeling like I was gearing up for showdown at the OK corral. Not only with my family, but also with Damon.

There were still too many questions bouncing around in my head so I ventured off in search of the truth and the one person who would give it to me—Queenie.

I found her bent over the gray cement sink, washing my bed linens by hand. I'd only spent one night on them. A clothesline was pulled straight as a ruler across the yard, one end tied to the mango tree, the other to the willow. Dangling from the line attached by dull gray clothing pins were an assortment of my finest lace panties and brassieres in every color from mustard yellow to mustang red. My cheeks warmed from embarrassment. I watched Queenie's hands as she squeezed and scrubbed the clothes with powdered soap. Squeak, squeak. Squish, squish.

"Queenie, those things weren't even dirty!" My cheeks warmed even more with the protest. Had she glimpsed my "friend" tucked in the far left corner of my overnight bag with the rest of my unmentionables?

Her hands kept right on moving. Squeak, squeak. Squish, squish. "Me knows that, Miss Kingston, but me just wanted to make sure."

I couldn't argue with that logic so amidst another squeak, squeak and squish, squish, I switched subjects. "Queenie?" Squeak, squeak. Squish, squish.

"Hmmmmm," she replied. Squeak, squeak. Squish, squish.

"Uncle Winston was telling me about Mama Grace's last days."

She hummed again, which I translated to "spit it out" and wrung the excess water out of the sheets with hands almost crippled by painful arthritis.

"He said Damon came to visit her."

"Awww! Yes, Miss Kingston. He was truly a blessing to Mama Grace. Yes, Ma'am, he was truly a blessing."

"I guess I don't understand, Queenie." I wanted her to explain it to me like I was a five-year-old. "Why was Damon here? I mean, I knew he was back on the island, but I thought he was in Montego Bay." I paused, letting the conversation hang.

Queenie picked up the loose thread and ran with it. "Well, he lives just down the street so," she replied as if the answer was obvious. "He fixed up his grandfather's house so nice, ya' see, added three rooms and a beautiful parlor—turned it into a clinic for the community. His granddaddy would be so proud. Damon has grown into a fine young man."

She hitched the tub of clean clothes up on her nonexistent hip, trudged over to the clothesline, and began hanging the sheets. She looked at the basket until she caught my gaze. Snorting, I picked up the end of a blue floral pillowcase with faded yellow daisies. So much for being the employer.

"Miss Grace asked for him to come and he did. Him come just as quick. Held her hand through the pain like it was his own mother. She didn't want anyone else to see her in such a state. So she called him. And he didn't hesitate. Yes, suh, that boy is a true blessing."

My pillowcase hung crookedly and Queenie nodded at it. I rehung it, anxious for her smile of approval. Her smile didn't quite reach her eyes, but we continued to hang the clothes in silence.

"You look like a lost pup," she said finally, putting her hand on the small of her back and stretching. "I know you have only me for company, but I can't take it anymore. Chile', why don't you go down there and thank Damon. I know Mama Grace would want you to. Plus, you just might make a new friend. I have some of those mangos I just picked from the tree that you can take to him. He loves Mama Grace's mangos."

Go and thank him? Make a new friend? She couldn't possibly realize what she was saying, or did she? No, she couldn't possibly know.

I slung a purple bra over the clothesline then snapped a pin over it. I tried to keep the anxiety from my voice when I said, "I already know Damon, Queenie. Remember Joanne, his sister? We used to play together when we were little."

Queenie looked up at the sky as if searching for an answer. "Oh yes, Ma'am. Now me remember. Well, there you go, even better. Now you can go catch up."

I gnawed on my lower lip, feeling torn. I couldn't exactly tell Queenie why I didn't want to go see Damon. I didn't want to lie either.

Just as I was about to flat-out refuse to go, Queenie pushed my shoulder non-too gently. "Go on, Chile'. He won't bite you and I'm just not going to be able to take you being up under me all day."

"Yes, Ma'am." I bit down hard to keep from saying anything else and walked along the gravel path that led to the house. "And fix yourself up. Put some makeup on." She called at my back.

I raised a hand in acknowledgment, but grumbled, "I'm not putting on makeup just to walk down the street," careful not to let Queenie hear. I stubbed my toe on a rock. *Shit!* Pay back.

The gilded mirror hanging in the narrow corridor mocked me as I walked by. I doubled back and squinted at my image. With nothing on my face, I looked about thirteen years old. All right, maybe a little bit of lip gloss. I nibbled on my lower lip and pinched my cheeks. And maybe a touch of blush. *Dammit!* I didn't want to care what Damon thought, but I did. I also didn't want to feel anxious about his reaction to me showing up at his house, but felt that as well.

I made a beeline for my suitcase. While searching for my makeup case, I spotted my new black Prada shorts that I had bought the previous summer in L.A. When I tried them on and pranced in the three-way mirror, I knew I had to buy them despite the one hundred seventy-five dollars price tag. They flattered my figure with rhinestones that danced across the bottom calling attention to my well-toned thighs. The cut of the material seemed to pull my stomach in and round my butt out. My female vanity kicked into overdrive and I slipped them on. I fingered a plain black t-shirt, but pulled the tube top that matched the shorts on instead. Finally, I brushed a touch of Lancome Glitter powder across my shoulders.

I dropped to my knees and ran my hand underneath the bed until I found my black stack sandals. Queenie must have pushed them under when she swept earlier this morning. I buckled the straps and studied my feet. The polish on the big toe on my right foot was chipped. A good pedicure should hold up better than this. I didn't expect to end up in Jamaica; so I had settled for a quickie job, thinking I had time later in the week. But once a Girl Scout, I was prepared. It only took me a minute to brush a new coat of Mardi Gras Red over each nail so they looked brand new.

Now for the hair. I pulled off the plastic band holding my hair, mussed it with my fingers until it fell gracefully around my shoulders, then added a bit of mousse to tame the flyaway tendrils at each temple. Preferring the natural look, I accented my lashes with just a touch of black mascara, MAC's gold bronzer across my cheeks, and Aveda's nude fantasy made my lips kissable. I sprayed perfume on my pulse points and then once in the air. I walked through the mist before twirling in the mirror so I could critique myself from every angle. Satisfied, I blew a kiss at my image.

Right on cue, Queenie's callused, bare feet came padding down the hall. "My, my, my," Queenie said, clicking her tongue as she peeked through the door to my grandmother's bedroom. I was standing in front of my grandmother's—my, I corrected myself—armoire. "You look like Cinderella off to de' ball." She handed me a bag filled with ripe mangoes and dull green avocados. "Go on, now." Queenie sucked her teeth as I hesitated, then pushed me toward the door. And with a ball of fire beginning to grow in my stomach, I went.

The sun had made it halfway through its orbit and the heat was merciless. In Kingston, cool breezes were few and I could already feel the skin at the nape of my neck growing moist. Kids were playing a modified game of cricket at one end of the street and a cart chase at the other. Motorcycles revved at the racetrack a few blocks over. I waved at a man selling flavored ice called ska juice in the vacant lot. Old ladies rocked in chairs on the porch, men worked shingling roofs, and babies played in their cribs in the front yard while their mothers tended to their gardens.

I trudged down the block to Damon's house, passing Maxwell Preparatory, the school my mother attended as a child. School was a generous term to describe the building, really just a house that was converted by a former nun who had been kicked out of the Convent for being too rebellious. Mom told me that she was having an affair with one of the married parishioners and got caught.

Uniforms—leftover from the days of British rule—were status quo on the island. I still kept two faded pictures of my mother in her school uniform—one taken with her class, one standing alone. In both photos, she looked shy, head ducked and hair pulled away from her face in two ponytails with ribbons tied on the end.

Too young to get a job after graduation, my mother went to a trade school and learned typing, short hand, and literary works. She worked and put herself through nursing school, but then got pregnant with me. Disgraced at being an unwed mother, she fled to America. Whenever we returned to Kingston, she would walk me to Maxwell. Standing outside and with misty eyes, she would tell me that this life had been easy, when life had been good.

Now the school was in shambles with only one red brick wall remaining completely in tact. The other walls were covered in graffiti: names of popular reggae artists past and present such as Bob Marley, his son, Ziggy, Chakademus & Pliers, Bongo and Yami Bolo, political slogans, and misshapen hearts with the names of boys and girls scribbled inside them. I walked inside the dusty schoolyard and kicked some rocks. The flowers had long been dead and there were no footprints in the dirt. A little girl was running on her way to somewhere more important, about twenty-eight pigtails tied at the end with red ribbon bounced around her head. As she passed by, her hand accidentally brushed my leg. She smiled. I smiled back.

Chapter 10

At six-years-old and with only two days carved out of my summer vacation, I was restless. I had already arranged and rearranged my dolls on the little twin bed that sat in the room just off the kitchen. The coloring books my aunt had sent for me were meant for someone much younger. Didn't she know I already knew how to color in the lines? Adults. They didn't have a clue.

The snacks that Mommy had packed were lined in the cupboard. I had already counted them twice this morning just to make sure no one was sneaking them but me. Pa-pa was taking his afternoon nap or I would have pestered him to teach me some more chess moves. Not that I really understood the game, I just loved spending time with him, one on one. He always made me feel like the most special little girl in the world and not just because he constantly told me, "Kingston, you are the most special little girl in the whole wide world." No, Pa-pa really cared about what I thought. He was the only grown-up who asked my opinion and then actually listened.

Normally, the majority of the summer would have been spent with Mammy, Mama Grace's mother, in Swift River—a little town that was nestled in the hills sitting opposite of the Blue Mountains.

All of my cousins would converge upon Mammy in phases: Lil' Winston, Stacia, Paulette, and Vivine would be there first. Next came Patrick, Pierre and Bianca. Finally, Adana, Andrew, and me.

This summer was different though. Mammy was sick and said her heart couldn't take the pressure of ten youngsters running through her house. The big Independence picnic wasn't going to happen until August—two months away—and that was more than enough excitement for an old woman, she said. So this summer I had been sentenced to three solid months in Kingston. Only being paroled for two things: shopping and church.

Mama Grace did most of the shopping at Coronation—a large noisy open-air market. Higglers dragged loads of bounty from all over the island: breadfruits, bananas, coconuts, plantains, yams, etc., and you had to barter with them for a fair price. Depending on the day, plus the mood of the market, multiplied by the heat, Mama Grace either made out like a bandit or felt like a fool—grumbling all the way home trying to come up with an excuse to give Pa-pa about why she went five dollars over budget.

Then, every Sunday, Mama Grace and I would walk to Coke Methodist Church on East Queen Street. Pa-pa never attended. He believed that most church folk were on the take and he could praise his God just as easily on his verandah while still wearing his short pants. My mother was not only baptized at Coke, but also confirmed and married there as well. I, too, was baptized there and hoped one day I would be married in the cathedral-style building. Occasionally, we'd go to a matinee if Pa-pa had the money, but those days stretched few and far between. So when Mama Grace suggested that I go out and play, I just looked at her. When she suggested that I go play by myself, I looked at her as if she were crazy. When she looked at me as if I were the one that was crazy, I straightened up my face. Mama Grace didn't play when it came to those looks.

I skipped outside. Children were whooping and hollering, playing an intense game of cricket. I walked slowly down the sidewalk, trailing my hand over the iron rod fence and studying the flowers that had just started to bloom. I noticed someone following me, dancing in my shadow. I whirled around, fully intending to give this intruder a piece of my mind, but her elf-like grin stopped me cold.

"Hi," she said simply.

"Hi."

"You Miss Grace's grandbaby." It was more a statement than a question. She cocked her head to the side. I was much taller than she was and she had to look directly into the sun to see my face. I wondered if that was what caused her eyes to cross in such a funny way or if it was natural. She twirled. The slogan on her t-shirt read, "Somebody who loves me visited the Big Apple and all they brought me back was this lousy shirt."

"My name's Kingston," I spoke in the same voice I used with the elderly ladies in church, exaggerated politeness with saccharin sweetness dripping from every syllable. "What's your name?"

"Kingston?" She grabbed her stomach and doubled over with laughter. "K-K-K-Kin!" She was laughing so hard she couldn't even get my name out. My eyes narrowed with every hee-hee-hee. "Who named you that?" She finally asked and I thought she was stupid.

"My mother named me, who else? Who named you?"

"My granny. I don't know who my parents are. They left my brother and me with my grandparents. I don't miss 'em though," she said defiantly. "Why would I want someone who doesn't want me? I live with my grandparents and I know them real well."

Suddenly we had something in common. "I don't know my daddy either," I said.

She smiled. She was missing both of her front teeth and one on the bottom. "My name's Joanne."

"Oh."

"Is that all you can say?"

"No," I said and once again she dissolved in laughter. When she finished, she took a deep breath, took my hand and I felt as if nothing could separate us. Little did I know.

The months of June and July passed quickly. My seventh birthday came and went and Joanne was the star in the play of my life. With her around, nothing seemed quite as boring, quite as slow or quite as uneventful.

August marched in and it was time to head up to the country for Mammy's Independence Day Picnic. We would be there for three days and I couldn't imagine a minute without Joanne. So I started in on Mama Grace early with arguments worthy of a high-priced lawyer.

"She's never been to Swift River, Mama Grace. And her brother lives in Hope Bay with her aunt so she'd get to see him. She hasn't seen him in a really, really, really long time. Isn't that sad?" I twiddled her apron strings around my fingers, eyes pleading just as much as my words. "And Mama Grace, I can show her Uncle Battle's goats. She's never milked a cow. It would be so much fun and then this way, you won't have to worry about me because Joanne will be there to keep me company, so you and Papa can play dominoes and I won't interrupt. You won't even have to walk me out to pee-pee. Joanne can go with me. And she knows how to swim so we can help each other in the river." It all came out on one whoosh of a breath as Mama Grace chopped the onions to go in the ackees and codfish we were having for breakfast.

"Hand me that little bowl behind you, Kingston." I did so then moved closer, wrapping my arms around her waist. "And finish wiping the table so that Pa-pa can eat before he goes to the store."

"Mama Grace?"

"I heard you, Kingston. I'm not deaf, ya' know." She was smiling, amused at my pain. She took my chin in her hand, her warm brown eyes meeting mine. "If Joanne's granny says she can go, then she can go. Pa-pa and I have already discussed it. We anticipated your request weeks ago." Her smile was crooked this time, as if she had just pulled a fast one on me. "I'll write a note for you to carry to her grandmother." I was out the door before she even finished the sentence, and almost to the gate when I heard her voice, sterner this time. "Kingston!" I put on the brakes. "You must finish cleaning while I write the note." She chuckled as she walked back into the house drying her hands on a towel.

When Pa-pa and Mama Grace finally announced that it was time for us to leave early Friday morning, Joanne and I had been waiting on the porch for almost two hours. We just sat there and listened to Mama Grace tidying up, Pa-pa feeding the dogs, the clattering of the breakfast dishes and a final walk through as they locked up the house—doing all sorts of unnecessary stuff as far as we were concerned.

As soon as we heard the key turn in the ignition, we ran to the gates to open them so Pa-pa wouldn't have to waste a moment getting out of the car to open them himself. He had borrowed the car from his cousin for one-hundred-fifty Jamaican dollars. Joanne was impressed.

Mama Grace was already in the front seat, adjusting the radio to pick up the morning news. Joanne and I flopped in the back seat next to a big box full of food—cooked and uncooked. Neither one of us had eaten breakfast, but the enticing aromas didn't stir a thing in our empty bellies. We were filled to capacity with excitement.

It didn't take us long to leave the city and soon we began our trek up the winding streets that would take us to the country. The drive from Kingston to Swift River normally took about two and a half hours; it took Pa-pa four hours. Never a man to hurry anyway, he was meandering at twenty miles below the speed limit. The steady rhythm of the car soon put us to sleep an hour into our road trip. When we woke, the car had just turned off the main road and was headed up the long winding hill that would take us to Swift River.

Mammy's house sat right in the middle of six family houses clustered together at the top of the hill. The large frame house loomed against the backdrop of the Blue Mountains. Beds of flowers were planted on either side of the long gravel driveway that led to Mammy's house, then splintered off into separate driveways like branches of a tree. Various fruit trees—oranges, tangerines, grapefruit, coconut, avocados, papayas, ackee, and mango—were sprinkled about the property.

Goats, chickens, and dogs ran wild in the front lawn. They were the lucky ones. The smell of blood permeated the air from the freshly slaughtered animals. Various forms of meat—pork, chicken, goat, beef—were already grilling on the pit, puffs of fragrant smoke wafting into the air with each turn. Some of Mammy's helpers were busy setting up tables and chairs for the more than three hundred relatives expected to traipse through this area over the course of the weekend. Most of the women were stationed in the outside kitchen connected to the far side of the kitchen, chopping, peeling, grating, picking, plucking, slicing, and dicing.

Various cars were already parked with families unloading suitcases at the respective houses. The kids had changed from their traveling clothes and were suited up in their country clothes ready to see who could get dirtiest the quickest. They were organizing games of dodge ball, tag, and cricket. Joanne just stood there with her mouth hanging open.

"Come on." I grabbed her hand. Pa-pa had already set the bags beside the car so we scooped ours up and raced toward the big house.

Mammy was standing in the middle of her huge outdoor kitchen orchestrating lunch. For a woman who had never worked a day outside her home, she had the organization and delegation skills of a CEO of any major corporation. Family members were in assembly-line formation, churning out sardine sandwiches, slices of bun and cheese, and shanty cola served in paper cups. Mammy's white hair snaked down her back in one long coil. She hadn't cut it in more than sixty years and it hung well past her backside. Her skin was soft and unwrinkled, making it impossible to believe she was more than ninety years old. She was assigning sleeping spaces and cooking chores when I pulled Joanne up to meet her.

"There's my Bumble Bee." Though her voice was soft, I never had to strain to hear her. The low, gravelly sound commanded full attention. She smiled, not caring that she hadn't put in her false teeth.

She took my face in her hands and presented each cheek for a kiss. I obliged with enthusiasm.

"Hi, Mammy. This is my friend, Joanne. She lives down the street from Mama Grace with her grandparents because her mommy and daddy are dead." Joanne was standing behind me, peeking around my waist.

Mammy opened her arms wide and I wrapped both my arms around her soft middle, her left arm pulling me close. Her right arm waited. "Come, Child," Mammy said. "You're one of us now." Joanne snuggled in close to me and was tucked safely in Mammy's arms. Before we suffocated in Mammy's ample bosom, she sent us on our way with a warning to stay out of trouble.

"Why does she call you Bumble Bee?" Joanne asked.

"She says when I was younger and we spent the summer up here, out of all the kids, I was the one who constantly buzzed around her like a bee so she started calling me Bumble Bee."

Joanne nodded, then said, "Bumble Bee."

I grabbed her arm. "There are some things only family members can get away with and calling me Bumble Bee is one of them. Plus, Mammy can do it because she's my elder."

"What's an elder?"

"Someone you have to respect no matter how crazy they are and you can't hit them, either, because they're older than you."

"Oh."

We traipsed across the verandah to the other side of the house and ducked in and out of rooms until we found the corner bedroom that had been designated as ours. Six twin beds lined up in a row in a space designed to only hold half as much.

"So whatcha wanna do?" This came from my cousin, Sheila. Joanne and I flopped across the bed adjacent from her.

It didn't take us long to figure it out.

Workers had been laboring over the past week to install a bathroom equipped with a shower on the inside of the house. It was located right outside of our room. We took turns running in and out of the spray, not caring that our clothes were wet.

After dinner, we played in the yard for a while then tried to convince the adults to let us go swimming in the river. It was our fifth attempt in two hours, but the adults refused to be worn down. They stood firm on their original position. We had to wait until the picnic tomorrow.

It was way past our bedtime and we were all fighting sleep. The slapping of dominoes and the shuffling of cards could be heard as the men entertained themselves while the women cleaned and prepared for the next day. The sweet smell of white rum and bread pudding teased us while we snuggled like sardines in the bed. A car stereo had been turned on to provide music for the teenagers. There was an occasional dog bark and crunch of tires on the gravel road that signaled even more relatives arriving. To this orchestra of sounds, we eventually drifted off to sleep.

We rose early the next morning, hastily tossing water in all the right places before heading outside to join the others. Breakfast was being made by the women while the men lined up animals to be slaughtered for the picnic.

Joanne and I had already demolished a plate of fluffy scrambled eggs and fried dumplings slathered with butter and guava jelly when we heard Pa-pa honking the car horn.

"Kingston! Joanne!" We stuffed one last spoonful of eggs in our already full mouths, grabbed another dumpling, and raced toward the car amidst gentle chastising from mothers who were overly concerned about our digestion. I broke my dumpling in half, stuffed part of it into Pa-pa's mouth and devoured the rest, all while jumping into the front seat beside him. Joanne settled in the back seat.

Pa-pa yanked on my ponytail and winked. "We going to pick up Damon?" she asked, her eyes dancing with excitement.

"Yes, Joanne," Pa-pa replied patiently, used to dealing with anxious little girls. He smiled at her in the rear view mirror. Her joy was infectious. We were all smiles and laughter as Pa-pa backed the car out of the yard and began the trek down the hill, heading for Hope Bay. By the time we reached the bottom of the hill, Joanne had expounded upon every single redeeming quality that belonged to her older brother, Damon.

Because he had gotten in so much trouble, Damon had been sent by his grandfather two years earlier to live in Hope Bay with an aunt. He was only eight at the time. When I asked Joanne what kind of trouble got an eight-year-old sent to the country, she just shrugged. She didn't want to talk about it. She and Damon were close and she guarded her memories of him.

Mama Grace said that Damon had been "acting out." She whispered that it was because his parents weren't around.

Joanne gave Pa-pa directions and soon we were turning into the gravel driveway that led to her aunt's beachfront home. It was bright blue with white trim and blended right in with sky. A gutted boat leaned on three huge rocks just a few feet from the side of the house, its rusty bow pointing east. Joanne explained that her uncle had been working on refurbishing the boat. Children's voices drifted from the house with a noticeably mature one giving directions to be polite and remain on best behavior.

"Damon," Joanne gushed on an awe-inspired breath and before Pa-pa could shift the car into park, she had thrust the door open and hit the ground running. Pa-pa and I followed a lot slower—him not wanting to intrude upon the family reunion, me, because I was jealous.

All summer long, I had Joanne to myself and now I was going to have to share her with someone else who I was sure she adored more than me.

But as soon as Damon, stepped from the house, all arms and legs with a grin so brilliant it took my breath away, all that jealousy faded and was replaced by something so spectacular I had to wrap my arms around myself to contain it. Damon walked back to the car, arm and arm with Joanne. He shook Pa-pa's hand, then enveloped me in a bear hug and kissed me soundly on the cheek. My heartbeat went into over drive and I knew.

At seven years old, I was hopelessly in love with my best friend's brother.

Chapter 11

The oversized knocker on the door to Damon's house sent echoes all through it as I bounced from one foot to the other. I wondered if Damon would look the same way, if the rhythm of my heart would beat the same way when he looked at me, would the butterflies that were now camped in my stomach flutter around the same way they did when he first kissed me.

Someone peeked through the peephole then the door swung wide. "Yes, Ma'am," she said.

"Hi. I'm here to see Damon Whitfield."

"Yes, Ma'am." She pronounced each syllable slowly as if extra concentration was needed for pronunciation. "Come in, please. The doctor's in the back. What time is your appointment?" The stout and sturdy woman opened the door wide and ushered me inside with a gesture of her hand.

The house smelled of furniture polish and pimento. The corridors were long and wide surrounded by walls that were paneled in heavy oak. On the right wall sat a small wooden stand with side extensions that flapped down and a small crystal bowl placed on top was filled with small, multicolored mints. A sign-in sheet attached to a red plastic clipboard hung next to it.

"I don't have an appointment. My name's Kingston. Kingston Phillips. I'm Mrs. Montague's granddaughter. I wanted to speak with the doctor."

"The one from the States? Oh, my. You're such a pretty girl. We were very sorry to hear about your grandmother. She was so loved in the community." Excitement caused her speech to become stilted and she fluttered her hands, looking slightly embarrassed at her familiarity.

"Thank you," I said and folded my hands together. "What's your name?"

"Tiny, Ma'am."

"Thanks, Tiny."

"Yes, Ma'am."

"Tiny?"

"Yes, Ma'am?"

"Please call me Kingston."

She nodded and showed me into the sitting room off the hallway. "Have a seat, Ma'am. The doctor will be right with you." I started to correct her again, but didn't. Ma'am didn't sit well on me, it was kind of like playing dress up in your mother's clothes. But pushing the issue would make her more uncomfortable.

The oak paneling continued throughout the house, the décor too warm to be a doctor's office. I sank down onto the over-stuffed maroon paisley settee, almost dropping the bag of mangoes that Queenie had shoved in my hands. The couch, catty-corner to me, was upholstered in an understated brown corduroy textured fabric, providing the perfect contrast. Even the bright yellow throw pillows seemed to blend right in. Large potted plants surrounded the other side of the couch; magazines covered the coffee table. I shifted, glancing at the pictures and artwork covering the wall. Some of the pieces seemed to have been chosen for artistic appeal, some sentimental. It only added to the homey atmosphere. The largest picture was of Damon's grandfather, framed with a small light shining above it. He was young, but still looked distinguished and stern as was the typical pose of that era. He had his white doctor's coat on with a stethoscope around his neck and Damon's strong chin.

Tiny hustled back into the sitting room—her navy and white flowered dress swishing against her bare legs. On a platter, she balanced a tall iced glass of tea. The heat already causing drops of water to run in rivulets down the sides and a sprig of mint was pinched on the rim of the glass. Butter cookies were arranged on a plate with a linen napkin folded into a small triangle.

"The doctor says him soon come."

"Thanks, Tiny." I accepted the glass. "How did you know I was thirsty?" I smiled and took a long sip. The mint tickled my throat. "Hmmmm. Delicious."

"Yes, Ma'am." Tiny ducked her plaited head and rewarded me with a shy smile. "Let me know if you need anything else." She left the room, head held high.

I picked up an old issue of *Essence Magazine* and flipped through it. An article caught my eye: "How to Rekindle an Old Flame." I put that magazine down and picked up the *Ebony*. On the cover, "Finding Love After 30." Not even. I tried *Jet* next. It automatically opened to the Society Wedding page. I was not interested in where Hope and Lance had spent their glorious honeymoon, so I gave up and started reading *The Wall Street Journal*. Prices were on the rise in China. I was halfway through the second article, learning more than I ever wanted to know about child labor when my whole world flipped upside down.

"Kingston." The voice was deep with timbre, so resonant it sent waves of remembered pleasure rippling throughout my body—an explosion that started at the very core of my being. Time stopped. The beat of my heart was the only sound I heard.

I hesitated before looking up, as if once I laid eyes on him, nothing would ever be the same. But then, nothing had been the same since Damon entered my life more than two decades ago. I thought about standing, but didn't know how my legs would hold up so I stayed right where I was, just raising my eyes to meet his.

Age had only made his already intense, dark eyes more determined and they held mine now with steady self-assurance. His locks had grown and were pulled back off his face. The sparse gray coming at his temples served only to make him more distinguished. Why was it men had it like that? He had maintained his body that had been so superbly fine-tuned from many years of playing football—American soccer. I imagined my fingers trailing across his chest, broad and strong underneath his form-fitting black shirt. Ten years had only made him more dangerous. I hoped now that I was capable of protecting myself.

I was glad my pride didn't get the best of me, glad that I took so much time with my appearance. I wanted him to kick himself all up and down Front Street for being stupid enough to let me go.

"Damon," I said, my heart pumping a mile a minute and my hands already moist. Then, my mind became my body's partner in the crime of betrayal. He used to tell me endlessly how beautiful he thought I was. What did he think about me now? Did he still find me attractive? Did I still turn him on? Did he anticipate my visit as much as I had dreaded it? Then, I kicked myself. It was too early in the game for this.

"It's been a long time," he said.

"Yes. Yes, it has." I shifted again in the chair, wondering if Damon was half as uncomfortable as I was, because quite frankly I wanted to be swallowed by the floor. Thoughts raced through my head—thoughts that I would never voice, wanting the past to remain where it was. Finally I stood up, feeling really stupid sitting there like a fifth grader.

But then standing presented a whole new problem. I didn't know whether to shake his hand or hug him.

Damon solved that, reaching out and enfolding me in his arms. My stomach jolted as a flood of memories rushed in as I inhaled his woodsy scent. Damon was never into commercial fragrances, preferring to walk up First Avenue in Washington D.C. to the Muslim store and select a variety of oils. He never just used one, tailoring a mixture of two or three depending on his mood—usually musk and jasmine.

After a brief hesitation, I wrapped my arms loosely around him. We had always fit perfectly together. At close to 6'3", he still towered over me when I wore heels, making me feel safe and secure. The hug lasted a few seconds longer than what was proper for casual acquaintances, even if they hadn't seen each other in awhile. But that's because that wasn't what we were or had ever been. Nothing had ever been casual about our relationship. Having his body against mine felt too good, too right; and for just one more fleeting moment, I stood there and enjoyed it before I worked to disentangle my limbs from his.

"It's been too long," Damon drawled slowly as he, too, pulled away. He looked at my hands clutching the bag of mangoes and avocadoes before turning those puppy dog eyes on me.

"Yes, these are for you. Queenie sent them. She also said to let you know that she'll be making some coconut tarts later and to come by and get some."

"If that lady didn't have a huge boyfriend, I would be her love slave just for her tarts. She knows how to make a man feel good."

Was he trying to tell me something? One of his biggest complaints when we were together was the amount of time I didn't spend in the kitchen.

After another second of uncomfortable silence, Damon took my hand and led me to the back of the house where he had converted one of the larger bedrooms into an office. Cumbersome pieces of oak furniture were lined up against the walls that had been painted in warm orange blossom. A multicolor area rug stretched across the middle of the floor and more flowery plants sat in all four corners.

"Have a seat." Damon gestured to a chair leaning against an overflowing file cabinet. He grabbed a standard office chair that was pushed under the desk, and rolled it right next to me.

"Thanks." I sat down demurely, crossing my legs so that Damon was shown a nice length of leg.

"So," he said slowly.

"So?"

"How have you been?" he asked.

"I'm good. What about you?"

"Really good," he replied, then paused. "I'm very sorry about your grandmother."

"Thanks." Relieved that we had gotten right to the point, I jumped into my rehearsed speech. "Actually, that's why I'm here. To thank you on behalf of the family."

"And here I thought you wanted to see me." Don't flatter yourself, I wanted to tell him. But I didn't. I was here to be nice. So instead, I gave a nervous chuckle and moved on. "As I was saying, I wanted to thank you for taking care of Mama Grace. It really means a lot to me because I'm not sure what it would have been like for her had you not been there."

He shrugged. "I was just doing my job."

"No, Damon. You were doing a lot more than your job. A lot more and I wanted you to know that I appreciate it. She didn't let on to us how sick she was."

Damon was now the one shifting uncomfortably. He had never been able to take compliments well and now, just nodded.

"So." That one word hung between us like the great divide.

"Yes, Kingston?" My name rolled of his tongue like a caress and I knew he was messing with me. I stood, fussily preparing to leave. Damon stood as well and gently placed a hand on my elbow. "Sit down. Please," he added. "We're not strangers. I want to know what you've been up to. It's been ten years."

I took my seat again and then became annoyed with myself for following his command so quickly. "I've been living my life, Damon." I added, a definite edge to my voice and he feigned offense at my comment.

"And what exactly does life consist of for you?"

I shook my head with annoyance. How was I supposed to fit ten years' worth of living into a couple of sentences? He must have seen the confusion on my face and began firing questions at me.

"What are you doing? Did you end up going into journalism? Where are you living? Are you married? Kids? Dog? Fish? Are you happy?"

"Whoa!" I said, waving in protest. "Are we conducting an interview? I feel like I'm on *60 Minutes*." He relaxed in his chair and gestured as if saying, "Okay, Ms. Thang, you handle it then."

I took a deep breath and my hands started doing their thing. My college acting coach called it, "overcompensation." Damon used to call it King-language, his silly spin on my name and the art of sign language.

For a moment our eyes locked and I knew he was thinking the same thing.

"Well, I'm in the entertainment field. I was a sales and marketing executive at a radio station, but there wasn't much room for growth so last year I decided to get into the record-label business. I convinced a major label to start an urban division in Chicago and let me head it up and I love it."

"Wow!" he said, raising his thick eyebrows. "That's quite an accomplishment. Your mother must be very proud."

"My mother is dead." The shock seeped from Damon like air from a punctured balloon—his eyes closed momentarily and his lips parted. He looked at me again before sinking back in his chair and dropping his head in his hands.

"I'm sorry to hear that, Kingston. I know how close you were. I'm surprised Mama Grace never mentioned that to me." He searched for some words of solace, but didn't come up with much of anything.

"Mama Grace probably didn't mention it because she never really got over my mother's death. It haunted her until she died."

"When?" It was a standard question, one I should have been used to by now; but the pain still hit me square in my gut at the slightest mention. "Two thousand and two, the eleventh of March."

A frown wrinkled Damon's forehead and I knew he was doing a quick mental calculation. "That was three months after I left D.C."

"Yes, and three months after you left me." The words left my mouth singed with bitterness and I was immediately sorry. I hadn't come here to do this.

"Why didn't you call me?" Damon asked, his voice strangely small.

My eyes turned into wide circles of disbelief. I opened my mouth, then closed it. Finally I managed, "Why didn't I call you?" He couldn't be serious. "Why didn't I call you?"

Damon nodded. He was serious.

"I did call you. I called you and I wrote you, Damon. You were never available to take my phone calls and you didn't respond to my letters. I left so many messages I lost count. When I found out my mother died, the first person I called was you. You were studying and I left an urgent message with the university for you to call me back, but I didn't say why. You don't leave something like that in a message. When you didn't call back that day, or the next day or the next, I gave up. I was tired of trying to keep our relationship together. And when I got back from the funeral, it took all the energy I had just to finish out the semester. Why didn't I call?" The tension hung between us like a thick cloud. I exhaled loudly and looked away; disgusted with the way the conversation had turned.

"I didn't know." Damon reached for my hand, lifting the back to his lips and tenderly kissing it.

A spark of electricity shot up my arm and I moved before the warmth could spread to other parts of my body. "It's history, Damon. Life goes on. It was hard, but I survived. And I'm happy."

Damon tapped his well-manicured index finger slowly against his pursed lips. I blinked, then looked away, focusing on a potted plant, as my thoughts took a sharp detour. A few more moments of unnerving silence passed before Damon spoke again.

"Married?"

"No," I said through clenched teeth.

"Boyfriend?"

"Not anymore." My eyes dared him to ask for an explanation. But I had never been able to intimidate him and he wasn't about to let me start now.

"Oh?" he continued, his eyes sparkling again. "Not anymore as of when?"

"Actually, as of about one day ago."

Damon nodded, leaned back in his chair and crossed one long leg over the other, like a psychiatrist studying his patient.

My eyes zoned in on the definition of his thigh beneath his summer slacks. "I've been focusing on my career." I could have kicked myself. I couldn't come up with a better explanation than that? "I'm not even sure I want to get married now." *Jesus, Kingston, could you sound more cliché?*

"What?" Damon's mouth fell open and he sat up straight, one arm flexed on the armrest of his chair.

"There's no need to be dramatic," I replied, my eyes now trained on his biceps.

"But you, not married? I can't believe it. Ms. Holly Homemaker with three-point-five kids."

"Things change. You, of all people, know that." As soon as the words tumbled out of my mouth, I wanted to shove them back in. No matter what went down with us in the past, I immediately felt guilty for repaying his kindness with rudeness.

"I guess they do."

"What about you, Damon? How long have you been back in Kingston? Last I heard your practice was in Montego Bay."

"You've been keeping tabs on me?"

He laughed at my expression, but answered, his eyes caressing mine. "I've been back in Kingston for about six months now, but I still travel back and forth. It'll probably take another few months to get my replacement in the Mo Bay office settled into the routine. After that, I'll be here full-time."

"You've done wonders with this house," I muttered for no other reason than to say something. "It's always been beautiful, but now it's amazing. And the way you've converted part of it into a health center—you've always wanted to come back to the community and do that. Plus it must be the perfect living situation."

"Yeah, Mon. It's definitely alleviated a lot of the pressure. My Aunt Brigitte from Hope Bay did the decorating. You remember her?"

"Yes. How is she?"

"Good. She actually planned the whole layout—construction, decoration, everything. Oversaw the whole thing, too. It took about nine months to complete."

"Wow!" That was a pretty quick construction job for Jamaica.

"Yeah. Auntie doesn't play around. She kept her foot in their behinds."

"She did a great job." I looked around again and tried to come up with something else to say. Awkwardness rolled in waves from one end of the room to the other.

"I'm not married either," he said, "and no kids."

"I'm sure you've been very busy. Your schedule probably doesn't leave much room for children and a wife."

"True. But I would make room for the right woman." He winked and my heart thumped wildly in my ears. "Speaking of which, how long do you plan on staying in Jamaica?"

"Well, Mama Grace's funeral is tomorrow afternoon. Then it will probably take another couple of days to settle her estate. I hope to be back at home within the week."

"So soon? You should stay a few weeks, relax, and take a vacation."

"That would be wonderful. Unfortunately, with this big deal on the table there's a lot of work to do. I can't stay around too long."

"I would've liked to spend some time with you."

The long beep that whined from the intercom startled us both and saved me from responding. Damon pushed a button and Tiny's voice followed.

"Excuse me, sir. Your next appointment is here."

Damon pressed the button again. "Thank you, Tiny. Please seat Mrs. Langston in the waiting room and offer her some tea. I'll be with her in less than five minutes." He looked at me and tilted his head to the side as if there was more that he wanted to say. Was that regret that flickered in his eyes? Good. Served him right.

We both stood at the same time and Damon took both my hands in his. "It was good to see you, Kingston. I didn't realize how much I missed you until today. I hope we can spend more time together before you leave." Then with a sheepish grin, he added as if only an afterthought. "Catching up, of course."

"Well, I hope to see you at Mama Grace's funeral and of course, there will be dinner at the house following." Damon's gaze turned intense, but he didn't say anything more. We could have probably kept the whole city of Kingston in lights for at least a month, maybe two, with the kind of electricity that was crackling in the room. He showed me out of his office and then followed me down the long hall to the front door.

"The funeral is at three o'clock at Coke Methodist."

"I'll be there," he assured me before firmly shutting the door behind me, leaving me to wonder what the hell just happened.

Chapter 12

Bianca was sitting in the middle of the living room floor surrounded by hundreds of pictures in and out of scrapbooks, her back facing the door when I returned. Her hair was piled on top of her head and she was wearing a pair of my shorts with a bikini top, her model thin legs bent in front of her forming a V. My arrival was announced by Toy jumping on the pile of photos, scattering them with her wagging tail.

Bianca swatted her away then went to work restoring order to her project. "It's about damn time you brought your fast ass home. Queenie told me you went to visit that doctor down the street. You couldn't have waited a few more days before turning the male population of Kingston out! And isn't old man Whitfield a little too old for you? Not that I'm knocking it. Old dick is better than no dick at all. And I should know." She punctuated all of her sentences with laughter, not bothering to allow me to respond. "Come here," she beckoned. "I found the cutest picture of us together when we were up in Swift River one summer. Here's a picture of us with your little friend. What was her name again?" She pointed at a little girl standing in the middle. All three of us dressed in colorful polyester.

"Joanne."

"Yeah. That's it. She was the one that …" She turned her head and looked me up and down with bulging eyes. Her hand flew to her mouth. "Wow!"

"Is that all you have to say? Wow?" I said irritably.

"Look, don't get testy with me!" She swiveled around and gave me another once-over. "What a way to get all dressed up just to visit the neighbors. You didn't give that old man a heart attack, did you?"

"First of all, you of all people should talk about how I look. You act like you're going to some blasted beauty pageant just to go to the grocery store. Second of all, if you must know, old man Whitfield as you call him has been dead for a very long time. It's his grandson, Damon—also a doctor I might add—that took care of your grandmother while she was on her sick bed. The least I could do was go and say thank you."

Bianca crossed her arms and rolled her eyes. "Uh huh. Sure."

"And you have met him before, Bianca. He's Joanne's brother. He was in Swift River the summer that picture was taken." I found a picture where he stood in the background. "Here he is." I stuck it in Bianca's face and tapped the photo with my index finger. "Remember?"

"Hmmmmm." She pulled the photo close to her face and peered down at it for a moment before she shook her head. "Nah, I don't remember him." She picked up a few more pictures and continued sorting through them. "You missed Aunt Bea."

"She came by?"

"In all her splendor. She had her 'going to church' clothes on. Her hat was fierce."

"You gotta be kidding!" I laughed, flipping my hair into a knot and securing it with a bobby pin.

"Nope. She said she wanted to see if you needed help with anything."

"And what did you say?"

"That you didn't need a damn thing from the likes of her!"

"Bianca, you didn't!" I gasped, amused and appalled at the same time. Bianca stuck her tongue out. "Nah, come on! I would never do that. I did tell her though that you needed about five thousand U.S. dollars to help with the burial and if she couldn't come up with it then she wasn't welcome here anymore!"

"Bianca, that's even worse!"

"You're such an easy target," Bianca said dryly. "She only stayed for a minute and I was nice to the old cow. Queenie fed her some iced tea and crackers and I told her that we'd see her at the service." When I tossed her a skeptical look, she shrugged her shoulders. "Honestly. That's all I told her."

I knelt down and started looking at the albums. "What're you doing?"

"Just going through some of Mama Grace's things before tomorrow, trying to put them in some kind of order. You gonna help or just sit there and look cute?"

I bent over and thumped her on the ear before jumping up and running to my room. She swiped at my leg, but I was too quick. Her laughter joined mine as I disappeared down the hall.

Queenie was standing on her tiptoes dusting the shelves that ran along the top of all four walls in my room. The overage of Mama Grace's knickknacks had been relegated to these shelves for years. I looked at the chipped burnt sienna polish on Queenie's toes and made a mental note to give her a pedicure before I left.

She ducked her head when she saw me. "I just wanted to tidy up a bit. I'll be done in a minute."

"Don't worry about it. I'm just gonna change."

"Mister Winston and his family are on their way over for dinner. He called while you were gone. They should be here any minute."

"That should be interesting, don't ya think?" I didn't expect a response. Queenie was way too discreet to comment. But it was no secret that she wasn't particularly fond of Uncle Winston either.

"Is chicken and spiced rice okay?"

"Yep. That's good."

"For you, curried catfish." She hadn't forgotten.

When I gave up red meat, Queenie had been very resistant to my change in diet—grumbling about fads and the new school way of doing things. During my yearly visits, I would leave pamphlets all over the house that contained illustrations of colons and arteries after a lifetime of fatty abuse.

"It's my favorite, Queenie, and you know it. Oh, and Damon said thanks for the mangoes. I told him to stop by later for some tarts."

"Good. I like that young man. Maybe he'll leave with more than some tarts!" With a conspiratorial wink, she left the room.

Dogs barked and the iron gate squeaked, signaling that Uncle Winston and his brood had arrived. I finished tucking my t-shirt in my jeans and joined them in the front room. Toy pranced around, sniffing everyone, her tail wagging so hard she almost knocked herself over. Uncle Winston picked up the pictures Bianca had put on the coffee table, while Auntie Dawn walked around fingering Mama Grace's crystal as though she was about to rack up during a red-tag sale at Macy's. Bianca was perched on a chair on the opposite side of the room, poised for battle. I took a deep breath to quell the anxiety swelling inside of me.

Let the games begin.

"My what a way you've grown!" Auntie Dawn said, clasping my hands tightly in hers. She looked smaller each time I saw her, her back noticeably stooped. She was close to sixty, only a few months older than my mother would have been. Her hair had more gray strands than black and the former fine lines of age were now thicker and etched at the corners of her mouth and eyes. Spider veins had claimed even more territory in the past few years, shooting up and disappearing underneath the wide openings of her lime green culottes. She had a handkerchief embroidered with antique lace tucked in her watch's wristband.

I hugged her and kissed her on the cheek. She smelled like peppermint. "It's good to see you, too, Auntie Dawn. I wasn't sure if I was going to see you before the funeral or not." I turned to my cousins. "Hi, Andrew. Hi, Adana." I hugged them, grabbing more air than person. Andrew seemed to hold on a little bit longer than necessary and I pushed him away, tousling his curly, jet-black hair like the little cousin that he was.

They said their hellos in unison then sat down together as if on cue. They always took that twin stuff too far, looking like carbon copies of each other with Adana now sporting a short, boxy haircut. Auburn tendrils curled against her forehead, drawing out the beauty of her face. Andrew looked exactly the same, except he had a mustache.

Auntie Dawn shuffled past the china before settling on the couch.

The peppery smell of curry invaded the front room, pushed by the warm evening breeze.

Bianca had cleared away most of the pictures and was looking over the program that Uncle Winston had picked up at the funeral home earlier in the day. The paper was parliament beige and two pictures covered the front—one of Mama Grace when she must have been in her twenties, clutching a bouquet of flowers, her smile brilliant, infectious; and the other picture was her and Pa-pa at their fiftieth wedding anniversary. Bianca and I must have been nine years old. That was two years before he died. The same picture had been on Pa-pa's funeral program.

Bianca's eyes watered and I grabbed her hand and forced memories of a happier time. I was going to need all my strength just to get through this. I would release the sadness in private.

I looked over at Uncle Winston and shook my head. Mama Grace always treated him well, but he definitely had not returned the favor. She took him into her house and cared for him as if he were her own; but when she needed him, he was nowhere to be found. And now here he sat with his money-hungry wife and idiot children, pretending like they actually gave a damn. Sniffing, I read through the program while Bianca seethed beside me.

"Looks good," I commented as I studied the front of the program again.

"Mama Grace had it printed up at the funeral home before she died. Seems she didn't trust us to take care of it." Auntie Dawn yanked a handkerchief from her pocket and wiped her nose. "She was always so independent."

Do ya really blame her? I wanted to scream, but instead said quietly, "I'm sure she wanted to alleviate some of the pressure from us. This way, we'll know that everything will be done exactly the way she wanted." I passed the program back to Bianca. "Have they printed up the copies?"

Bianca's teeth clamped down on her bottom lip. As crazy as it sounded, it was almost comforting that she was taking this as hard as I was. I was also glad that she had enough respect for Mama Grace not to turn this into an out-and-out brawl.

Uncle Winston crossed the room and collected the program. "Yeah, Mon. The only thing we have to do is show up. She had Queenie set some clothes aside before she died. I took them over to the funeral home before I came to pick you up yesterday."

"I wonder why she didn't want to have a viewing before the service? Did she say anything to you about it, Uncle Winston?" Bianca asked.

Auntie Dawn answered with a humph. "We tried to talk her out of it. But she wouldn't hear of it. Mama Grace wasn't quite right toward the end."

"Wasn't quite right toward the end?" Bianca repeated, edging closer to the tip of her chair. The clock in the front room chimed on the half hour. They hadn't even been here thirty minutes and it was already on. "What's that supposed to mean? Not quite right?"

Auntie Dawn pulled the handkerchief and dabbed at the corners of her eyes. "I just mean that as she got older, she wasn't quite as sharp."

"And you would know this how? I mean, let's think about this, Aunt Dawn. How much time did you actually spend with her to come to this brilliant conclusion?"

"Well," Aunt Dawn hedged.

But she was waved off by Uncle Winston. "Don't go getting on your high horse, Bianca. You weren't exactly a regular visitor either."

That one must have hurt considering our conversation last night. But she handled it. "You're right. I wasn't here like I should have been, but at least I have the guts to be honest about it. And I'm not the one looking for handouts now that she's gone. You don't even bother to come around while she's alive; but then before her body is even cold, you swoop through here like a bunch of vultures. She's probably turning over in her grave right now. No, I take that back. Mama Grace is probably resting easy. She expected this. That's why she put Kingston in charge of her estate and not you." Bianca's voice broke with tears.

Auntie Dawn was fanning herself at full speed, her thin mouth still hanging open. Over the years she had turned looking offended into an art form. Adana giggled a bit behind her hand, which earned her a swat from her brother. Neither one of them really had a clue—they were just sitting there with stupid looks on their faces, both legs crossed, feet swinging in the same direction. Twenty-five years old and still living at home. They worked for their father at his printing company and didn't even have management positions. Uncle Winston said he wanted them to learn and work their way up from the bottom. Eight years later, they were still hovering closer to the bottom than top. They'd never even left the island without either their mother or father —normally a rite of passage for Jamaican teenagers with relatives in the states or in Europe. But then, they had always been different, as if the sins of the father have marked them as well.

When my mother was alive, she encouraged me to keep in touch with all of my first cousins; so I would painstakingly write letters and cards, making sure they were tailored for each cousin. Horses for Bianca. Ballerinas for Terry Anne. Anything dead or bleeding for Steven. For Andrew and Adana, I sent generic stuff like baseball for him, rainbows for her. But they never bothered to answer a letter, never sent a card. After my mother died, I gave up trying to keep in touch. Still, I couldn't help but feel sorry for them. They'd probably be pretty nice people if their parents didn't have so many problems.

Queenie bustled into the room at just the right time. She had lemonade, sliced fruit, and crackers with three different kinds of cheeses laid out on a silver-serving tray. Setting it down on an end table, she left the room just as quickly as she came. "Dinner soon be ready," floated over her shoulder.

Uncle Winston looked at the food as if trying to add how much of his inheritance Queenie was spending. Auntie Dawn was pricing the silver tray. I looked away in disgust.

Turning to my cousins, I asked, "So Adana, Andrew, how's everything going?"

Both looked at me like a deer caught in headlights, as if they'd never anticipated being asked such a question.

"Well," they both started then stopped together. Adana nodded to her brother and he finished the sentence, "Things are fine."

"What are you guys doing now?" I continued already knowing the answer while Bianca sucked her teeth.

"Well …" again in surround sound. Andrew nodded to his sister.

"We're still working with Daddy."

Bianca steepled her fingers underneath her chin. "Do you think you'll be moving out of mommy and daddy's house anytime soon?" Her venomous words were packaged with wide-eyed innocence —she was determined to get something started.

Her question made Andrew and Adana hem and haw while Auntie Dawn sped up the fanning process.

Then, Uncle Winston slithered to the rescue again. "My children are more than welcome to stay with me until they are married or ready to leave. It doesn't make sense to waste money on rent when there is plenty of room at our house."

The twins bobbed their heads absently.

"Obviously," Bianca said. "But how do you expect them to meet anyone if they can't leave the house without you holding their hand?" She smiled and paused.

Adana giggled behind her hand again while Andrew absently slapped at a mosquito.

Auntie Dawn sent them an admonishing look before narrowing her gaze on Bianca. "Speaking of parents, where's your mother, Bianca? I'd think Lonnie would want to be here."

"Mommy's at home. She and daddy will be here tomorrow. They wanted to come sooner, but couldn't get away." Bianca's tone was matter of fact, but she crossed her arms in front of her like a shield, containing the rage bubbling beneath the surface.

Auntie Lonnie had been a not-so-undercover closet alcoholic most of her life. Uncle Lee had the same problem, but functioned much better.

Uncle Winston aimed directly for Bianca's most vulnerable spot. "I see," he rolled the words slowly around on his tongue. "Is your mother not feeling well, again?"

She was ready. "Actually she feels just fine considering the fact that her mother just died. But then, you wouldn't know how that feels, would you, considering you don't have any idea who your mother is?"

"You know I've had just about enough of you, young lady." The wind off Auntie Dawn's fan was so strong that it sent some of the pictures flying from the coffee table to the floor. No one moved to pick them up.

Bianca flopped back in her chair, a smug grin distorted her face, satisfied that she'd gotten a rise out of someone. "Have you? Then leave."

Uncle Winston jumped to his feet with Bianca on hers right behind him. Obscenities flew back and forth with Auntie Dawn adding her two cents every few seconds. Andrew and Adana cowered against the back of the flowered settee. Even Toy had left her post outside to check out the commotion.

I counted to ten before saying, "Enough," but the word didn't even make a dent in the ruckus. "I said, enough!" I shoved my hands on my hips. "Why can't we be in the same room for more than fifteen minutes without it turning into a WWF wrestling match? Mama Grace is dead, but this is still her house. Now, you may not like it, but you owe her more respect than this. Y'all are acting like a bunch of little kids!"

"But, Kingston …"

I held up a warning finger in her face. "Don't try me, Bianca. Now we're going into the dining room, sit at that goddamn table and eat whatever Queenie has cooked and we're going to act like a family. I don't want to hear a word that is not polite even if you have to lie through your teeth. We're burying Mama Grace tomorrow. All hell can break out after that. I don't give a damn; but until then, there will be peace and quiet or all of you can get the hell up out this house."

No one responded—each one picking a different spot on the floor to study. A red blush slowly made its way up from Uncle Winston's scrawny neck. I turned on my heel and went in the dining room.

One stubborn tear fell and I rubbed at my cheeks until no sign of it remained. And they wondered why Mama Grace wanted me to oversee her estate. Didn't anybody else in this family have any sense? I understood that Bianca was just defending me, but she was the main one starting the fight, not knowing that you had to pick your battles. Today's fight didn't add up to anything but a waste of time.

The war that really needed to be fought would start after we buried Mama Grace.

Dinner had already been laid out and the table was well on its way to looking like Martha Stewart had flown in to set it for royalty. I could only hope nobody ended up throwing any of the good stuff. The spicy aromas from the chicken, rice and catfish danced slowly from each dish, and set my stomach to growling.

As Queenie finished folding the napkins, dismay was etched on her face. She had heard every word. She had probably spent more time with Mama Grace than any of us and simply showed her allegiance to me by smiling and nodding. Her eyes said, "You done right by Mama Grace."

I grabbed the silverware from the china cabinet and helped her finish setting the table. It was so quiet you could hear a mouse dancing in Africa, but I knew everyone was still here—sitting in the same place, staring at the same spot. They had too much pride to leave.

"Dinner's ready, Ma'am and I'll clean up after dinner. Tray is coming for me in a couple of hours."

"Thanks, Queenie," I said, "For everything you did for Mama Grace and for me." Emotions swelled, threatening to overwhelm us as I hugged her. She tensed, then embraced me back.

"Mama Grace was always good to me. Gave me a job when I didn't know how I was going to feed my babies. Staying now is the least I can do." She smiled. "Yes, Lord, it's the least that I can do." Her bare feet sounded her quick retreat on the cold kitchen tile.

"Dinner's ready," I yelled, forcing a lightness that I hoped would help reset the tone; but when everyone filed in like they were headed for their last meal, I knew it wasn't going to be easy to turn this evening around. They kept shuffling, playing musical chairs until I assigned seats. Bianca sat between Auntie Dawn and Andrew. I pulled out the chair separating Uncle Winston and Adana who were seated on the opposite side of the table. No one sat at the head of the table—one less power struggle. Bianca shot me a look full of piss and vinegar. We were just about to bless the table when Toy started fussing up front.

Before I could push my chair back and stand up, Queenie whisked past me headed towards the front door.

"I'll get it, Ma'am," she called.

Bianca scooped some callaloo on her plate and added a generous portion of scotch bonnet peppers. She started to replace the bowl, but I cleared my throat and she passed the bowl to Auntie Dawn with a slight scowl, careful to avoid the slightest contact between hands. I wanted to remind her that frowning inspired a faster onslaught of wrinkles, but feared for my safety as she attacked the rice and peas, digging into the bowl as if they personally had placed her in this unfortunate position. When she was finished and passed the bowl, I smiled, nodding as if rewarding a child for a new behavior learned.

"So," I directed to no one in particular, "I heard all the way in the states about the Prime Minister's education-reform package. I was impressed. Is it being received well?"

Uncle Winston angrily swiped a piece of rice from his mustache with the napkin and swung a half-eaten chicken bone around like a sword. "P.J. Patterson and his reform package are full of rubbishness! Only an idiot would think that putting more money toward after school-activities is going to improve the opportunities for our youngsters when they graduate. Jamaica's going to hell in a handbasket with Patterson in the driver's seat and I've said so since Michael Manley left office, isn't that right Dawn?"

As Auntie Dawn nodded, I said, "It works in the states. Sometimes kids just need something to do other than hang out on the street."

"Well, if their parents took control of their families like I did, we wouldn't need any kind of after school nothing."

Bianca and I both looked at Andrew and Adana. I should have known that politics was not a safe topic of discussion. Next time I would stick to the weather and the uses for pick-apeppa sauce in Jamaican cuisine. I speared another piece of catfish and stuck it in my mouth.

As we sat at the table, Queenie tried in vain to hush Toy's excited barking. Soon another voice joined Queenie's—this one with more bass. Even before they entered the living room, I knew it was him.

When Queenie came back into the dining room with Damon and pulled out the chair at the head of the table for him, my recently consumed rice and peas tumbled in my stomach like Mexican jumping beans on speed.

"Good evening, all." Damon placed his hands on top of the walnut-back chair, and his class ring sparkled from his pinky finger. He looked like a king about to address his advisors. His locks were unbound and touched his shoulders; he wore a yellow linen summer suit that flowed around him like sunshine. It might have looked feminine on any other man, but only added to Damon's regal carriage. His forearms were bare and the fine hair that covered them glistened with sweat. A vision of his left hand covering my right breast caused licks of fire, hotter than the curried catfish, to shoot downward and I had to cross my legs.

"Good evening, Damon," Uncle Winston said and made introductions all around.

"An evening that just got better." Bianca angled closer. "Hello, Doctor Damon." His name oozed from her lips and in her mind, I knew Bianca was already sporting a three-karat wedding ring and signing Christmas cards from Dr. and Mrs. Whitfield. I restrained myself from kicking her under the table. Barely.

"Glad you could make it, Damon." I assumed the role of gracious hostess, even going so far as to get up and scoop generous helpings of each dish onto his plate.

"Thanks, Kingston." He sat down and bowed his head slightly before picking up his fork.

"No problem," I murmured, my left breast grazing his right shoulder as I poured his lemonade. He smiled up at me—his teeth still perfect rows of enameled white pearl—and my breath caught in my throat.

Damon sampled the curried catfish and Queenie hovered until a satisfactory smile spread across his face. He touched fingers to thumb and brought them to his lips, kissing them in salute and sending her away with a schoolgirl blush as if the Pope had deemed her meal the next best thing to heaven. Damon had always had charisma more powerful than a magnet. Even Toy had taken up court at his feet, resting contentedly.

Bianca continued to flirt, asking Damon every dumb blonde question under the sun except maybe, "What's your shoe size?" Damon was cordial, but didn't seem to feed into it. Everyone else concentrated on eating with the exception of Uncle Winston, who offered a few comments just to keep things interesting. And even though Queenie had outdone herself, I too was giving more attention to the food than necessary until Uncle Winston began once again to stir things up.

"I was telling Kingston that I thought you and Bianca should meet. Maybe go out sometime. I didn't expect introducing you two was going to be this easy."

Bianca had the nerve to duck her head coyly. I rolled my eyes and smothered the urge to hit her.

Damon looked at Uncle Winston, his gaze then moving over Bianca before resting on me. "Now that would be interesting," he said pointedly.

Chapter 13

"Girl, this fine dude is heading your way and you look an absolute mess," Essence squealed! "Come here, wipe your mouth, you got some stuff taking up residence in the corners."

I stopped slurping on my chocolate shake, rolled my eyes, and lazily ran the back of my hand over one corner of my mouth and then the other. Essence sighed and re-wiped my mouth; the only thing missing was the spit.

"Kingston, you really are beautiful and I know that it's become trendy to do that whole natural-girl thing, but men don't like a woman who doesn't bother to put on a little lip gloss or something, you know comb your hair, for Christ's sake! Be a lady."

My standard reply, "Men also like to know what they're getting without having to scrape through a ton of makeup."

"You would buy into that theory," she replied. "Trust me, you gotta get a man interested enough to want to look beneath the ton of makeup." She no longer pushed the issue as vehemently as she once did. I had never been one to do something just for the sake of vanity and no amount of lecturing from Essence was going to change that.

"Yeah, Kingston," Keela said. "He's so cute and has been asking questions about you all day. He's got Terrance all worked up, that's for sure, drilling all his boys for information."

I'd been with Terrance for a while now only because I couldn't find anything wrong with him. He was intelligent, outgoing, sexy as hell, and brought no drama to my life.

Keela and Essence had money riding on this one. But I knew better, just like a Christmas toy in March, eventually he, too, would be thrown to the back of my closet, long forgotten as my focus zoned in on a new and improved model. Dating to me was more like a past-time, a hobby. It was not the main event.

"Me?" I pointed to my chest, my finger grazing Howard University's logo emblazoned in yellow, green, red, and black stitching.

"Yes, you!" Essence replied as if she could hardly believe it herself, and plopped down in a chair, flipping her long tresses over her shoulder in one fluid movement.

Blackburn Center—the hub of student life on Howard's campus—was a scene of constant movement, a flurry of activity; studying, socializing, debating, making out, breaking up, making up, strategizing, politicking, recruiting, or just chillin' out. Howard was a sweet mixture of twelve thousand of the best and the brightest students from all over the world.

Just imagining the achievements of alumni such as Thurgood Marshall, Debbie Allen, Ralph Bunche, David Dinkins, Vernon Jordan, Toni Morrison, Jessye Norman, Phylicia Rashad, L. Douglas Wilder, and Andrew Young and what they meant to African Americans and the nation—put me in the mindset to conquer the world.

Amidst the melody of clanking silverware, banging trays, and groans from students used to a more edible selection of culinary delights, a fierce game of spades was underway in one corner of the cafeteria. In another, the student ambassadors were conducting a tour for potential high school students. Our usual table had been pushed against a wall far away, but close enough not to miss even the most minute bit of gossip always in the air.

We had been friends for three years now. Essence, the stereotypical glamour girl was born and raised in the good part of Los Angeles; her father, a prominent entertainment attorney, and her mother, a talent scout for a major movie company. Even with those connections, Essence didn't want anything to do with the business. She didn't aspire to be a model or actress even though she sure looked and acted like one. Waking up beautiful, her skin was a radiant tone of light copper that looked as though it had been kissed by the Goddess of Sun. With hair, long and straight, her ethnicity was hard to determine; guesses ran the gamut from Puerto Rican to Ethiopian. A bit on the thin side, the extra weight she did carry was settled nicely in her chest and butt. But her most redeeming quality was her straightforwardness. Essence shot it to you straight from the hip, no sugar coating and no chaser. "The truth is the truth," she would say, "no matter how pretty you package it, bows, ribbons, and all that shit. When you unwrap it, it's still the truth."

Keela was just as beautiful and just as oblivious to the effect her strong African features had on people. Her cheekbones sat so prominently on her perfectly round face even Grace Jones would have been jealous. Her skin looked as if it had been colored with the burnt end of an artist's charcoal stick, dusted softly with a glimmer only seen on African royalty. Her hair was cut in the short, sassy style like Toni Braxton's, with spikes gently cupping her face. Keela's hairstyle was an accident though, the result of a relaxing job done in a dormitory room. When her soft, fine hair began to fall out, I thought we would have to admit her to a mental ward, or worse, jail for killing the "incompetent ho" as Keela so eloquently put it. It turned out well though; the haircut marked Keela's entry from her teen years to the legal status of twenty-one. Whereas Essence was long and lean, Keela was short, chunky, and proud of it. We called her the poster girl for "Big Girls Need Love, Too." Her favorite saying: "Why would a dog want a bone when he can have prime rib?"

"That's why black men are dying at such an alarming rate of high cholesterol," I shot back just as quickly.

Keela would laugh. "Yeah, but they die happy."

Keela packaged all her extra stuff well. What I spent on books in a year, Keela paid out four times that in a month on clothes, not including the shoes. Her clothing allowance was financed by her on-again, off-again drug-slinging boyfriend in Detroit.

Essence had labeled her "relationship disabled." Keela was brutally raped when she was sixteen and now had a hard time relating to and trusting men. She continually invited men into her life who walked all over her like a welcome mat, and raped her not physically, but mentally and emotionally.

I fit smack dab in the middle. Average height, average weight and in my opinion, average in appearance. Of course, this only fueled Essence's argument for cosmetic enhancement. I was not quite as down to earth as Keela, but I was more sensitive than Essence. I'd tell you the truth, but try not to hurt your feelings. Like Keela, I knew what it was like to be overweight, but had long since lost the baby fat and worked out like a maniac to keep it that way. Tragedy had also touched my life, but I was able to push the memories to a small corner of my mind. It was only at night when I could not fight back the darkness.

When I asked, "What does he want?" Essence slapped her palm to her forehead.

"Kingston, if I have to tell you, then there's something really wrong. That boy's been sniffing after you like a dog in heat."

Keela nodded and pulled a notebook from her backpack. "He's from Jamaica and has those dread thingys everyone's starting to wear. I don't see why anyone wouldn't want to comb or wash their hair."

"They wash their hair," I said with a huff. "Wearing dreadlocks is a statement of cultural and religious beliefs. The dreadlocks on a Rasta's head symbolize the Rasta's roots, contrasting the straight, blond look of the white man and establishment." My speech was practiced from delivering it to Keela alone.

"Yeah, yeah, yeah," Essence retorted, then added with a sniff, "It's still nasty. 'Nuff respect to Bob."

"I think he plays soccer," Keela said.

"And you guys don't know his name?" I asked, searching my memory database. I'd attended all of the Caribbean Students, the West Indian Culture Club, and the H.U. Jamericans Association meetings faithfully since my freshman year. There weren't many West Indian students on campus that I didn't know.

"Isn't that what we've been saying?" Essence pushed her hair off her face with irritation. "I checked him out, but he didn't do anything for me. So I'm passing him on to you." The natural assumption with Essence was that every man wanted her. As her friends, we just let her arrogance ride. We understood that when she said, "He didn't do anything for me," that really meant he didn't give her any play.

"He is sooooo cute," Keela reiterated, giggling as she bit into a steaming polish, with onions, sauerkraut, and chili piled high on top.

"Shhhh. Shhhh. Here he comes." Essence fluttered prettily then positioned herself on the edge of the round table. Keela checked for mustard. I held my breath.

He is cute, was the first thought that popped into my mind. And he did look familiar, but I dismissed that thought. Of course the man looked familiar. We attended the same school. I must have seen him around campus, in the library or hanging out on the yard.

The stranger looked as though he had walked straight off the playing field, still dressed in his red, white, and blue Howard University soccer practice jersey—their nickname "Booters" tagged on the bottom—and torn black Umbro shorts. The rip in the shorts allowed an enticing game of peek-a-boo with each step. His legs bulged from his thighs all the way down to ankles, hidden by thick white sweat socks bunched artfully around the top of his cleated shoes. His short, neat dreads bounced as he came closer. As he stood before me, his succulent lips parted to display the most even, whitest set of teeth I had ever seen. But they were not as brilliant as his warm brown eyes. For a moment, we were suspended in time, like some weird Star Trek episode. He was the one to break the silence.

"It's been a long time, Bumble Bee, but I would have known you anywhere." His speech was slow and his accent controlled, but leaving no doubt in my mind that he was Jamaican. "Ya' know, Star, you still look as pretty as you always did."

Someone sighed and without looking, I knew it was Keela, the romantic. Then the stranger scooped me from my chair, wrapped long, sinewy arms around me, and pressed me hard against his chest. I'm not sure whose mouth hit the floor the fastest, but I was the first to recover and Keela, the first to smile.

But Essence was the first to speak. "Who in the hell is Bumble Bee?"

"That would be me," I answered, gently pushing at his chest—anxious to reclaim my space. "What I can't figure out is how you know my nickname. I mean, I haven't been called Bumble Bee in years." I turned to Keela and Essence. "My great-grandmother, Mammy, used to call me that." I turned back to the stranger. "Come on, you gotta' give me something to work with here. How do we know each other?"

The man tossed his head back and laughed, deep in his belly before moving closer to my face. "You don't recognize me?" The grin slid from his face and he stuck out his hand. "Damon," he said. "Damon Whitfield. Joanne's brother." He took another step back and opened his arms as if to say 'in the flesh.'

Then, all the memories flooded back, washing over me like a Mexican tidal wave, and knocking the breath out of me. Joanne, my best friend from the summer I spent in Kingston. Damon. Joanne's brother. The little boy from Hope Bay who spent Independence Day weekend with my family in Swift River. Damon. Joanne. Damon.

"Does someone want to tell us what the hell is going on?" Essence forced us back to the here and now. Both she and Keela had their hands on their hips. Keela had even put her hot dog to the side. Drama took precedent over food.

"We're old friends," Damon offered by way of explanation. "I met Kingston one summer in Jamaica. My sister, Joanne, and Kingston were playmates." He was talking to Essence and Keela, but his gaze never left me.

The silence crackled between us. Under other circumstances, I would have inquired about an old friend. Ask what Joanne had been up to. But in this situation, I didn't. I couldn't. I couldn't because I already knew.

"Wow!" said Keela breaking the trance. "That's deep."

"Damon, these are my best friends, Keela and Essence. Ladies, this is

Damon." Smiles floated all around.

"How long has it been?" Damon asked, his eyebrows pinched together.

I did a quick mental calculation. "Fifteen years."

"Well, isn't that cute?" Essence made a production of grabbing her leather book bag and Gucci purse. She slipped on her tortoiseshell sunglasses. "I would really love to see how this little *Brady Bunch* episode turns out, but I have to get to class. Ciao." With a fragrant burst of perfume trailing her, she was gone.

Keela polished off her hot dog, then started in on her fries, clueless to her third wheel status. Finally, I tapped her shoulder and she looked up. One glance at my face and she got it.

"Well, I gotta run, too. It was nice meeting you, Damon. Hopefully, we'll see you around more often." She gathered her books in one hand, and balanced her tray in the other.

"Same here, Keela. Need some help?"

Keela practically swooned at Damon's chivalrous gesture. "Oh, no. I'm fine. Trust me, I've had to juggle more." And then, she left after dumping her trash, and waving goodbye.

"You'll have to forgive me for not recognizing you, but it really has been a long time. It's a shock to see you. I didn't know you went to school here."

Damon pulled out a chair and sat down, dropping his book bag to the floor. "Yeah, Mon. I'm actually in my third year of med school. I've been in D.C. almost seven years."

"Seven years?" I squirted some ketchup on my plate, dabbed a French fry in it, then popped it in my mouth. "Why haven't I seen you? Did you know I went to school here?"

"My grandfather died over the summer and while I was home, I went to check for you and your grandmother told me you were attending school here."

"Sorry to hear about your grandfather." I murmured, the French fry becoming like lead in my mouth.

"Just a part of the life cycle. It was to be expected."

"I guess I'm just surprised that in four years I haven't seen you around."

"I don't have much time to socialize." Damon leaned forward and picked a French fry off my plate. He doused it with ketchup, then stuck it in his mouth. "I work two jobs. I'm trying to complete my four years of medical school in three. It doesn't leave much time to hang out. The studying alone takes up most of my evenings. And since I won't be staying to do my residency here, I'll have to put in additional hours at the hospital before I graduate."

I narrowed my eyes when he reached for another fry. "Help yourself."

He grinned an apology, wiping his hands on a napkin. "I'll do my residency back home in Kingston. My grandmother is old and I need to be there to take care of her. Howard and The University of the West Indies have worked it out so I can finish here and do my residency there."

"Wow, that's great! I'm sure your grandmother will love having you so close." I took in Damon's gear. "I see you find time to play soccer."

"When I can. I was on the team when I first got here, but it got to be too much. Now I only work out with the team every once in a while. Gotta stay in shape." He slapped his flat tummy and it sounded six-pack hard. "You must be in your last year, right? What're you studying?"

I finished the rest of my Pepsi and actually used a napkin to wipe my mouth. "Uh, yeah. I'm studying Broadcast Journalism."

"I can see you on TV reporting the five o'clock news."

"Nah, not me. I'd much rather be behind the scenes calling the shots. I'm doing some work right now for the campus television and radio station."

Damon laughed. "I remember that. Even at six, you was a bossy little thing."

The statement brought back blurry scenes of the past. It sobered both of us and stopped me from making a sarcastic comeback. I flipped my wrist over and looked at my slim gold Timex. Only ten minutes to make it to my Media Law class, all the way on the opposite side of the campus. "I really have to go or I'm gonna be late."

Damon snatched a napkin off the tray of a passing student. He scribbled down his contact information in large, loopy scrawl. "That's my home phone number and cell. There's no excuse not to give me a call. We'll catch up and talk about old times. I may even feed you. Do you still put away the food like you used too?" He flashed a toothy grin.

I stuffed the crumpled up napkin in the front pocket of my Levi's, hooked my backpack over my shoulder, and gave Damon the once over as I ran a tube of cherry gloss over my lips. "Have a good day, Damon."

"Call me."

"Sure," I responded with a nonchalant wave of my hand. I didn't have to turn around to know that Damon was watching me.

"Kingston," he said again, "Call me." I glanced back and his hopeful eyes once again held mine hostage, the left side of his mouth tilted upward in a goofy grin and I was hooked. I nodded before dashing up the stairs two at a time and heading outside into the courtyard. Students leaned casually against trees studying or talking. The wind was light, the sun hidden by stubborn clouds. I turned the corner and found Keela, as I knew I would, leaning against the red brick wall.

"Told you he was cute," she said.

"I'm going to call him."

She smiled in response and we strode across the yard in the direction of the Journalism school. "Why didn't you ask about his sister? What was her name? Roxanne?"

"Joanne."

"Yeah, why didn't you ask about her?"

A leaf floated down gently from overhead and I stopped. I followed its graceful dance with my eyes before looking at Keela. "She died," I said. "She drowned when she was six." I resumed my trek to class. I started to say more, but Keela was no longer by my side.

By the time I turned around, looked up, and took a breath, it was December and half of my stuff had been moved to Damon's two-story flat on the northeast side of D.C. My toothbrush resided next to his, strands of my hair could be found on his pillow, and I used the bathroom with the door open without a second thought. My extra VCR was plugged into Damon's small television so I could work on television projects while he wasn't there. He didn't have to be home, I just liked being in his space. We hadn't put a label on our relationship, but we didn't need one. "We" just worked.

The transition from our first meeting to "now" had happened so smoothly and subtly that there no longer seemed to be a time when Damon and I weren't together.

And together was exactly the way a blustery Sunday morning in mid-December found us, snuggled tightly under two quilts and one blanket because Damon was trying to save a little on the heating bill. The frost was etching patterns on the windows and icicles hung from the windowsills, growing longer with each melted drop. I fitted my chest even more securely against Damon's back. He had been tense all weekend and was resistant to my usually successful attempts to relax him. I ran my foot down the length of his calf and worked my fingers more firmly into the bunched up muscles in his biceps. Being naked on a Sunday morning felt as natural as the sun rising in the east. The only worry was whether to make waffles or omelets for breakfast. I knew Damon's answer would be, "Why not make both?" Of course, he wouldn't be the one to dig the gunk out of the little squares in the waffle machine and scrape burnt egg edges from his cast iron skillet. Not that I minded. I got a kick out of taking care of my man.

The only arena that I had yet to tackle was the sexual one. Damon and I had yet to make love even though we had spent numerous steamy nights perfecting the foreplay stage—kissing, licking, sucking, nibbling, and rubbing until Damon would roll over with a moan that said "put up or shut up." Until now, I had taken the second option, not because I didn't desire to be intimate with Damon. I did, fearing sometimes that the yearning would consume me. Maneuvering around my invisible chastity belt had been frustrating, but Damon stayed understanding, often joking that he would rather make love to his books before standing in the shower under a cold spray of water.

But I was a virgin and had a desire to wait until I was married. My mother often said, "Why buy the cow when you can get the milk for free?" Not that I put any stock in that. I just wanted my first and last time to be with the man I planned on sharing my life with.

So I wasn't discouraged when I moved seductively against him and nothing happened. Damon was about to enter his last semester of medical school. He was so worn out, his five o'clock shadow creeping up on eight o'clock and dark rings constantly circled his eyes. At three o'clock this morning, I could still hear him turning pages and clicking the mouse of his computer as he worked on the study guide for his board exams. Knowing I only had him for a few more months made my stomach clench and my mouth go dry. The thought of a long distance relationship scared me; with Damon as far away as Jamaica, it seemed damn near impossible. Damon wouldn't even entertain such negative thoughts. He said that if we were meant to be, then we would be. Easier said than done. I'd rather have a plan of action than sit back, kick my feet up, and enjoy the ride.

As if Damon read my thoughts, he sighed and rolled over facing me. He kissed my furrowed brow and pressed his nose against mine. "Frowning will give you wrinkles and make you look like an old woman before your time."

My forehead bunched together even more. "That's what I tell you when you're hunched over one of them damn books."

Shaking his head and laughing, he said, "You make me happy."

I smiled and kissed him on the tip of his nose, then teased the corner of his mouth with my tongue.

"Kingston." He cupped my face in both of his hands. "We need to talk."

A churning began deep in my stomach. I tried to pull away, but Damon held me in place. An argument was brewing and space is what I needed. This is one area where Damon and I stood in direct opposition. His belief was the closer we were, the faster we'd be able to solve our issues.

"Baby, hear me out."

I tried not to pout. My listening skills were an area that I'd promised Damon I'd work on. I'd be so anxious to show him that I understood that he never got to finish what he had to say. And that frustrated him.

"My aunt from Hope Bay called Friday."

Relief eased through me. His news was nothing major. "I know. You told me that already."

He sighed at my interruption and smoothed a thumb over my right eyebrow, before rubbing the frown that had returned. I bit the soft part in the inside of my mouth to prevent any further outbursts.

"Well, it's not good news. My grandmother has taken a turn for the worst."

"Oh, honey, why didn't you tell me?" I scooted closer and planted a kiss on the corner of his mouth. "What do you need me to do?"

He took my hands in his before bringing my hands closer to his face and nuzzling my knuckles. "I needed to work it out in my mind. Figure out what I needed to do."

"And?" Once again the insides of my stomach churned.

"And I'm gonna have to go home, Kingston." He traced my cheek with the back of his hand, as if the action could soften the blow.

"Well, of course you do. You need to check on your grandmother. I'll look for flights. I may be able to find a really cheap one." The producer in me needed to do something and I immediately kicked into action, swinging my long legs out of the bed, wrapping myself in a sheet, and looking for my cell phone. "When do you want to leave and when do you want to return?"

"No, Kingston, you don't understand." The urgency in his voice made me stop, phone in midair to my ear.

I turned and sunk back on the edge of the bed, now flipping through the Yellow Pages looking for the section on airlines. "What don't I understand?"

"Stop moving!" His eyes briefly flashed anger and his hands clenched. "Honey, this is going to be more than a visit. I'm going back to Jamaica for good."

"For good? As in forever?" I asked, as if phrasing it differently would help my brain digest what the words would mean for us and our relationship. I wasn't ready for forever. There were still so many things that I wanted to do with him, things for us to experience together.

"I'm not disappearing off the face of the earth, Kingston," Damon said, wrapping his arms around me.

"Yes, but it won't be the same." I protested, leaning into him. "When are you leaving?" I managed to squeak the words past the lump in my throat.

"In three days," he said, and my eyes began to water. "The doctors are not giving my grandmother much longer than a week. She hasn't been the same since my grandfather died; and my aunt says that she's been asking for me, so I need to get there as soon as possible. Three days will give me time to finish my exams and take care of other business. I'll hire someone to box my stuff up and ship it. I've already booked my flight. I leave Thursday morning."

"You did all of this without talking to me?" I pulled the sheet tighter around me and wrapped my arms around myself, trying to shut off the pain.

"I knew you'd be upset and I wanted to get as much out of the way before I told you."

"Never mind that," I said, plastering a smile on my face. "I'll go with you. I can afford to take a week or so off and I'm sure my professors will be flexible since it's an emergency. I want to be there for you, Damon."

His face softened briefly, then the hardness returned. "I thought about that and I don't think it's a good idea. I need this time with my grandmother. Alone."

I wanted to argue the fact that my own grandmother lived right up the street from his and that visiting with her would keep me occupied, but his stone face told me that his mind was made up and nothing short of a memo from God could convince him to change it. So instead of belaboring the point, I began to clean, straighten and sort. Anything to keep from looking into his eyes that were mirroring the sadness in my own.

"Three days," I repeated and nodded as if I totally understood, but inside I was screaming against the unfairness of it all. He needed me, but he wouldn't open up and let me in. And I didn't know how to make him. Still in too much shock to cry and with us both consumed in our own thoughts, I slowly got dressed and for the first time in more than four months, I went home and slept in my own bed.

The next few days passed like a splash of grease in a hot cast iron pan—you knew it happened, but it was so quick you had to check to make sure. We were consumed with Damon's impending departure. I tried to be helpful without getting in the way and refused to shed tears in front of him lest it be interpreted as a female's underhanded attempt at a guilt trip. Not that he would have noticed. Damon remained focused; making sure everything was in order. Bank accounts were closed, newspaper delivery stopped, the message on his voice-mail changed, and an ad was placed in the paper to lease his two-flat until a broker could arrange to have it sold.

Damon was leaving for the rest of his life.

I packed his clothes and shopped for the hard-to-come-by supplies that he would need in Jamaica. I bought a ton of cards and wrote quirky little sayings in them, funny memories, and the things I loved most about him before stashing them in different suitcases and boxes so he would discover them as he unpacked. I cooked all of his favorite meals and took three rolls of pictures of myself and of us together. I massaged his temples after two long nights of studying and kissed him twice on the forehead for good luck before sending him off to take his exams. I had a bath waiting for him each evening and rubbed him down with scented oils to ease the pressure that was steadily building in his muscles. For me, I took a blue oxford shirt before he could take it to the cleaners, a pillowcase that still carried his scent, one of his favorite pens, and a bottle of Red Stripe beer to store in my refrigerator. I was looking for anything that would surround me with his spirit. As meticulous as Damon was about his possessions, he never said a word.

Our quality time was slammed between his school schedule and preparations to leave. He never said what he was expecting from us once he left and I was too chicken to ask. His grandmother's number was scribbled in two different address books and I bought ten calling cards for each of us. Fifty self-addressed envelopes that I had taken to the post office to make sure they had the correct postage sat on my computer stand. I wanted to make the keeping-in-touch as easy as possible for both of us. I dreamed of the flowery prose he would write, detailing the extent of his missing me and the plane tickets he would send because he had to see me. I reassured myself that being apart would only make the bond between us stronger. I was optimistic. I was in love.

White containers of Chinese food covered a blanket that had been spread in the middle of his empty living room. I scooped generous helpings of Shrimp Egg Fu Yung onto flimsy paper plates while a bottle of wine chilled in a Styrofoam ice cooler, our Dixie cups already filled to the brim with the first round. Will Downing was crooning in the background. Damon jumped up and dimmed the lights. The candles flickered as he returned to the blanket and accepted the paper plate I handed him.

"It couldn't be more perfect," I said. With only one night left, I was determined to show Damon how I felt about him.

"I couldn't agree more, Kingston. I couldn't agree more," he repeated, lifting a glass in salute, his brown eyes darkening as they held mine until I no longer recognized time or place. His eyes conveyed to me all the things he hadn't been able to say. And for now, that was enough.

I didn't remember us finishing the food or drinking a whole bottle of wine. What I did remember was pushing the carton and the bottle aside and Damon pulling me to lay alongside him on the faded green army blanket. He wrapped the edges around us then rolled onto his back, pulling me on top of him. He caressed my face before bringing it closer to his and nibbling slowly on my bottom lip, his tongue darting out to tease the corners of my mouth. I held out as long as I could before I kissed him in the way that turned him on. I wished that it could last forever, but Damon was restless and the blanket was a hindrance so he tossed it to the side before rolling us into the reverse position, pinning me beneath him. This time he lovingly tortured my earlobe before traveling down to my neck, leaving a trail of kisses over my collarbone and between my breasts before he lay his head on my chest. I held on, content to feel his heart beating against my stomach.

"Awwww! Kingston," he breathed. "I need you so much tonight." His hands wormed their way beneath me and cupped my butt, pulling me upward until I was certain about the intensity of his need.

"I need you, too, baby," I replied just as breathless. He was still for a minute longer before sitting up and pulling his t-shirt over his head in one fluid motion. Looking at him was a joy and I indulged myself before following suit. Soon, our clothes were scattered around us. As I reached to unfasten my bra, Damon stopped me.

"Let me." He stood up before reaching down and pulling me to my feet. His eyes drank me in and I was glad that for once I had listened to Essence and bought a new bra and panty set from Victoria's Secret. His finger trailed down the lace eyelet that trimmed the cream bra cup. One hand rested lightly in the sweet slope right above my hip. He turned me around and lifted my hair, kissing the back of my neck, then unhooked the clasp of my bra before turning me back to face him. I slowly slid the straps over my shoulders and let the bra drop carelessly to the floor.

"You're so beautiful," he said before teasing my right nipple with his tongue. My navel was next on his list of things to do. I never knew someone could enjoy a belly button so much. I soon learned about other things that he liked more. When Damon's tongue dropped lower, much lower, I had to brace myself to keep from exploding.

"I want you to make love to me, Damon," I said; and before he answered, I kissed him again, becoming intoxicated on my own essence.

"Kingston, are you sure?" I took his hand and moved it until my wetness seeped onto his hand. "I don't think I could deny being sure, even if I wanted to."

"You gotta be sure, baby." He paused. "I mean really sure. You've always said you wanted to wait."

"And I did wait. I waited for you and now I'm ready to share everything with you. Don't deny that you want me."

He shook his head as I ground my hips against his, molding my body to him. The next kiss lasted as if we had all the time in the world. "You won't regret it, Kingston. I promise," Damon replied and sank himself inside of me.

After another thirty minutes of exquisite torture I thought, "Damon sure is a man of his word."

Dulles International Airport buzzed with the stream of holiday travelers. It was early Thursday morning and Damon was wearing a red Howard University baseball cap and a blue nylon windbreaker; he held his laptop computer carrier. A briefcase rested by his feet.

Everything else would be shipped later that day. Damon's life had fit neatly in no more than ten U-Haul boxes.

There were no words, no promises, but I could feel his heart breaking against mine as I grabbed two fistfuls of nylon and tugged him into me, held my breath, and tried to keep my heart from exploding. His lips moved against my hair, my ear and he whispered, "Kingston, my love," over and over again. I pushed my teary face further into his neck and tried to contain my sobs.

When a whiny airline employee announced, "Last boarding call for Air Jamaica Flight 427, nonstop to Kingston, Jamaica," over the intercom system, it startled us both.

Damon was the first to pull away. He took my face in his hands and as I cupped his face in mine, I fought against the urge to beg him not to leave. He wiped away the wetness stinging my face as a lonely tear rolled down his. Unashamed, Damon let it slide down his cheek and over his chin. I dabbed at the streak it left with a tissue. "We're gonna be a mess," I said with a slight smile.

"You've made me so happy, Kingston. I love you," he said, kissing my quivering lips. Then he walked away, never once slowing his stride, not turning back for a final glance.

I felt his absence as strongly as if a limb had been sawed off. What I didn't know was that his absence would be more than temporary. Damon was walking out of my life for good.

A gust of air whooshed from my lungs as if I'd been sucker punched. It happened from time to time when I contemplated my loss or tried to figure out what I had done to make Damon end our relationship. When I realized that I had no choice but to untangle his future from mine, I wondered when had Damon become such a part of my life that I doubted I'd ever be able to go on without him. Broken hearts make you stop and second-guess everything. I thought I'd go crazy with the questions that marched though my head twenty-four hours a day. What was he thinking? What was he doing? Was his heart twisted in as much pain as mine?

One never knew what pain was until you've had your heart broken: Til you got a lump so big in your throat that you doubted that you're going to be able to breathe again; Til the tears started to fall and you didn't think they'd ever stop. Enough tears to fill the Mississippi River two times over. You couldn't put a Band-Aid over this kind of pain. Phone calls to my mother didn't even help.

"Kingston, no amount of kisses from mommy is gonna take the sting away," she said with her lilting Jamaican accent as I sobbed on the phone one Sunday. "I know you're hurting, baby. This is something every woman deals with at least once in her life. Mine was when your father left. I still get angry when I think that man I loved so desperately left me all alone to face Pa-pa with you in my belly.

"You can't go around it, over it, or under it. The only way is through it. Suck up the hurt, Kingston, and do your best to go on. And remember, there are three versions to every story: yours, his and the truth."

It wasn't what I wanted to hear at the time. My world as I knew it had dissolved. By February—two months since Damon left—I had only received three postcards and two phone calls, initiated by him; one call to report his arrival and the second to inform me of his grandmother's death.

I wept my way through Valentine's Day with not a peep from Damon. Holding one of the postcards in my hands, I read it one more time before passing it to Keela and Essence, making them read it again for the umpteenth time. On the front was a picture of Dunn's River Falls and on the back, scribbled in his lazy scrawl: *Kingston, I love you. Forever and three days. Damon.* I had no idea how short forever really was. Blowing my nose loudly, I crumpled the tissue and threw it into the wastebasket.

"Two points." Keela giggled through a mouth full of cheap wine.

"This is serious, Keela."

We were sitting on the living room floor of my apartment. My pink cordless phone sat in the middle of the circle surrounded by scattered candy bar wrappers. And as I silently willed it to ring for the millionth time, Keela at least had the decency to look properly chastised.

I shoved another piece of candy in my mouth. "I mean really, why is it that a dude just can't call when he says he's gonna call or do what he says he's gonna do? It only takes a minute to pick up the phone and let a woman know something. Honestly, not knowing is worse than anything." Damon's last phone call was seven days ago and I had already called him eighteen times, but left only four messages. I wasn't going to call him again.

Essence was filing her nails. "Maybe men and women are talking a whole 'notha language like that dude says in his book, *Men are from Mars, Women are from Venus*. It's even harder for black people, because we have to figure Ebonics into the mix."

Keela giggled again, droplets of wine flying from her mouth.

"You can't have anything else to drink, Keela. You're already silly enough. Alcohol just makes it worse," Essence commented.

I looked at the phone for good measure and as I tugged on the cord to see if it had been pulled out by accident, I knew that I had hit an all-time low; amazing the depths that a woman in love would sink to.

Another pain ripped through my heart. Essence finished with her fingernails, then painted her big toe in Maybelline's Outrageous Orange.

She wiggled it for approval. I nodded while Keela shook her head. Essence didn't pay any mind to us; she just concentrated on her toes.

"Are you two listening to me? I'm in crisis over here. Why don't men just do what they say they're gonna do? If they'd do that, then we wouldn't be so damn crazy.."

"You ain't nevah' lied!" Keela was always on my side.

Essence blew on her toes and looked at us with a smirk. "My question is: why are you sittin' around waiting for some dude to call when you *know* he's trifling like that? My motto: leave them before they leave you and sleep with one of their friends just for good measure. Ain't no man gonna do for me what I can do for myself. I'm looking for perks, ladies. Diamonds, furs, a nice thick," Essence paused. "Well, you know what, and a man that knows what to do with it and then he can take his ass home when he's done. I ain't looking for no phone call or sweet promises that don't add up to a hill of beans."

It took a lot to see through Essence's bullshit, but somewhere inside was a scared little girl who believed in fairy tales. I needed to believe that or I wouldn't like her so much.

Essence picked up a wide-tooth comb and a small gold container of Kemi Oil then motioned me over. I dropped between her legs and she parted my hair in four equal sections and began tuggin' through the tangled strands. "Essence, don't you ever just want to be in love, get married and have babies?" I asked, but before the question left my mouth, Essence was swiveling my head so that I was looking up at her.

She grasped my chin and with her eyes bearing down on mine, spread one arm wide and said, "And ruin this beautiful body? You gotta be out of your mind! Marriage, babies, and happily-ever-after is a trap. Men marry you, get you pregnant, then you're trapped at home with a baby to take care of and what is he doing?" Essence didn't wait for a response. "I'll tell you what he's doing. He's out living his life as he damn well pleases—going out with his boys, sleeping with women who have no stretch marks, playing golf, schmoozing and cruising. Meanwhile, you're at home with a baby attached to your saggy breast. Ladies, I ain't the one."

"But, your parents are still together." Keela stood and traipsed into the kitchen to grab a soda and another bag of potato chips. She dropped back on the floor and pulled the bag open with a satisfying pop.

"And? What's your point?" Essence roughly massaged the oil into my scalp. She was planning on braiding and then twisting my hair into a French roll. I had a series of job interviews scheduled in the upcoming week and I wanted a no-fuss professional look. I tried to hold my head as still as possible. With my sensitive scalp and Essence's heavy hands, if she got any more passionate, I wouldn't survive.

"Well, they seem so happy when they come to visit." Keela poured some chips on a napkin and passed them to me.

"That's part of the brainwashing. My dad has my mom believing she's happy. She's got three great children, she's never had to work and only does that talent scout thing because she wants to, she's got a huge house, an extensive wardrobe, and all the diamonds her heart desires. On the surface, it's a life any woman would envy. But it's a farce and my mom has bought into it. My dad's had a girlfriend since I was twelve. She's young, gorgeous, and doesn't have to work either—not outside the house anyway. Her job is to please dear old daddy until his brains fall out. Holidays and babies are not in her contract. Face it, ladies," she said as she finished off one braid. "Men run the world. The sooner you guys figure that out, the better off you'll be."

Keela rolled her eyes. This topic was a sore spot with her since she tended to attract men who were either married, had a girlfriend, horny for someone else, or happened to meet that someone special while with Keela. At the end of the relationship, all Keela had was a drawer full of empty promises.

She sucked the salt off a finger. "I don't see what the attraction is. Why would you want to be relegated to sneaking in back doors, checking into hotel rooms under assumed names, and accepting only stolen minutes? I mean, it's really becoming an epidemic, especially with black women; and I, for one, am tired of seeing families ruined by women trading one straying husband for another, tired of children who are depressed because daddy doesn't live here anymore. How can we teach our children to seek the truth when we as women are lying to everyone including ourselves? We not only owe it to ourselves, but to other women to honor vows and commitment. What happened to family structure and just plain old-fashioned values? Black women have sacrificed since the beginning of time, during slavery so our kids wouldn't be sold off to another plantation, and we sacrifice now because we want our children to grow up in a two-parent household. Married women stand by their men because they made a commitment before God, but what about the commitment to our sisters? We can't expect others to respect us when we do not respect ourselves. A home should be a family's sanctuary. Cheating is single-handedly sabotaging our families."

I'd heard it all before and the pained expression on Essence's face told me she was thinking the same thing.

But Keela was on a roll. "I mean, how can a woman give her best when she's burdened by heartache and pain?"

Essence clapped slowly. "If you believe that, then I'm the Queen of Sheba." She sucked her teeth. "Sharing men has been a reality since the beginning of time. Some women just don't want all the drama that comes along with a relationship. I'd rather have a man I can send home to his woman. That way he doesn't have to be all up under me. Get used to it, ladies, no matter how faithful you think your man is, there's always someone else."

Keela grabbed my arm, the proverbial light bulb flashed above her head. "You think he's found someone else?"

"Thanks, Keela, Essence, for this enlightening conversation. As if I'm not dealing with enough already," I said. The thought of Damon finding someone new or renewing a relationship when he returned to Jamaica had crossed my mind; but until this moment, I didn't have to acknowledge it. Denial can be a wonderful thing until someone brings the thought to light through spoken word.

Essence said, "Men never fully sever ties with a woman they like, or more specifically a woman they like sleeping with."

"Yeah, but there are some lines you just don't cross."

Essence put the final touches on my hair and said, "Go check it out."

I walked down the hallway into the blue-tiled bathroom, flipped the light on and glanced in the mirror. "You are the bomb!" I hollered at Essence. "Even if you are a bitter ho!"

Her deep-throated laugh danced all the way to the bathroom. "Now see if you can do something with the rest of you," she yelled back.

I stared at the puffy eyes and red nose. I did look pitiful and splashing cold water over my face didn't change much.

"Two more days," I promised the image in the mirror. Two more days and I planned to be over him. Why should I be worried about some man who didn't give a shit about me? As I continued to look at the pathetic image staring back at me, I knew unless I did something now, two more days wouldn't change much. "Forget the friggin' two days," I grumbled. I'd been saying that for more than two months. There was no time like the present.

"Ladies," I yelled, "Who wants to get their groove on?"

March rolled around bringing buckets of rain and not much else. The pain of Damon being gone had dulled to a tolerable ache. When I reached to rewind the tape I was editing and mastering for my "Elements in Journalism" class, a jolt of pain shot up my spine—the latest in a long series of aches. I hadn't been taking care of myself, neglecting the gym and pushing myself ten times as hard as I normally would, working until I was brain-dead—all part of the twelve-step program to kick my Damon habit. I figured if I didn't have time to eat, sleep, or breathe, then I wouldn't have time to obsess over him.

The phone rang, the Caller I.D. registered from Missouri. Irritated, I looked at the clock—a little late for my mother to call.

"Kingston?" a strange voice mumbled after I answered the phone.

"Oh, I'm sorry! I thought it was my mom."

"It's Aunt Malinda. Kingston, I have some bad news. Are you sitting down? Are you alone?" Aunt Malinda was my mother's best friend and she gulped loudly when I responded "yes" to both questions.

"Oh, geez, I don't know how to say this."

"Just say it, Malinda," her husband bellowed in the background.

"Lord, Jesus," she said. "Okay, here goes. Your mother was in a very bad car accident."

"Is she okay? Is she at home? No, you wouldn't be calling me if she was at home. She's still in the hospital? Barnes Hospital, I hope. That's the best one. What's the room number? I'll call now." My words tumbled out faster than my thoughts. Convinced that if the words kept going, then everything would be the way it was supposed to be. My mother would be fine and life would be fine because God knows without her, my whole world would fall apart.

"Kingston, listen to me, honey. She isn't okay. You're going to have to come home."

"Was she hurt bad? It must be bad or you wouldn't be telling me to come home. Man, I've got this documentary that has to be done by Friday so after that I will catch the first flight home." *Keep talking, Kingston*, I told myself. *Just keep talking.*

"No, Kingston. You have to come home now. Your mother was killed upon impact. The police said she didn't suffer at all so that's a blessing." The sobs that Aunt Malinda had been working so hard to stifle exploded as she began to chant the Twenty-third Psalms. "She didn't suffer, baby," she repeated.

I was still trying to figure out how it is a blessing that my mother was dead. How was it a blessing that I was now alone in the world? A blessing that I never got to say goodbye?

"Okay," I said numbly, trying to think back to the last words I said to my mother. Nothing came to me. I lay the phone down on the table, never bothering to hang up.

"Kingston! Hello! Kingston! Are you still there? Kingston!" Aunt Malinda called. "I think she hung up, Dennis. Kingston!"

I closed my eyes and for the first time since Damon left, shed a different kind of tear—a tear filled with the sorrow of loss that lessens with time, but never fully goes away. Curling into a ball, I cried for my mother and wished for Damon.

He'd know what to do.

Chapter 14

Dinner passed quickly and painlessly enough considering the circumstances. Damon was responsible for carrying the conversation as any good quarterback would—initiating topics of discussion and then, passing the ball to those open and willing to participate. Queenie served brandy with dessert; and with each sip, Bianca's shameless flirting got worse. Damon handled it well, spinning suggestive barbs into group discussion. If anyone noticed my silence, no one bothered to mention it.

Uncle Winston and his brood were the first to leave; Auntie Dawn loaded down with the majority of the meal's leftovers. Damon, Bianca, and I retired to the front room. Bianca was draped over the rocking chair, her snifter refilled, swaying back and forth with her legs thrown over the arm of the chair, showing ample amounts of buttock and thighs. Damon and I sat opposite her, also enjoying more than our share of my grandfather's aged E & J Grand Reserve, along with the view Bianca provided; Damon more than I. He didn't seem in a hurry to leave. The clock ticked in the background, marking each passing minute.

The phone rang and I welcomed the distraction, answering on the third ring, beating Queenie by half a second. She headed back to the kitchen, drying her hands on a dishrag. Her boyfriend had arrived and was waiting outside, leaning against the mango tree, the sweet scented smoke from his marijuana-laced cigar filling the air. She was eager to finish cleaning up.

"Montague Residence."

"May I speak to Kingston, please?" Just hearing Essence's voice improved my mood.

"It's me, Essence. You didn't recognize me with my Jamaican accent?" I laughed faintly but Essence wasn't fooled.

"How's it going?" she asked.

"It's going," I said, my swell of excitement deflating like a balloon.

"Well, it's obviously not going well. I talked to Keela. She says that you haven't given up the punany yet, that all the men in town are still safe."

I laughed. "What is with you guys? Just like I told her, this is not a sex fest. I'm here for my grandmother's funeral."

"And? What's your point?"

"When I talk to you, Essence, pretty much, I have no point."

"Exactly, you don't have a point because I know all and you know nothing when it comes to matters of the punany. I mean I know you're there for your grandmother's funeral, but who says you can't kill two birds with one stone?"

Still smiling, I sat down, picked up a pen and started doodling on a notepad. "There's no sense in arguing with you."

"I'm glad you're finally figuring that out." Essence paused and I heard muffled whispers: "Who are you talking to?"

"Nobody," she said quickly, then, "Keela also says Damon is there. Have you seen him yet?"

"He's here right now."

Essence's voice rose an octave. "And you've waited this long to tell me?"

"You were too busy giving sexual advice." Now I would torture her, dangling this information like a carrot in front of a horse.

"Don't play with me, Kingston. This phone call is too damn expensive to waste talking about trivial stuff."

"But I was just listening to you," I protested with a grin.

"Just tell me what's happening," Essence said; and since I really wanted Essence's no sugarcoating take on things, I gave in.

After I had covered everything from being made executor of the will to my discoveries about Damon, her call-waiting feature beeped twice. "You gonna get that?" I asked.

"Hell no," Essence replied. "This is better than a soap opera."

My voice lowered as I began to give the real dirt. "Earlier today I went to his house-slash-health center to thank him."

"How does he look?"

"The same, only ten times better."

"Really?" Essence squealed. "So he's totally delicious!"

"Totally. Age has been good to him. His dreads are longer and he has a bit of gray at the temples. He looks very," I searched for the word, "distinguished."

"And the body?"

"From what I saw, that, too is even better than before, if that's possible."

"Damn." Essence mulled that one over. "Was he surprised to see you?"

"A little. He must have known I was going to be in town, but I don't think he expected me to come by. But he was happy. He was definitely appreciating me as much as I was appreciating him. You woulda been proud of your girl. I had it laid out."

"It's good to know that all my work has not been in vain," Essence yelled. "Y'all talk about anything important? Like why didn't he return any of your phone calls ten years ago? Why did he leave you just hangin'? There's more, but that's just off the top of my head."

"We didn't get into any of that. And I really don't want to. It's history."

"Tell it to somebody else. You've had questions pounding in your head for ten years now, so while he's there, might as well ask him."

"We'll see," I responded, trying to end her interrogation. No such luck!

"So back to my original line of questioning, think you're gonna hit that before you come home?"

"Essence!" And the conversation in the front room halted. I cupped my hand over my mouth. I continued to protest, not ready to admit to myself, much less anyone else, that Damon still stirred something tribal in me. I knew there was a lot of work to be done, but I did want to talk to him, see if anything could be salvaged, if only a friendship. Like it or not, I still missed him.

"I'm not like you, Essence. I can't just make love to a man, then walk away. I need to have some sort of feeling to even want to be intimate with someone. With Damon, there's so much pain and hurt. Besides, I'm at the point in my life where I need more than just a good time. I need romance."

Essence sighed, "All right, honey. Be open to the possibilities and do what's best for you. I just want you to be happy."

"I know, and I love you for it."

"Before I go, did Keela tell you what's going on with her?"

I had filled up a whole piece of paper with my doodling and was dismayed to discover it was all about Damon. I crumpled the paper into a ball. "No, she told me she had some news, but that she wanted to wait until I got back. What's up?"

Essence laughed. "No way am I going to spill the beans and have her upset at me."

"Am I gonna be mad or glad?"

"A little of both. All I'm gonna say is that all that women's lib rhetoric that she's been spouting since college hasn't sunk into her psyche."

"Well, then I don't want to know until I get home." I placed my head in my hands. "I've got enough on my plate."

There was more muffled noise in the background. "I'm gonna have to cut this gab session short, but I have one more thing to say. I know we have different perspectives on relationships and men and I respect that, but I do know this. Randy was nowhere near good enough for you. I don't believe in fairy tales but if you like it, I love it. And if you want it, then you deserve it and I want you to have it. But Randy is scum."

I smiled. Essence had built such a wall around herself that it was hard to see how big her heart was, but when a little of her softness broke through, it shined like a bright ray of hope. "Thanks, baby." I sniffed in a not-so-fake show of sentiment and Essence giggled as I asked, "Who's the sucker tonight?"

"Girl, the new player for the Bulls. He just signed a five year, twenty-five million-dollar contract. I'm trying to help him spend some of that. He doesn't play like Michael Jordan, but he sure looks like him and that's good enough for me. He's taking me to the Signature Room in The John Hancock Building. I know it's kind of passé, but you know he's gotta pass the test."

I shook my head, well aware of the test. On a first date, Essence liked to be taken to a very expensive restaurant. This way she could judge her date's reaction to the prices on the menu. The less shock he showed, the more money Essence knew he would drop. "All right, girl, don't hurt him too much!"

"It's his ex-girlfriend I'm talking about hurting. Can you believe she's calling me already?"

"Why?"

"'Cause women are haters. Women don't want to see another woman doing good. Whether it's in the workplace or in a relationship, women just don't want to see another woman making it. Instead of congratulating a sister, they're too busy trying to figure out if she has a weave. Do you know how many dirty looks I get in the club because some insecure chick thinks that I'm gonna take her man? Women are petty and insecure—haters. Well, I'm here to tell you, play with me and I'll take your man."

"See, that's why they're hating on you."

"I gotta have some fun, too! By the way, I dropped your flea bag of a dog off at the doggy hotel." We laughed together before Essence added, "And tell Damon I said hello."

After agreeing to pass the message and assuring Essence that I didn't need a ride home when I returned to Chicago, we hung up.

In the living room, the conversation between Damon and Bianca was going strong. Bianca's words seemed slightly slurred and I couldn't tell if it was from the brandy or just for effect. I got my answer when I spotted the dry canister on the floor by the rocking chair. As I turned the corner, I also saw that the seating arrangements had changed. Bianca was lounging next to Damon on the couch and I thought I heard the words "physical examination" slip from her pouty lips.

Damon's head shot up and his mouth dropped open when I entered the room. Bianca didn't even notice. She was too busy rubbing her leg up and down Damon's and angling herself to get closer to him, her left breast almost exposed. Damon tried to untangle her limbs from his, but from where I was standing, he wasn't trying hard enough.

"Don't mean to disturb you. I mean, I see you're getting to know each other. I just came to say good night." My words sounded catty, even to my own ears; and even though I knew that Bianca was unaware of my history with Damon, I was offended at an invasion of my territory. Damon on the other hand, knew better.

Bianca purred as Damon pushed her gently to the side so that he could stand.

"So early?" the idiot asked.

"The funeral is tomorrow so I want to get some sleep," I replied. "Goodnight to you both. And Bianca," I inserted an overdrawn pause, "desperation is not attractive on a woman." As she gave me a blank stare, I turned to Damon. "At least, not to most men." Cattiness wasn't attractive on a woman either, but I pushed that thought to the back of my mind. As I walked away, I heard Damon stuttering my name, but I didn't turn around, the tears of remembered hurt welling up in my throat, causing a painful lump that burst, sending tears streaming down my face.

Chapter 15

The edge of the sharp rocks sliced into the pads of my toes as I worked my way down the sandy bank. Warm blood oozed, mixing with the sandy earth to create a reddish mud. I sank deeper into the giving soil with each step, while the wind whistled through the willowy trees, providing the perfect soundtrack for the blurry neon-colored images that swirled in front of my eyes.

It was the dead of summer, but a definite chill permeated the air, making it so thick and heavy that I could hardly breathe. As I moved closer to the river's edge, the chill reached out to me with long fingers and icily caressed my cheek before invading my body, my mind, and finally my soul. The water stretched in front of me, lapping softly on the bank, taunting me with its misleading innocence. It seemed that for as long as it had been in existence, generations of my family had been served well by Swift River, named so because of its deceptively fast current. For years, it had provided the only source of water for bathing, cooking, and washing clothes. But that was no more. The river had turned the tables and belying its innocence, taken something very precious from me. As I looked closer, a watery smile mocked me, laughed at me for trusting and believing it was my friend. And I had believed, still wanted to believe because not doing so would unveil a reality too frightening to fathom.

I continued down the embankment, navigating more carefully because the leafy green moss was still slick from the morning dew. Every ragged breath I drew brought me closer to my newfound nemesis. The coolness in the air continued to shimmy up my spine, doing an almost deathly dance, its tapping toes moving one vertebra at a time. The wind now joined the fray, whipping leaves and branches in an upward spiral. The three-quarter moon bounced off the water, making the thick blanket of fog that hung above seem almost translucent. The waves continued to lap slowly against the shore. I went closer still. A promise of a new beginning beamed down from the moon but that promise soon died to a twinkle, and then an occasional shimmer as time and time again it was rejected and sent spiraling to the water below. My breathing was now shallow, my pulse beating a distinctive calypso rhythm in my ears, my fingers curled, bending into a fist. My eyes focused and the blurry visions became clear. A scream started to work its way up my throat, beginning on disbelief and ending on a name.

And I couldn't breathe. I couldn't breathe because the memory of the two of us standing in front of Mammy's mirror, her twirling with arms wide and me making funny faces to make her smile. I told her how pretty she looked and not to worry 'bout her little potbelly. "Gwan' now," I urged her. "A likkle' fat make ya' look healthy." She laughed over her shoulder as she ran out the door. I slowly followed. Thinking about something—obviously not of importance now—but thinking nonetheless as I often did. That was earlier. Before we made it to the river where the picnic was being held. Before we stuffed ourselves on bammy, crispy fried fish, and fat plums. Before Mammy yelled that we had time for one more swim in the river while the adults cleaned up and readied to head back up the hill to the big house. Now everyone was looking at me. I felt their eyes attempting to hold mine, but I kept my gaze on the ants that were burrowing holes in the ground. I scrunched my toes in the damp sand. Already, I had seen enough. Their sorrow was reflected in the single fat tear that rolled over my cheek and down my chin. My knees buckled and I thought how sweetly fragrant the earth smelled as it rose to meet me, to provide comfort for me—if only for a little while. Then, "Why didn't you take me? I am the only reason she's here."

Hands stronger than my nightmare tightly gripped my shoulders. My name pricked my subconscious and I opened my eyes. A shadow blocked most of the red glow being cast across my bed by the rising sun. I blinked, believing that I was still dreaming; but I wasn't. Sitting on the edge of my bed was my real life knight-in-shining-armor, Damon.

"Kingston? Can you hear me, baby? Are you awake? Talk to me, honey!" Concern pulled at the corners of his mouth and resonated in his voice as he shook me gently, then caressed my back.

"I'm awake." I moved closer to him and my tears mixed with the dampness of Damon's shirt. My body relaxed as I once again got used to the feel of Damon's arms around me. His sweaty scent was causing warm sensations in the pit of my stomach. Damon's breath whispered across my collarbone. Shockwaves rippled through each of my limbs as my soft chest rubbed against his hard one. My cotton nightgown provided friction, not protection.

Damon shifted his weight and pulled me even closer, smoothing damp tendrils of hair that were plastered to the side of my face. Butterfly kisses followed, beginning at my temples before slowly tracing the line of my jaw. His touch was familiar and overwhelming.

My mouth was dry and I swallowed deeply before I spoke. "Why are you here, Damon?"

"I was jogging past the house and heard you screaming so loud, you had the hairs on my neck on end. I thought someone had broken in or something. I came to check and noticed your window was cracked, so I jimmied it wider and crawled through."

Now the damp t-shirt, musky scent, and knee bandage made sense. Too many years of football on the rocky streets of Jamaica with inadequate shoes had caused major damage to the cartilage in his knees. He eventually had surgery, but still needed to wrap one knee for support. Damon slowly separated his body from mine and immediately I sensed the loss. It felt unnatural—as if our bodies were destined to be intertwined. But the separation didn't last long, Damon switched positions, then settled me on his lap before cradling me to his chest once again.

"Tell me about it," he said.

The words danced about in my head, but it was hard to vocalize them. It's been haunting my dreams since that fateful summer in Swift River. More than two decades had slipped away since I'd talked about it. Just the thought made me tremble and Damon tucked me more securely under his armpit. The bond between Damon and me went so much deeper than the relationship we had at Howard University. Damon and I would be attached forever, linked by the death of his sister and my friend, Joanne.

"I have nightmares," I said. Damon's heart beat wildly beneath my ear and his cheek rubbed the top of my head as he nodded in agreement. "Very bad nightmares about Joanne."

"I figured as much. I knew while we were at Howard. You would talk in your sleep—mumble Joanne's name. I would try to broach the subject, but it was like you wouldn't even hear me. It was as if you had blocked out the experience in Swift River while you were awake, but re-lived it while you slept. It's been twenty-five years, Kingston; you need to let it go. Yes, she died a horrible death, but it was an accident. She wouldn't want you to suffer so. She'd want you to be happy."

"I know," I said, shaking my head. "I just keep picturing her posing in my swimsuit, laughing and playing without a care in the world. She made that summer so special for me. The way she looked at things and accepted me no matter what. We were so different, but yet, the same. My grandmother would say, there goes Fric so Frac must not be far behind. I know she wouldn't want me to be in so much pain over it. She'd probably be pretty pissed, actually. But still, I can't help but feel guilty."

"What do you feel guilty about?"

I pulled back and looked into his eyes. "It should have been me." I shrugged, and repeated quietly, "It should have been me."

"You weren't the only one there, Kingston. It was a picnic full of people. No one understood what was going on until it was too late."

"Yeah, but I'm the reason she was in Swift River. I'm the reason that she went swimming so soon after eating, that she went so far out. I didn't realize that she was so tired, didn't check to make sure she was behind me. I should have taken better care of her." I breathed deeply; the words that had played nonstop in my head like a broken record since her death were now out in the open. "It should have been me." Sobs racked my body as the well of stored-up pain released from my soul.

Damon was murmuring nonsensical words against my ear, then my neck, finally my hair; words that comforted in their repetition. He cupped my face in his hands and asked, "Kingston, how can you say it should have been you? Do you have a direct line to God that you haven't told me about? Everything happens for a reason. Whether good or bad, there is a reason. Maybe we were supposed to learn something or be motivated to do something. You know that I am not a religious fanatic, but just as the sun rises in the east and sets in the west, I believe that there is a natural and divine order. The real pain in life comes when we fight against that order. Losing Joanne was a tragedy, but it was a tragedy that didn't happen to you because it simply was not supposed to. He spared your life. God must have something pretty important for you to do. Have you stopped to figure out what it is?

"All of us felt bad about what happened. Why do you think I became a doctor? Why do you think I was so hell bent on coming back to Jamaica to practice, continue with my grandfather's health center? So that there are no more Joannes, no more deaths that could have been prevented by just a little bit of knowledge.

"Health care is so lacking in Jamaica because everyone wants to practice abroad to make good money. But if we aren't willing to stay and help our own, who will?"

I felt the passion in each rise and fall of Damon's chest.

"Why do you think it was so easy for me to leave you and come back after my grandmother fell ill? I didn't have a choice, Kingston. I owed it to Joanne. I feel the guilt, too. I was her older brother. If anyone was supposed to protect her, it was me. But I was only ten and you were seven. We were just kids ourselves, too young to shoulder such a heavy burden."

And as we sat there, rocking gently, the sun rose, shining so much light that there was no room for darkness to hide. In this kind of light, healing began and I fell into a deep restful sleep.

When I woke up, Bianca and Queenie were already moving around. I stretched lazily and inhaled, the only things left from my encounter with Damon was an imprint on the bed beside me and Damon's familiar scent that still lingered. It enfolded me in a brief and comforting embrace before my bare feet hit the cold tile floor and reality rushed in like a splash of cold water against my face.

Today we would be putting my grandmother in the ground.

Chapter 16

I moved through my early-morning rituals mechanically, all while trying to wrap my mind around the fact that we would bury Mama Grace shortly. Today seemed like every other day. The sun was shining. The birds were chirping and the normal hustle and bustle was taking place right outside our front door. As if my rock, my very foundation, my Mama Grace hadn't been snatched from me.

The salty smell of codfish mixed with the sweetness of fried plantain, lingered in the air. Queenie was laying out a veritable feast—fortifying the troops for the battle that lay ahead.

Clad in a silk floral kimono, Bianca was seated at the table, nibbling on a triangularly cut piece of hard-dough bread toast smothered in guava jelly. She had bypassed the traditional ackee and codfish, spicy pork sausage, bubbling grits with pats of butter floating on top, sardine and cheese omelets, fried plantain, and homemade dumplings Queenie had placed on the side serving table.

The steam from her coffee cup swirled lazily upward, adding to the humidity already thickening the morning air. Her bare legs were crossed and a strappy, silver sandal dangled from her swinging foot, the Jamaican Gleaner newspaper spread out in front of her.

"Mornin'," I said. The anger from last night tagged along, ebbing out the joy left by my time spent with Damon. It would serve her right if she had one hell of a hangover. And she did. She grumbled her response, then grabbed her head with a slight moan.

"How ya' feeling?" I kept on, filling my plate with ackee and salt fish, hoping the smell would aggravate my traitor cousin.

"I had a bit too much to drink last night," she responded, flipping a page of the newspaper.

"I would say it was more than a bit too much."

"I haven't had a hangover like this since I was a teenager."

"Yeah, well you had much more than a hangover last night."

"Hmmm?" Bianca grunted before taking another sip of coffee.

I sopped up some ackee with a piece of dumpling and shoved it in my mouth. "Is that all you have to say? Hmmm?"

"What do you want me to say, Kingston? You're obviously fishing for something."

"You made a fool of yourself last night with Damon."

"Says who? You? I didn't hear Damon complaining."

"You were too drunk to hear anything."

"What's wrong? Mad because you didn't get to it first? Mad because once again a man was more interested in me than you?" She casually flipped another page.

"You really think he wanted you? Damon was being polite. If you weren't so conceited, Bianca, maybe you could see that!" I stood up so quickly the blood rushed to my head and my plate almost overturned.

Bianca felt the impending onslaught and buried her face in her hands.

"Why does somebody always have to be jealous of you? That's always the answer for you, isn't it? If something doesn't go your way, you always find a way to work it back around to them being jealous. Well, that's not what this is about. I'm not jealous, Bianca. Trust me, you are more than welcome to your sad, little lonely life. Thirty years old and you still walk around flipping your hair, flashing your diamonds, and bragging about your interracial heritage as if that's supposed to impress people. Newsflash: it doesn't anymore. It's the new millennium, sweetheart. Step into it. Being light-skinned doesn't make you better. Being rich doesn't make you better. And looks will fade. It's your heart that matters. What does your heart look like, Bianca? In the end, that is what's going to count."

At her muffled sobs, I softened. "Bianca, there's more to you than being beautiful and rich. You are kind and generous and most of the time fun to be around. You're the only one who doesn't know it. So, no, Bianca, I'm not jealous of you. Because when it comes to Damon, been there and done that. We dated for almost a year at Howard." I sat down and pushed the rest of my breakfast around the plate.

Before Bianca could respond, Queenie bustled into the room her apron swishing around her legs, her red scarf tied neatly as if she were expecting company.

She paused, her brow furrowed. "Well, aren't you two a fine pair this morning? I heard the bickering all the way in the kitchen. And on your grandmother's funeral day too. God rest her soul. You should be ashamed of yourselves." She reprimanded in a harsh whisper and a suck of her teeth. "Your family will be arriving soon, so I suggest both of you pull it together." With a flounce of her skirt, she left just as regally as she'd entered. Queenie had spoken.

The sun was no longer shining as brightly as it was earlier this morning. Fat, angry, gray clouds gathered, pregnant with the possibility of severe thunderstorms, reflecting my mood perfectly.

The white limousine pulled up curbside at the cathedral at ten forty-five—Mama Grace's funeral scheduled to begin promptly at eleven. The majority of attendees were already seated with the exception of a few people lingering on the tall, concrete steps leading to Coke Methodist. They strutted like peacocks decked out in their Sunday finest as if this were their party, content to take their seats after they were sure everyone else had been seated.

Planting my classic black-leather pump on the sidewalk, I stepped into the heavy Jamaican air. People strolled up and down the sidewalk attending to their day-to-day business. Bianca was next from the limo and we linked arms as soon as she stepped out. Her mother and father exited, followed by Uncle Winston, Auntie Dawn, Andrew, and Adana. Aunt Bea had opted to be chauffeured by a friend, pooh-poohing the need for, as she called it, "such ostentations transportation."

That was it for immediate family. The phone calls from other family members started early this morning. Calls saddled with the expected, but still pitiful excuses. She was in death as she was in life, with few gathered around her. But it didn't matter. As mama used to say, "One monkey don't stop no show."

We were dressed in stoic black. Bianca added a hat with a veil and I wore sunglasses. We were trying to conceal our eyes, already brimmed red from crying. We paused briefly before starting up the steps with resigned hearts—we presented a united front—accepting stale hugs and kisses delivered by the peacocks as we stopped to thank them for coming.

Standing beneath the arched, stained-glass doors leading to the sanctuary stood Damon, his hands crossed formally in front of him, looking so handsome in his tailored, navy blue summer suit. He smiled, his warm brown eyes embracing mine and I realized that I was actually proud of the man that Damon had become.

"I was waiting for you," he said before easing between Bianca and me, escorting us through the doors.

In contrast to our attire, a sea of color greeted us in the form of hats and suits fit for Easter Sunday. Church issued fans advertising for *The*

Royal Bank of Kingston waved back and forth, doing little to alleviate the overwhelming heat. Gossipy conversations were whispered behind gloved hands. Children sat prim and proper, on their very best behavior, legs crossed at the ankles, swinging back and forth. Activity ceased immediately upon our entry. Two ushers dressed in white and black rushed to meet us. They turned and marched ahead, leading the way down the aisle passing the stained-glass windows lining each side of the sanctuary.

Mama Grace's coffin rested in front of us—smooth, dark, rich mahogany lined elegantly with ivory satin. The ushers parted in perfect formation, each going a different way and there we stood in front of Mama Grace. Clad in her best silk violet dress, hair coifed and curled under, pale pink on her lips, she looked as beautiful in death as she did in life and even more peaceful. I wiped away a tear, Damon's hand reassuringly rested on my waist. I knew that she was in a better place, smiling down on us and that provided some comfort. Still, shock and a sense of abandonment stomped through me as if another piece of my soul had been ripped away.

The Very Reverend Arturo Pegue descended grandly from the pulpit, greeting us with perfunctory kisses on each cheek, and then releasing us into the capable hands of the ushers who directed us to the front pews. Despite the fact that he was not family, no one blinked twice when Damon sat, sandwiched between Bianca and me. Aunt Bea was already seated and dabbing at her eyes. I slid next to her and she tilted her head, presenting her overly rouged cheek to be kissed. I obliged, cringing when my lips met her leathery skin that smelled of Dove soap and olive oil. Damon reached out with one hand and held mine while throwing the other arm around my shoulders.

The organ kicked into high gear and on cue, the peacocks flocked from their perch on the steps and filed into the sanctuary.

The Reverend's voice boomed over the congregation, his shiny, purple robe reflecting the light and starched white collar standing at attention. With wagging jowls, he welcomed us to his church, waving a bible in one hand and grasping the podium with the other.

"Saints," he sang.

"Yes, Lords" and "Amens" sprang up like dandelions from the congregation. "Saints!" he yelled with more vigor this time. "This scripture is from the book of John."

Damon squeezed my hand before letting it go to flip open a program, a long finger following the text as it was read.

The Reverend continued, "Jesus said 'I am the resurrection and the life, saith the Lord; he that believeth in me, though he were dead, yet shall he live: and whosoever liveth and believeth in me shall never die.' And I want us to remember that as we gather here today to commemorate the home going of Grace Marie Montague, a beloved member of this congregation for more than sixty years. She has been a beacon of light to her family, friends and community. Let's lift our voices in celebration of Mama Grace's life as the choir leads us in singing one of her favorite hymns, 'Amazing Grace'."

The organ zipped to life, the organist's fingers danced over the black and white keys as the congregation stood. "Amazing Grace, how sweet the sound, that saved a wretch like me. I once was lost, but now am found; was blind, but now I see."

When the hymn was finished, Reverend Pegue looked at the family. I nudged Bianca and whispered, "It's your turn."

She stood and scooted past us, heading to the front. Bianca tried her best to keep her composure, reciting one of Mama Graces's favorite poems. She'd heard it at Her Majesty Queen Elizabeth's funeral, loved it, and saved it for her own ceremony. Bianca now held the same piece of paper on which she'd written it in her hand. "You can shed tears that she is gone or you can smile because she lived. You can close your eyes and pray that she'll come back or you can open your eyes and see all she's left. Your heart can be empty because you can't see her or you can be full of the love you shared. You can turn your back on tomorrow and live yesterday or you can be happy for tomorrow because of yesterday. You can remember her and only that she's gone or you can cherish her memory and let it live on. You can cry and close your mind, be empty and turn your back or you can do what she'd want: smile, open your eyes, love and go on."

After Aunt Lonnie and Uncle Winston finished saying a few words about Mama Grace, I read the obituary and thanked everyone for attending before turning the podium back to the Reverend. He reclaimed it with zeal, concluding the service with a fiery monologue designed to save our souls from a damned eternity before saying a final prayer. "May God in his infinite love and mercy bring the whole Church, living and departed in the Lord Jesus, to a joyful resurrection and the fulfillment of his eternal kingdom; and the blessing of God Almighty, the Father, the Son, and the Holy Spirit, be upon you and remain with you always."

Once again, like magic, the ushers appeared and led us back down the middle aisle of the church and out of the sanctuary.

Many "How do you dos?" and "Thank yous for coming" and "Yes, Ma'ams, she sure will be missed" were exchanged in the foyer before our group—still including Damon—was once again tucked in the limo and headed for the cemetery.

The skies had opened up, as if they too were grieving for Mama Grace, and very few people braved the weather as we committed Mama Grace's body to dust. The solemn words of the Reverend Arturo Pegue punctuated the still, damp air. "In gratitude, we bid farewell to a greatly loved woman. For her grace, humanity, and sympathy, for her courage in adversity, for the happiness she brought to so many, for her steadfast pilgrimage of faith, for her example of service, and for the duty which she rendered unflinchingly to her community, we thank and praise Almighty God. As we commend Grace Montague, his servant, to God's mercy, let us especially pray for her family."

I leaned on Damon as I picked up a handful of dirt and tossed it onto the lowering casket. I felt alone, the same as when I had done this for my mother. Sobs ripped through my body and I swayed against Damon. The clouds burst again, rain falling steadily as he wrapped his arms around me and turned me from the pile of dirt that would soon cover my grandmother.

Chapter 17

The one upside to a funeral: when it's over, you get to throw one hell of a party. Queenie had stayed at the house preparing for the onslaught of family, friends, and neighbors that would occupy every space at Mama Grace's eating, drinking, and catching up.

An impressive crowd had gathered when we returned. The glorious blend of curry, pimento and ginger met us at the door, wafting on the Calypso music that played softly. Dominoes clicked on card tables, and children laughed as they chased Toy around the yard. It had been an exhausting day and drained from the roller coaster ride of emotions, I wanted to lie down. Damon offered no solution, shrugging helplessly as he kissed me on the cheek before setting out in search of food. It would have been politically incorrect to shut myself in the room and wallow in self-pity, so I squared my shoulders, sucked in a lungful of air, and allowed myself to be dissolved into one perfumed hug after another.

Two plates and three hours later, I was sipping my fourth rum punch and filling the fifth person in on what I'd been "up to."

Aunt Bea held court in the corner with her whispers loud enough to be overheard, but not quite loud enough for anyone to comment. "The high yellow one is her granddaughter, too. You know the one that fools with them horses and such. She stood there looking like the devil when she was talking about Grace. A hypocritical devil, that's what I say; and if Grace had been here to see it, she would have just died. I tell you, it's them kids and grandchildren that put her in her grave. Worried her to death, that's what I say. And now they're standing around with their hands out, knowing they didn't do diddly squat for Grace while she was alive."

When Aunt Bea realized I was staring her down, she had the decency to blush. But that didn't stop her from adding a parting shot behind a cupped hand, this time too low for me to hear.

With a chuckle, I excused myself from the current conversation. Auntie Dawn had held me captive—waxing over the finer points of antique silver when I spotted Uncle Winston and Aunt Lonnie beckoning me to follow them to the kitchen. I shook my head in disgust. I already knew the topic of this discussion. Bianca stopped me midway. "You look vexed," she observed. "How ya' holding up?"

"Okay. What about you?"

"Same. It's good to see everybody, but …" Bianca shook her head. "It's going to be hard without her here. I think that's finally beginning to sink in. I wonder what's going to happen to all of us now that she's gone. Mama Grace was the one that held us together. Well, as together as we could be, anyway." Sniffing, her almond brown eyes were surprisingly sad. "And I'll miss you. We only get to see each other a couple of times a year as it is. It was so nice spending this little bit of time together, even if you did yell at me today." She smiled and took another sip from her chilled glass of Rum Punch.

"I'm sorry about that, Bianca. It wasn't you I was angry at. Damon and I have a lot of history and not all of it's good. But I shouldn't have taken it out on you. And don't worry; you and I will be fine. We just have to be better about staying in touch, not forget what Mama Grace stood for or all that she has done for us. As much as I hate to say it, Bianca, that's going to be pretty much left up to us."

"Yes." She agreed. "We are certainly going to have to be better at communicating." She paused and looked me squarely in the eyes. "And we can start with you and Damon. Why am I just now hearing about this juicy affair?"

"Because it was over before it started." I said, the explanation sounding lame even to me but Bianca was gracious enough to move on. The understanding clear in her expression. "But yes, we will be better about communicating." I leaned in closer. "And maybe you could try to spend more time with Adana and Andrew, they could use a strong role model."

Bianca rolled her eyes as my gaze landed on the twins. They were seated between Aunt Dawn and Aunt Bea on the settee. All four held over-flowing plates of food. Andrew and Adana were giggling and hitting each other on the arm—in on some secret joke. They really did need help.

"Just think about it, Bianca. I'll be right back, okay?"

Bianca followed my eyes, then turned to me with raised eyebrows. She understood what was about to happen.

"Yes, Uncle Winston?" I stepped through the narrow door into the kitchen where Uncle Winston and Aunt Lonnie paced. With all of us there, it was more than a tight fit. Aunt Lonnie pulled the sliding door shut behind me, and they wasted no time in getting to the point.

"We," Uncle Winston began, then looked to Aunt Lonnie. She nodded before he continued, "We wanted to know how you planned on handling tomorrow."

"I don't plan on handling tomorrow," I replied, my back arching like a cornered cat.

"You know what he means," Aunt Lonnie said, her chin lifting.

Uncle Winston placed a hand on my shoulder. "We just want to know what you're planning to do after the will is read."

"I don't know what the will says, Uncle Winston. The attorney will be here at eleven o'clock. Until then, I don't know what else to say." Then it occurred to me; they must know something more, so I asked, "Am I missing something here?"

The look the two exchanged was quick and dripping with guilt. Aunt Lonnie rushed to answer. "No, of course not. We know Mama Grace set some money aside for family members and we want to make sure everything is distributed fairly, that's all, Kingston." If Aunt Lonnie thought she was doing a good job of cleaning this up, she was mistaken.

"I'm sure Mama Grace was very fair and tomorrow we will see just what her idea of fair is. But I don't think now is the time to have this discussion. We have guests out there." As I closed the sliding door behind me, I felt steam rising from the top of my head. How dare they try to turn this into a showdown? Whatever sliver of unity we experienced this morning, had disappeared like a puff of smoke. I would have even less support than expected as executor of Mama Grace's will. I couldn't even imagine what Uncle Winston and Aunt Lonnie expected; but if it turned out even half as bad as they thought that it would, it was not going to be good.

"Whoa! Where's the fire?" Damon grabbed my arm and I spun to face him. He was still wearing his navy suit, but now a few of the buttons loosened on his white shirt, a hint of chest hair poked out, and his dreads fell loosely around his shoulders.

"Funerals seem to bring out the worst in people." I paused. "No, I take that back, money brings out the worst in people." I leaned forward. "I think my aunt and uncle have gone mad! They're trying to figure out what their share of Mama Grace's money is going to be."

Damon laughed and kissed me on the forehead. "Sad, but true; and this is only the beginning, Kingston. Same thing happened when my grandmother died. Not many family members were in favor of my turning the house into a community center. Most wanted to sell it, then split the money. No one could see the good that could come from it.

Thank God, my aunt was there to fight with me."

"I can't deal with this right now, Damon." I threw my hands up, my voice breaking from the tears I was fighting to keep back.

"So don't," he said and gave me a conspiratorial wink. "Let's get outta here. You've put in your time. Let's go relax, have some fun."

An automatic red light went off in my head. I laughed out of nervousness.

"Scared?" he teased.

"Of course, I'm not scared. Scared of what?" I sputtered. Damon raised his eyebrows up and down, a corner of his mouth pulled into a lopsided grin, the word DARE written all over his face.

The red light started flashing; but never one to back down from a challenge, I wasn't going to start now. "Do I need to bring anything?"

"Just you."

"Where are we going?"

"Trust me on this one, Kingston. Just trust me."

Now that was easier said than done.

I placed my hand in his and dared myself to trust him—and myself— just a little bit. I whispered in Bianca's ear that I needed to get some air, which wasn't exactly a lie. I just didn't tell her that Damon was going to be sharing some of that air space. It was a small omission, a lie by omission.

The evening air was dank—warm and humid—with the smell of smoke lingering. I regretted not changing from my Ann Klein suit and heels into something more casual. I hadn't wanted to give Damon the idea that I was concerned about my appearance.

It was five minutes before I realized where we were going. "Your house?" I asked, looking up at Damon, one hand shielding my eyes from the stubborn sun.

"That okay with you?"

"Fine," I replied, nibbling on the inside of my jaw, but I didn't feel fine at all. A whirling sensation in the pit of my stomach caused a lightheadedness that made me want to sit down. My palms were sweating and I didn't feel as if my legs were going to carry me too much further.

"Good," Damon said and grabbed my sweaty hand in his. I had

forgotten how affectionate Damon could be. While it was comforting at the funeral, it now felt like a lover's gesture and that didn't sit well with me at all. I was enjoying the attention way too much and the last thing I needed was to get used to Damon being in my life. After all, I'd be on a plane to Chicago in a few days.

The rest of the distance was covered in silence, giving me plenty of time to reacquaint myself with the community. Children were outside playing, kicking a worn soccer ball and jumping rope. A woman passed, her arms full of groceries. She nodded warmly at Damon and gazed at me with open curiosity. A group of men were standing in front of the Chinaman's corner store, swigging cheap beer and swapping cheaper stories. In the distance, a baby goat baahed. Coconut trees bent under the weight of their bounty. A breeze prickled against my sweaty neck. It was a typical Jamaican evening.

Damon led me around the side of his house to the backyard. A privacy fence had been put up so it looked like a tiny piece of a tropical heaven had been captured, then stashed away for his pleasure. Rows of fruit trees—orange, ackee, and pear—lined the yard while a myriad of potted plants decorated the wide, wooden deck. In the middle of it set an in-ground hot tub that started bubbling when Damon flipped a switch.

"My, what a way we've come up," I said under my breath, trying not to appear impressed. "It's beautiful."

"Thanks, but don't go getting the wrong idea about the hot tub, Kingston. It's strictly for therapeutic purposes and tonight a chilled glass of wine and a nice long soak in a hot tub is what the doctor ordered."

My eyebrows shot up, but my lips gave me away, curving into a flirtatious half smile. "Oh really?"

"Yep. So I'm going to give you a few minutes to get undressed and climb in while I get the wine."

"I don't have a bathing suit." I gestured with my arms, highlighting the obvious. "I don't have anything."

"I know, Kingston," he bantered over his shoulder while unlocking the padlock on the wrought-iron porch door. "Neither do I." Then, he disappeared into the house.

Just call me the Mario Andretti of undressing. I set a record getting out of my clothes. The thought of getting in the hot tub naked just to freak Damon out did cross my mind; but in the end, I left on my sheer black bra and thong panties. I folded my clothes and draped them over a wooden bench. I stuck my big toe in the water and closed my eyes in ecstasy. "This is going to be heaven," I whispered to the stars, sinking down so far into the water that the bubbles kissed my chin. My hair was piled on top of my head and secured only with a wish; one false move and it would come tumbling down around my shoulders.

Damon returned, carrying a bottle of wine in a bucket of ice and two glasses. "I'm sorry, but there's nothing prepared to eat."

"It's okay. I ate more than enough already."

"Same here. Queenie's amazing when you let her loose in a kitchen."

It was nervous conversation; small talk, nothing more. Damon poured the wine. He had changed out of his clothes and was wearing electric blue shorts with funky orange squiggles that complimented his cocoa brown skin. And I was right, he was in better shape now than ten years ago.

This is a potentially explosive situation, I told myself and wondered how it had gotten to this point. Less than five days ago, you couldn't have told me that I was capable of having a civil conversation with Damon much less be in a hot tub, damn near naked, drinking wine and thinking lustful thoughts.

"Here you go." Damon handed me a glass of wine, then lit three candles before climbing into the hot tub. "Let's drink to the beauty of Jamaica." We clinked glasses.

"It is a beautiful country," I murmured, lowering my eyes and focusing on the wine. I couldn't look at him, his gaze was too intense.

"And you too are part of the beauty of Jamaica."

That did it. Things were going too far. "Damon, please stop."

"You're a beautiful woman."

Flustered, I shook my head. "I'm not talking about that. I mean the wine, the candlelight, the hot tub, the sweet words. What exactly are we doing?"

"We're two old friends catching up."

"Two old friends, Damon?" I repeated incredulously.

"Okay, more than two old friends. But I still want to catch up."

"We did that when I came down to your house. There's not too much more to catch up on."

"I think that there is." Damon put down his wine glass. I took another long swallow, swirling the cool liquid in my mouth.

Damon scooted closer to me. "Do you know how many times I wanted to call or write you? I wondered what you were doing; wondered if you were married with three babies and a white-picket fence, wondered about everything, really. I've missed you." He pushed at a few strands of hair that were stuck to the moist side of my neck. His stroking my neck was too intimate a gesture, and I moved to reclaim my personal space. It bothered me that Damon could still push my emotional and physical buttons so easily.

"I hate when people say that, Damon," I replied, pushing his hand away. "Because it's nothing to pick up a phone and call somebody. It's nothing to drop them a postcard. It was not my intention to have this conversation. There's no point to it. What's done is done. There's nothing you can say to excuse what you did."

Damon reached for me again, but then drew his hand back as if he were afraid to touch me. "You don't think I realize that? And I'm not going to give you excuses. As a man, I'm not proud of what went down; but at the time, I didn't know what else to do. My grandmother was dying and not being able to help her brought back all the feelings that I had about Joanne and I went into a meltdown. I had all of these responsibilities that I was not equipped to handle and it emotionally drained me.

"After my grandmother died, I went to Montego Bay to get away from all the crap that was going on here. I started my practice and worked myself until I was too exhausted to think or feel anything. I had nothing left for you, Kingston. You deserved everything and I had nothing to give you. It was as if I just couldn't hold on to the women in my life. Joanne. My grandmother. You."

Damon's words chipped away at the rock solid barrier that I was trying hard to keep around my heart. I could better understand where he was coming from, but I still couldn't let go of the pain, the hurt and lonely nights. "A phone call, Damon, that's what I deserved more than anything—a simple phone call. The worst thing about what happened was the not knowing. You could have told me that you needed space, or that you were too busy or whatever it was. But I deserved to know something. Yes, it would have hurt. Yes, I would have been mad; but I would have been able to start the healing process a lot quicker than I did." My breath was coming in spurts as I shook my head. "I would sit around praying that you would call me. I'm not proud of that, but I loved you so much.

"My mother told me to only be a fool for love once. You were my one time. I won't do it again." My words added another layer to the tension between us. "And for the record, I would have never left you. Joanne and your grandmother, they didn't have a choice. I did, and I chose you."

Damon's shoulders slumped. "I loved you, too, Kingston. It took working with underprivileged children in Montego Bay for almost three years before I could come to terms with everything that had gone on in my life: from my parents leaving, to losing Joanne, to losing you. But after so much time had passed, it seemed like it was too late for apologies."

"It is never too late for apologies, Damon. It's never too late to try to right a wrong."

"I really loved you, Kingston. I need for you to hear that."

"How could you have loved me, and done that to me—just leave me like that? Your walking out made me question everything about our relationship and some things about myself as a woman. For years, I couldn't go out with a man and not compare him to you. I was miserable and I was bitter. I hated that I gave you so much power." I dragged my hand through the water watching the bubbles reappear in the path left by my fingers. Anything was better than looking into Damon's eyes.

"It was an honor to have you in my life, and I'm sorry for causing you so much pain. I didn't mean to abuse the trust you had in me."

I waved off any more apologies. "I've come to peace with what happened. Well, as much peace as I could. Ten years is a long time. I guess we just weren't meant to be." I steeled myself before looking at him. "I do have one question, something that still bothers me. And be honest, Damon. I mean, what can it hurt now, right? Was there someone else waiting for you when you got back? Did you have another woman?"

Damon's mouth went slack. "No. There was no one else, then or now," he said, a frown flashed against his face.

"You don't really expect me to believe that."

"I didn't say I lived like a priest. I've dated." He shoved his hand through his hair, dreads wrapping around his fingers. "But no one has ever come close to capturing my heart the way you did. I don't think anyone ever will. You stay in the back in my mind, not letting anyone else in."

"Damon," I started, then shook my head. I didn't know what to say. It was too much to take in at one time.

He took my hand in his. "I know it's been ten years. But I still have to say it. Forgive me, Kingston, please."

"I forgave you a long time ago." At the hopefulness and untainted love reflected in his eyes, the dam broke and tears flowed down my face. This conversation had been the cherry on the top of a heart-wrenching day. The embarrassment I felt for crying in front of Damon made matters worse and I cried even more. Damon put his arms around me and pulled me close. I resisted for only a moment before melting into his warmth.

"It's all right, sweetheart," he whispered over and over, punctuating each statement with a kiss. And then the clincher, "I meant it when I said the feelings never went away. I still love you."

Our chemistry exploded like instantaneous combustion and I could no longer hold back, no longer wanted to hold back. I returned his kisses with urgent ones of my own, moving my hands hungrily over every part of his wet body and memorizing every inch of his anatomy. Damon's hands searched just as purposefully, sliding the straps of my bra off my shoulders and down my arms. He placed a hand over each breast, rubbing gently at first and then more forcefully causing my nipples to blossom under his attention. I kissed him again, this time slow and lovingly. I nudged his lips open with mine and allowed my tongue the freedom to tease and caress. Damon groaned deeply into my mouth and placed his hands on my waist, picking me up and positioning me so that I faced him, straddling his lap. Our hips moved in a circular motion and when I felt his need pushing against me, I tried to angle closer to him.

"You're killing me," Damon moaned.

I laughed throatily as he kissed my neck, sucking gently before leaning lower so he could capture my nipple in his mouth. I threw my head back, and my hair spilled around my shoulders. Damon seized the opportunity, tangling his fingers in my hair and holding me captive as his tongue tormented first one nipple, then the other. It was my turn to groan and I pulled him closer, as he tried to scoot out of his shorts without unseating me. I laughed at his clumsy attempts. His third try was successful. My undergarment was much easier to deal with. Damon ripped it off with a breathless promise to buy me a new one. I didn't care. Only one thing mattered right now and with one push, Damon handled that, too. After what seemed like a lifetime, we were united again as fully as two people could be.

Every ounce of energy I had was gone. Between the heat from the hot tub and our fierce lovemaking, I could barely move. Damon repositioned me so that he could cradle me in his arms. Slowly, the reality of what had just happened washed over me. I felt raw, vulnerable—and scared.

"I've got to go," I said, jumping from his arms and the hot tub.

Damon's smile faded and he started to climb out after me. "Why are you leaving so soon? I thought we could have more therapeutic sessions inside, maybe make love in a real bed. We've never done that."

"No," I protested. "I've got to go." I slipped my skirt and jacket on and stood holding my shoes in my hand. I'd put them on later. Damon started to follow me, but I stuck my hand out. "Don't," I told him, running toward the front of the house.

"Kingston, please don't go," he said; but it was too late. I'd already faded into the darkness of the black Jamaican night.

Chapter 18

When I woke up, I changed my flight. It cost a pretty penny, but the other options could cost far more. Pacing the length of that back porch, I drank my second cup of coffee while Uncle Winston, Auntie Dawn, Andrew, and Adana sat on the porch. Aunt Lonnie and Uncle Lee were in the living room, listening to the late morning news on the radio from Pa-pa's room. Aunt Bea roamed the yard inspecting the garden, clicking her tongue at the weeds. Bianca was still asleep.

Toy's barking signaled the arrival of the attorney, eleven o'clock, right on the dot. The bedsprings squeaked as Bianca got up, her bare feet padding on the floor as she walked down the hall to the bathroom.

Queenie had earned the day off, staying late to help last night. Plus, I thought it would be best with only family present. I rinsed my coffee cup while the rest of the family chitchatted with the lawyer in the front room. Everyone was ready to get this over with, not all for the same reasons, though.

Bianca slipped through a side door, yawning and joined me in the kitchen. "I was worried about you last night," she said giving me a brief hug.

I returned her hug; worried that Bianca could smell the lingering aroma of sex clinging to me. A short laugh escaped my lips. "No, you weren't. You're nosey and wanted to know what I was doing. I was fine, just needed a little fresh air."

Giving me a sly grin, she asked, "So, just how fine are you? I kinda' put two and two together when I noticed you and Damon were gone at the same time."

"We had to put some things to rest." A blush warmed my cheeks. "I'll be leaving to go back to Chicago later this evening. If you're not in too much of a hurry to get home yourself, I'd love for you to take me to the airport."

Bianca's intuition kicked into overdrive. "That must have been one heck of a conversation. You'll have to tell me the story one day."

"I will, over another bottle of wine and bag of cheese popcorn."

Bianca grimaced. "I'll stick to fruit punch next time. And, yes, I would be more than happy to drop you at the airport on my way home. I'm anxious for things to get back to normal too." She looked into the dining room where everyone had gathered, then turned back to me. "Ready to do this?"

"Ready as I'll ever be." I squeezed her hand. Ten minutes later with everyone seated around the dining room table, the attorney, Mr. Bartlett, pulled some official-looking papers from his briefcase and shuffled them around.

I studied him from under hooded eyes. Not quite what I had expected, Mr. Bartlett appeared to be about the same age as Mama Grace and meticulous with everything, including his dress. Although the temperature already hovered at ninety degrees, he wore a light beige tweed suit, with a light blue handkerchief folded in the pocket, and a starched white shirt. He stood before us like a teacher about to lecture an unwilling class, smoothing his unruly, white mustache and adjusting his spectacles. Uncle Winston tapped his foot while Aunt Lonnie darted sideways glances at me. We were trapped, so we waited in silence until Mr. Bartlett decided to begin. Everything that pertained to this transaction was going to happen according to his timetable and not one minute before.

He cleared his throat. "Good afternoon, Ladies and Gentlemen. Today, this sixteenth day of December in the year of our Lord two thousand and thirteen," he began. "We are gathered here to read Grace Marie Montague's Last Will and Testament."

Toy's sudden bark startled us and all heads turned to watch her scurry out to the front porch, her nails making a scraping sound on the tiled floor. A few seconds later, she came trotting back, followed by Damon. Shocked silence greeted him, but no one was more surprised to see him than me. Uncle Winston started to rise in objection, but it was soon obvious that Damon was supposed to be here and Uncle Winston sank back into his chair with a blush slowly making its way up his neck.

"Hello, everyone. Sorry, I'm late. I had an unexpected patient stop by the clinic and I couldn't turn her away." Damon shook Mr. Bartlett's outstretched hand. At least someone seemed happy to see him.

"It's good to see you again, young man. You're just in time. I was afraid I'd have to meet with you separately."

Damon claimed the empty chair next to Andrew, directly across from me. Andrew looked puny compared to Damon, not just in a physical sense, but also in an overall manhood kind of way. Damon was dressed causally in jeans and a button-up shirt with his hair pulled back. He glanced at me and smiled, oblivious to the turmoil his mere presence was causing inside of me. I didn't smile back. What the hell was he doing here?

Mr. Bartlett continued, "As I was saying, in order to lend a more personal feel to her last wishes, Mrs. Montague wrote a letter to dispense of her monetary and physical possessions. Granddaughter, Kingston Phillips, has been deemed Executor of Mrs. Montague's estate and will work closely with me in order to make sure that her wishes are carried out accordingly." His gaze skimmed over me, sizing me up as if to see what I was made of, as if this was going to be the single most important task that I'd ever undertake. And it just might be. When I passed his approval, he said, "If we are all ready, then we shall proceed. I have made copies of the letter for each of you so you may follow along if you wish."

He took several sealed envelopes from his briefcase, then passed them around. When Uncle Winston eagerly started to open his, the attorney held up his hand, brought out a tape recorder and set it in the middle of the table. "Mrs. Montague made a tape recording of her wishes. Before you open these, I would like to make one thing perfectly clear—despite this Last Will and Testament being partially in letter form, it is still legally binding." Mr. Bartlett's eyebrows rose threateningly. "And in my fifty-four years of practicing law, I've never had a will contested."

With that said, he nodded and envelopes were ripped open. Aunt Bea pulled out her white napkin tucked in the sleeve of her shirt. I ran my finger over the words that Mama Grace painstakingly wrote in anticipation of her death. Still standing, Mr. Bartlett picked up his own copy of the will, pushed the play button on the tape recorder and Mama Grace spoke from the grave.

"To my sister, children, grandchildren, and their spouses. This is my Last Will and Testament. I know you may be anxious to get to the monetary issues, but I will reach there in my own sweet time. First, I want to impart some good advice, which, if you follow it, will bring you better returns in the hereafter.

"Money is a curse and the source of most evil, but a necessity to get on in life. I, however, do not want to be guilty of leaving too much of this evil to any one person. I think as I get more into the division of assets, you will be surprised at how much wealth I have amassed in my life. Your grandfather and I, with the aide of our attorney, have made some very wise investments. So, I died a rich woman. But I have also been poor and have found that no matter how much money you have, there is no real happiness on this earth. Earthly pleasures are only for the moment. Real happiness must be lasting.

"I have also learned that nobody is sent more crosses than he or she can bear and there is always enough grace sent to bear them if you

ask. If you bear all your crosses willingly and even ask our Lord for more to bear, you have then derived a sense of happiness to which the best pleasures of this world cannot compare. Always bear your troubles willingly.

"My darlings, be good, do good, and you will always have peace and be on the right road to heaven. I have found that much unhappiness is caused by family disputes. Stubbornness runs in our family so you got it honestly, from both sides of the family. As soon as you notice you are not getting anywhere, you need not give up your point of view, providing you are sure you are right; but you must stop arguing, shut up, and listen. You will be surprised how much quicker your argument is settled.

"Love the Lord thy God with all your heart, mind, and soul. Also love your neighbor as yourself. But to truly be at peace, you must love God above all things. It is always better to give than to receive. Charity should begin at home. And charity does not necessarily mean financial assistance. A pleasant smile and a good disposition at all times, also a desire to do a good deed whenever you get the opportunity, is good charity. Try and do at least one good deed each day.

"If I could live my life over again, there is a lot that I would do differently. But all of that fades away when you are on your deathbed, when the only reason you would live life over again would be to advance your salvation. So why gamble the first time, when there is no second time. Try and live your life as you would live it a second time, and you will derive a sense of happiness, which cannot be compared to the earthly pleasures you now get out of life. Everybody should be glad to be on this earth and have a chance to attain the great happiness in Heaven. This life is only a preparation for the next. See that you make it the best it can be. I have lived a long, good life and I have learned many things. I can only pray that you listen and apply them to your own lives."

Mr. Bartlett pressed the pause button on the recorder to stop the tape. He looked out at his captive audience over his horn-rimmed glasses. "Any questions before we continue?" No one spoke, so once again the tape rolled and Mama Grace's voice filled the room.

"To my granddaughter, Kingston, who I have named Executor and Trustee of my estate, I leave the house located at 2 1/4 Blossom Street and all of its possessions therein with the exception of those that will be detailed later. If Kingston chooses not to live in or maintain said residence, the proceeds from the sale of the house and its contents will revert back to the estate trust fund that has already been established and will be explained later by my attorney. It is my sincere hope, Kingston, that you will not sell the house, but would choose at my urging to reside here at least part of the year in order to oversee the estate fund. I know it will be a sacrifice, but I hope you will discover it to be a worthy endeavor.

"To my remaining sister, my children, and my grandchildren, I leave twenty-one thousand dollars each with the stipulation that those not living in Jamaica must return to the island to receive it. It is further stipulated that one-third of the above-mentioned twenty-one thousand dollars must be donated to a charity of your choice. Any funds unclaimed after ninety days will revert back to the estate trust fund.

"All of my remaining possessions, bank accounts, stocks, and bonds will be liquidated or sold and the proceeds will revert to the estate trust fund. My attorney, Mr. Bartlett, has in his custody all of the papers needed to make this happen.

"From the estate trust fund, Kingston as overseer will be paid a yearly stipend to be disclosed at a later time by my attorney for the remainder of her life or until such time as she is unable or unwilling to complete her duties. Also from the estate trust fund, Queenie McDowell will be rewarded for her loyalty with a yearly stipend of twenty thousand dollars to be paid bi-weekly, for the remainder of her life. If the house is not sold, she will be allowed to continue in her duties if she so desires.

"Furthermore, from the estate fund, a charitable foundation will be established in order to help underprivileged girls further their education here and abroad.

"From the estate fund, a yearly stipend of thirty thousand dollars *will be paid to Damon Whitfield for the sole purpose of maintaining the community health center and its charitable works.*

"In closing, other than the funds and possessions stipulated in this Last Will and Testament, no further moneys or possessions will be dispensed to family members. I feel I've given each of you a sufficient amount of money in order to help you accomplish some things in life, whether it be going back to school, starting a business, or paying off some bills. But I will not support in any way your viewing my death as an occasion for you to profit. I love each and every one of you and wish you all the happiness in the world. I'll be watching."

Mr. Bartlett reached over once more and with a click stopped the tape. The silence was deafening. Aunt Bea's mouth hung open in shock while she dabbed at the corner of her eyes with the already damp tissue. I looked at Damon, but he was staring at an invisible spot on the table, and I realized he had no idea that Mama Grace was planning to leave him anything in her will, and certainly not something so substantial. I was happy that she did, but from the scattered whispers around me, not all shared the sentiment.

Bianca nudged me. "I had no idea Mama Grace was so loaded."

"Neither did I," I admitted, still recovering from shock.

"Does anyone have any questions before I depart?" We had forgotten that Mr. Bartlett was still here.

Uncle Winston raised his hand and waited until he was acknowledged with a curt nod. "So, if I'm to understand things correctly, the majority of Mama Grace's fortune is to go into some estate trust fund?"

"That's correct, Mr. Montague. The fund was established at the time your stepmother drafted her will."

"Exactly how much is in this fund?"

"Let's just say that there's more than enough money to support its designated endeavors on the interest alone. Kingston will have the authority to establish charitable projects as long as they fit within the guidelines set by Mrs. Montague."

"So basically," Uncle Winston said as he rose from his chair, "Kingston has sole control over all that money."

"No, Mr. Montague," Mr. Bartlett started, as if he were about to explain physics to a two-year-old. "Kingston is in charge of administering the funds as instructed by Mrs. Montague. Kingston does not have access to the fund for personal use."

"Exactly how much is in this fund? I think we have the right to know," Aunt Lonnie muttered.

"According to the terms of the will, that cannot be disclosed. Besides myself, only Kingston and the accountant will have access to that information."

"It must be well over a million dollars," breathed Auntie Dawn while Aunt Bea moaned into her tissue.

"My, my, my," Aunt Bea said, "Bless Grace's heart, giving all that money to charity."

"What about her family?" Uncle Winston fired at Aunt Bea, causing her to shrink in her chair.

"And who will be in charge of making sure Kingston does what she's supposed to do with all that money?" Auntie Dawn asked.

"It's my job to make sure that Mrs. Montague's will is executed legally," Mr. Bartlett replied, his chest puffed out. It was one thing for everyone to question my credibility. It was another thing entirely for them to question Mr. Bartlett's. "And as I said earlier, Kingston will not be able to use that money for anything other than what has been approved by Mama Grace." He paused, then scanned the room again. "If there is nothing further, I will take my leave. I have other clients to see today. My office number is printed on each copy of the will. Feel free to call me with any questions."

After placing the tape recorder and the remainder of his papers in his briefcase, he turned to me. "Kingston, I will need to speak with you in the next couple of days; so please forward your contact information to my office as soon as possible." He snapped shut his briefcase and tucked it under his arm. I wanted to tell him that I was already unwilling or unable—depending on how you looked at it—to complete my duties because I was catching a flight in less than three hours. But by the time

I opened my mouth, Mr. Bartlett's stiff back was disappearing through the front door.

Bianca waited until she heard the front gate slam and a car motor start before she whirled to face her mother. "Mommy, how could you?" she wailed. "I would have expected that he would act a fool," she said, tossing her head in Uncle Winston's direction. "But not you. None of this is Kingston's fault."

"Not now, Bianca." Aunt Lonnie looked pointedly at Damon.

Bianca crossed her arms in front of her. "I don't care if we have company. Besides, it's too late for 'not now,' Mommy," she returned in a high-pitched voice designed to mock her mother. "You should have thought 'not now' while you were trying to make Kingston seem like a criminal, like she's stealing something from you. Kingston's your niece."

Deciding that it might be better if I step in before the situation escalated into an all-out catfight, I placed my hand on Bianca's arm to stop her from continuing her tirade. "Bianca, it's okay. I understand that everyone is still grieving and sometimes when you're grieving, you say things you don't really mean." Bianca's head snapped back and her eyes widened in surprise. Then suddenly her face softened. She realized I didn't mean a word of what I just said and backed off. I wanted to laugh at her sheepish look. We'd grown closer in the last two days than in all the years growing up.

Uncle Lee took Aunt Lonnie by the arm and steered her in the direction of the door, her gold bangles jingling. "It's time to go," he said. "What's done, is done."

"That's a poor choice of words considering the circumstances we find ourselves in," I commented. I waited for Uncle Winston to follow suit, gather his brood and just leave, but Uncle Lee wasn't finished.

"After all, we really don't need the money like some others," he snorted and they stomped out, car doors slamming within seconds.

Damon took that as his cue. "I have patients that need to be seen today, and I don't want to intrude any further." Damon scooted his chair back. "It was nice seeing all of you." He smiled, then turned to me. "Kingston, could you walk me to the door."

I hesitated, taken aback by his nerve, then followed him out to the porch.

"You look beautiful," he said before we were even out of earshot.

I smoothed a hand over the front of my linen pants and frowned. "Damon, don't do this."

"Don't do what?" he asked. "Compliment an absolutely delicious woman?"

"Don't act like we're going to pick up right where we left off last night."

"Giving you a compliment isn't doing that. This," he whispered "is acting like we're picking up right where we left off," then swept me into his arms and kissed me. And not one of those regular old kisses, either. This was a Scarlett O'Hara, *Gone with the Wind*, kind of kiss—long, passionate, and delicious.

So delicious, I almost forgot that we were standing on the porch with all to see. Almost.

Sure that Aunt Bea, Uncle Winston, Auntie Dawn, and the two brats were getting more than an eyeful, I pushed at Damon's chest until he let me go, then grabbed his arm, yanking him down the steps until we were as far away from the house as possible.

"I really didn't want you to do that," I spat out, still feeling the imprint of his mouth branded on mine and knowing that my body had definitely betrayed me.

"Yeah, I could tell." Damon laughed. "You weren't enjoying that at all, were you Kingston? Do I have lipstick on me? That shade of red looks good on you, but I'm not sure it's my color." He wiped his mouth.

I sighed. He was hopeless. "This isn't funny."

"I don't mean to make fun." He planted a kiss on the corners of my pouting lips. "I miss you, that's all and I want to see you. Tonight. I'm figuring I'll be done about seven. Maybe a little dinner and even some dancing. They have this new night club for the over-thirty crowd that I hear is very nice."

"I'm leaving, Damon," I said, not beating around the bush. I looked from the pained expression on his face to the slim Movado watch on my wrist. It was easier. "My flight leaves in less than three hours, so I need to get ready to go." I started to rattle off the list of things that I still had to do.

"I thought you were staying until at least tomorrow. And maybe even longer after hearing what your grandmother wanted."

"My life is in Chicago. I need and want to get back to it. I just can't forget about all of my responsibilities and stay here."

"What about the Will?"

"I haven't figured that out. Don't worry though, I'll make sure you get your check on time."

The smile vanished from Damon's face. "That's a low blow, Kingston. You know that I'm not concerned about the damn money. Obviously, it'll help me do more in the community, but I can survive without it." He paused, then ran a finger down the side of my face and tilted my chin until my eyes met his. "I'm concerned about you. You've gone through a lot and I want to help you deal with it. Plus, I was getting used to the idea of you being around. I have quite a bit to make up for. Besides, if I didn't know any better, I would say that your grandmother was playing the matchmaker, giving you the house so you could stay here and be with me."

"Why would you say that?"

"Let's just say your grandmother and I had a lot of conversations before she died and most centered around you."

I turned and leaned on the front gate. I wasn't happy to know that Damon and my grandmother had been discussing me behind my back, but I didn't want to make the situation worse by getting mad. I forced my lips into a smile. "Well, whatever the case may be, I'm glad that we talked. And I am glad that we got some things cleared up. But that other thing that happened last night was a mistake."

Damon laughed and shook his head. "You can't even say it? We made love, Kingston. That's what happened last night and it was incredible."

His words brought back the steamy images with the force of a mack truck, and a fiery warmth started in my stomach before exploding through my entire body.

"Okay, I admit it." I lowered my voice to a whisper. "We're definitely compatible in a sexual sense. But that's not enough for me. I won't compromise what I believe."

Damon placed his hands on my shoulder, his brown eyes smoldered. "What compromise? I still love you, Kingston, as much, if not more than, I used to. I know this sounds cliché, but that kind of love just doesn't die."

"It may not have died, but something happened to it. I don't owe you an explanation, Damon, I just need more."

"You're not giving it a chance to be more."

I poked my finger in his chest and replied through clenched teeth, "No, you didn't give it a chance to be more. Goodbye, Damon." I turned and walked back into the house, managing to pass the open mouths and prying stares with my head held high. But when I reached my bedroom, I threw myself on the bed and dissolved into tears. My head was telling me that leaving Damon was the right thing based on what had happened in the past; but my heart was screaming, "not again." Because like it or not, I had fallen back into Damon's trap.

The pain, loneliness, and despair came rushing back the same as it did ten years ago. I knew that the heartache would go away. I'd learned that lesson well. No matter what, there was always an end to the pain; always an end to the heartache.

When the stream of tears dried up five minutes later, I packed my bags, and let Bianca drive me to the airport.

Chapter 19

"All right, girl, give me the news. You've made me wait long enough."
I snapped my seatbelt in place, then flipped the visor down and checked
the mirror. My hair and makeup were still in place—even after the long
flight; but out of habit, I brushed a coat of raspberry lip-gloss across my
lips.

"No small talk?" Keela joked as she looked in her rearview mirror
before switching on her left turn signal. She was doing her best to
navigate through the congested airport traffic.

"Keela," I growled in warning.

"My goodness, aren't we tense?" she joked as I rummaged through
my purse for a piece of gum. She was stalling, trying to deflect the
attention back to me. I stared at her until she took a deep, fortifying
breath. "Well, here goes … I'm pregnant. You're going to be an auntie."
She glanced at me out of the corner of her eye.

I nearly choked on my Doublemint. "What! Get outta here," I
exploded, socking her in the arm.

"Ouch," she said, massaging the bruised spot.

"Why did you wait so long to tell me? When? How?" I paused.
"Forget that. I know how."

"Take a deep breath, girl." Keela giggled. "I know it's a shock. But this is a good thing. I'm ready to be a mommy."

"How far along are you?"

Keela wrinkled her nose and shrugged. "About eighteen weeks now, halfway through my second trimester. I was trying to wait before I told everyone. My doctor says that first babies are tricky, that they don't always stay, so I wanted the risk of miscarriage to go down before I started spreading the good news."

"I'm not everyone," I protested.

"I know, sweetie, but you had so much going on. I wanted you to get through that first, then tell you face to face." Keela merged onto the highway, traffic flowing well for this time of day. "I'm gonna be a mama," she said, gently patting her tummy.

"You're going to be a mommy!" I inhaled the wonder of it, let the enormity of the situation settle in and happiness flooded my heart. If anyone deserved to be a mother, it was Keela. She was a nurturer, a caretaker.

Keela continued to take side-peeks, gauging my reaction, waiting for me to explain the frown that now furrowed my brow.

"Go on and ask me," she said quietly. "You're dying to know, so go on and ask me who my baby daddy is."

"I didn't know there was a baby daddy. I thought you went to a sperm bank and was going to list 'test tube' as the father on the birth certificate," I suggested with a half smile, though secretly wishing that really were the case.

"Oh, you got jokes?" Keela blustered as if she were upset, but couldn't quite pull it off. Soon her whole body was jiggling and covering her mouth couldn't even contain the giggles.

"So?" I prodded.

"So, what?"

"Who's the baby's daddy?"

"Brandon."

"Brandon who?"

"What do you mean, Brandon who?" Keela's face screwed up and suddenly the thought of Brandon being the baby's father pissed me off.

"Like I said, Brandon who? You must have met somebody new, because I know you are not talking about Brandon Charles: Brandon, 'I can't keep my hands off other women,' Charles; or Brandon, 'I need more, so I dumped you after you slaved over Christmas dinner for two days,' Charles; certainly not Brandon, 'I'm thirty-eight, but still don't have anything to call my own,' Charles; not the same Brandon Charles who had two of his other women three-waying you just to call you all kinds of sluts and hos non-stop for a week? Stop me when I've got the wrong Brandon Charles."

Keela didn't respond, but one look at her told the story. Her eyes shone with unshed tears and my heart sank. I saw the sadness in her eyes and knew I needed to find the sweetness in the situation. I didn't want to see this as just another mess that Brandon Charles had created.

"Oh, honey." I covered her hand with mine and gave it a gentle squeeze.

"I can't help that I love him, Kingston." She gave me a watery smile, the tears splashing on her cheeks.

"I know, Keela. And I'm sorry. I just worry about you, and this relationship has not been the most solid. I wonder how healthy this is going to be for the baby."

"Just be happy for me."

"I am, but ..."

"No buts, Kingston, be happy for me. We didn't plan to have a baby, but Brandon says he wants us to be a family, and for my child, I'm willing to try. If it doesn't work, I'll handle it. Regardless of the outcome, I need you and Essence more than ever."

"And you know we've got your back, no matter what. And I am happy for you, Keela. No more lectures, promise." I held up my hands in a gesture of peace.

"I'll believe that when I see it," Keela said, exiting from the Dan Ryan and turning onto 47th street. "Now tell me about the trip. I'm dying to hear about Damon. And don't leave out anything, Kingston. Not a damn thing—I want to know everything!"

I sank down in my seat and looked out the window as we passed the Java Hut coffee shop on the left, Lee's Nails on the right and two bums standing on the corner ahead. The snow had melted to a grayish slush that had dulled the normally brilliant glow of the city; but it was good to be home.

"Kingston," Keela said as she braked at a red light and looked at me. "You're not saying anything."

I shrugged and picked at some chipped polish on my nails. "Sorry, but there's not much to tell; just a lot of family drama. It's sad the things relatives will do over money—money, no one even knew Mama Grace had." Adjusting the vents on the dashboard, I said, "But I can't be worried about that. I'm have to call my grandmother's attorney in the morning, break down my situation and see what he says. As far as Damon goes, well, he's the same old Damon. I'll tell you everything when we see Essence so I don't have to repeat it. I'm just glad to be home and away from all that mess."

"Have you called Randy?"

"No, and don't plan on it." Randy hadn't crossed my mind in close to three days and I didn't want to think about him now. Of course, I left out the part that Randy hadn't bothered to get in touch with me either.

Keela started to push for more details, but one look at my frown and she let it rest, rambling about baby stuff for the remainder of the ride home. Vertebrae by vertebrae, I relaxed. Now that I was home, I could work on trying to get some semblance of normalcy back into what had become my life.

Two hours later, after making a drive-by stop at my house to dump my suitcases and calling Jonetta to let her know I had made it home—Essence, Keela, and I sat around a high round table at a local pub on 51st street. We smiled as the waitress set frosty mugs of Margaritas in front of us. Essence and I had requested ours be made with double shots of Grand Marnier while Keela's was non-alcoholic.

"I'll be right back with your appetizers." The waitress flashed a dazzling smile before swishing off to the next table.

After two sips, Essence turned to me. "Start talking."

"You guys don't waste any time, do you?" I kidded. "Can I take a sip first?"

"Yes," she answered with a straight face, "but just one."

"You are a trip!" I threw my head back, laughing so loudly that people sitting near us also looked to see what the commotion was about. Essence didn't find it funny at all.

Clearing my throat, I said, "Everything was a mess. Come to find out during the reading of the will, Mama Grace was a millionaire. Can you believe it? A millionaire," I repeated as their faces reflected their shock. "I was sending her money every month like she was barely scraping by and she was sitting on a truckload of dough. Apparently, she saved all of her money and invested wisely."

I took another sip, the lime from the margarita tickling the roof of my mouth. "She put the majority of the money into an estate trust fund, designed to support different programs like scholarships, but here's the kicker—she allotted thirty thousand dollars a year to help Damon with his clinic. And to top it off, Mama Grace chosen me to be the administrator. She left me the house and everything. So you know my aunt and uncle are up in arms because they feel they've been cheated out of some huge inheritance."

Keela and Essence sat back, taking it all in. Their eyes widened when I mentioned the part about Damon, but they didn't say anything. They would work their way back to that juicy tidbit, wanting to clear up the preliminaries first.

"How are you going to be the administrator of a fund in Jamaica when you live in Chicago?" Essence raised an eyebrow. Before I answered, the waitress placed our Buffalo wings and mozzarella cheese sticks on the table.

I filled a plate. "I have no idea. I'll be talking to the attorney first thing in the morning. In her letter, Mama Grace said that she left me the house in order to," I used my fingers as quotation marks, "encourage me to stay and take care of the estate fund. But I can't see giving up my life here. Damon thinks she did it to bring us back together."

"Why would he think that?" Keela munched on a hot, spicy chicken drummette, licking stray sauce from the corner of her mouth.

"Isn't that going to give you gas?" I asked, concerned at the amount of wings Keela was consuming. "I've heard about how delicate the stomachs of pregnant women can be."

"Trust me," Essence cut in. "That hasn't been a problem for her. She eats like food is going out of style." She twisted her nose and looked at Keela's belly. "You're gonna be so fat."

Keela made a face and kept right on eating. "Don't try to change the subject, answer my question."

"Apparently he spent a lot of time talking to Mama Grace while he was taking care of her and I guess some of those conversations were about me."

Essence wiped her mouth with a napkin. "Yeah, but to think based on those conversations, she would leave you the house just to get you and Damon back together seems like a stretch. There's got to be more to it than that," she concluded, signaling the waitress for another drink.

I blushed and stuffed a cheese stick in my mouth. "I knew it! There is more," Essence declared, clapping her hands and pointing at me. "Why do I always have to pull teeth with you, Kingston?"

"All right." I held up my hands in surrender. "There's more. Damon and I talked after Mama Grace's funeral. We went back to his house where he tried to explain why things happened the way they did. It wasn't the best of explanation, but I guess it was better than nothing."

"Yada, yada, yada," Essence said and motioned with her hands. "Get to the good part."

"She's working her way to it, Essence, be patient," Keela chastised and put her hand lightly over Essence's mouth.

"We talked in his hot tub," I admitted, ducking my head.

"See, I told you. That's what I'm talking about, Kingston." She slapped palms with Essence, then held her hand up to me for a high five, which I gave to her half-heartedly, still a bit ashamed that I let my guard down so easily.

"We talked in his hot tub and then, we didn't talk in the hot tub." I popped another cheese stick in my mouth.

"You did the nasty with Damon! Such a slut!" Essence said, before sticking a finger in her mouth, then touching it to her butt. "A sizzling hot mama!"

"Shhhh, Essence, people are staring," I said and leaned forward. "It started innocently enough. We were drinking wine and talking, then he told me he loved me and it was pretty much over."

Essence put her face right up in mine and tugged on a stray curl of hair. "So, let me get this straight. All he had to do was tell you that he loves you and you fell right back into step?"

I slapped her hand away. "I wouldn't put it like that. I agree I got caught up in the moment. But I'm not falling back into anything and I made that clear to Damon."

"But he said that he loves you," Keela offered with a raise of her eyebrows as if that was supposed to make everything better.

"So what?" Essence sneered. "We're back to happily ever after and all that shit?"

"He left me and for ten years never said a word. 'I love you' does not always make it better. I'm a single woman thanks to Randy's trifling ass and I'm going to enjoy it, not jump right back into anything—with Damon or anyone else."

Keela's eyes danced. "So, how was it? Good?"

"Mind blowing," I said, nibbling on a carrot, laughing at their shocked expressions.   Essence snapped her mouth shut, then asked, "Really? That good?"

"Better than it was ten years ago, if that's possible. He wanted me to spend the night and I didn't want to leave, but then I started thinking of the pain I went though when he left and just couldn't. I was tempted, though. It was like we were in some kind of time warp, like we were back together again." Images of Damon's sweaty body covering mine popped into my mind and my eyes closed automatically, every nerve tingling.

"Oh girl, you are so gone." Essence balled up her napkin and threw it on top of a stack of clean chicken bones.

Nodding, I picked up a celery stick and dipped it in the bleu cheese dressing. "I know, but there's nothing I can do but get over it—again.

How in the world can Damon and I be together now?" I finished off the last of my Margarita and pasted on a smile that made my mouth hurt. "Such is life."

We sat in silence for a few minutes, finishing what was left of the food.

"When are you going back to work?" Keela finally asked. I dabbed at a spot of hot sauce on my sleeve. I had just bought this shirt and already it was ruined. I swore softly before answering. " I need a couple of days to think, get my head together, but tomorrow's Sunday so if I can get some rest, figure things out, I may be ready to go back to the office on Monday. With everything that needs to get done, now is not the time for me to be out for too long. Besides, I'm really itching to get Scooby's project off the ground, and laying around feeling sorry for myself is not going to make that happen."

"Ooh!" Keela exclaimed and with excitement flashing in her eyes, dropped her voice to a conspiratorial whisper. "I forgot. Remember my girlfriend Lola Baker? She said she saw Randy at his company's annual Christmas fundraiser. Her current man works in the same department as Randy or something like that. She told me that Randy was all over that white girl—lots of public displays of affection. Didn't he always tell you that he was against that—kissing in public and stuff? Well, Lola said that she had on this little piece of triangular material that didn't leave anything to the imagination, had all the old white managers drooling. If you ask me, Randy is using her to help him climb the corporate ladder." She sniped, "What happened to the modeling career he was so fired up about?"

"I'm not thinking about Randy," I retorted. "Don't get me wrong, I wish him well, but I've never been able to remain friends with an ex— they're exes for a reason. I'm certainly not going to waste any energy helping him further his career. Handling my own career is enough. Add everything else in there..." My words trailed off as I thought about Mama Grace and her will, then about Damon, and all the energy drained out of me.

Keela smiled sympathetically as I shrugged my shoulders and fought back the tears. "You've been through a lot. Just relax. If you're not ready on Monday, then you're not ready."

"Keela's right, Kingston. Lord knows I need a couple of days off."

I shook my head. "You always need a couple days off."

"Working gives you wrinkles," she shot back.

"Are you really needing some time off or are you just trying to sneak off with your new man?" Keela asked Essence as she unfolded a Wet Ones and proceeded to clean the hot sauce off her hands.

"What new man?"

"You know what we're talking about," I replied.

"No, I don't." Essence puffed up and pushed her plate to the middle of the table. "We almost ready to go?"

I slurped up what remained in my glass then looked for the waitress. "I want one more drink."

"Okay. Be back, gotta potty." Essence grabbed her purse and headed for the bathroom.

"Anything for you?" I asked Keela after placing my order with the waitress.

"No, I'm good. I can feel the other two already kicking in. It's my turn to teach Sunday school at church. Gotta be ready for the babies in the morning."

"Yours didn't have any alcohol in them," I reminded her.

"Yeah, but I think they gave me a double shot of strawberry." Keela started to search through her purse for her wallet when a cell phone started vibrating on the table. "Yours?" she asked.

"Nope, I left mine in the car on the charger. I'm not trying to talk to anybody right now." The waitress set my drink in front of me, then checked the bill before sliding it on the table.

"I'll take it when you're ready," she said before hustling off to the next customer. The phone vibrated again.

"It's Essence's cell." She grinned. "Watch this." Picking up the phone, she spoke quietly, mischievously, trying to disguise her voice. "Hello?" Her smile disappeared and the light faded from her eyes. Her lower lip quivered. When she spoke again, it was with cold fury. "Why the hell would you be calling Essence? Whatever. God, I hate you," Keela whispered before hanging up and replacing the cell phone on the table, the rage bubbling in her eyes.

"What's wrong, Keela?" I covered her hand with mine, but she yanked it away.

"Nothing." She threw fifty dollars on the table, then stood up so suddenly she almost knocked the stool over.

Oblivious to the curious stares from those around us, I repeated, "Keela," but she just looked at me before turning on her heel and storming out of the restaurant.

"Keela!" I yelled after her, but she didn't even pause. I ran to try and catch her when Essence walked up and grabbed my arm. "What just happened?" she asked. "Keela flew past me as I was coming out of the bathroom and didn't say a word."

"I have no idea." I shrugged and pointed to the phone on the table. "We were getting our stuff together, your cell phone rang and playing around, she answered it. Then she flew outta here. It must be something the person said to her." I grasped at straws, "but she didn't say who it was."

Essence snatched her phone before I finished my sentence and scrolled through the menu to find the last call received. Her eyes became as wide as saucers, and her hand flew to her mouth. "I gotta go after her. Explain things." She slammed her phone in her purse and walked away, her face pale, as if she had seen a ghost.

"Wait!" I screamed. "What is going on? Who was on the phone? Tell me something." My voice echoed through the room. Once again the click and clanking of utensils and glasses ceased, and I felt all eyes on me.

Essence stopped dead in her tracks and spun to face me.

"Who was it?" I roared at her again.

"Brandon."

"Keela's Brandon?"

She didn't answer, but then again she didn't have too. She lowered her eyes and when she looked at me again, they appeared hollow as if all the joy had been chased right out of them.

My heart sank.

Chapter 20

Lake Shore Drive was a mess. Thick flakes of snow fell in sheets, blanketing the roads, causing cars to slide every which way. Traffic was at a crawl.

On an emotional roller coaster for almost a week now and with this latest bump, I was tired; tired and confused. I couldn't reach either Keela or Essence on their cell phones, so I was in the dark about what had transpired after they had run off into the night. I watched the windshield wipers swoosh across the glass, making perfect arcs out of the snow, as I asked the same question that Keela had posed to her boyfriend while on the phone earlier.

Why the hell would Brandon be calling Essence? And if it had been an innocent call, why wouldn't Essence just offer an explanation on the spot? It made her appear guilty. But guilty of what? I stopped myself before even trying to answer that question. I didn't want to get ahead of myself. I knew Keela and Essence. I mean, really knew them. We'd been best friends for almost fifteen years. I knew what each of us was capable of and what lines wouldn't be crossed under any circumstances. *Didn't I?* Sure, Essence had been known to date a married man or two.

Yes, she had slept with other women's boyfriends and not even blinked. I slung the uncertainties to the back of my mind and concentrated on the road. With no proof that she had crossed that invisible line, there was no use in getting all worked up. All I had right now were assumptions.

Hoping for some distraction, I flipped on the radio and sang along with Mint Condition, but nothing could take my mind off the earlier scene in the restaurant. I merged into traffic, exiting onto 47th street and checked my cell phone, but the display flashed zero new calls. Not wanting to be alone, I pointed my car south and drove to the kennel.

Open 24 hours, the Paw House Hotel looked just like a miniature Holiday Inn. A painting of a droopy-eyed beagle with a Toucan parrot sitting on its back was plastered just perpendicular to the front door. Other than a blue Volvo with a dented rear bumper, the parking lot was deserted.

Barks blended with meows greeted me as I stepped through the door, my arrival announced by a tinkering bell. Legs were propped on the counter, a hand thumbed through a calculus book, and a head bobbed to a silent beat. By all appearances, the front desk attendant couldn't have been any older than sixteen.

"Can I help you?" Snatching a pair of headphones from her head, she asked the question with a pop of gum and bounced to her feet. Her brunette ponytail swayed as she punched some keys on the computer, scrolling through several screens. I peered at her crooked nametag. Missy. I should have known.

"I'm here to pick up my dog, Cocoa."

"The chocolate Lab?"

"That's her." I pulled out my Visa as she punched a few more buttons, then yanked a freshly printed sheet from the machine behind her and laid it neatly on the countertop.

"Here's your bill. Why don't you look it over while I go get Cocoa and we'll get you all checked out?" The pair of Reebok Crossfits disappeared around the corner and I glanced at my cell phone again. Still nothing. Heartworm pamphlets were displayed next to the computer and I made a mental note to schedule an appointment for Cocoa's annual checkup.

Toenails clicking on the green tile floor brought a smile to my face. Cocoa bounded around the corner, dragging Missy behind her. She picked up my scent and her tail started whipping, almost causing her to turn in a circle. Dropping to one knee, I suffered through a fierce tongue lapping spurred on by ear scratching and baby talk.

"Everything okay?" Missy asked as she swiped my Visa through the credit card machine.

I nodded, stuck the receipt in my purse and turned to leave.

"By the way, your friend's boyfriend is gorgeous. He oughta be a model or something. But then she looked like one, too." She smiled and fitted her headphones back over her ears.

Certainty settled like a lead weight in my stomach. I couldn't believe Essence could stoop so low.

"Come on, baby." I tugged gently on Cocoa's leash. "Let's go home."

I twisted my bright orange scarf around my neck and braced myself against the cold. Since the parking lot hadn't been shoveled, I was forced to ease my 2009 Lexus in between two Toyotas on the street perpendicular to my house, which put me a good two blocks from my front door. It also meant trudging through four-inches of snow, Cocoa by my side, the whipping wind stinging my cheeks. A neighbor was struggling to carry two bags of groceries, and I waved, when I noticed someone waiting for me inside my gate. My heart lurched and out of reflex, I dropped Cocoa's leash. Forever the protector she trotted ahead of me, growling. But instead of attacking, she ran right up to the stranger, placing one paw on a covered knee.

My heart settled when I saw that it was Keela sitting on my doorstep—a solitary figure—shaking, tears streaming down her face. "I-I-I-I didn't know where else to go." She stood up, her arms wrapped tightly around her middle.

"It's okay. I'm glad you came here," I said, fitting the key in the lock. "Come on, let's get inside where it's warm."

The phone rang as I ushered her through the door, then stood aside so Cocoa could get in. She dashed upstairs, sniffing everywhere, familiarizing herself after four days away. The phone continued to ring, but I refused to answer it. I already knew it was Essence. Yes, my friends needed to talk, but it wasn't up to me to make it happen. Keela would have to do this on her own timetable.

My still-packed suitcases were on the couch. I pushed them aside before heading to the kitchen to put on a pot of water. Keela didn't say a word and I didn't force conversation. I wanted to get her upstairs, calm her down, then try to sort out the truth.

Sugar, cream, and packets of Chai tea were gathered and placed on a serving tray. Keela's arms and legs were drawn together in a protective ball, her nose bright red, and tears streaked down her face, leaving crisscrossing trails through her make-up. Cocoa climbed on the couch, circled once, then settled beside her.

The shrill whistle of the chrome kettle startled Keela and prompted a fresh wave of sobs. My eyes welled, too, my heart was breaking along with hers. I set the tray on the coffee table and dunked a tea bag in the steaming cup of water before adding heaping spoonfuls of sugar and cream to her cup; sugar only to mine. When I shooed Cocoa from the couch, she scurried under the coffee table, dropping her nose on one paw and falling asleep.

"This will make you feel a little better," I said, handing Keela the cup, then grabbing a plaid, woven throw from the arm of the couch and wrapping it around her. This time when the phone rang, I crossed the room to pick it up and switched the ringer to off.

"Is it her again?" Keela asked.

"Looks like this is the fifth time she's called."

"I don't know what to say, Kingston. I don't know what to do." Her voice broke and she pressed a ball of tissue to her nose as if that would contain the sadness.

"Well," I began. "We need to figure out what's going on and not jump to conclusions. Any more than we have already," I amended as she trained her sorrow-filled eyes on me. "Have you actually talked to Brandon or Essence?"

"They've been calling non-stop, but I haven't been answering." She pulled her cell phone from the pocket of her sweater and showed me the number of missed calls. Sixteen.

"That might be the first step, Keela."

"I know, but who do I talk to first and who do I believe? They're not going to tell me the same thing. Hell, I may never get the truth. I already know Brandon's a liar and a cheat, but I never thought Essence would stoop this low."

"That's my point. We don't know that she's done anything wrong yet." I lifted my hands. "We don't know what's going on, which is exactly why you need to get both versions of the story."

"I don't want to talk to either one of them ever again." Her lips pouted, her voice as small as a two-year-old's. "Love shouldn't hurt like this."

"Love doesn't hurt," I said, studying a recently-bought painting hanging right above the fireplace. Shadowy outlines of a muscle-bound man and a robustly curved woman twined together. The longer you stared, the more the couple became one. That was what love is all about.

"This is really messed up."

"It is. I'll give you that much. Listen, Keela, I know you're upset, but there may be a good explanation behind all of this. We won't know until you talk to them. I understand that it's difficult, but you are going to have to at least hear what they have to say."

The internal struggle of emotions played across Keela's tear-swollen face—her eyes sparked with bitterness, darkened with intense anger, finally just looked empty.

"You're right." She reached for a fresh napkin. "But for the record, I don't buy that there is a 'perfectly good explanation.' You know as well as I do that something very foul is going on. And no matter what they say, I don't think I'm ever going to get the truth."

I agreed. The situation stank, but I couldn't believe Essence would betray Keela or our friendship. After all this time, she deserved the benefit of the doubt.

"So?" I asked as her phone began beeping. "You gonna answer it?"

She frowned. "I'm not sure who this is? I don't recognize the number."

Her brow furrowed into the shape of an M, but she pushed the Talk button and said hello. Rolling her eyes, she held the phone away from her ear and mouthed "Brandon," then pressed the speakerphone button and the sound of a voice begging mid-sentence blasted into the room. "Baby, you just gotta listen to me." A long pause. "Are you still there? Baby?"

Keela exploded. "I'm still here, you cheating son-of-a-bitch and I'm listening; but maybe not for too much longer, so you'd better start talking fast. I need to know what you're doing calling Essence? And no more lies. I'm fed up." Tapping her finger on the phone, she looked at me through hooded eyes, her mouth pulled into a smirk. "Baby, it's like this-"

"Don't tell me what it's like, okay? I want to know what it actually is. Maybe this question will be easier for you: Are you and Essence sleeping together?"

As Brandon stammered some more, I crossed my legs Indian style, picked up a pillow and pressed it to my chest. I was ready for another cup of tea, but didn't want to miss a minute of the conversation.

"It was a mistake, Keela." His voice dropped to a whisper. "I didn't mean for it to go down the way it did. It just happened."

If I didn't know Brandon, I might have believed him, fallen for what he was saying, thought that he actually was sorry. But I did know Brandon; and I wasn't buying his story, and apparently neither was Keela.

"Just so we're clear, you're admitting that you slept with her?"

Brandon released a harsh sigh. "Yes, Keela, I slept with her."

Surprised at how forthcoming he was, I wrote "That was too easy" on a piece of paper and showed it to Keela. I had been prepared for at least five minutes of begging before the "truth" came out

She nodded at my note, then said to him, "Of all the women in Chicago, why my best friend?" Keela took a deep breath. "How long, Brandon? How long have you been sleeping with my best friend right under my nose?"

"Calm down, Keela," Brandon said as if he was talking to a toddler throwing a tantrum. He was struggling to control the anger that simmered like lava just beneath the surface, but he wasn't about to unleash and risk messing up a chance of getting through to Keela. "It hasn't been that long and doesn't mean anything. You know that you're the one I love. We have a baby on the way. I want us to be a family."

I stuck my finger in my mouth and pretended to gag. Keela's stern expression broke into a slight smile.

"No, Brandon, I have a baby on the way. You don't have anything to do with this anymore. The only person you know how to love is yourself, so the baby and I are better off without you. I don't give a damn what you try to say or do. You won't be a part of our lives. Leave me alone or I'll disappear so fast it'll make your head spin. Don't call, don't come by. It's over."

I gave her the thumb's up and nodded encouragingly. Brandon's game was good, but Keela was proving to be stronger.

"Keela, you're mad and it's understandable. But don't say things you're going to regret later. I'll make this up to you, I promise," Brandon pleaded, his voice at a dangerously seductive level.

"You've made too many promises and haven't kept any of them. Why should I believe you now? It's a whole new ballgame and I have more to worry about than just me. It's taken me a long time to realize it, but you're no good for me, Brandon."

Brandon's tone darkened and his fury seeped through the phone. "Get off your fucking high horse, Keela. You're getting exactly what you want—me forever."

"What the hell are you talking about?" Neck rolling, the strain was beginning to show—Keela was approaching the end of her rope.

"I'm saying that getting pregnant on purpose is not going to get you nominated for Angel of the Year!"

"Brandon, you're starting to sound like a badly written soap opera. Why would I get pregnant on purpose?"

Brandon snorted, "So you would have me tied to you for the rest of my life. In your twisted mind, you probably thought I would drop to one knee, place a diamond on your finger, and beg you to marry me."

"Marry you?" Keela laughed. "That's rich. I deserve better than a fifty-year life sentence to a no-good man that can't keep his pants zipped up. Times are not that damn hard. This baby deserves the best of everything and I plan on providing it."

"I'll take you to court and have you declared an unfit mother," Brandon growled—the threat an empty one, but Keela paled nonetheless.

I gave her hand a reassuring squeeze and she forged ahead with false bravado. "Mothers are always given preferential treatment. I'm a substitute teacher, active in my church. Do you think the courts are going to believe you over me? Trying to smear my character isn't going to work, so don't mess with me, Brandon."

"No, don't you mess with me. I'll make your life a living hell. And for the record—Essence was a much better in bed than you ever were. And unlike you, she loved sexing me. No wonder you could never keep a man," he hissed. "Ask her about her technique, maybe she'll teach you a few things." His comments were mean, but the laugh that followed was pure evil.

"You can't hurt me anymore," Keela said. "It's over and I'm hanging up now." Keela calmly ended the call, but she was shaking like a leaf. I put my arm around her and pulled her in tight.

She let her head drop on my shoulder and sighed. "That's the real him," she said. "Everybody saw it but me. I wanted to think the best of him. That he may treat other people like crap, but never me. I was just fooling myself." Keela looked at me, then placed her hand over my mouth. "Don't say I told you so."

"I wasn't, but you still need to talk to Essence. Are you okay?"

"I'm fabulous, Kingston." And to my surprise, she beamed up at me. "I've never felt so good in my life." I looked at her skeptically. "All right, that's a lie; I feel like I've been hit by a train, but breaking up with an asshole can be a pretty empowering experience." She took a sip of her lukewarm tea and smiled at me over the brim of the cup.

I was worried. "Keela, are you sure you're okay? You're not going to freak out on me or anything, are you? I mean you're kinda' scaring me."

Keela threw her head back and laughed, which concerned me even more. I'd read about the signs when someone was in danger of spiraling into a nervous breakdown and I wanted to head this one off at the pass.

She stood, stretched before starting to furiously pick up various pieces of scattered tissue. "I'm perfectly fine, Kingston. Honestly. Don't get me wrong, I'm itching to kick Essence's ass, Brandon's, too, but what would that solve? They say things happen for a reason. I needed this wake-up call."

I cradled my head in my hand and watched her scurry about. "I don't know about all that. Brandon could have been honest with you and told you that he wasn't ready to be committed. If he wanted to be with someone else, he should have said so. Sleeping with Essence breaks all the rules. That's not a wake-up call. That's a stab in the back. And I'm disappointed that Essence would roll in the mud with that pig. All of this is so hard to believe." I took a breath and added one more realization. "You're going to be a single mom."

"Millions of women have done it. I'll just make it a million and one. Besides, I'm gonna have the best Godmother in the world to help me out. That's if she doesn't leave and go to Jamaica."

I sighed. I'd forgotten all about that. "Too much is happening, Keela. I don't know which way is up."

"It's going to work itself out," Keela said, her hands perched on her widening hips.

"Now, I think we ought to invite Essence over. We have some things that need to be worked out." She spotted more tissue on the floor and bent to pick it up. She reminded me of Mama Grace—always cleaning.

"Maybe tomorrow would be better," I suggested, following Keela's lead, folding the blanket and fluffing the pillows back in place. "I still can't believe that she'd do something like this. Maybe Brandon's being vindictive."

"Being vindictive about what?" Keela shook her head. "He's telling the truth. We need to get everything out in the open. Tonight. It can't wait until tomorrow." She peeked around the corner into the living room and snapped her finger. "Call Essence and invite her over. There's a lot more truth that needs to be told." I could hear her opening cabinets and rumbling through one after the other.

"There's more?" I asked, but Keela didn't respond to that, instead hollering, "Hey, Kingston you got any chocolate in here—cookies, donuts, anything? I need something to go with this tea."

"In the cabinet over the refrigerator," I answered, puzzled. This was not the response I expected, but I had a feeling that despite Keela's seemingly good mood, things could still get ugly. But despite the warning bells ringing in my head, I picked up the phone and called Essence while Keela jammed two Oreo Cookies in her mouth.

Chapter 21

Essence accepted a cup of tea, but didn't take a sip and didn't sit down. Hair uncombed and clothes uncharacteristically wrinkled, she seemed pinned to one spot by Keela's piercing brown eyes.

Cocoa circled nervously from the tension in the room, so I walked her upstairs and shut her in my bedroom. She scratched once on the closed door before jumping on the bed, making the springs squeak.

"I'm glad you called." Essence was serving up the peace offering like a delicate pastry as I walked back downstairs, still standing by the staircase, trying to feel Keela out.

I was, too. While we waited for Essence, Keela would say nothing about the impending conversation. Talking about everything from baby booties to types of formula, not a word was said about Brandon or how she was feeling. No trace remained of the tears that had flowed in abundance before. Her make-up had been touched up and she glowed, with renewed fire in her eyes.

I still wasn't sure if the conversation with Essence was a good thing, but Keela was insistent that everything be "taken care of" tonight. "The air has to be cleared. And if what I think is true, then things had been going on for way too long." Never elaborating on what things she was talking about, I got the feeling it was more than the Brandon/Essence situation.

Keela paced back and forth, rubbing her tummy, and Essence shifted from foot to foot, while I sipped more tea. The snow was falling with tempestuous force now, the pitter-patter of it blowing against the windows.

"I'm glad you came," Keela finally responded. "Not everyone would have been woman enough to face up to this mess. But I wanted to give you a chance to tell me your side. I've already talked to Brandon, so I know that you slept with my man," she said evenly, but Essence still flinched. "All I wanna hear is why would you do this. You're my best friend. We've been to hell and back and I never thought we'd be having this conversation."

"What did Brandon say?" Essence asked, her voice trembling..

"Just tell me why, Essence," Keela fumed, throwing her hands up in the air and making her way to the couch. "Don't try to confuse things or take time to get your story straight. Trust me, I'm not the one today. You slept with the father of my baby. What was the problem? You weren't happy with all the other men you'd been playing? You had to have mine, too?" Her mouth twisted with contempt.

"He was no good for you," she replied with a straight face.

"What do you mean? Who died and made you God?" Keela's stone wall started to crumble and her voice rose. Suddenly her eyes opened even wider with understanding. "Oh, I get it. Brandon is the new guy you've been seeing. He's the one you've been sneaking out of town to spend time with. Right?" Keela prodded before wailing, "Why, Essence? Make me understand why," she demanded, slamming a fist into her palm, her eyes welling up with fresh tears.

"Keela, it was a mistake and I'm sorry it happened, but I can't change it now. I would understand if you hate me, but I hope you don't."

"Trust me, this would be a lot easier if I could hate you." Keela leaned back and crossed her arms beneath her "A" cup breasts. "The only thing I feel right now is pity. You have a problem and you need to talk to somebody about it. A therapist or somebody—anybody, but you need to get help. God, I want to strangle you!"

Essence burst into giant sobs that didn't move Keela. "It's too late for tears, you've done too much dirt. Remember when you spent the night at my house after Bitty's birthday party at the Estate Club? Well, when you went home you left a card on my kitchen table. A love card from what I know now is a mutual friend." At the look of open-eyed shock that flashed across Essence's face, Keela smiled the kind of smile that could get you committed. "You know what I'm talking about. I bet you went crazy trying to figure out where you left it. Unfortunately, I didn't put two and two together until tonight, but now the initials on the card make sense, so I think you need to explain some things to Kingston."

Essence walked to the coffee table where she placed her cup, then hightailed it right back to where she was standing. She sniffed and patted at her wet cheeks with the backs of her hands.

Keela's words had snapped me to attention. "To me?" I asked, pointing at my chest. "How the hell did I get into this?"

"Ever heard the saying, 'when it rains, it pours'? Well, the storm has only just begun, right, Essence?" Keela was on her feet now, pacing back and forth, throwing cutting glances at Essence. "Either you tell her or I will," she threatened.

Trying to figure out what to do, Essence stared at Keela, her eyebrows lifted, her eyes darkened and she twisted her hands together.

"Somebody better tell me something." My back stiffened, I crossed my arms in front of me, and I tapped my toe, ticking off time as my head swiveled from Keela to Essence then back to Keela.

"Brandon's not the only boyfriend that Essence has helped herself to," Keela supplied as she placed her hand on my shoulder, bracing me for more. "Apparently she and Randy have spent quite a bit of time together. The initials on the card were R.B." She turned her eyes to me. "I'm sorry that I didn't realize sooner that the card was from your Randy."

I was on my feet lightening fast; and when she didn't answer, I took a menacing step, forcing her to take a quick step back. "Essence?"

Her trembling hands flew to cover her face and she moved her head from side to side. "It's true," she said, her head hung low.

"What do you mean, it's true?" I felt as if I'd gotten in the way of a moving train. Flattened. "Do you realize what you've done?" I raged.

Instead of something resembling apologetic, Essence bristled. "Look, it's this simple—Brandon and Randy were losers. I'd told you that over and again. I was beginning to sound like a broken record. I'd told you all the different ways I could and you still weren't hearing me. I was getting sick of sitting around watching the two of you get hurt, so I took action. Seeing is believing right?" she asked, a wild look in her eyes.

My stomach lurched in disgust and I threw my hands up. "You sound crazy."

"I was looking out for the two of you—my best friends. I couldn't stand watching you in pain, hearing you cry over the phone; especially not over some no-good man."

Yes, Essence sounded crazy—and looked crazy too, her eyes not only wild, but blurred over, hands in constant motion while trying to make her point.

"You're the one causing the pain and the betrayal. It hurts twice as much coming from you, because we had faith in you. And you threw it away like it was yesterday's trash. I never thought some man would come between us." Keela's eyes welled up again.

"So you're going to let some men, who didn't really want you anyway, break up our friendship?" Essence asked, exhaling loudly. "I did it for you guys. Doesn't that count for anything?"

"You didn't do it for us. You did it for you. You're a selfish, conceited woman who has no conscience. You're the one who damaged this friendship. You don't care who you hurt." I waved my finger at her. "Something has really fucked you up along the way. I don't know if it's your parents' relationship or if you have some kind of weird addictive behavior that prevents you from controlling your sexual impulses, but whatever it is, you need help." When Essence didn't respond, I shook my head. "You don't get it, do you? You don't think you did anything wrong?"

"You're not even trying to understand what I'm saying," Essence whined.

Keela's eyes narrowed. "There's nothing to understand. You're wrong, own up to it. You've betrayed our trust. But I guess we should've known that if you'd do it to other women, you'd eventually do it to us." She paused. "I just wanted to talk to you face to face, give you the benefit of the doubt."

"And I appreciate that," Essence said. "But what about Brandon and Randy? I didn't do this alone."

"Brandon and Randy have already been dismissed," Keela said, her voice steady. "You were the last piece of business to be dealt with. We gave you a chance to say your piece, and now I'm done with it." Keela started picking up long-forgotten coffee cups and crumb-filled napkins. "Kingston's tired and needs to unpack." She carried the items into the kitchen.

"Are you telling me to leave?"

"That's exactly what I'm telling you," Keela retorted.

"I want to get this resolved," Essence responded, her hands on her hips, before turning to me, "Kingston?"

"It's not about you right now," I said. When she suggested that we meet for breakfast, I rolled my eyes. "I don't think so, Essence. We'll call you when we're ready to talk. Respect that." I stood my ground and Essence assented, but I saw something else brewing in her eyes. I wasn't sure if it was denial or anger, but to me it spelled trouble. She paused before turning sharply on one heel and walking down the stairs. Neither Keela nor I spoke until we heard the front door slam behind her.

"I am really sorry, Kingston," she said as she turned on the water in the sink and began washing the dishes.

"There's no reason for you to be sorry." I waved off her apology, falling back onto the couch with a thud, my legs about as firm as Jello now. "I had my suspicions about Essence, but I couldn't let myself go there, especially with no proof. I'm not tripping off Randy, but I hate feeling like a fool." I dragged my hand through my hair. "My whole world has changed in the space of a few days. Yours, too, huh?" I hated the hollow feeling that was eating away at my insides. "So, what do we do now?"

"We just go on, I guess. What is it they say? Time heals all wounds? It may not be today, it may not be tomorrow, but we'll be fine." Keela dried her hands on the towel hanging over the faucet before joining me in the living room. She squinted her eyes, then asked, "There's nothing that you need to tell me, is there?" softening her question with a wink.

I laughed and hit her on the leg. "Hell, no. What about you?" Her laughter joined mine and soon we were howling so hard, tears streamed down, making our faces a soggy mixture of sour betrayal and sweet friendship.

Chapter 22

Clad in one of my old t-shirts, Keela spent the night, passing out in the guest room before the lights were off. For me, sleep did not come as easily. I let Cocoa out to use the bathroom, unpacked my suitcases, watched some TV, worked on my proposal for Scooby's album, but still couldn't wear myself out. After another hot shower, I crawled into bed. Stretched out, I lay on my back, then my side, then my stomach, turning my sheets into a tangled mess. When I did ease into sleep, it was restless, disturbed. Then, the phone rang, at three o'clock in the morning!

I said, "hello," hesitantly, pulling the sheets over my head until they made a tent, feeling like I was fifteen again, sneaking in a phone call.

"Were you sleeping?" Golden brown honey, disguised in the form of a voice, glided over me.

I pushed my hair out of my face. "Damon?"

"Yes, baby. I didn't wake you, did I?"

"Uh, no, not really," I stuttered, rubbing the sleep from my eyes. "I was having some trouble falling asleep."

"Still having nightmares?"

"Not since the other night. I think I've put Joanne to rest."

"I'm glad. That's just one less burden for you. You try to be so strong, Kingston."

"Why are you calling, Damon?"

"Straight to the point, huh?" He chuckled. "I couldn't sleep either and I needed to hear your voice. I miss you, Kingston."

"Really?" I asked, not wanting to be pleased, but I was.

"I guess it would be too much to expect you to tell me that you feel the same way."

My lips curved lightly. "Yes, that would be too much."

"In time." He was confident—overly so—but that confidence turned me on. "When are you coming back to Jamaica?"

"I just left," I replied. Damon's eagerness was also a big turn on. Not in a demeaning way. But his it signaled that the tables had turned and now I had the upper hand.

"It seems like you've been gone forever. But forget about me, you have Mama Grace's business to attend to. Trust me, everybody's anxious to see what you're going to do."

"I know." Groaning, I burrowed even further under the covers. "Dammit, my life is here. My career is starting to take off. How could Mama Grace expect me to pick up and leave? I have a house, friends ..." I hesitated, my thoughts flickering to Essence. Disbelief and shock, the heavyweight contenders in the boxing ring that had become my life. I wanted to tell Damon everything, but was scared I'd be opening myself up to even more heartache.

"Maybe she knew where your heart really lies. Your spirit is Jamaican through and through. You should be here basking in the golden sunshine, swimming in the blue waters, shopping in the market place, continuing the legacy Mama Grace worked so hard to establish, and ..." Damon's statement hung in the air unfinished.

"Be there with you?" I asked.

"That, too," he said, then added teasingly. "But that would be considered a perk."

"You're so damn arrogant." I flipped over.

"Not arrogant, just sure. Sure about you. Us."

I tried to force down the desire that was rising in me. But it just sat there swelling, expanding and threatening to consume. Just when I thought no words would escape, I asked, "And what makes you so sure?" Even to me, my voice sounded seductive, and I wanted it that way, wanted him to be turned on as much as I was.

"Hmmmm, you sound delicious, sleepy and sexy at the same time. I want you here so I can make love to you until the sun rises, then sets again." His words continued fanning the fire that had been ignited.

"What about your patients?"

"They can wait. I need a healing that only comes in the form of you."

My heart jumped in my throat. I sat up and wrapped my arms around my naked legs. "This is a bad idea."

Damon sighed. "Whether you want to accept it or not, I still love you. No matter how hard I try, I can't get you out of my mind. When I saw you again, all the feelings I had for you ten years ago came flooding back ten times stronger. The way you smell, the way you taste, the way you looked while I was making love to you in the hot tub."

I closed my eyes and shared the same vision: Damon and I, water glistening in the moonlight, our bodies joined as one. My breath started coming in short pants, forbidden juices dampened my inner thighs.

"I can see the perfection of your nipples, feel the fullness of your breasts in my hands, remember how your legs wrapped themselves around me while I was buried deep inside of you. Jesus, Kingston, I'm getting hard just thinking about it, thinking about you."

I licked my lips and imagined it was Damon's tongue tracing their outline. I closed my eyes, gripping the phone as if it were my lifeline and squeezed my legs together, trying to contain an explosion that just might be inevitable.

"What are you doing?" Damon's voice sounded muffled as if he were fumbling with the phone.

"Listening," I answered weakly.

"Can you imagine me there next to you? Kissing you? Touching you?" he asked. And when I answered, "Mmmm hmmm," I knew I had crossed the threshold of no return. My pulse quickened with every word that floated from his mouth.

"Will you touch yourself for me? Run your hand over your breasts and your nipples, slowly. Do that for me."

I groaned as I followed his instructions, an overwhelming need to please and comfort him took over, just as he was pleasing me.

"Good," Damon murmured. "Can you feel my lips on your breast, my tongue teasing your nipple?"

I nodded, not trusting myself to speak; still not quite willing to let myself totally go.

"Kingston?"

"I'm here," I said softly.

"Now your belly. I remember how sweet your belly was—sweet and ripe like a mango—how I loved kissing it, tracing the fine line of hair with my finger; it starts at your belly button, then leads me to paradise." He inhaled. "Move your hand lower. Imagine my warm tongue licking you wherever your hand goes. Does that feel good? All I want to do is make you feel good."

My hand hit the target and I groaned, moving my hand lower still. My knees clenched together, trembling, trying to stand strong in a battle that couldn't possibly be won.

"It's okay, Kingston," Damon offered, sensing my hesitation. "I'm here with you and never plan on letting you go again. Now move your hand lower. That's a good girl. You're so hot and wet, so ready for me. It's only for me, right, Kingston? It's all mine, right? Let me hear you say it."

"It's all yours, Damon," I repeated, trying hard not to explode, although holding it inside was killing me.

When he asked, "Remember what it was like for me to be inside of you?" my resolve broke and I couldn't hold back any longer. The pressure was building faster than the speed of light; the ache between my legs so overwhelming that I had to let go. "Oh God, Damon," I cried as the dam broke, turning my head into the pillow to suppress my sobs.

"Give yourself to me, Kingston, like you did in the hot tub." This time it was Damon who groaned and I knew he was in the same predicament as me. "Oh, God!" he echoed with such animal ferocity that it triggered something more in me and I let go again—jumping on the roller coaster ride with him, diving over the edge, hand in hand. All of the pent up anger, frustration, sadness, and desire rolled themselves into a huge, red ball spinning wildly before it got so hot that it simply disintegrated. And I lay spent, still clutching the phone in my sweaty palm, inhaling my own musky odor and listening to Damon's heavy breathing.

Eventually, my breathing slowed and my body floated gently back to earth. I blocked the regrets that pushed at my brain and dried my face with the blanket. "Damon?"

"Yes, love?"

"No matter how much I try to stop wanting you, I only end up wanting you more," I admitted, pushing damp hair from my face.

"What are you so scared of?" Damon's voice was quiet, reassuring, and I melted again. "Being hurt like I was before."

"It won't happen again, Kingston. It's different now."

"Yes. It is different now. So different you wouldn't even believe." I closed my eyes, steeled myself, then placed the phone back in its cradle and curled into a ball, pulling the covers over my head. Thoughts still raced through my mind, but my body was drained; and as proven just minutes earlier, the body sometimes wins the battle over the mind. And soon, blackness edged out the light.

The nutty aroma of fresh coffee brewing woke me long before I was ready. The sweet, buttery smell of waffles mingled with the smokehouse scent of frying bacon had me reaching for my robe. I grimaced as my bare feet hit the cold, hardwood floor. I trudged into the bathroom to splash some water on my face, then brushed my teeth while thoughts of what had occurred in the past forty-eight hours slowly came back to me.

The weight and pressure that had been heaped on my shoulders from all directions settled firmly back on like a familiar coat. Damn, I should have stayed in bed.

Keela smiled as I walked into the kitchen, her expanding waistline was cinched by an apron. Her enthusiastic, "morning," was even brighter.

"Yeah, yeah," I replied, reaching for the coffeepot. The fresh brew was still perking, but I pulled it from the warmer anyway and poured a steaming cup as drips of coffee hit the hot burner with a satisfying sizzle. I doctored it up and after a passionate slurp, I was fit for company. "Good Morning."

"That's more like it." Keela grabbed a plate and started piling on scrambled eggs, waffles, and strips of bacon. "Hungry?" she asked after the fact, setting the full plate on the high round glass table occupying one corner of the kitchen. Silverware wrapped in a paper napkin and a small glass of fresh orange juice soon joined it. This was better than service in a restaurant.

"Aren't you eating?" Spearing a nice chunk of the fluffy egg mixture, I jammed it in my mouth, followed quickly by a piece of bacon. "Hmmmmm, just the way I like them." I doused the waffles with syrup and was halfway through them before Keela sat down with her own plate. "I didn't realize how hungry I was," I mumbled around another mouthful of bacon. I broke off a burnt end and dropped it into Cocoa's open mouth.

"I figured that. You haven't had much time to eat or do anything else."

"True." I smeared the last piece of waffle across the plate and soaked up the remaining syrup. "It's been hectic for both of us." I paused, looking at the icicles hanging from the outside balcony, melting under the persistence of the mid-morning sun. "You hangin' in there?"

She pursed her lips before taking a sip of orange juice. "A good night's sleep and a hot breakfast can make the worst situation seem a whole lot better. My dad used to say that all the time. I lost the father of my baby and my best friend at the same time. I think that qualifies as the worst situation."

"It's not like they died," I pointed out.

"No, it's worse, 'cause I can't bury their asses without going to jail!" She giggled before rising and clearing the table.

"No, let me," I said, finishing off the last of my coffee. "You cooked so I'll clean up." I loaded the dishwasher and powered it up. Leaning one hip against the countertop, I contemplated another cup of coffee.

"What are you going to do today?" Keela asked.

"Go back to bed, get another couple of hours. Then I need to go to the grocery store."

"Me too. I'm having cravings for foods that I've never even eaten before. How do you explain that? I actually was dipping my pepperoni pizza in maple syrup the other day. Some of my cousins down south used to do it when we were little." Keela laughed at the grimace on my face. "Don't sleep on the pizza and syrup combo, it was pretty good. I'll spare you the rest of my cravings. I'm going to take a quick a shower, then I'll be out of your hair."

"You're welcome to stay as long as you want."

"No offense, but the bed in your guest room is not all that comfortable. I want to curl up in my own bed. Plus, I have to prepare lesson plans and all that good stuff. Did you decide if you're gonna go into work tomorrow?"

I sighed and wiped off the table. "I'll be bored if I stay at home all day. I have a huge opportunity with Scooby, and I'm not going to blow it."

We headed up the stairs together; and as I lay in bed, I heard Keela taking a shower and tidying up the room. When I woke up, she was gone.

Three hours later, my cart was already half full when I rounded the corner and headed toward the fresh produce aisle. The Co-op was busy for a Sunday afternoon; I suspected people were getting ready for Christmas dinner. Shelves were being stocked, then restocked. Sales papers littered the floor and over-sized signs trimmed with cheap garland advertising the store's famous "ten for ten" sale hung in every aisle.

Juan, the twenty-something Hispanic produce manager, arranged first the watermelons, then the cantaloupes before looking up, smiling when he spotted me. His dark hair was moussed off his face and his goatee needed a trim.

"Ready for the holidays?" he asked when I got closer, wiping his hands on his dirt streaked khakis.

"Nope," I said. "They always seem to sneak up on me. You?"

"Same." He worked at scraping some of the dirt from under his fingernails, then pointed at the oranges. "We got in a shipment of Valencia oranges—sweet for this time of year. And we got those bags of ready-made salad on sale. Buy one, get one free."

I smiled, tossing a few oranges in a plastic bag. When he smiled back, it was a different kind of smile, his eyes warmed with interest.

"Are you trying to tell me I need to be on a diet, Juan?" I teased, laughing when a deep blush stained Juan's neck and cheeks.

"Oh no, I didn't mean to imply that at all. You know you're a beautiful woman." He nodded with appreciation. "Everything's right where it's supposed to be." At my raised eyebrows, he began sputtering, "Well-well-well," then waved his hand. "You know what I mean."

"I know, Juan, I was just teasing you. Thanks for your help." He waved again, turning his attention back to the melons.

I wheeled my cart past the meat department, picking up two packs of frozen chicken breasts when I spotted an acquaintance with her two children in tow. All three were going in different directions, a mess of arms and legs. I ducked in the cereal aisle so she wouldn't stop me for conversation.

Apple Jacks or *Frosted Flakes*? It had become quite the deliberation when a hand settled on my shoulder and squeezed gently. I turned and found my self face-to-face with Randy. I couldn't catch a break.

He grinned, looking like two shots of tequila poured into a faded pair of Levis—all warm and golden brown—begging you to take a sip, but coming back to haunt you if you drank too much. Right now, I felt as though I had swallowed the whole bottle.

"Randy," I said, exasperation sharpening my tone as he placed a cool kiss on my cheek.   He said, "I didn't know you were back in town." His gaze traveled up and down my frame —inhaling the fitted baby-girl shirt and hip-hugging sweats beneath my leather bomber— before looking me square in the eye and whistling softly. "I'd almost forgotten how fine you are."

"Give me a break, Randy, I've been gone less than a week. Your memory is not that bad." I stepped to the side of the aisle, scooting my cart over to allow an old lady enough room to get her cart and cane around me.

She smiled. "Thanks, baby," she said, whistling slightly through the toothless gap in the front of her mouth. She reached for a box of *Grape-Nuts* cereal, the stretch causing her skirt to rise above her rolled-down knee-highs. I crossed to the other side and pulled the box down for her. It was more than my being helpful, I was trying to put some space between Randy and me. She mumbled her thanks again, and continued pushing her cart up the aisle. A heartbeat passed before he grabbed my hand and pulled me so I was standing next to him.

Not wanting to make a scene, I discreetly yanked my hand away. But that didn't stop me from being rude. "What?" When he didn't answer fast enough—just leaned against his cart, head cocked sideways, grinning—I continued, "Look, I don't have time for this, Randy. I've got things to do and as I've heard, you've been quite busy yourself, so let's not continue to waste each other's time."

I left Randy standing there with his mouth hanging open. Moving through the self-check-out lane at the speed of light, my hands trembled with rage. I fumed as I stuffed my groceries in the bags. I fumed as I shoved my cart out to my car, and I fumed some more when I spied Randy leaning against it, his arms casually crossed in front of him.

"Damn, Randy, what do you want?" I snapped through clenched teeth, my face creased in a frown as I unlocked my trunk and started tossing the bags every which way.

"It seems like you're really not all that happy to see me. What's up with that?"

"Nothing's up. You spoke. I spoke. What else is there to do?"

"There's tension. I don't want it to be like this every time we see each other. I'm sorry things didn't work out, but can't we move on and be friends?"

"Why would I want to maintain contact with you—friends or whatever?"

"Why wouldn't you?" he countered.

I slammed the trunk shut and pushed the cart into the holding area. "Because you're a jerk," I said matter-of-factly. He blinked in surprise and his mouth snapped shut. "Look, Randy, let's just cut to the chase. It's bad enough that you were messing around with your ex-girlfriend; but no, you had to go and sleep with my best friend, too." This time he couldn't keep his mouth from falling open. "Yeah, I found out about that. Did you really think you and Essence could keep this little secret tucked between you forever?"

Randy followed me to the door. "Essence told you?"

"I wouldn't say she told me—more like she was forced to admit it. I may never have found out if some other events hadn't come to light. Besides, you're not the only boyfriend that Essence has helped herself to. But it's all good. Our relationship was over before I found out this little tidbit, so I'm not trippin'. I just don't want you to be under any misconceptions that we're going to end up all buddy-buddy."

Randy shrugged. "I was just doing what comes naturally to a man. You can't expect me to pass up on something that was practically thrown at me."

"Actually, call me crazy, but as my boyfriend—I did expect you to pass up on it. But I guess we have different ideas of what a relationship should be. The fact that you think a man is just following his natural urges when he cheats is plain crazy. Ludicrous. Pathetic. Insane." I rolled my hand as if I could continue forever.

"I get your point," Randy inserted. "But I don't think you get mine."

"I don't want to get your point. What's done, is done. I've learned my lesson. I'm just glad you didn't waste too much of my time." I slid into the front seat of my car and backed up, praying that I'd snare Randy with my left bumper, but he was already heading to his car—and already waving at some other woman. I took a deep breath and exhaled the negative emotions, released them into the atmosphere.

Randy was not worth the stress

Chapter 23

The house was quiet and the evening sun bathed the small office I had fashioned out of a corner in the guest bedroom in a golden glow. I'd spent the past two hours whipping up dinner. A mixture of finely chopped onions, green peppers and scallions simmered with diced tomatoes, ground beef and Italian sausage, now sat, just begging to be tossed with rotini pasta. Add a salad, and dinner was done.

That was for later, now it was time to get down to business. I was not going to allow tragedy, cheating boyfriends, or triflin' best friends to throw me off schedule. I was not going to block my blessings.

Sorting through the mail was at the top of the agenda, picking out the Christmas cards, setting them to the side, tossing the junk flyers, and organizing bills. E-mail was next. Jonetta had sent a list of things that needed to be done, all of which could be taken care of tomorrow. My reply included instructions to set up a phone conference with Mr. Mansini for ten o'clock in the morning and to start formatting the outline for Scooby's proposal so I could input information as I got it. I ran my naked toes back and forth over the fuzzy, round rug and winced when I snagged a rough piece of skin; definitely time for a pedicure.

The phone rang. Swiveling the chair, I stretched across the desk and looked at the display. The area code was 876. Jamaica. Mama Grace's attorney, Mr. Bartlett, wasted no time with formalities.

"I hate to disturb you on a Sunday, but you left the island without us talking about the plan of action for your grandmother's estate. I can't proceed without instruction from you." He cleared his throat.

I leaned back in my chair. "Something urgent came up at work. Sorry, I wasn't able to contact you before I left."

"Returning to Jamaica anytime soon?"

"To be quite honest with you, Mr. Bartlett, Mama Grace's decision to put me in charge of her estate was totally unexpected."

Again, he cleared his throat. "I asked Grace to relay her wishes to you beforehand so that you would be better prepared. She was categorically against it. I know it's a difficult position to be in, but a decision needs to be made so we can move forward. If no one contests the will, I'd like things to be in place by the end of January."

I sat forward, my heart quickening. "You think somebody's planning on contesting the will?"

"Even if they do, they won't win." Pages flipped. "How about we touch base tomorrow evening, around six? You can give me your decision then."

A day to make a major life decision? I made a notation on my desk calendar. "Do you think it would be possible to oversee the estate from here?"

He hesitated; I could see his eyes squinting behind those wire-rimmed spectacles. "I think it would be possible, but I think it would undermine the spirit of what your grandmother had envisioned. And I think it would be stressful for you. Overseeing an estate this size brings a lot of responsibility and social commitment. It will be important for the people to feel that you're part of the community." Once again, he cleared his throat. "But of course, that's your decision."

"Of course," I echoed, then clicked off. I stared out the window. Everything was so upside down, confusing. I had a blossoming career here, but a golden opportunity there. Neither one outweighed the other. I just wanted to do the right thing.

Opening my address book, I searched with an index finger for a number. Punching the ten digits, the phone rang once, twice, three times before Bianca answered.

"Well, it's about damn time you called," she said.

I smiled. "Are you busy?"

"I'm trying to finish up my Christmas shopping, but I end up buying more stuff for me. I'm on my way home from the store now." Horns honked and Bianca swore under her breath. "Sorry."

"I just got off the phone with Mama Grace's attorney. He wanted to know when I was going to come back to Jamaica?"

"What'd you tell him?"

"Same thing I've told everyone else. I think my biggest problem is I don't know how to let go of everything that I've established here to move to Jamaica and start all over."

"But you wouldn't really be starting over. You'd have a job, a house, your family's here, and it sounds like running the estate will be flexible enough for you to travel to Chicago whenever you want. Is whatever you have there worth letting go of what Mama Grace had been planning for many years, something she could only trust to you?" Bianca inhaled. "Plus there's Damon to consider."

I clenched my teeth. "He has nothing to do with this."

Bianca laughed. "I saw your eyes light up whenever he walked into the room. I saw the way he held your hand at Mama Grace's funeral. You can't fool me. You guys have the kind of love that only comes once in a lifetime."

"Not anymore," I said. "If I do come back to Jamaica, it will be for Mama Grace, not for Damon."

"Tell yourself whatever you like. I, for one, am hoping that you decide Jamaica is where you want to be."

"For purely selfish reasons, huh?"

"Yep," she replied. "Merry Christmas."

"Merry Christmas to you, too." I hung up and leaned back in the chair, lacing my fingers behind my head. I felt the tug of a migraine and moved my fingers to my temples, massaging gently. It eased the tension a bit, but not enough. Cocoa trotted into the room and nudged me with her nose. When that didn't move me, a more vigorous scratch with her paw followed.

"All right, let's go out for a bit." I grabbed the leash, my down-hooded coat and Timberland boots. We made a trek around the courtyard, long enough for Cocoa to work out some friskiness and to start my nose running. My immediate neighbor struggled to haul a suitcase through the front door while balancing her daughter on one hip.

"Hi, Kingston," she called when she saw me, setting her daughter down, then poking her head back outside. "I was sorry to hear about your grandmother. The Townhouse Association sent out a notice."

I unleashed Cocoa so she could prance freely in the small, gated yard. "I just got back yesterday so I'm still trying to settle in."

"Teeka was at her daddy's house all weekend so I'm pretty much doing the same thing—he don't do a damn thing when he's got her. She hasn't had a bath all weekend and he didn't feed my baby dinner," she looked at her watch, "and it's almost seven o'clock. Damn. So now I gotta try to throw something together." Teeka wrapped her chubby arms around Sharneesha's legs and began whimpering.

"Mama's coming. I know you're hungry," she said, smoothing the little girl's unkempt hair, then looked up at me. "I need to go find her something to eat."

"Does Teeka like spaghetti?" I asked. "I just made a big pot and I can't eat it all." I leaned over the fence, speaking directly to Teeka. "Would you like to come over and eat spaghetti with me and Cocoa?"

Teeka looked up at her mother before nodding. "Can I feed Cocoa?" she asked before ducking her head behind her mother.

"You most certainly can, sweetheart." I turned to Sharneesha. "Is it okay?"

She nodded gratefully. "We'd love to join you for dinner."

"Great. Put your stuff down and come on over when you're ready. All I have to do is warm up the spaghetti and toss the salad. I'll leave the door open."

"I'll be just a sec," she said before picking up Teeka and disappearing into her house.

I had just finished setting the table when Teeka's head popped up around the corner. Sharneesha was right behind her, panting from the climb up the stairs. "You don't know how much I appreciate this." Sharneesha could stand to lose about fifty pounds, but still had a pretty face, all the extra weight packaged well. Her hair was stylishly cut, spiky and short—so short a thought could comb through it, and her clothes were in line with the latest fashion; not the top of the line brands, but good knock-offs. A pair of cheap leather pumps stretched from wide feet. Teeka's hair had been combed into dozens of neat braids that fell around her face. Her almond shaped eyes set deep in her face and a dimple appeared when she smiled.

"It's no problem at all. I'm happy for the company. It gets lonely sometimes with just me and Cocoa."

"Wow!" Sharneesha looked around. "You opted for the open floor plan. It works really well with your furniture."

"I loved the airiness of it. It gave the illusion of space without me having to buy a bigger townhouse."

"I feel ya' on that. When I found out how much these places were worth, I almost fell out." At the confused look on my face, Sharneesha explained. "Oh, I don't own my place. I rent. I'm on Section 8 with the Chicago Housing Authority." That meant she was paying little to nothing for a home worth more than two hundred-fifty thousand dollars. Tax-paying citizens were picking up the majority of the bill. Sharneesha said, "It's a well guarded secret. How many people would buy a house in such an exclusive community if they knew they could be living next door to Section 8 tenants? They wouldn't," she answered, her eyes rolling with disgust. "Like poor people aren't deserving of a nice place to live."

A blush of shame spread up my neck. I felt like a snob. "I guess people look at their house as an investment. They'd probably think that this would drag their property values down."

"And how messed up is that," Sharneesha commented under her breath, careful that her daughter didn't hear her.

I agreed, adding, "That's life."

"Yeah, and life can be pretty messed up at times."

Nodding—I was learning that lesson well—I transferred plates of steaming spaghetti to the table. We all sat down, Teeka perched on a stack of magazines so she could reach the table. Her mother leaned over and cut her spaghetti. "Say your grace."

The little girl folded her hands together and bowed her head. "God is great. God is good. Let us thank Him for our food. 'Men."

"Very good, Teeka," I said, while Sharneesha tied a napkin around the little girl's neck.

"She's a bright little girl when she wants to be. Sometimes she can just be so hardheaded though."

"I can see that. About the bright part, I mean." I handed the wooden bowl of salad to Sharneesha. "One day I hope I have a little girl just like you," I said and meant it. I briefly thought about having Damon's child growing inside my body; a perfect little baby girl with Damon's smile and my eyes. Cool shivers of pleasure danced up my spine.

After dinner, Teeka sat in front of the television watching Nickelodeon while Sharneesha and I tackled the dishes.

"So what happened with you and Teeka's father?" I dried another glass and put it in the cabinet.

"I couldn't deal with the other women—so many women I lost count, the lying, the drama. It was too much."

"How'd you find out?"

Sharneesha snorted and vigorously scoured a pan. "Please, he didn't bother trying to hide it. I found numbers in pockets, noticed he was taking showers as soon as he got home, he started doing his own laundry—all the typical shit. I shouldn't have stayed as long as I did, but I loved him."

"There ain't that much love in the world." Wiping the table off, I threw the paper towel in the trash.

Sharneesha finished the last dish, handing it to me. She sat back down at the table and sipped her water. When she looked up, she was frowning. "No disrespect, but I hate when people say that. You can't judge another person's situation until you've been in it." She flicked a long red fingernail. "What you may be able to tolerate, I may not and vice versa. I had a child to think about. I did what I thought was right at the time."

Once again, I felt like a judgmental idiot. I put the leftovers away, then leaned against the refrigerator door. "What changed?"

"When I got pregnant the second time, the doctor told me I had herpes. Wasn't hard to figure out how I got it." Sharneesha massaged the back of her neck, rolled it to release the tension. "The trust had been gone long before I found out I had a STD. But after I lost the baby, I knew I could do better by myself."

I sat down. "A friend of mine is going through that now, being pregnant and the father not in the picture."

"Tell her to settle in, she's got a long road to hoe."

Sharneesha jerked her head at Teeka who was bouncing on the couch while Cocoa danced around her legs. "I mean, it's hard being a mother, period. I have married friends who still feel like single mothers. No matter what your situation, as a mother, the burden falls on you." A thud caused Sharneesha to rush from the kitchen. She shook the book at her daughter, then bent down and whispered something in her face.

Feeling slightly embarrassed, I said, "Don't worry about it. No harm done. Cocoa probably knocked it off. Sometimes she gets overly excited."

"Just sit still and watch TV, Teeka," Sharneesha said in a too loud voice before returning to the kitchen, still mumbling underneath her breath. It took a moment before she focused on me again. "Like I was saying, I know there are some great fathers out there and even some men that have sole custody of their children, but the majority don't do shit."

Still taken aback, I bobbed my head. "She's strong and I'll help."

"She's lucky to have you. Most of my friends gave up on me while I was with Teeka's father."

"Then they weren't really your friends."

She finished her water and wiped her mouth with the back of her hand. "Trust me, I've learned a lot of lessons the hard way." Her shoulders slumped and it took a minute before I realized she was crying.

"What's wrong, Sharneesha?" I rubbed her back and waited for her sobs to subside. I passed her a napkin, worried that her daughter had overheard her outburst. Luckily the television was up loud enough and a giggling Teeka was none the wiser.

"I'm sorry. Lately, it seems like if it's not one thing it's another. For most of my life, it's always something." She sniffed, then dabbed at her eyes, but the wet tissue was powerless to stop the flow of crocodile tears. "But lately, it has gotten to be really bad."

"What's going on?" She looked at me with sorrow-filled eyes I grabbed her hand. "Talk to me. Maybe I can help."

"I was fired from my job almost three months ago. I've wiped out all of my savings—what little there was, ain't got no money coming in. I'm barely able to buy groceries. My boyfriend was helping out, but I guess it got to be too much for him and he split. Said me and my baby had become a liability.'"

I frowned and handed her another tissue. "Screw him. What about unemployment?"

Sharneesha sniffed and wiped her nose. "I was fired for stealing less than one hundred dollars from the petty cash drawer. Can you believe that? The company is fighting my unemployment benefits over one hundred dollars and now I can't feed my baby." She broke down in fresh tears as she gazed at Teeka who was now asleep on the couch. Her tiny legs curled into her chest and her hands folded under her plump cheek. The picture of innocence.

I lowered my voice to a whisper anyway. "Stealing, Sharneesha?"

"I didn't do it, Kingston. I mean, I'm struggling, but I'm not going to steal, especially not that little bit of money. Trust me, I'm not as ghetto fabulous as I look." Smiling, she crumpled both napkins and dropped them on the table. "I just happened to be the most convenient black person to pin it on. They had no proof, which is why they didn't pursue criminal charges. Of course, it would have been politically incorrect to accuse the manager that did it. Money came up missing and the rumor was that it was me. They fired me; problem solved." Pointing at her ample chest, she continued, "So you're looking at the fall-guy. And the white girl, well, she got a promotion."

I shook my head in disgust.

"Isn't that the way it always goes?" She ticked off on her fingers. "So here I am, out of savings, no unemployment; and with this economy, all of my attempts to get a job have produced zilch. I haven't been able to pay this month's rent or my car note. I gotta keep moving my car all over Chicago so the repo man doesn't get it, and the sheriff'll be by any day to put my stuff on the curb."

"Did you explain the situation to the people you're renting from?"

Sharneesha snorted. "Girl, them people don't care about why I can't pay my rent. They want their money. It's a business to them. They own about ten other units. They can find someone to put in there tomorrow, so why keep me around?" She paused and looked at Teeka. "I do have a friend that's a social worker and she was able to speed up the paperwork at the welfare office, so I've been collecting that for over a month, but it's not enough to keep up with all the bills I have."

Sighing, she said, "You can't imagine how humiliating I felt going to some office and sitting on those small plastic chairs and answering personal questions that don't have nothing to do with nothing. Asking about Teeka's father and whether he's paying child support. If there's another man in my life giving me money. Like they need to know all my business. There are some days when I don't think I can do it anymore. When getting out of bed takes all the strength I have."

Sharneesha dropped her head in her hands, rubbing the tears from her eyes, only to have them fill with more. "I've even thought about ending it all, but then I think about Teeka and I could never leave her with the legacy of a mother that committed suicide. Then there are those other days when I know as sure as I'm breathing that God has something in store for me. I'm a survivor and I'm going to take care of my baby. You best believe that."

"I believe you," I said. And I did. As I rubbed her hand and looked into her eyes, there was a spark. She was hungry and when you're hungry—you're dangerous. I decided to step out on a limb. "If I could wave a magic wand and give you anything, what would it be?"

"That's a tough one." Sharneesha rubbed her chin and hunched her broad shoulders. "I think I'd like to move somewhere else, somewhere warm. I can't take much more of these Midwest winters. Maybe live in a culturally diverse neighborhood where Teeka can learn about different kinds of people. I want to buy a nice little house for my baby and me. And I want a job where I'm helping someone. And I'm not talking about helping rich people get richer as I was at the Chicago Board of Trade. I have a Bachelor's degree in Business Administration and a Master's degree in Public Policy. I want to use my education to make a difference in somebody's life." Her smile faded. "But right now, I'd settle for a gig that pays my bills. People think you can't rise above your circumstances, but I know it can be done," she said, more for her benefit than mine.

"Well, don't give up on your dreams. You never know. They just might come true." I said, the wheels in my mind spinning.

"You say that like you know something."

I walked to the utility closet and dug in my petty cash jar. "I just may, Sharneesha." I winked, a smile spreading across my face as I scribbled my home and cell phone numbers on a piece of paper and shoved it along with one hundred dollars across the table into her waiting hand.

Chapter 24

I navigated my way down the sandy bank, sinking deeper into the giving soil. The wind whistled through the willowy trees.

Inching closer to the river's edge, I stared at the black water stretched out in front of me, gently lapping against the bank. I rubbed my arms, trying to warm them as the coldness descended.

The moonlight bounced off the water making the thick blanket of fog that hung above seem almost translucent, the boughs from the gnarly trees lining the bank holding the dense sheet of fog in place. I moved closer. A promise of a new day rode the white-capped waves that rushed against the bank more forcefully each time.

The memory of the two of us standing in front of Mammy's mirror, her twirling with arms wide and me making funny faces to make her smile. I told her how pretty she looked and not to worry 'bout her little potbelly. "Gwan' now," I urged her. "A likkle fat make ya' look healty." She laughed over her shoulder as she ran out the door. I followed more slowly. Thinking about something – obviously not of importance now – but thinking nonetheless as I often did. That was earlier. Before we made it to the river where the picnic is being held. Before we stuffed ourselves on bammy, crispy fried fish, and fat plums. Before Mammy yelled that we had time for one more swim in the river while the adults cleaned up and readied to head back up the hill to the big house. Now everyone was looking at me. I scrunched my toes in the damp sand. Already I had seen enough and I wanted to cry. Before the tear could make it's way down my face, it was wiped away and a finger lifted my chin until I was looking into smiling brown eyes. No words had to be said. Peace radiated in waves of light and they warmed my spirit. I reached out to hug her, but she glided away. She looked happy as she smiled one final time over her shoulder before she simply floated away. She waved before disappearing into the mist. And I waved goodbye as well.

When I woke up, I knew in my spirit that she was gone. That even though the nightmares were unpleasant, they were my way of holding on to Joanne, my way of keeping her with me. But I no longer had the heaviness of guilt weighing me down. Joanne was free. And so was I.

Free to make one of the hardest decisions of my life.

For as many reasons as I had tried to come up with to stay in Chicago, there were twice as many to return to Jamaica and fulfill Mama Grace's wishes. So much good could come from it. Not just for the community, but for me and for those that I loved.

I rolled over and buried my head in my pillow. There was a lot to do and I wanted to get at least two more hours before it was time to get up and rearrange my life.

Chapter 25

I snapped open my compact and looked at my image with a critical eye. My lipstick was too dark. I pursed, blotted and glossed before setting my cosmetics bag back in the top drawer of my desk. A quick stop at Lee's Nails before coming into work left me less than satisfied. The usual Mardi Gras red looked gaudy, wrong, as if my hand now belonged to someone else. No matter how I tried to fight it, the slick "big city, go-getter" skin, that once clung as snugly as a worn pair of jeans, had dried up and slipped away once I stepped foot on Jamaican soil.

Now that I was home, it no longer seemed to fit.

The early morning chill still clung to me and I rubbed my arms through my cream turtleneck sweater. A fierce wind pressed against the window, whistling.

"Line 2's still holding for you, Kingston," Jonetta buzzed through on the intercom. "I need a hit. I'm gonna run out to Starbucks. I'll bring you back the usual." With a jangle of keys, she was off.

Surveying my cluttered desk, I sighed, thinking, 'good, I need a hit, too. Not one of my hands had touched the stack of paperwork, and mail that had accumulated while I was gone, and I'd been in the office close to an hour. Tension was pooling in the small of my back, expanding and growing, threatening to overtake.

It was going to be a long, tedious day and I was already wanting to go home.

With a press of the speaker button, Keela's lilting voice floated into the room. "A friend of mine just called and told me she had to go to Cosmetology Summer School. Guess what I asked her."

"Whadya' ask her?" I rubbed my temples and flexed my foot under the table. My legs were cramped from my early morning five-mile run. For a treacherous sixty minutes, it was woman versus machine, a pounding frenzy of wills. Judging from the amount of pain I was in, the treadmill had won.

Swearing softly, I tried to shake the gloom and doom off. I was beginning to complain as much as Uncle Winston.

"Was it a makeup course?" Keela tittered and I imagined a hand covering her mouth, trying to smother the giggles.

"Keela, it's eight o'clock in the morning and I'm staring at a pile of paperwork with a deadline that's about to smack me in the face—I don't have time for this," I paused. "Is that a true story?"

"Heard it on the radio."

"I sure hope it was funnier then," I said, my voice flat and uninspired and hopefully not indicative of how the day would play out.

I pulled the Billboard Magazine from the middle of the pile, scanning over the top one hundred albums. Hip-Hop superstar Jay-Z was still holding the number-one spot. Scooby would soon change that. Fame and fortune was his for the taking. A rush of adrenaline shot through my veins.

"You need a cup of coffee."

"I need more than that, Keela." I frowned at my own rudeness. "Sorry, I didn't get much sleep." I tossed the magazine to the side. "I bumped into Randy's sorry ass at the grocery store yesterday."

"Did you say something about Essence?" Keela's earrings bumped against the receiver.

"Of course. He sounded as stupid as the rest of them." I mimicked in my whiny voice reserved for punks and other spineless creatures. "How could I resist what Essence was serving up on a silver platter. Typical. They must give all of 'em a handbook when they leave the womb so they know exactly what lame line to repeat in any given situation."

"A book would be good and the name has to be really stupid. Something like *Bullshit Lines for Men 101*. That way it properly reflects the content."

I snickered, wrote that down on my desktop calendar and underlined it twice. "You got it." The front door slammed and Jonetta swished in, setting down a cup of coffee and a raspberry croissant on my desk. "So, tell me, how are you?"

"I think I'm still in shock. I feel numb most of the time, and the rest of the time I feel sad for the baby. It seems like the poor thing is already starting out life with one strike against her."

I perked up. "You called the baby a her. You know it's gonna be a girl?"

"Oh, no, I'm waiting. I want to be surprised, that way it will be a little like Christmas. I need something to look forward to." Keela laughed, but the joy had seeped out somewhere along the way.

I frowned and picked up the phone. "Are you sure there's not something you want to talk about?"

"It's just that I have this doctor's appointment and Brandon had promised to go with me 'cause I'm getting an amniocentesis today. I'm a little nervous so I don't want to go by myself. I hate needles so please, please, please say you'll come. The appointment is at three, but the doctor's a brother so you know how that goes."

"I can meet you there at five."

Keela laughed. "They're not that bad. As long as you're there by three-thirty, we should be okay."

"Call me about an hour ahead and I'll meet you." I hung up and pressed the intercom. "Jonetta, can you come here, please?"

A minute later, she peeked through the door. "What's up, boss?" Her hair was contained in twisted rows, then burst into two fluffy afro puffs. The slashes of blue across her eyes, and bright fuchsia on her lips appeared neon against her dark skin. She must be going through an experimental phase. She looked like a Pam Grier throwback—on crack. I suppressed a smile. "What time is Mr. Mansini calling?"

Jonetta consulted a small white pad. "In about an hour or so and he wants an update on where you're at with Scooby's projections."

"I e-mailed some figures to his secretary earlier."

"I'll call her and see if she received them." She scribbled a note, then stuck the pen behind her ear.

"I want to at least have something in place before the holidays start slowing everything down."

"Christmas is two days away," Jonetta reminded me.

I sighed and shook my head. "I know. I'm a little out of it."

"Understandable, with your grandmother passing."

"It's more than that."

At her raised eyebrows, I quickly filled in the blanks. Jonetta leaned against the wall, then put a finger to her head. She studied the floor for a minute before speaking, "Let me get this straight—you got a house, a job, and both are in Jamaica?" I bobbed my head. "I should have such problems."

I stretched my arms out and gestured around me. "I just convinced Mr. Mansini to start this operation, how can I just up and leave?"

"Girl, please. I'd be outta here so fast." Jonetta twirled her finger in the air.

Laughing, I cocked my head to the side. "You would just pick up and leave your whole life?"

"Yeah, and start a new one—in the glorious sunshine with all those gorgeous Jamaican men." Jonetta shivered. "If you decide not to go, let me know where to apply. I could sure use a Dexter right about now."

For her, it was a rare display of humor and laughter bubbled up inside of me. "You need to get your groove back, Jonetta?"

A broad grin broke across her painted face, her lips a petunia in full bloom. "I need to get something back—my groove would be a good start. Oops, the phone is ringing." She cupped a hand over the receiver and hollered from her desk. "It's Scooby!" So much for formalities.

I sat up straight, waiting sixty seconds before picking up the phone, and forcing festivity into my voice. "It's about time you returned my phone calls. I've left you a ton of messages."

Scooby breezed over my reprimand, with the easygoing nature of a twelve-year-old. "Awww! You know how that goes," he yelled over the noise in the background. Apparently, the party was still going on. I pictured him hanging onto his oversized pants with one hand and gripping the phone with the other. "What's up, *Mami*? Whatcha' know good?"

"I know we got you one hell of a record deal."

"Oh, it's about to be off the chain, *Mami*! We're about to blow this shit up for real."

"I heard the celebration was really something."

"Yeah, we set it off—blew off some steam and what not—y'know how I do, but I'll be ready to get down to business when you are."

"I hope you mean that, the hard work is about to begin."

"I know all about grindin', Baby. You must have forgotten where I come from. Surviving the streets is the hardest thing I'll ever have to do. This here's cake."

"I'm looking forward to a little bit of cake."

"Oh, that's a done deal, believe that." The signature hard-core raspy edge left so quickly, I had to wonder if it had been there to begin with. Now he sounded more like an R&B singer about to croon a love song. "Anyone as sexy as you deserves all the friggin' cake you want and I'll be more than happy to be the one serving it up to you. Ya' feel me?"

"Slow down, Scooby," I said, keeping it professional. I had enough of that, dealing with Mr. Mansini. "Right now, the only thing I want served up to me is a double-platinum album."

"That's a done deal, *Mami*. I've got five smoking joints just waiting to be laid, ya' heard? I got some tracks that are on fire."

"I hear you, Scooby, and can't wait to listen to them; but don't get your heart set on anything until we hash out the details."

"This producer will blow you away, guaranteed. I'll have my manager e-mail you a clip so you can check 'em out."

"Cool. I have a conference call with Mr. Mansini today, then I'll give your manager a call and let you know when we'll need you in the studio."

"I'm ready when you are."

"You better be." I hung up the phone.

More time was spent during the conference call with Mr. Mansini trying to finagle my trip to New York, than on actual business. I hung up feeling as if I needed to take a shower to wash off the innuendos and double entendres. Mr. Mansini had no idea what to do with a Hip-Hop label and was content to see how far I could take it, giving his blanket approval to everything; including the producer that Scooby had chosen. "As long as you're comfortable with it, Kingston," was all he'd say.

The rest of the afternoon was spent putting together marketing plans, advertising budgets, recording schedules, and booking studio time. I even scribbled random ideas for album covers. Mr. Mansini wanted this project done within two months, and we'd be on point even if I had to work straight through the holidays.

That is if I decided to stay.

A measly seven days ago and I'd have been clicking my heels together, singing with elation at the free reign. But now, guilt was weighing me down like an anchor; knowing that with the other things that I had going on, I might have to walk away from this project and from Scooby.

I rubbed my eyes and leaned away from the computer screen. The snow was falling gracefully, like in the snow globe. Shake it up and there'd be a moment of confusion before everything settled into peaceful perfection, just a few stray flakes sticking to the container.

A wrecking ball swung in front of my office window before burying itself into a dilapidated building—clearing out the old to make way for the new. Sort of like my life, I mused.

Jonetta stood in the doorway and tapped her watch. "Five minutes to three. You better get going or you'll be late. Keela called and left the address and phone number for the doctor." She laid a piece of blue paper on the desk in front of me. I stuck it in my purse, then scooped up my briefcase, tossed my coat over my arm and headed out the door. She leaned into the hallway. "I forgot to tell you, a Mr. Bartlett called while you were reviewing things with Mr. Mansini. He didn't say it was important and I didn't want to bother you, so I just took a message."

"It's okay, Jonetta. That's my grandmother's lawyer. He keeps calling to find out about my decision. He acts like I'm making a decision on what to eat for lunch or something."

I pressed the button for the elevator and heard the rickety doors close below; then muttered, "I know it's his damn job, but he's starting to irritate me." The frustration was wearing at my already frayed edges— ripping and tearing at my sanity. I didn't need the pressure. "Aaaargh!"

Jonetta's eyes bucked and her grip tightened on the door. I knew I sounded crazy, probably looked it too, but afterwards I felt better.

"What your grandmother's trying to do is important, Kingston," Jonetta asserted. "You're an intelligent woman, but this decision may have to come from your heart, not from your head."

I didn't like being told what to do even if Jonetta was right; and to my own ears, my protests were starting to sound a tiny bit on the selfish side. I thought about Sharneesha and the children starving in Africa. Things could be worse.

I slid between the elevator doors before they opened fully. "Just hit me on the cell phone if you need me," I said before the doors squeaked shut.

The decision had been made in my heart when the lawyer read Mama Grace's will. My head just needed to catch up.

Chapter 26

"Wait, slow down, Sharneesha, I can't understand what you're saying." I punched the volume button on the cell phone—even though it was already loud —and pushed the earpiece further into my ear.

Edging away from downtown Chicago's Magnificent Mile, I watched the parade of feathery-soft furs, heavier shearlings with a few butter-soft leathers mixed in, hunkered down beneath the whipping Chicago wind. Shopping was the main draw of the Magnificent Mile and despite it being the middle of the workday, the jet set was out in droves.

Leaning forward, I squinted up at the street signs that were partially covered in snow. It was bad enough that I was in unfamiliar territory, but being lost in a snowstorm was akin to having your tooth yanked without anesthesia. I was negotiating the maze of streets that made up Chicago's near north side with blinders on.

"They're giving me three days," Sharneesha stammered, a sniffle followed every other word. "Three more days until the sheriff comes to put my stuff out in the street."

"That's the day after Christmas," I pointed out. I smoothed the small piece of paper on my thigh and looked at the address again. If I had just spent the extra two hundred dollars and bought the car with the navigational system, I'd probably have been there by now.

"It's bullshit; that's what it is. How can you do that to someone during the holidays? Where the hell am I supposed to go?" Sharneesha's voice faded off in another torrent of tears. "Why do these things always happen to me?"

I held the phone away from my ear as Sharneesha sobbed. She should have been better prepared—eviction was a long process and she'd been well aware that this day was coming - but not wanting to pour salt in the wound, I didn't tell her that. Besides, it didn't matter now. What we needed to talk about was a solution.

"Just try to calm down, Sharneesha. Being hysterical is not going to help." I looked around for a familiar landmark, but didn't see one. Why Keela couldn't find a doctor in the hood was beyond me. "There may be a way that I can help, but I don't want to get into it right now. I have to meet my girlfriend at her doctor's appointment. I'm already late and I think I just missed my turn." I squinted up at the street signs and made a quick right. I passed the plaque with "Health Care Center" embossed in blue. I made three more quick rights and started looking for a parking spot.

"Is everything okay with …?"

"Keela," I supplied. "Everything's fine. She's getting some testing done and is a little freaked out about it. She has me driving all over God knows where to come and hold her hand." I fumbled with my keys as I tried to grab them and my purse at the same time while not dropping the phone. I accidentally slammed my coat in the car door.

"I'll let you go. This is the second time that I have completely broken down on your shoulder."

"It's okay, all part of the sisterhood. When we put our heads together, we'll come up with something. Believe me, everything's going to be fine. There's no way that you and Teeka are going to end up on the streets."

"I'm just so tired. Life shouldn't be this hard." Sharneesha sighed.

"Yeah, well it is. Trust me; you're not alone. Bad things happen to good people all the time. The difference is how you handle it. You gotta have a little bit of faith, Sharneesha. Faith will bring you through any situation."

"I know, I know."

"Look, why don't you come for dinner tomorrow? It's Christmas Eve. I'll cook, make some drinks and we can celebrate together. Keela will be there; you can give her some pointers on motherhood. Plus, I'd like to see Teeka again. I think the bright spot in this holiday season is going to be finding a Christmas gift for her."

"You've done enough already," Sharneesha protested.

"Girl, please. I need something to take my mind off what's been going on with me. In fact, I think it may be good for all of us."

"Here," I said, handing Keela the zip-locked bag of Gold Medal flour with one hand while turning on the stove burner with the other. "Start flouring the chicken so I can fry it. Seasonings, spices, etceteras, are in the cabinet about the stove. And don't put too much Lawry's in it," I warned as I transferred the cast iron skillet full of oil from the kitchen island to the red-hot burner. "You know you got a heavy hand when it comes to salt."

Keela sucked her teeth, but only added a few shakes before screwing the cap back on the bottle. "Why did you decide to fry chicken instead of making a turkey or something anyway?"

"Are you complaining? 'Cause if you're complaining …" I gave her a stern glare that only caused Keela to giggle.

"I never, ever complain about a free meal. I was just asking a simple question."

"Today just felt like a fried chicken day. Good down home comfort food to soothe the soul. I wonder if that's why they call it 'soul food'?" Keela's face twisted as she thought about it way too long. "Anyway, I threw together some homemade macaroni and cheese, green beans, spaghetti, catfish for me and tossed a salad. Hell, I even made the monkey bread and chocolate rum cake from scratch."

"Not the famous Mac n' Cheese." Keela had the nerve to open her mouth and gasp. "With some extra *Velveeta* thrown in?" I nodded, lining up the paper plates, cups and utensils on the counter. "It must really be a special occasion. All right then, Bettina Crocker. It smells divine in here." Keela pulled open the oven, took a whiff, and then sighed with dramatic pleasure. Cocoa sprang into action, prancing into the kitchen and sniffing the air. Keela shooed her back into the living room with an oven mitt.

"Chocolate rum cake, Kingston? I just gained ten pounds. You sure got enough food here. It looks like you're expecting an army."

And I was expecting an army—sort of. Over the past couple of days, the festivities of four had ballooned to over twenty invited party guests. The holiday spirit was starting to catch up with me. The whole day had been spent hanging garland, wrapping presents, cooking dinner, and stringing Christmas lights. I even went so far as to buy a pre-decorated tree that now blinked from its designated spot in the corner.

"Not quite an army, but I did invite a few extra people: Jonetta from the office, Darryl and Henry that live just down the way—Oh! I forgot you met them when you got your hair done at their salon—Brigitte, the lady that does my nails, and her sister, Bertice." I waved my hand as if the list went on and on. "Just a slew of folks. Oh, and my next-door neighbors, Sharneesha and her daughter Teeka. You're going to love Teeka. She's just the most adorable little thing."

"Oh, it's gonna be a party up in here." Keela squealed, then stopped short and stooped over, placing her hand on her belly and motioning for me to come closer. I placed my hand on the side of her protruding belly. "Now just wait," she instructed and ten seconds later, I felt a whisper of movement. "Did you feel that?" she asked, her eyes shining.

I bobbed my head in wonder.

"Pretty cool, huh? The first time that it happened, I thought I had a gas bubble or something, but now this baby is rocking and rolling. Sometimes she keeps me up at night."

"That's the second time with that girl thing." I gasped as the baby moved again then gave her tummy a final pat. "Amazing. Maybe you should sit down."

"If I had to sit down every time this baby moves, I'd be on my butt all day long. Our ancestors used to have their babies in the field while picking cotton—no drugs or comfy hospital beds—no, suh, they'd just squat and plop; then they'd go right back to picking cotton and you want me to sit down because the baby moved. Girl, puh-lease."

"Excuse me if I'm a little in awe over here. You're creating a life, Keela. You are the epitome of woman right now, fertile ground."

"Fertile ground?" Keela exclaimed. "What the hell is wrong with you, Kingston?"

"I don't know—maybe a little jealous." Waving my hands, I tried to fan away the tears that stung my eyes, then swung away and started dropping pieces of chicken in the pan.

"Awww! Sweetie, your time will come. Everything happens when it's supposed to."

"Yeah, yeah!" I pursed my lips. "My luck with men ain't too hot right now, so I'm not gonna hold my breath."

"Hey, I'm not exactly batting one hundred over here either."

"Have you talked to Brandon?"

"He's left about a million messages, but I don't want to talk to him about anything but child support and a DNA test."

"DNA test? Brandon asked you to take one?" I gulped. The idea that Brandon could question the paternity of Keela's baby snagged a bit on the way down.

"Hell, no. It's my idea and I don't give a damn what he thinks," she said, slamming the oven mitt down on the counter. "I'm not going to risk him waking up one day and trying to say this baby isn't his so he can get out of paying child support or some nonsense like that. I want proof. The court will order it if he refuses."

"Maybe he'll do the right thing and take care of his kid."

"I'm not taking any chances." Keela tilted her head and looked at me. "You know, maybe it's not such a bad thing it only being us. We're single, educated, black women doing our thing. Who cares that we haven't met the elusive Mr. Right? We don't need a man to make us complete. We're fine the way we are, so let's not throw a pity party. Especially not tonight."

"All right." I flipped the chicken, inhaling the down home smell of seasoned flour and *Crisco*. It reminded me of Mama Grace and the warm summer nights when homesickness would hit me like a wave of nausea, rolling around in my belly.

She'd rub my back while I bawled for my Mama, then tease me until I ate. "Come now, Pickney, I may not be the Colonel, but my fried chicken's not that bad." I shook my head to clear the cloud of nostalgia. "People should start coming soon. Can you handle this while I go set up card tables?"

"I know how to fry some chicken, Kingston." She pulled an apron from the drawer and tied it around her waist. "Girl, give me those tongs and go do what you got to do. I got this!"

"I don't want you to accuse me of slave labor. I'm trying to be considerate of your delicate condition."

"Kingston," she warned.

"I'm going."

"And don't forget to look for the dominoes. I may feel like slapping some bones!"

"You not ready for the bones, Keela. Don't forget, I'm from Jamaica where they breed real dominoes players."

"You know you talk more trash than a little bit."

"That's the first sign of a true domino player. Talking trash allows me to get into your head. Once I get into your head, the game is over."

Keela laughed and pulled the last piece of chicken out of the pan, setting it on the paper towel-covered plate to drain. "And by the way." She waved the greasy tongs at the kitchen wall. "The oversized wooden spoon and fork are played out. Come on, Kingston, move into the 21st century with the rest of us."

Five hours later, the music was pumping full blast and we were well into our fifth spades game. Henry and I were partnered up against Sharneesha and Jonetta and to say that we were in the process of whooping up on them would've been an understatement. I was about to run a Boston when I felt a tug at my leg. Teeka was smiling up at me, with her pink barrettes that dotted her head.

I brushed *Oreo* crumbs from her chin. "No sucking your fingers, remember?" I clucked as perfectly as any non-mother hen, while gently pulling her finger from her mouth.

"I'm thirsty, 'ingston." My heart melted into a syrupy, gooey substance and I bent down so my face was closer to hers. "I think I have some Kool-Aid. Or would you rather have a glass of milk?"

"Got boo ooo-aid?"

I shot a questioning glance at Sharneesha for interpretation. "Blue Kool-Aid," she said.   "No, blue Kool-Aid. I think it's strawberry."

Teeka's face fell with disappointment before her eyes brightened. She nodded, barrettes bouncing. "Okay." Apparently strawberry Kool-Aid was better than no Kool-Aid.

"Okay what, Teeka?" Sharneesha corrected, her voice unnecessarily harsh, and I looked at her. A frown creased her forehead, her eyes narrowed to slits and Teeka looked like she was going to cry. The air grew heavy and the music faded into the background.

"It's okay," I said, instantly in motion. "I understood what she meant."

But Sharneesha ignored me. "Teeka, how do you ask for something?" Her words were punctuated with sharp movements of her head.

"May I hab' sum ooo-Aid, pease?"

"That's better," Sharneesha said, her face softening. The cloud of awkwardness disappeared in a puff and things slid back to normal.

"Hold that thought," I said as Henry raised his hand ready to slap a card on the table. "Let me take care of my little buddy. And before I hear someone calling my name, allow me to make this clear—all y'all are grown and no longer company, so get your own damn drinks." And away I stepped, snapping my fingers to R. Kelly's "Fiesta" all the way to the kitchen.

The party had shaped up nicely: Sharneesha, Jonetta, and Henry at the card table looked like three bookends from three different sets. Sharneesha was wearing a body-hugging, long-sleeved cat suit that must have been picked up in the Junior's section and the gold tint she had added to the tips of her hair sparkled as brightly as the Christmas tree. Jonetta was clad in the same dark brown sweater with flicks of green, red, and orange and a light brown corduroy skirt she'd worn at the office. Her eyes still coated in blue. As fashionable as any model from a GQ magazine, Henry wore his Gucci sweater and Gucci jeans and black Prada shoes. Darryl was perched on the arm of the sofa. Squeezed up like pigs in a blanket on the couch were Bridgett, Beatrice, and two male friends, one slurping up Sharneesha's curves as though he was in the middle of the Sahara desert and she was water. The other man was slumped so far down in the sofa cushions, I thought he'd fallen asleep. The coffee table overflowed with dirty paper plates and half-empty cups. Bridgett frowned at Darryl, but he didn't get the message.

I was still dancing as I stirred the Kool-Aid to the beat of Bruno Mars.

"Get it girl!" Darryl hollered and readjusted himself on the arm of the couch where he was doing his best not to ruin the crease in the slacks or muss the cashmere sweater he may have to take back to the store the next day.

"Yeah, you go, girl!" Henry echoed as he flipped through my CD case. "Hey, we need to put some real Hip-Hop on; maybe some Jay- Z or Tupac or something, get this party jumpin'."

Laughing, I tossed a few ice cubes into Teeka's Sippy cup. "I ain't even gotten started. Watch me work." I executed a twirl, dip, squat move, laughing on the way up.

Henry whistled. "Yeah, you workin' it. All we need to do now is get you a stripper pole and put you to work for real."

Keela had curled herself around a bowl of popcorn in the overstuffed brown recliner that had been shoved into the corner to make room. "Don't talk like that in front of the baby," she said.

But Teeka was in her own world as she followed me from the kitchen, slurping happily, a red ring forming around her mouth.

"What do you say, Teeka?" Sharneesha pushed at Teeka's arm. She faced me as I sat down at the table.

"Thank you, 'ingston." This was delivered with a delightful blink of her precious brown eyes.

"You're very welcome, Teeka."

"Now go back upstairs, finish watching your cartoons. And don't spill your juice, do you hear me? You can't pay for nothing around here." Sharneesha sent Teeka toward the stairs with a pop on the butt.

"Yes, Mommy."

Henry slammed down an ace of spades, winning the book and the game. "We are the champions," he sang, cabbage patching in his seat.

Sharneesha threw her cards on the table. "Puhleeze, that was nothing but luck."

"Don't hate," Henry said and I high-fived him, almost knocking over my eggnog.

"This has been too much fun, but I think it's time for us to get out of your hair." An odd mixture of hiccups and giggles popped from Darryl's mouth. "Get it? Get out of your hair?"

Jonetta stood and stretched, her mouth twitching with laughter. "Don't quit your day job." She reached for her purse. "I think that's going to do it for me, too."

Bridgett, Beatrice, Vincent, and Leroy followed and Sharneesha pushed back her chair. "I'm gonna go check on Teeka."

Henry waited until he could no longer hear Sharneesha's footsteps on the stairs before angling his elbow in Darryl's side.

Darryl said, "Now Kingston, you know I don't mean to get into your business, 'cause I don't want to be accused of being a busy-body."

"Ask her, already."

Darryl cleared his throat again. "How long have you known Sharneesha?"

"We just started getting to know each other. Why?"

"Well," the word was drawn out through tightly clamped lips, "people have been kind of talking."

"Wait a minute." Keela moved from the recliner to plop down in the chair that Sharneesha had vacated.

"Like?" I said, rolling my hand in small circles. "This must be pretty good dirt if it's taking you this long to get it out."

"Never mind, I'll tell her." Henry waved a dismissive hand at his partner and leaned in close, one hand splayed on the table. His diamond pinkie ring winked at me. "I have it on very good authority," he said slowly, "that the police have been asking questions about her. Plain clothes policeman. Drugs were mentioned." His voice lowered to a whisper as if the juiciest tidbit of gossip was about to be bestowed. "Plus, she doesn't even own the place. She's a renter."

Keela sucked in her breath and a hand flew to her chest. "She doesn't look like a drug addict or a renter."

I looked at Keela and shook my head, not knowing whose ridiculous comment to address first.

"If what you say is true, why wasn't this brought up at an association meeting? As many rules and regulations as they have in our handbook, I'm sure there's something against criminal activity," I said, looking at Keela, "and renting."

Henry snapped his fingers. "I can't know everything, Kingston. I'm telling you what we heard. Watch your back," he said as he stood up.

Henry and Darryl brushed air kisses against our cheeks and wished us a Merry Christmas. Keela and I looked at each other as I locked the door behind them.

"What do you think?" she asked.

"I don't know what to think." I walked to the living room and started picking up dirty paper plates. Keela brought a garbage bag from the kitchen and we began loading it up.

"She doesn't seem like she's into drugs."

I shrugged. "You never know about people. I think that's been demonstrated in the past couple of days."

"Still, I don't get that impression from her." We cleaned in silence, giving the rumors just enough time to take root before Keela said, "She's taking a mighty long time up there."

"Don't be silly." I laughed and carried the stuffed garbage bag

downstairs and sat it in the garage. Then the rumor bloomed, maybe I
didn't know enough about Sharneesha to invite her and her daughter to
move half way across the world with me.

I wiped my hands on my jeans. "I had intended to talk to both of you,
actually, but now..."

Keela looked up from wiping the coffee table. "About?"

"I'm about 90 percent sure that I'm going to Jamaica," I paused.
"Well, maybe 98.5 percent. I don't think I could live with myself if I
didn't. And if I do go, I plan on leaving pretty quickly, maybe before
the end of the year, depending on how soon I can get things wrapped up
here. So, what I was thinking is that maybe you and Sharneesha could
…"

"Sharneesha could what?" Sharneesha asked as she walked into the
kitchen. She looked at Keela, then me.

"Is Teeka okay?" I asked, hanging the dishrag over the faucet.

"She's fast asleep on your bed."

"Good. Let her sleep. Both of you guys come sit down." I twisted my
hands together. "I was thinking it might be a great opportunity for both
of you to come to Jamaica with me. I'm definitely going to need people
to help me with the estate, we have a place to stay, it's perfect."

"Move to Jamaica?" they said together.

I looked at the confusion on both of their faces and decided to try
easing in a different way. "What's keeping you here? Sharneesha,
you don't have a job and in two days, they're going to set your stuff
out on the curb, and Keela, you're about to have a baby so you're not
going to be working for a while. I thought this would be a way we
could help each other. It's a big step, I know, but Sharneesha you were
saying how you wanted to move to a place where you've never been
before, where there's warmer weather all year long. How you wanted
to be in a culturally diverse neighborhood so Teeka can be exposed
to different kinds of people. And how you want a job where you are
helping someone—so you can use your education to make a difference."
I almost quoted verbatim.

"Yeah, but I thought we were just dreaming. You know talking about in a perfect world and all that shit. I never thought it would really happen."

"Maybe it could be a perfect world or at least a perfect solution to the situation you're in."

"Yeah, but move to Jamaica?" Keela repeated.

"Why not?" Neither one answered so I kept going. "I could see if you had a job, but you don't. Even if you come for a few months and don't like it, but don't just shoot down the idea without thinking about it."

"Maybe it's the hormones talking or the holiday spirit, but I'm really touched that you would be so concerned about me that you would want me to come with you to Jamaica." Tears welled up in her eyes. "I feel a bout coming on." She paused. "It's a big step and I need a little bit of time to think it over. I'm not ruling it out. I just need time." She seemed to be getting more upset so I backed down.

"Trust me, I went through the same thing myself so I understand. Just thought I'd put it out there, see what you all thought." I tried to hold in my disappointment. Keela and Sharneesha were not as excited as I thought they would be, but I did understand. I was in the same place not two days ago.

I held out a hand to each of them, which they grabbed gratefully. "Take your time, think about it and let me know. I want the best for both of you and if there is anything I can do to help, I will."

Now everyone's eyes brightened with emotion. "Not many people would go out of their way like this for someone else. I'm not used to being able to lean on anybody. It makes me wish we'd gotten to know each other sooner."

"We can't live this life on our own," I said.

"You're right about that." Sharneesha stood and stretched, a guttural sound escaping. "I need to get Teeka home. Can't party like I used to and I'm sure you want to get some sleep, too." She smiled, then leaned down to hug me before running up the stairs.

"Wanna crash here?" I asked when Sharneesha was out of earshot.

"Nah, I think I'll go home."

"Okay." The word came out elongated, as I paused, reaching for more time. "Keela, you know my asking you to come to Jamaica was for purely selfish reasons. I don't know how I am going to survive without my best friend."

Before she could answer, Sharneesha came downstairs carrying a still-sleeping Teeka. "Can you grab her coat for me?"

I picked up the purple Barbie doll fleece jacket and held it open so that Sharneesha could maneuver Teeka into it without waking her up.

"I'll walk out with you." Keela grabbed her purse.

Just as I was about to open the door, the bell rang.

"Are you expecting anybody?" Keela asked and reached for the door.

"Don't open it," I whispered and pulled both of them back toward the stairs. I jumped as the person rang the bell again and then, started knocking on the door.

"Most burglars and rapists I know don't ring the bell," Keela said, with a slight smile.

That made sense. "Well at least, ask who it is."

But before she could open her mouth, a voice with bass warm enough to melt even the coldest of souls, slid through three inches of solid wood. At the same time, my heart soared and my blood boiled.

Damon.

Chapter 27

Thirty minutes later, standing with a fist planted on each hip and my foot tapping a tribal rhythm on the hardwood floor, I said, "Dammit, Damon, where do you get off just showing up like this? It's two o'clock in the morning."

"I wanted to surprise you." Damon raised his hands in a gesture of innocence, leaning in the recliner, his corduroy-clad legs propped up and crossed at the ankles as if he were at home in his living room, and not sitting in mine uninvited. He had graciously endured the kisses and questions from Keela, then the sexy looks from Sharneesha before I pushed both of them—and the still sleeping Teeka—out.

Damon, however, insisted on walking Sharneesha to her house and Keela to her car. It was the right thing to do, but the gentlemanly gesture piled irritation on top of shock and anger. If Cocoa hadn't needed to go outside and take care of her business, I might have locked the door and gone up to bed. But Cocoa did need to pee and I'd been forced to wait.

Now, here he sat filling up my space with his overwhelming presence. I was on the verge of exploding.

"Surprise me?" My fists clenched and I felt a neck swerve coming on.

Damon flashed his signature playful grin. "Yeah, I thought I could be your Christmas present. Pretty good-looking package, eh? Wanna unwrap me?" He winked and opened his arms wide.

I stood there looking at him in disbelief. *This fool has lost his mind.*

"And while we're talking about packages—you ain't doing too bad yourself."

I crossed my arms in front of me as Damon's eyes soaked me in. Chill bumps prickled every square inch of my body. The sexy, winter-white, Calvin Klein halter-top that I had thrown on earlier with a pair of skintight denims and high-heeled boots seemed like a good idea, but now I wasn't so sure. I felt exposed.

"Damon, it is two o'clock in the morning." I stamped my foot for good measure, my finger shaking as erratically as my pulse. "Do you hear me? Who shows up on someone's doorstep at such an ungodly hour without calling first? I'll tell you who—a crazy person—that's who!"

One corner of his mouth twitched and a bushy eyebrow jumped as Damon struggled to keep a straight face. "So I take it you're not happy to see me?"

"Dammit, Damon, where do you get off sashaying in here, wearing my favorite cologne, charming my friends, and trying to take over my life?" I wailed, throwing my hands up and stalking over to the window. Staring outside was a lot less unsettling than looking at Damon.

The snow had picked up momentum, looking close to becoming another winter storm. The sidewalk and parking lot were covered with at least three inches of fresh snow. "Trying to take over your life? Don't you think that's taking it a bit far?"

"Take over my life," I repeated. "Did you ever even consider whether or not I wanted you here? I mean, I thought I had made myself clear on where I stood about us before I left Jamaica. And then here you go, showing up on my doorstep at two o'clock in the morning." As I whirled to face him, I knew I was taking the drama to a whole 'nother level. Most of my anxiety had nothing to do with Damon just showing up. It had nothing to do with him and everything to do with me.

But Damon didn't know that. His face constricted with regret as he sat up and folded his hands together. "I'm sorry Kingston, I didn't mean to intrude. I thought you'd be happy to see me. I never meant to upset you."

The fortress that I had worked so hard to build up was destroyed in two seconds by the sorrow in Damon's eyes. My shoulders started twitching and my eyes burned with tears. Before I could reel in my emotions, I broke down.

"I am happy to see you. I just, I just …" I stammered. "I don't know what's wrong with me." I went into the kitchen to grab a napkin, blew my nose loudly, then tossed it into the wastebasket.

Damon walked up behind me. "Two points for Kingston Phillips," he mimicked in his best impersonation of a basketball announcer.

"It's not funny." Punching him lightly in the chest, I dissolved into more tears. "I think you make me crazy."

Damon watched me for a few more seconds—long enough for the tears to slow and my composure to return. "Come here." He grabbed my hand.

Following him back to the recliner, I crawled into his lap like a baby. "Mama Grace is gone and I gotta move to Jamaica and I found out Essence was sleeping with my boyfriend and ..."

"It's okay, sweetie. I'm here. Just let it all out." And with each circle that he rubbed on my back, I did just that, releasing more and more until I felt like a mound of jelly.

"Why do I always fall apart when you're around?" I asked into his chest.

Damon's arms tightened around me. "Because you feel safe with me."

"But why is that when you've hurt me more than anybody else?"

"I think you know that it's not in my heart to intentionally hurt you—that I was only doing what I thought was best at the time. I hope you know that."

"You always sound like you're reciting the words from a Bob Marley song."

"You mean like this?" And he broke into a shaky rendition of "No Woman, No Cry" that would have Master Bob putting the ganja pipe down.

"'Nuff respect to Bob." He chuckled.

I shifted trying to get as close as possible to the source of his joy, laying my head over his heart. "Why are you here?" I asked quietly.

"A colleague of mine invited me to spend the holidays with him in Atlanta, so I decided to rent a car, stop in Chicago, and see you first. I'll leave first thing in the morning to drive to Atlanta." Damon crooked a finger underneath my chin, tilted it up. "I forgot about how the winters in the states could be. I don't know how you stand it; you could freeze your cute little butt off here. I thought it got cold in D.C., but this is ridiculous."

"So I'm just a pit stop? And here I thought I was special."

"I don't think you know how special you are." He kissed me tenderly, quickly, causing me to bluster and search for a change of subject.

"What's the name of your colleague?" I asked, filling my nose with his scent.

"Dr. Alan Baker. He's a professor at Meharry Medical College in Nashville Tennessee."

"I've heard of him. Didn't he invent a new procedure involving heart transplants in newborns?"

"Very good," Damon said looking at me with raised eyebrows. "It's called the Baker Maneuver."

"I saw it on *60 Minutes*."

Damon rubbed his hand up the length of my calf and over my thigh and then back down again. "I met Dr. Baker at a conference that he holds every year in the spring. The convention is considered one of the most highly regarded among minorities in the medical community. We connected at the first one I attended; now he's not only a mentor, but also a great friend." Damon paused and now he changed the subject.

"I didn't know that Calvin Klein's 212 was your favorite cologne."

"How could you know something like that?"

"Did you buy it for your boyfriend?"

"No." The underlying jealousy in his tone amused me.

"And Essence was sleeping with him?"

"Yes." And then, I filled him in on the events of the last forty-eight hours, enjoying the feel of his muscles flexing beneath my hands. I also asked him if Essence had gotten to him.

"Women like Essence can only do things like that with men who allow it. She knew better than to try me. I wouldn't have tolerated her disrespecting you or me." He paused. "Did this boyfriend break your heart?"

"It would have hurt more if it had been you." If I could have shoved the words back in my mouth, erase them from the atmosphere, I would have. I reeled at how honest my statement was. With tiny bits of perspiration beaded across my top lip, I started backpedaling. "Well, you know what I mean. With Randy, it was more of something to do than some great romance. You and I were in love; so, it would have hurt more."

Damon nodded. "Where do you and Essence stand?"

"We don't stand anywhere. She also slept with Keela's man. Not sure if you could tell or not because she had on such a big coat, but she's pregnant; about 18 weeks." Damon exhaled, his breath ending with a slight whistle. "And here I thought she was still a bit on the chunky side. Whew! That must be rough for her. Did she kick both of them to the curb, too?"

"This wasn't the first time, but Essence was the last straw." I shrugged. "So now the three musketeers are just two peas in a pod."

"So have you decided about Jamaica?"

"No," I lied and ducked my head into the crook of his throat—the fragrant spot was begging me to kiss it.

"I bet the pressure from that isn't helping any. I'm sorry you've had so much pain in your life."

His words burrowed deep, touching a place that had been locked away for so long. There was nothing to say; nothing that could adequately express how I felt. Hell, I couldn't even explain it to myself; so with a slight sigh, I moved closer into the circle of his warmth and willed my mind to be still. I had done too much thinking already.

The snow sailed downward past the window like tiny angels on their way to something important. The flames flickered and the smell of burning wood hung heavily in the air. I felt the pulse in his neck beating strongly beneath my lips. I let memories wash over me and tried to be at peace with them. We were so still for so long, I thought he had fallen asleep.

Then, he said, "I'm going to kiss you, Kingston." It was a statement of fact.

"Not if I kiss you first," I teased. Tilting my head back, I placed my hand behind his neck, and drew his lips to mine. I expected overwhelming passion, but this kiss was long, leisurely. It reminded me of smoldering embers that could explode into flames, but didn't. We cuddled and kissed in that old recliner until the sun peeked over the balcony.

"Is it okay if I take a shower and crash for a few hours before I head out?" That was the question his mouth asked, but his eyes were saying the opposite.

"Sure." I nonchalantly lifted a shoulder, knowing that if the desire in my eyes hadn't given me away, then the wetness moistening my inner thigh sure would. Climbing off his lap, I pointed upstairs. "The bathroom is that way. I'll grab you some towels. The guest room is already made up, so make yourself at home." I made a production of yawning. "I need to get some sleep, too. I'm exhausted."

Damon nodded, heading downstairs to grab his overnight bag, then up to the bathroom without even a second glance in my direction. I was unprepared for the aching void that he left in his wake or the rejection, as if that made any sense at all. Damon was feeling the same way I was—frustrated. I knew that. I also knew that if I had pressed the issue, we would still be in that recliner, testing to see if the spring devices were as good as the television ads professed them to be. But I hadn't pressed the issue and neither had he.

The shower water ran and I still hadn't gotten the towels.

When I knocked on the door, there was no answer. I knocked again more loudly, but still nothing; so I went in, picked up clothes that were scattered over the beige marble tiled floor, folded them and laid them on the countertop.

The bathroom was filled with steam, but the outline of Damon's naked body was still visible. Bent at the waist, he was lathering himself with the same sure movements that he used to introduce me to ecstasy. I watched him work on legs that were thick, strong, and sweetly bowed. My gaze wandered over his soapy chest before following the curly dark hairs that tapered down his stomach and disappeared into his groin. My knees buckled. I leaned on the sink to keep myself from falling and knocked over the soap dispenser.

At the clattering, Damon looked up. When our eyes met in the mirror, I wanted to look away, but couldn't. I should have walked right out the door, but my feet remained glued to the floor. Sweat trickled down my neck caused by the heat from the shower, and from the electricity that shot between us. I either had to do something or be consumed in the fire.

Damon's gaze gave me no choice. I slowly moved my hands to unfasten my halter-top. He licked his lips as it fell to my waist and finally to the floor. I peeled my jeans from my body, Damon's eye widening when he saw my Brazilian-cut G-string bikini panties. I didn't even remember slipping off my boots and socks before stepping into the shower.

"I could look at you all day," Damon said, tossing the washcloth to the side.

I smiled as if it were an everyday occurrence to have a naked man in my shower. Stepping into his embrace, I traced a moist trail with my tongue from his strong neck to his navel, planting kisses everywhere in between. Damon's grip tightened on my shoulders, turning me and backing us underneath the spray of the shower. His hands explored my slippery body. Smoothing the wet hair off my face, he moved his lips down the curve of my jawbone. When he turned me to face the mirror, I tried to wiggle away, but he just pulled me closer.

"I want to see you," he said, as he opened the shower door so that he could get a clearer view. The outlines of our body reflected in the foggy mirror and my breath quickened.

"Awwww! Sweet Jesus, I could easily become addicted to you." He wrapped his arm around my waist, laying one hand flat against my stomach, the other hand cupping my breast before he moved it lower, then lower and lower still. His lips were hot against my ear as he nibbled on the lobe. "I love you so much, Kingston."

"I love you, too." The words danced out of my mouth and dissolved into the steam from the shower before I could suck them back in. But then, I wasn't sure I wanted to anymore.

His fingers worked their magic, causing me to moan and look up through hooded lids. With the steam of the shower and the passion, I could almost swear that I was standing in the outside shower beneath the blackness of the Jamaican night broken only by the twinkling of stars.

Chapter 28

Damon wrapped us in a fluffy towel and gently dried me off with the loose ends. I moved closer to him, touched by the tender gesture.

He chuckled. "We still haven't managed to make love in a bed yet."

I laughed, too, and wiggled my hips enough to elicit a response. "It's not too late," I said.

"And you wonder why I love you?" Damon swooped me into his arms, covering the space between the bathroom and the bedroom in two long strides before flinging me on the bed and jumping on top of me.

After another two hours of lovemaking, we had fallen asleep, exhausted—a sweaty tangle of arms and legs. And now he was doing his best to ruin it.

"I want you to move back to Jamaica."

"Damon, this doesn't change anything. Just because I like having sex with you does not mean that we're back together and that I'm going to move to Jamaica to be with you." I pushed the sheets back. "You're like that piece of candy that my mama told me I couldn't have, but I snuck and got it anyway. I couldn't resist it; but trust me, when my mama found out, there were consequences that made it not so worth it in the end."

"Well, I'm giving you permission to have that piece of candy." He pointed to his bare chest. "I'm the candy and I'm telling you to eat me."

"Candy's not good for you. Makes you fat and your teeth fall out," I said before getting up and heading toward the bathroom. I brushed my teeth and washed my face before rummaging through the dirty laundry for some t-shirts, sweatpants, and a sweatshirt to run in. I put on about five layers of clothing before I walked back into the room.

"I would run with you, but I really need to get on the road. I didn't plan on sleeping as long as I did."

"I didn't ask you to run with me."

Damon recoiled as if I had picked up a rifle and shot him. "You can be so cold sometimes, Kingston. When we make love, it's like magic— you're so warm and sweet and giving; you operate totally on how you feel, then two hours later you turn into a different person. Yes, the sex is unbelievable, but I want more than your body. I want your heart, mind, and soul, too. I want all of you. When are you going to start doing what your heart tells you to do, and forgive me?"

"Well, you can't have all of me. So just take what you can get or don't take anything at all." I picked up my headphones and mini iPod off the dresser. Cocoa was scratching at the guest room door, waiting. When I opened it, she bounded in and jumped on the bed licking Damon eagerly on the face.

"Cocoa," I said in the voice usually reserved for pooping on the carpet or some other offense. "Let's go." She got in one last lick before skulking off the bed and lying obediently by my feet. I glanced at Damon, his naked body, only key parts covered, and willed myself not be weak again. "Lock the door on your way out." I trotted down the stairs, listening not to my heart or my head, but my pride. Ego wouldn't let me give in.

Grabbing Cocoa's leash, I wrapped it around my wrist, locking her in. She stood by my side and the look on her face said she wouldn't betray me again.

I heard Damon call, "Merry Christmas," just before I slammed the front door.

Most of the day was spent packing and ignoring calls from Essence and Randy, who were phoning under the guise of wishing me a Merry Christmas. The first couple of times, okay, I knew they were trying to clean up dirty laundry. The holiday spirit had moved them to want to make amends, but after my blow up with Damon, I was not in the mood.

After the sixth call, I was ready to alert the police and report them as stalkers.

More socks were tossed into the suitcase that lay open on the couch already surrounded by a myriad of other clothing. From the corner of my eye, I saw the note that Damon had left on the table. I imagined him placing it there before hopping in his rental and driving to Atlanta. The stark white paper had been folded once, then folded again. Next to it sat a tiny box that was wrapped in gold paper and topped with a green satin bow. Both were untouched. I hadn't worked up the guts to open either one.

During my hour and a half run, I had come up with a plan for Mr. Mansini and once again I was going to present it with no option for being turned down. I was moving to Jamaica, but still wanted to head up the urban division of MMG, with Jonetta playing a much larger role in day-to-day operations. That way I could live in Jamaica, run the estate, and be free to travel to the states when necessary. The technology available today would make it more than possible. Jonetta was capable and organized enough to handle the additional responsibilities. I also knew that Mr. Mansini and the board of directors had too much invested in this project to just scrap it. With just one artist signed to the label, daily presence in the office would not be required. The situation could definitely work.

So anxious to start the process that right after my run, without even bothering to shower, I booked my flight to Jamaica online, scheduling to leave Saturday morning at five forty-five. That would give me enough time to take care of my personal business, but not too much time to over think my decision. I faxed my flight information to Mr. Bartlett's office along with a short note letting him know that I would be taking control of Mama Grace's estate, then called Bianca and left a message asking her to pick me up at the airport. Normally, that phone call would be reserved for Uncle Winston, but it was time to start some new traditions. After wishing her a Merry Christmas, I hung up filled with a sense of finality. I couldn't believe that everything was about to change. Cocoa bounded into the room and I rubbed her behind the ears. She was the one constant in this whole thing. The phone rang again and I rolled my eyes toward heaven. God grant me strength.

I tossed a load of dirty clothes into the washing machine, then went upstairs to rummage through the closet to pick out the shoes I would be taking with me. Two rows of various types of boots—from hiking boots to eel-skin Prada spikes—would no longer be of any use. I grabbed ten different pairs of sandals and three pairs of tennis shoes. Only taking the necessities, I packed as if I were going for a couple of weeks as opposed to the rest of my life.

The phone rang again. I took a deep breath and tried to calm my nerves before picking up the phone. "What do you want, Essence?"

"Just called to wish you a Merry Christmas."

"Oh, that's it? Well, Merry Christmas to you, too. Bye."

Essence screamed at the top of her lungs, "Wait, Kingston. Don't hang up! Please!"

I placed the receiver back to my ear and cradled it with my shoulder, but didn't say a word. I continued to pull clothes from the dresser drawers and put them in a pile to pack.

"Are you there?" she asked. "I know you're there, Kingston. I can hear you breathing."

"I'm here."

"All right, so I called for more than to just wish you a Merry Christmas. I needed to tell you how sorry I am. These past few days without you and Keela have been torture. I feel horrible about everything."

"I bet you do. But I think you feel bad because you got caught, not because of what you did. I'm not sure anymore if you're even capable of being remorseful about the things you do."

Essence sighed. "You know I never apologize for anything, and I definitely don't ask for forgiveness. My whole life philosophy is take me or leave me—bullshit and all. But this is different. I can't even begin to tell you how much I want forgiveness from you and Keela."

"Yeah, well I can forgive you. That's the easy part. It's the forgetting that I can't do, at least not right now."

"I miss you guys. I'm not ashamed to say that."

"Look, Essence, I'm not in the mood for weepy confessions. I know you're sad. So am I. But what's done, is done."

Essence sucked her teeth. "I think you're being a baby about this whole situation. I knew Keela would whine for a while, but I thought you'd be able to move on quickly."

"What happened to the pitiful 'I'm so sorry' routine?"

"Look, I messed up. What more can I say? I'm not gonna sit here and beg for your forgiveness for the rest of my life."

"Then don't," I said simply, then hung up the phone. Almost immediately I picked it back up and punched in my boss's number at home.

He wasn't happy about it. "It's Christmas Day and I'm in the middle of spending time with my family. We were about to sit down to dinner. This better be good," Mr. Mansini growled and I felt put back in place, like a mistress who had overstepped her bounds.

"I'm sorry to interrupt, but I wouldn't have called if it weren't important. I need to talk to you." Mr. Mansini listened as I spilled my guts, relating the tale of Mama Grace's estate in one long rambling breath.

"I'm not sure what to say, Kingston."

"I know I'm putting you in a very awkward position, but I've thought this through and I believe I've worked out a viable plan."

"I don't believe I have quite as much confidence as you."

"Just hear me out. We'll keep the Chicago office and I'll set up another one in Jamaica. With technology, it'll be as if I'm right here. Traveling won't be a problem, so I can be in Chicago or New York as often as necessary. Of course, I'll need some extra help. I haven't mentioned anything to Jonetta yet, but I think a pay raise would convince her to take on added responsibilities."

Mr. Mansini's voice turned cold. "There isn't room in the budget to give Jonetta any more money. Scooby has potential, but he hasn't earned this company a dime yet. I took a big chance on this venture and on you and now it looks as if I've made a bad decision."

"No disrespect, Mr. Mansini, but there is more than enough money in the budget to give Jonetta a raise. I know; I'm the one who put it together. But if you need to, you can offset the extra money with a portion of my salary." I thought was a fair offer, but I still sensed hesitation on Mr. Mansini's part. "You've trusted me this far, Mr. Mansini, and I've delivered on everything I've promised, haven't I? Can't you trust me for a little bit longer?"

The air was heavy with Mr. Mansini's discontent, but I smiled. I could feel him wavering in his silence.

"I'm sticking my neck out for you, Kingston, I hope you can appreciate that. We'll do a six-month trial basis. That should give you time to complete Scooby's project and get it in the stores. When we see what the first two weeks of sales look like, we'll re-evaluate. Don't make me look bad in front of the Board of Directors, Kingston. More than anything else in the world, I hate to look bad."

Drowning in a sea of multi-colored packing boxes was a cruel way to die; almost as cruel as hacking myself to death. In the space of three hours, two of my fingers had almost been lost in a packing tape incident. Still sucking on one, the other covered in a Band-Aid, I answered my cell phone when I felt it vibrate against my bare leg.

"Merry Christmas, sweetie." Keela's voice was filled with jingle bells and mistletoe.

"Merry Christmas to you, too. Having fun at your grandma's house?"

"Uncle Noonie got drunk again and Daddy had to throw him out. He called Aunt Yvonne a ho, but she drove him home anyway and

Grandmama got mad at her for being a wide open idiot—her words, not mine—and told her not to come back."

"She's a nasty cuss! Umph, umph, umph!" It was Keela's grandmother. Her voice so loud, I thought her mouth was pressed to another phone.

"What's a cuss, Grandma?" Keela asked, laughing.

"Don't be a smart mouth, girlie." Her grandmother harrumphed again. "Yvonne's a cuss and she can stay her behind at her house with that crazy man of hers. How he gonna bring his narrow behind up in my house and show out like that?"

Keela said to me, "She acts like Noonie ain't never got drunk before and acted a fool. He did the same thing at Thanksgiving. She gets all upset, but it's funny as hell to everyone else."

"Sure hate I missed that." I sealed another box and moved it to the side.

"Yeah, I'm sure you are. What're you up to?"

"Packing. I leave on Saturday."

She paused before saying, "Wow! That soon? You're not playing, huh?"

"Once I make up my mind, I go ahead and do it before I start getting second thoughts."

"When I grow up, I want to be just like you. These past few months, I've had trouble picking out what I want to wear in the morning." She laughed.

"Listen, if you're not going to Jamaica with me, Keela, just say so. I'll understand if you don't want to."

Another pause. "It's not that I don't want to go. I don't see how I can. You know my mom would be heartbroken if she missed the birth of her first grand baby. I couldn't do that to her."

"Keela, you don't owe me any explanations." I tried to stop the flow of attitude, but couldn't. It flooded right through the phone.

"See, I knew you'd be mad."

I tossed a few paperback books in a box filled with bath towels. I wasn't in the mood to figure it out. "I'm not mad."

"You sound mad."

"I said I wasn't mad, Keela." Once again the words had come out too sharply. "I'm sorry. Guess I'm not much in the holiday spirit; but really, I'm not upset that you're not going. I'm disappointed and scared and nervous, but not upset. It would have been nice to have my best friend along for the ride."

"Oh, that's great, Kingston, make me feel even worse by piling on the guilt."

"Oh, stop it! I'm not trying to make you feel bad and you shouldn't; there's no need to. If my mother was still alive and I was about to have a baby, I'd want to be close to her, too. Women need their mothers at a time like this."

"Every day I have a question about something." Keela waited until her grandmother finished a sentence full of cuss words I'd never heard before. "Maybe Sharneesha will still go. Have you heard from her?"

"No, but I suspect she's gonna say the same thing as you."

"You'll be okay. Besides," she said, and I could see the smile spreading over her full lips. "You have Damon. Don't think I wasn't going to bring that up. Is he still tucked away in your bed? All naked and delicious?"

"Don't make me hang up on you, Keela," I warned; but the threat held no weight, and she knew it 'cause she pressed on.

"Well, is he?"

"He was only here for a minute. He left to visit some friends in Atlanta." The undisclosed information on our lovemaking session swung like a pendulum between us. But I wasn't saying a word.

"I bet he was happy to hear about you coming to Jamaica."

"I didn't tell him."

"He didn't ask?"

"I lied." I exhaled. "He asked me and I said I didn't know."

"But Kingston, he's gonna find out. You'll be living right down the street from the man!"

"Don't you think I know that? I just didn't want to deal with it right now."

"That's because you knew how happy he would be and the assumptions he would make."

"And I was right, seeing how he just showed his ass up on my doorstep."

"He loves you." Keela —always the hopeless romantic.

"Yeah, well, that's not my problem. So since you're not coming with me do you think you can handle some things for me here?"

"Like?"

"I'll call the movers and the real estate agent tomorrow and get everything set to sell the townhouse, and put my stuff in storage. I just need you to make sure everyone does what they're supposed to do."

"I can handle that. Mom's calling me. I bet she's gonna try to get me to make the spaghetti even though she knows I hate doing it."

"Stop grumbling and go make the damn spaghetti. I'll call you later." I clicked off the phone—still laughing.

And I thought my family was crazy.

Chapter 29

I was two hours behind on my packing schedule. Dismantling the desktop computer and printer and packing it in a box with all the hardware had taken longer than expected. It was due to be shipped tomorrow, so it would arrive in Jamaica shortly after I did. The doorbell rang and after glancing at the clock, I wondered, who could be ringing my bell at this time of night? It was only eight, but still. A surge of adrenaline shot through my body and my breath caught in anticipation. What if it was Damon again?

Cocoa trotted down the stairs ahead of me, anxious for an opportunity to escape the friendly confines of home. I peeked out the window and my heart sank. It wasn't him.

I pulled the door open anyway. "Hi, Sharneesha. Merry Christmas."

"Merry Christmas. I brought you a plate from my mom's house. Wasn't sure if you were going to cook or go somewhere for dinner."

"That was sweet." I accepted the plate. "I am a little hungry. Wanna come in?"

"Just for a sec."

"Where's Teeka?" I asked as Sharneesha stepped into the foyer.

"At her grandmother's house—her dad's mom. She's gonna spend the night there."

"I have something for her and I forgot to give it to her last night."

"You didn't have to do that."

"I know, but that's why they call it a gift, 'cause you don't have to do it."

"Teeka's going to be so excited." Sharneesha shifted from one foot to the other and looked down at the floor. "Listen, I've been thinking a lot about it and I'd like to go to Jamaica with you. You're right, there's nothing to keep me here. A judge took pity on me and I got an extension on the eviction, but only until after the New Year. My mother even said she'd put the airline ticket on her credit card, but I have to sign an I.O.U."

I clapped my hands with glee. "See, things are starting to work out and it's only going to get better. I am so happy. Keela wants to stay and have the baby here, so I'm really going to need your help."

"I'm excited. It'll be a new beginning for us. I'm not used to accepting help from other people." She gave a short laugh. "I didn't know it would be this hard."

"You're going to be helping me as much as I'm helping you. Besides, it's going to be fun and a wonderful opportunity for you and Teeka. Let me go write down my airline information so you can book on the same flight." I ran upstairs, put the plate in the refrigerator and grabbed Teeka's present before copying my travel details. Cocoa had returned from outside and was wagging her tail furiously as Sharneesha patted her behind the ears.

"Here you go. Let me know if you have any questions or if you need help with the ticket. It might be expensive since it's last minute. I think Teeka should be able to fly free, though."

"I think I'll be straight on the money, but I'll let you know. Seems like I have to keep saying thank you."

"Don't think of this as charity, Sharneesha because I'm definitely going to be working you."

"I'll let you know what happens with the flight," she said with a tiny smile.

"Keep thinking positive thoughts, Sharneesha and give Teeka a kiss for me." Sharneesha waved as she disappeared into her house.

"Come on, girl," I said to Cocoa. "Let's go eat." The news that Sharneesha and Teeka were going to Jamaica had lifted my spirits. Any concerns about her extracurricular activities had been pushed to the back of my mind; probably somebody with nothing better to do than stir up trouble, started the rumor.

I was headed to the kitchen when Damon's note and gift caught my eye again. I don't know why I was so scared to open it.

After picking up the note and holding it for a few minutes, I flipped it open. Damon's familiar scrawl jumped off the paper.

Christmas 2013

My dearest Kingston, I can't say much more than what I've already said. Looking at you while you were sleeping, beautiful and innocent, just re-confirmed what I already knew, that I'm hopelessly and utterly in love with you. And I know that you love me as well. I understand that you have doubts because of what happened before, so I'm leaving the next step up to you. I don't want you to feel as if I'm pressuring you. Have a happy New Year. I hope that it brings you everything your heart desires and more. I already know what I want. I've enclosed my heart for you to keep. It will always belong to you. Call me if you need anything.

Love, Damon

I laid the note in my lap and tore the wrapping paper from the box, pulling off the tiny top. Nestled in dark blue velvet was a thin silver necklace, on it a delicate, floating heart rimmed in diamonds. Running a finger along the outside of the heart, a tear rolled down my cheek. I was overwhelmed with sadness. I'd lost so many things in my life: my parents, my grandmother, Damon and Essence. Maybe life was offering me a second chance. Fate was dangling the brass ring within my reach, but I couldn't make myself grab it. Sighing, I went upstairs—my appetite gone. I clasped the chain around my neck and flopped down on the bed in the same spot where Damon and I had made love just hours earlier.

"Mama, tell me what to do," I whispered into the darkness. With the covers pulled up under my chin, I cried, soon falling into a troubled sleep.

Chapter 30

"Look, someone's at my door so I gotta go, but it's imperative that you have the house packed up by the first of the year. The real estate agent's putting the house on the market January 3rd so don't mess me up on this one, Leroy. Keela has your number, so she'll be the one to contact should you have any questions or problems." I hung up the phone, suddenly uncomfortable about my decision to go with a smaller, black owned mover versus a major moving company. The company, appropriately named "Leroy and Four Dudes," was already having issues, and I wouldn't be here to put out any fires.

Calm down, I told myself, things were going to be fine. Besides in less than eight hours, I'd be on a plane to Jamaica, sipping Rum Punch, and it would be out of my hands.

I stepped around an overstuffed garbage bag, two huge suitcases, and Cocoa's airline carrier to open the door.

When the outside light flipped on, it pushed back the darkness revealing a small figure huddled inside a coat that was too big. Teeka stared up at me with wide eyes, holding her purple Barbie doll backpack with shaking hands.

"Hi, Teeka." I leaned out the door and looked around. There was no sign of Sharneesha. Kneeling down in front of the little girl, I asked, "Where's your mother?"

Teeka shrugged and whimpered. The frigid wind blew her small braids against her cheeks; her nose was starting to run. "Come on, sweetie." Wrapping my arm around her shoulders, I drew her inside and sat her down on the bottom step. Cocoa stood guard as I shrugged on my coat and slipped into a pair of fur-lined boots. "Wait here," I instructed before walking outside. I made a quick trek around the courtyard with the wind pushing at me from every direction. I balled my hands up and stuffed them in my pockets. There was still no sign of Sharneesha or her beat-up Toyota Corolla. I circled back and stopped at her front door. An eviction notice was tacked to it. I tried the knob. Locked. Pressing my nose to the window, there were no signs of life inside. And no furniture. My head spun with confusion and the ball of anxiety snowballed inside as I trudged home.

"'Ingston, where'd mommy go?" Teeka asked as soon as I walked in, her voice breaking with tears. I rubbed my hands together, blowing hot air onto them before pulling off Teeka's mittens and warming her hands in mine. "I think maybe she had to run an errand or something, but we'll call her and find out when she's coming back, all right?"

Teeka laughed as Cocoa licked her on her cheek; tears magically drying up.

"No kissing, Cocoa, remember?" I shooed both of them up the steps.

"Are we going on a trip? Mommy said you were taking me on a trip."

"Yes, sweetie, we're all going on a trip," adding, "your mommy's going, too," even though my intuition was whispering that something was very wrong.

"Can I watch cartoons?"

"Of course you can. We'll watch them together."

"Is Cocoa gonna watch cartoons, too?" Teeka sat on the couch and Cocoa settled on the floor at her feet.

"She sure is. Watching cartoons is one of her favorite things." I clicked the television set and flipped through the channels. An old re-run of Disney's *The Proud Family* was on and Teeka perked up. I left her clapping at the characters' antics while I paced in the kitchen.

Sharneesha's home phone had been cut off and her cell phone was going straight to voice mail. I didn't bother to leave a message. I tried to quell the hysteria swelling inside like a tidal wave, and I dialed both of her numbers again—still nothing.

"Teeka, your mom didn't tell you where she was going?" I sat next to her on the couch.   She shook her head, gaze glued to the TV and her finger stuck in her mouth. When I realized she wasn't going to be any help, I went back downstairs. My nose was open like an investigative reporter. My plan: search the Barbie suitcase.

The contents of the suitcase were typical for a four-year-old girl—all pink and frilly. I picked through the t-shirts and denim shorts and found nothing. But buried beneath Teeka's nightgown was an envelope.

I slit it open and my stomach dropped to my feet. The items contained within: a birth certificate and passport, an electronic plane ticket and a letter giving Teeka permission to travel with me were self-explanatory. Also enclosed was a short note written on a sticky note:

"Kingston, please take Teeka with you. I can no longer take care of her. She's better off with you. I think you've figured out why. I will contact you when I know that you've arrived safely in Jamaica. Please tell Teeka I'm sorry. Sharneesha."

Fury surged through me. I started to dial Sharneesha's number again—just in case I had misdialed the other times. But what would I say? Where the hell do you get off abandoning your daughter on my doorstop? I dropped the phone back in its cradle. I had a bigger problem right now. How in God's name was I supposed to break the news to Teeka? That the one person who was supposed to love her more than anyone else in the world had kicked her to the curb? The abandoned little girl inside of me ached for Teeka, knowing how it felt to be alone in the world. At least my mother hadn't left me by choice.

My fists clenched as initial shock began to give way to anger and resentment. And who said I wanted to take on the full responsibility of someone else's child? Sure, I wanted to be a mother someday. But someday wasn't today and it certainly wasn't the day before I stepped off the edge of my world into the unknown.

The wheels started turning. Maybe there was somewhere to safely drop Teeka off, let somebody else deal with the situation, but that idea was dismissed as quickly as it had come. The chances were too great that Teeka would end up another victim of the child welfare system.

I walked back upstairs, when something else occurred to me. If Sharneesha really didn't think she could be a good mother, then maybe she was right. Things could turn out much worse if I did track down Sharneesha and force her to take back her own damn kid. The *Chicago Tribune* had run a story a few months back about a mother who jumped into Lake Michigan, taking her two young children with her. All three of them drowned. I didn't want a tragedy like that weighing on my conscience.

I sighed with frustration. Frustration worked up into a third wave of rage until I stepped onto the landing and looked into the face of sweetness and innocence, and a burst of maternal warmth surged inside of me. No way could I leave Teeka behind to face life on her own, to feel alone and unloved. Sharneesha was free to screw up her own life, God bless her, but I wouldn't let her screw up Teeka's.

Picking her up, her arms and legs wrapped tightly around me, I said, "Well, I talked to your mommy and she's not going on the trip with us after all."

"Why not, 'ingston?" Teeka wailed. "I want my Mommy to go, too!" Her legs kicking in protest as I carried her upstairs.

"I know you do." I gathered her close to me, bony knees angled against my rib cage. "But she's got this great new job and can't leave right away. But she'll join us as soon as she can." The lies came too easily, but I refused to feel bad; at least they were for a good cause.

"But who's going to take care of me? That's what mommies do." Teeka's eyes brightened with tears and her mouth quivered.

I kissed her on the forehead as she laid her cheek on my shoulder. All

I wanted to do was reassure her that she would be safe.

I tilted her head until she was looking at me, her eyes deep pools of confused sorrow. "I'm gonna take care of you. Sometimes mommies need a little bit of help. That's all." I grabbed an extra blanket from the closet, covering her with the thick fleece, pushing the edges underneath. "Tuck, tuck, night, night, everything's going to be all right," I sang the same way my mother did for me and she smiled before rolling over and facing the wall.

"'Ingston?"

"Yes?"

Brushing a hand across her burrowed forehead, tweaking an ear on the worn bunny she held in her death grip. She looked at me again, her eyes still blurry with confusion. "Where Mommy go?"

I avoided her eyes, didn't want to face the pain and disappointment that were surely reflected in them. So with no answer to give, I simply kissed her on the cheek and turned off the light. Wishes of sweet dreams caught in my throat, knowing that neither one of us would have any of those tonight.

When I checked on Teeka for the fifth time, she was humming softly from her nose and sucking a finger contentedly, as if there wasn't a care in the world. But for me, her words, "Where Mommy go?" still hung in the air and sleep was not coming easily.

"I'm going to take care of you," I reaffirmed in the darkness, but my words sounded dull and far away as if they belonged to someone else. The blackness caused my fears to scurry around like rats before light hits them.

Who was I fooling? I didn't know squat about taking care of a four-year-old and my certainty about not letting anything happen to her was wavering. Hell, I wasn't even doing that great of a job of not letting anything happen to me.

Padding to the bathroom, I turned on the light, leaving the door cracked so if she needed to, Teeka would be able to find the bathroom. When I returned to my room, I sank to the floor beside my bed, dropped my head into my hands and cried until I was too tired to care anymore. I cried for Mama Grace, I cried for Essence, but mostly I cried for myself, feeling weak and powerless to fight against the sense of betrayal seeping into my bones.

As much as I had tried to stave off the pain I felt at what Essence had done, it now swept me up like a level five hurricane, then tossed me back to the ground, just an empty shell. In its wake, I was faced with a startling realization: maybe it was so hard for me to forgive Damon because I had never forgiven my father for doing the same thing. The feelings of being ugly and unwanted had been worn like a pair of broken in shoes for most of my life.

So I cried for myself, but I wept for Teeka. It took a long time for sleep to claim me. When it did, it was restless and washed black, the color of pain.

Chapter 31

"Bring your suitcase back here, Teeka," I said, leading the little girl to the same room that I slept in when I was her age. "This is going to be your bedroom," I whispered, choking back tears as a hesitant smile lit across her face. My own luggage waited down the hall in Mama Grace's room. As weird as it felt, my grandmother's room was now mine.

"And my mommy can sleep here, too, when she comes." With an earnest look on her face, Teeka touched the bed, pushing at the squares on the patchwork quilt almost as if she didn't believe it was real.

"Yes, she can," I lied, running my hand over her rainbow colored barrettes. She gazed around with wide eyes, twirling a braid with her finger. Everything to her was new and magical—from the plane ride to her new home in this tropical paradise. She was curious about it all; the strange accent, the odd smells, and the interesting people.

But the most fabulous thing of all was her new Auntie Bianca. I had called ahead and warned my cousin that I wouldn't be arriving alone. With nothing more to go on than that, Bianca's jaw dropped when I showed up with my motley crew of two—a four-legged animal and a four-year-old girl.

She recovered nicely though, hugging first me, then Teeka, patting Cocoa on the head. On the way home, Bianca bought Teeka an ice cream cone and promised her a manicure complete with pink polish. That was all it took. Teeka was a fan for life.

When I flopped onto the couch in the front room, Bianca crossed her eyes and stuck out her tongue. "Seems like things have been jumping in your life." Tossing her head toward the window—where Teeka was outside playing with Cocoa and Toy—her corkscrewed curls of hair dancing around her shoulders.

Between the barks and peels of laughter, I wasn't concerned about Teeka overhearing me, but I lowered my voice anyway. "Teeka's mother was my next door neighbor. She was having some problems, lost her job, was about to be evicted, really going through a rough time. To help her out, I suggested that she come with me and she agreed; but then last night, she just dropped Teeka off on my doorstep and disappeared. I couldn't just leave her."

Bianca glanced through the window again. "Of course, you couldn't. You're not that kind of person. How well did you know Teeka's mother?"

"Please," I said, snorting. "I didn't know her at all. We lived next door to each other for almost a year, but never talked. It was just hi-and-bye until a few days ago." I crossed my arms, the corners of my mouth drawn down into a sneer. "It blows my mind that a woman could carry a baby for nine months, feel life moving inside of her body, and then leave her with a virtual stranger."

At that, Bianca sat up, her face screwed up with intensity. "I don't understand that either, but I guess some women are just not fit to be mothers. Teeka's mother proves that." She relaxed against the covers with a disgusted humph. "Have you figured out what you're gonna do?"

"Keep her," I said with more certainty than I had felt about anything in a long time. "I can't bear the thought of her alone in the world. There are too many abandoned babies already. I mean, look at her, who wouldn't want to have her as a daughter?"

Teeka's face was lit up with joy, while playing tag with the dogs, peeking from behind one tree before running and hiding behind the next one.

"She's definitely a cutie. It's going to be a lot of work, though. Being a mother isn't as easy as it looks."

"Like you would know." Laughing, I flicked a piece of lint off my leg. "Trust me, we're going to have our challenges. She's already told me at least ten times that I'm not her real mother so she doesn't have to listen to me, and I thought we were going to have to restrain her when it was time to board the plane. She didn't want to leave without her mother and who can blame her? I'd feel the same way." Shaking my head, I watched her through the window. "She can throw quite the little attitude when she wants to, but I figure I can outlast her," I said, then smiled. "Thanks for being so nice to her. I don't want her to feel uncomfortable at all, and you put her at ease right away."

Never one to accept a compliment well, Bianca waved plum-pink colored fingernails in the air. "It's nothing."

"Well, it means everything to me. Family means everything to me. Are you planning on hanging out here for awhile?"

"Yeah, I'll stick around for a few days. Help you get situated. When do you meet with the lawyer?"

"I haven't called him yet, but I want to get things underway as soon as possible. If I'm here to do good, then I want to get to it before I change my mind. Plus, I want him to look into how I can legally protect us from Teeka's wishy-washy mother. I'm not sure how things work now that we're in Jamaica. But I found out that Teeka's father signed away all his legal rights when she was born."

"Are you thinking about adoption?"

I nodded hard. "Definitely. I think that's the only way to ensure that Teeka is going to have some stability in her life. But I'm doing it for myself, too. I'm already bonding with her and I definitely don't want to set myself up for heartbreak."

"Nothing's foolproof," Bianca pointed out.

"I know, but I don't want to be a straight-up fool either."

"I hear ya'." Bianca fussed with a curl before looking at me slyly. "By the way, did you get a surprise visitor?"

I threw her a suspicious look, then rolled my eyes. "Did you have something to do with that? You gave Damon my address in Chicago without telling me, didn't you?"

She smiled and shrugged her shoulders.

"Thanks," I snapped, then took a deep breath and let it go. No use in getting upset. Raising Teeka and running both Mama Grace's estate and MMG's urban division were the most important things and I had to stay focused. I didn't have time to run up after some man, especially Damon.

I walked over to the window to check on Teeka. She had moved Papa's chess table to the middle of the verandah and had set it with pale blue plastic dishes that Queenie had given her. Any minute I expected to see the dogs with teacups in their paws sitting daintily at Teeka's tea party. I parted the curtain. "How about some fruit punch, Teeka?"

She said something to the dogs before skipping inside. I wiped the dirt from her knees and headed to the kitchen.

"Bianca, are you thirsty, too?" I called.

"I'd sell one of my breasts for a glass of Queenie's fruit punch." In anticipation of her day off tomorrow, Queenie had stocked the pantry and the refrigerator with enough food to last a month.

"We wouldn't want you to go to extremes," I replied, pouring three glasses of the frothy concoction, adding a plate of cookies to the middle of the table.

Bianca took a long swig, then wiped her mouth with the back of her hand. "Don't I get some cookies, too?"

I almost choked on a mouthful of punch. After clearing my throat, I asked, "Anything interesting going on with family? I know there's gotta be some juicy rumor ready to be spread around."

Bianca giggled. "Uncle Winston's still so mad about this whole estate thing, he's practically peeing in his pants. Aunt Bea said he was thinking about suing the estate."

"What the hell is wrong with him?" I shoved my fists into my hips. "He's always starting some sh. . ." Teeka blinked at me, mouth barely able to contain the three cookies she had crammed in it. "Some stuff. Doesn't he realize that all of this mess takes away from Mama Grace's memory?"

"I think there's still some confusion about where all the money's going. They, Uncle Winston mainly, think because you're running the estate that Mama Grace's fortune," exaggerated quotes made in the air when she said fortune as if a million dollars were no big deal at all, "is being deposited directly into your pockets. He's not going to make too much noise, though. Aunt Bea said once he found out how much the lawyer's fees were going to run him, he abandoned that idea. Plus, Auntie Dawn said she'll divorce him if he proceeded with the case."

My mouth popped open. "What? She actually took a stand?"

"Gave him an ultimatum and everything. Aunt Bea said the bastard backed down so fast. I'd have paid good money to have seen that one."

"Good, I'm too tired for a fight."

"Well, I hope you're not too tired for a party, 'cause that's what we're going to have." Bianca held up a finger when I started to protest. "Wait, just hear me out. I've thought this whole thing through. We can have food, music, and games for the kids. It'll be great." Bianca waved her hands enthusiastically, a determined look in her eyes. "Can you think of a better way to introduce Mama Grace's estate to the community than to hold a carnival or how do you say it in the states? A block party?"

"Who's going to pay for it?"

"It'll be exciting to write your first official check from Mama Grace's estate fund, doncha' think?"

"Bianca …"

"Don't worry, just leave it to me." She nodded before wrinkling her nose and smiling at me. "I'm gonna take care of everything."

I rolled my eyes. "That's *exactly* what I'm worried about."

Uncle Winston crossed one leg over the other, pulling long and hard on a Kool cigarette. The sun had long since risen and now bounced off the layer of Soft Sheen that covered his grayed head.

It was one week later and Queenie had polished the verandah the day before as a part of the pre-carnival cleanup.

The "block party" had turned into an extravaganza of enormous proportions, starting before noon and lasting until the wee hours of the morning. Bianca had strewn paper lanterns, steamers, and balloons across the entire block. The entire community turned out in their Sunday best and devoured an abundance of food and drinks and the festivities had endured despite the persistent swarm of mosquitoes and smoldering heat. Games were the same as we used to play in the states, but with far more interesting names like: Brown Girl in the Ring, Dandy Shandy, and Stucky Ketchy.

We were all sluggish. Cocoa was curled up on the step next to me, snoozing off and on, both of us content to watch the human tug of war between my uncle and the lawyer. Even Bianca was awake, hovering nearby while picking gold tinsel from an overgrown bush. Teeka was the only one granted a reprieve. Under the pretense of taking a nap, she was jumping on the small wire framed bed, squeaks and squeals meshing together.

Mr. Bartlett had scheduled the meeting with me. I had no idea how Uncle Winston found out about it, but the frown deepening the lines on the weathered face of Mama Grace's attorney showed he was less than pleased.

And he almost said as much when Uncle Winston met him at the gate, then cornered him on the verandah. Uncle Winston wasn't all that happy either; he slumped back in the wicker chair with a groan of resignation as Mr. Bartlett once again reviewed the finer points of Mama Grace's will. His one hundred dollars-an-hour attorney fees had whisked through the five hundred dollars retainer and still hadn't been able to find a loophole that would make Uncle Winston the rich man he thought he deserved to be.

So, after fielding endless questions, Mr. Bartlett was prepared to cut a check just so Uncle Winston would go away. But of course, he couldn't do that without my approval.

That was a delicious thought. I savored it, allowing a few minutes of silence to pass. Just when I thought Uncle Winston was good and ready to burst, I gave the official nod.

Mr. Bartlett yanked his glasses from his long nose and wiped them with his pinstriped tie, amidst a promise that the check would be in the mail first thing in the morning. Finally, in a finely tuned impervious tone, he asked, "If we're done, sir?"

Uncle Winston stubbed his cigarette with two fingers, ashes falling carelessly to the ground. Queenie would not be happy. After pulling his baseball cap low on his forehead, and giving Mr. Bartlett a final once over, he hopped in his pick-up truck and drove away.

"I don't envy you," Bianca whispered as I followed Mr. Bartlett inside. Luckily, our business was dispensed in less than an hour and he was on his way, a neat stack of paper requiring my review and signature left on the dining room table.

I pushed them to the side and powered up my laptop. Just as I had suspected, there were at least five e-mails from Jonetta that needed my attention, one from Keela. I opened that one first. I was halfway through Keela's long list of pregnancy complaints when Bianca strolled into the dining room with Teeka. They both looked like sunflowers, Teeka in a gathered yellow sundress and Bianca in yellow shorts and matching halter-top.

"Wanna walk to the market with us?" she asked, adjusting the band of her top so it covered more of her belly.

"If you have to keep pulling on it, then it's probably too small," I muttered, opening up an e-mail attachment that contained the budget projections that Jonetta had inserted into a spreadsheet.

Bianca rolled her eyes, making Teeka laugh.

The invitation was tempting, but someone had to be responsible. I had someone else to worry about besides myself.

"Don't be a sourpuss," Bianca said.

"I've got work to do." I didn't even spare her a glance, instead I skimmed through the numbers; pleased with what I saw. Everything seemed to be on target for an early spring album release. I couldn't wait to tell Scooby.

I grinned at Teeka. "Next time," I said, patting her cheek. "Just bring me back some candy, a chocolate bar or something. I've been craving something sweet all day."

"The need for chocolate has been directly linked to the lack of S-E-X," Bianca spelled for Teeka's benefit.

"Be good, sweetie." Ignoring my cousin, I pulled Teeka in for a hug, not at all discouraged by her body's sudden stiffness. "You're in charge of picking out a candy bar for me, okay?" I pulled twenty Jamaican dollars from my pocket and pressed them into her hand.

"Okay, 'Ingston." She pulled at Bianca's hand. I smoothed some of her hair back into her ponytail and then, they were gone.

I turned to the stack of papers that Mr. Bartlett had left. I knew the majority of it contained information about the adoption. Thumbing through the thick stack, the light fan of air hit my face. I sighed and settled more comfortably into my chair. This could take awhile.

Chapter 32

A plate clattered to the ground followed by a squeal and the sweetly whispered promise of a quiet morning was broken. A whirlwind consisting of Teeka, Cocoa, and Toy swept into the tiny bathroom. Queenie dashed behind them, a dishtowel whooshing through the air as she chased the two dogs from the house, her carefully spoken English flying out the door with them.

"Pickney and dawgs dem' eatin' from de' dayum dinner table. Jeesum' Peeze'! Who ever 'eard of such a ting? Dawgs eatin' in de' kitchen," she exclaimed in disbelief. "Lawdamercy! Child's gwan' make me lose muh religion." The rag sliced again before she looked at Teeka, shook her head, then tisked all the way back to the kitchen, her sturdy legs shaking.

Teeka stuck her tongue out at Queenie's retreating figure before barreling into my chest, her body quivering with sobs. "Don't let Queenie catch you doing that," I chastised, even as my hand flew to cover my laughter. Shampoo ran close to my eyes as I grabbed the nearest towel and wrapped it around my hair before guiding Teeka to the side of the chipped pedestal bathtub, it groaned beneath both our weights.

Queenie had long since lost the patience needed for a four-year-old under foot. I don't think I ever had it. But I was learning.

"Teeka?" I gently peeled her away, and tilted her chin up.

"But they were hungry and my mommy taught me to share," she whined, her words rushed together. "I was sharing with Cocoa and Toy, 'Ingston. That's all." She pushed her face back into my chest. "Queenie's just mean and I don't like her. Neither would my momma."

I sighed, wiping her running nose. The mentions of her mother were coming fewer and farther between, but they still hit me like fat drops of water from a slowing faucet. Understanding Teeka's confusion and pain was not hard, loving her through it was the challenging part. But in her round dimpled face, I saw myself, I saw Joanne and every other little girl who had been left by a parent, and that was enough to recharge my determination to stick it out. My words were firm, softened with a slight smile. "I know, sweetie, and your mom's absolutely right. You should share with others, but dogs are not allowed to eat from the table. You can help us put out their food in the mornings, but you need to eat your own breakfast and let them eat theirs." My smile deepened. "And mind Queenie. No more sticking your tongue out behind her back. I'm sure your mom also told you about listening to others and being nice, right?" My eyebrows remained raised until she nodded grudgingly, but her lip shot so far out I was afraid she might trip over it. "Now go back and finish eating your food." Teeka rolled her eyes and stomped all the way to the kitchen, her bare feet slapping against the hardwood floor.

I fought the urge to yank her back and give her one of those time-outs child experts seemed so fond of. It had been almost a week since our arrival and neither Teeka's attitude nor my mood had improved. This mother thing definitely took some getting used too.

I towel dried my hair, releasing fragrances of strawberry and citrus. I was determined to enjoy a few minutes of peace with a novel and cup of coffee on the verandah before Teeka finished her breakfast. She was already sitting at the kitchen table, legs swinging, waiting for the lumps to be beaten out of the batter. Queenie had resigned herself to making pancakes and sausage for breakfast, and sometimes lunch, almost every day depending on which way Teeka's wind was blowing.

I laughed softly, not seeing the shadow stretching across the burgundy carpet until it was too late.

"Hey, slow down." Damon's hands reached out to steady me, a warmth flowed from his body to mine. "Where's the fire?"

"Ohmygosh!" I pressed my hand to my chest and took a few quick breaths to quiet my thudding heart. "Damon, you scared the mess outta me."

He threw his head back and laughed. I batted away his lingering hands, snatched the towel from my head and tried to work my damp clumps of hair into something halfway presentable.

Sunglasses fitted his face, an easy smile graced his lips, and a multi-colored beach ball was hooked under his arm. "Thought you could sneak back into town without me finding out?" Damon pulled his lips back and chucked my chin with his finger. "I knew the minute your sexy butt stepped foot on the island." Damon's eyes traveled past my face taking in my too small tank top and unrestrained breasts that pushed at it. A warm white oozing pleasure spread through me at the appreciation that shone in Damon's eyes.

"Just showing up is becoming a bad habit for you," I said with my hands resting on my waist, determined not to shrink beneath his gaze. My French-manicured toes curled into the soles of my tan beaded flip-flops to keep from flying up and kicking him.

The eyelet curtains that dissected the two front windows lifted and rippled from the moist mid-morning breeze. A slick humidity coated the city and I pressed the edges of the towel against the dampness sliding down my forehead.

Damon's smile broadened, non-plussed. He took a step back. "Do you remember my Aunt Olivia?" he asked and it was only then that I noticed the tiny woman at his side. Her shimmery, pale pink lips—the color of well-chewed bubble gum—parted to reveal a gap between her two front teeth. Subtle shades of gray and silver were scattered throughout her short, feathered haircut. Thick brown age spots covered her face like continents on a map. Her green floral culottes swayed against her skinny, pecan-colored legs.

"Of course. How are you, Aunt Olivia?" I leaned down for a jasmine scented hug, pulling away with the fragrance still clinging to me.

"Please just call me Olivia. I've been trying to get Damon to drop the aunt for years. Makes me feel too old." Her voice was wispy, full of extra breath as she shoved a foil covered Bundt cake into my hands. "Sorry, I wasn't able to make it to your grandmother's funeral. I couldn't get a ride in from Hope Bay. The roads were rained out that day, y'know?"

How could I forget? It was my grandmother's funeral. Every minute detail of it had been branded into my memory. That's what I wanted to say, but I nodded politely. I spied the book and cup waiting for me out of the corner of my eye. The window of opportunity for a few moments of peace had just been slammed shut.

With a resigned sigh, I plastered a bright smile on my face and ushered them both inside. I picked up some of Teeka's toys—a neon-colored snail that counted out loud and her book, *Walter the Farting Dog*—from the sofa and chairs, clearing space so they could sit. As I sat the cake on the dining room table, I cut my eyes at Damon with a look that said, I'll be talking to you later. I wanted him to know that Olivia's presence was the only thing keeping me on my best behavior.

"So what brings you this way?" I said more to her than to Damon, but he responded with excitement.

"We're on our way to the beach and thought you might like to go. Let me see you in a bikini." Damon waggled his eyebrows, causing Olivia to titter and clutch her handbag to her chest, as if that would keep the laughter from spilling out of her bosom.

"Is that why you're wearing those ridiculous swimming trunks?"

"You don't like them?" Damon looked down and seemed to really take notice of the colorful cargo shorts. "I guess they do look like they were finger-painted by a group of one-year olds. But since my Aunt Olivia gave them to me as a present, they hold a special meaning for me."

Olivia shrugged and studied the shorts with an intense gaze, adding matter-of-factly, "I think they bring out the color in his eyes." Inwardly, I groaned. Maybe if I counted to three, the floor would swallow me up.

"Sooooo," Damon continued, his voice resonating like a drill sergeant rallying his troops. "The boats come in at eleven o'clock; so if we want to see them, we need to get a move on."

Teeka was still in the back room eating, her knife and fork clanking against the plate as she made mincemeat of her stack of pancakes. A day beneath the sun, breathing fresh ocean air would be a welcome change from the smog and dirt of the city. I knew that Teeka would love a day at the beach. But my day had already been scheduled.

"Today's not good for me. I'm supposed to meet with the lawyer to discuss the estate. Studio time has to be scheduled, along with a number of other things. I do have a record label to run as well." I narrowed my eyes. "Maybe next time you could give me a little notice."

"Awww, come on! You can meet with your lawyer anytime. As far as that other stuff is concerned, big time record label execs deserve a day off, too, right?" Crossing the room to sit next to me, he placed a hand on my thigh. "Think about it: the sun beaming down on your face, water rushing against your toes, crispy fried fish, sweet bammy, not to mention the company."

Damon spread his arms wide while Olivia fluttered her hands and crossed her legs at the ankles. "He's got a point, Kingston. No sense in being cooped up in this house all day. Besides, I'd like to spend some time with you." She wrinkled her nose as if something smelled funny. "Y'know, have some girl talk."

I blew a long stream of breath, sending a damp piece of hair up only to fall back over my eye. I knew Damon was not going to accept no for an answer. "I'm not by myself," I said, the words had barely tripped off my tongue when Teeka walked back into the room, her lip still jutted out, the smell of melted butter and syrup following her like a fragrant cloud.

Damon's charm went into overdrive. "I heard there was a new princess in town, but no one told me how pretty you were." Teeka stuck her finger in her mouth and ducked behind my leg, snaking out every few seconds, staring at Damon with a mixture of curiosity and admiration. I suspected it was the same expression I wore on my six-year-old face when I first laid eyes on him.

Damon's eyes flashed as he knelt in front of her. "What's your name?"

"Teeka."

"Princess Teeka." Her name slipped off Damon's tongue as sweet as candy. "It's nice to meet you." He extended his hand and she shook it like royalty before giggling and ducking again.

"Teeka, this is Mr. Whitfield. He's a doctor and lives down the street. And this is his Aunt Olivia."

"Hi, sugah'," Olivia clucked. "Call me Ti-Ti and just call him Damon. None of that Mr. Whitfield, Aunt Olivia stuff, okay, precious?" She waggled her bejeweled fingers, cooed some more, and blew pink bubblicious kisses.

Damon slanted his head and bestowed Teeka with yet another smile before rubbing his chin thoughtfully, and saying, "So, Princess Teeka, I'm having a little bit of a problem here and I think that you are the only person in the world that can help me with it. Aunt Olivia …"

Olivia cleared her throat. "Ti-Ti."

"I'm sorry, Ti-Ti and I are going to the beach today and we'd really like for you and Kingston to go with us. Would you like to go to the beach?"

Teeka nodded, sucking her fingers in earnest. Then, her eyes lit up until they beamed like the Fourth of July. She tugged on my shorts, gently at first then harder and harder as the magnitude of a day at the beach and all that that entailed weighed in on her.

My eyes darted between Teeka and Damon, amazed at how fast the tag team routine had come together.

"But she says she's too busy to go." Damon frowned and Teeka frowned right along with him. "So we have to convince her that going to the beach is a great way to spend the day. Any ideas on how we can do that?"

Teeka opened her eyes wide and stopped sucking as if the last thing she had expected was to be asked to participate in the discussion. Damon scratched his head, then suddenly snapped his fingers.

"I say we tickle her 'til she pees on herself," Damon said and pounced, wrestling me to the ground, his fingers digging into my ribcage.

The beach ball flew through the air, ricocheted off Olivia's forehead and knocked a picture crooked. Teeka dropped to her knees giggling and clapping.

Damon's dreads hung in my face, teasing my nose and I reached up and pulled on one—hard.

"Ouch! Fighting dirty?" he asked, rubbing the sore spot. The tickling began again and soon I was laughing so hard my bladder pressed down heavily.

"Okay, okay! I give, I give!" I sat up holding my side. "You win. We'll spend the day at the beach."

Damon whooped and hollered, holding his hand up for a high five.

Teeka slapped his palm as he grabbed me around my waist, pulling me into his side for a hug. The soft, lingering kiss that came next was as natural as breathing with the exception of Olivia eagle-eyeing us the whole time.

Damon stood, then pulled me to my feet. With my hand tucked under his arm, he said, "Then, let's go." And half an hour later, we all piled into Damon's gold Land Cruiser and backed out of the driveway, tires crunching on the gravel.

I thought of my ridiculously small white bikini and wondered if it had been a good choice. Knowing if I held it up against Teeka's pink striped two-piece, hers might be bigger.

I rolled down the window until the struggling air conditioner kicked in, and listened to the rhythmic sounds of our beach bags bouncing merrily beside a small blue cooler. "What's in the cooler?" I asked.

"Red Stripe."

"Don't they sell Red Stripe at the beach?"

"Only in plastic cups."

"And?"

"No self-respecting Red Stripe lover would drink it out of a plastic cup. Ruins the taste. Gotta be in a bottle."

I formed the word "Oh" with my lips and settled back in my seat. Who knew there was a philosophy behind drinking beer?

Damon flipped on a local reggae station and Chaka Demus and Pliers bolted from the speakers, then danced their way through the car.

It was just as hot as it was bright, but that didn't slow down the activity in the streets. A group of young boys kicked around a battered football in the schoolyard, where more reggae music blared from a nearby system. Children skipped in and out of houses while women swept dirt from the sidewalks into the street with put-together brooms that were barely staying put together.

I pointed out the goats to Teeka who giggled behind her hand, then stuck her head out the window and made baaing sounds. Damon stopped at the end of the street to allow a colorful mixture of people and animals to cross.

"Everything crisp, doc?" asked a man before he bobbed in front of the truck and headed up the opposite side of the street.

Damon waved a hand. "As crisp as a new dollar bill."

We continued through the maze of narrow streets, Damon occasionally acknowledging someone he knew, while I endured the whistles from male passersby, all to Olivia's amusement.

"Which beach are we going to?" I yelled over the noise of the rumbling engine.

"Hellshire."

Memories of spending time with my grandfather and my mother at the beach made me smile. "I haven't been there since I was about twelve."

"Then this should be a treat." He winked, the simple gesture causing flames of desire to shoot through the core of my body, but my eyes narrowed anyway.

I could tell Damon was up to something. His words seemed to hold some sort of double meaning.

Thirty miles southwest of Kingston lay the white sandy beaches of Hellshire. As we traveled Garvey Drive, the inner city congestion and the rows of tenement blocks began to thin. We skirted the Kingston Freezone and crossed the causeway. To the right, across the Hunts Bay Lagoon, lie Caymanas Park Racetrack and the mouth of the Rio Cobre at Passage Fort. This was the seaport for the ancient capital of Spanish Town and the place where the British force landed to capture the island in 1655.

Next, Damon pointed out the historic Fort Augusta that sat on the left.

"It's now a women's prison. They keep drug runners, prostitutes, and thieves there; maybe even a murderer or two. All sorts of nasty women," Aunt Olivia whispered from the backseat, her hands over Teeka's ears.

Acres of rusting roofs of corrugated metal sheets that slanted atop huts whizzed by. The grim structures were crowded on top of each other with a few feet of ground in front, fenced with wire, tin sheets, or rotting wood. Some had yards where children played. Others were patches of a dying garden, now overgrown with weeds, that used to burst with yams and eddoes once grown for subsistence. Round shaped women hauled buckets of sloshing water with fat babies toddling after them.

"We're almost there," Damon shouted. Minutes later, we turned left at the next roundabout and the prevailing smell of fish along with the collection of oversized umbrellas and parked cars confirmed that we'd arrived.

As the car slowed, Damon said, "It's about the only nice beach left in Jamaica that's still owned by Jamaicans. Isn't that right, Auntie?"

Olivia gave a serious nod as Damon pulled into a parking space.

We unpacked the car before Teeka and I headed to the changing rooms.

When we emerged, clad in cover-ups and jeweled flip-flops, Damon had already quarantined a section of the beach guarded fiercely by Olivia. He, however, was nowhere in sight. I looked around as memories of lazy days, jelly sandwiches wrapped in wax paper, and my mother's carefree grins assaulted me from every which way.

The government's many efforts to give the beach a facelift that would leave it resembling other more commercial beaches hadn't happened. Hellshire residents had resisted, so there was still a certain roughness to the beach that only added to its charm.

Wood shack structures selling food dotted the beach mixed with boats anchored to decaying docks and cars that no longer ran and had been long forgotten. Men with bare feet, soles hardened from years of working in or by the water, skinned fish before packing them in ice. A thick woman pulled up her skirt and danced in the water to the cheers of the men behind the bar before dropping her scarf-covered head shyly.

Tourists in big straw hats and over-priced sunglasses took pictures and pointed with their children. They treated the island like their playground and as a result would be nursing inches of peeling skin when they returned home.

Olivia was perched on a lounger, slathering her hairy forearms with thick white sunblock, her nose already dotted with the crème.

"Come let Ti-Ti rub some on your arms," she said to Teeka as I shrugged out of my cover up and settled on a matching lounger that was missing more than its share of slats. Struggling to get comfortable, I pulled a book from my bag.

I was only a couple of pages in when Teeka tapped me on the shoulder, her skin slick from coconut oil. "I wanna get in the water 'Ingston."

"Let's wait until Damon gets back."

Teeka muttered something under her breath that I ignored. I pulled out a pail and shovel, instructing, "make a sand castle," while trying to hold on to what was left of my patience.

"Where is he anyway?" I asked, as Teeka plopped beside me, almost toppling us both and sending the sand in her scooper flying. I brushed some from her chunky thighs before tending to my own.

Olivia's eyes were closed and covered by a white sun visor.. "To get some fried fish and bammy. Hopefully, they have some festival today. They don't always have it. You'll like festival, Teeka." She opened one eye and glanced around. "Here he comes."

We all looked up to see Damon negotiating the hot sand with bare feet and hands full of flimsy paper plates. His shirt had been removed and Olivia had obviously attacked him with sun block as well. His well-defined chest glistened like that of a body builder.

"Food is served," he said, depositing his bounty on a small red plastic table designed more for show than use. "We're in luck, Auntie, they did have festival."

Olivia clapped like a schoolgirl and peeked under the napkins stained brown with grease.

Then his eyes rested on me. Damon whistled, his caressing gaze traveling the length of my body before wandering back—taking in every naked inch—to capture my eyes. "You better be glad we're in mixed company, girl," he said. "So I can't say what I really want to. But don't worry, I'll tell you all about it later."

I blushed, but was too proud to cover up.

"You look good," he finished, capturing me in his spell for a few magical seconds before it dawned on me that we were not alone.

"Are you hungry, Teeka?" I asked, inhaling the delicious tapestry of fat, cholesterol and calories, and ignoring Damon.

"I wanna go swimming, "Ingston," she repeated; her lips poked out.

"Well, if that's what Princess Teeka wants, then that's what Princess Teeka gets."

"I'm not even sure she can swim, Damon. She's only four." The protests rose in my throat like bitter bile. Tears threatened as the colors of Teeka's swimsuit blurred into colors from a time long gone. I inhaled as an overwhelming anxiety squeezed my heart. It was too much like before, I realized, with Teeka twirling, just as Joanne had before we'd run unknowingly into the river. If it happened once, it could happen again and I shook my head. Just as I was about to verbally refuse, and lock Teeka safely in my arms forever, Damon placed a calming hand on my shoulder.

"It's okay. I'll be with her." Despite my continued hesitation, he scooped Teeka up, making her laugh as he ran toward the water. She waved happily, Damon whispering in her ear.

"Eat something." Olivia handed me a paper plate. "Try not to worry."

"She just reminded me so much of Joanne."

Olivia's sigh of sympathy was drowned out by Teeka's gleeful cries.

I broke off a piece of fish and shoved it in my mouth while she piled her plate high with some of everything, dousing it all with hot sauce. For a space of time, we ate in silence before Olivia pulled out a bottle of beer and offered it to me. I shook my head and plucked a bottle of grapefruit soda from the cooler. I propped my book open with one hand.

Olivia took a long swig of Red Stripe. "I'm not going to beat around the bush, Kingston. Of course I don't look it, but I'm much too old for that." She looked at me long and hard, chewing slowly until her mouth was empty. "I want to know what your intentions are with my nephew."

It took a minute before her words were absorbed, understood. I sputtered on my drink and for the second time, almost toppled out of my beach chair with laughter. "You want to know my intentions?"

Aunt Olivia pursed her lips as if my question offended her. "Well, I think I have the right to know. I practically raised that boy out there and I'm pretty much all the family he has left. His heart has seen enough heartache to last a lifetime. So I don't want to see any more piled on by the likes of you."

Something inside me flared at the accusatory tone in her voice. I worked at overlooking it, chalking it up to good intentions.

"Damon's a big boy," I said, closing my novel so I could focus on Teeka and Damon playing tag with the ocean, tempting and teasing the incoming tide. It was a better option than seething at Olivia.

As Teeka smacked her tiny hand against the water and watched the spray, a swell of nostalgia pushed through me. I couldn't get over it. Teeka reminded me so much of Joanne with her courage and spunk.

Damon waved reassuringly and I relaxed. But the sense of peace was cut short when Olivia hurled her empty plate into a nearby trashcan.

"I know Damon's a big boy," Olivia snapped, diverting my attention back to her.

I leveled her with a look that forced her retreat.

She placed her hand across her chest and took a few breaths. "I'm worried about him, that's all. Now he was wrong all them years ago. He handled things poorly." My sharp intake of breath hardly gave her pause. "Yes, he told me about it and I gave him a stern talking to, let me tell you. He was raised to be more of a gentleman. But it all stems back to not knowing his parents and losing Joanne at such a young age. Poor boy doesn't know how to be happy, that's what I think. Having something of his own scares him half to death."

"So if you know what happened, why are you lecturing me? Damon's the one that you should be talking to."

"I'm sorry, pumpkin. I guess I get passionate when it comes to Damon. Like I said, it's like he's my own child." As her eyes watered, I softened and reached over, pressing her hand with mine.

My words were just as gentle. "I have no intention of hurting Damon. I love him as much as you do." The admission shocked her as much as it did me and that shock spread over her face like a wildfire.

"That's a relief to know," she said before reclining again. "Just wanted you to understand how everything's affected him and maybe why he acted the way he did."

I nodded my understanding and gave myself over to the delicious feeling of loving Damon.

Sitting on the beach watching him and Teeka jumping through the white-kissed waves, splashing and laughing in an ocean that stretched to the end of the earth, it was way too easy to lay back and pretend that the three of us were a family. As I closed my eyes, I held that fantasy tight. I wanted to enjoy it as long as possible.

When the excited sound of Olivia's voice woke me, I was disoriented. For a second, I hadn't realized that I'd fallen asleep. Her lips moved and I knew that she was saying something. In the time that it took for me to sit up, I knew something was terribly wrong.

I followed her frantically pointing finger and heard the shouts that echoed from all directions and my body froze. Teeka was no longer in view. Damon was diving in and out of the ocean surrounded by a crowd of onlookers, but there was no sight of Teeka. I dropped to my knees, only slightly aware of the sand cutting into my skin. Time slowed as Damon sliced through the water. He went under for the third time and came up holding Teeka's small body.

My heart jump-started, then began racing, the thud in my ears blocking out any other noise.

I ran to meet them as Damon trudged up the beach before laying Teeka on a towel, set there by a stranger. I watched as Damon bent over Teeka and administered mouth-to-mouth resuscitation until she coughed up a lungful of saltwater. But I was no longer in the here and now; I was trapped by the memory of a rushing river and a lifeless girl.

He sat Teeka up gently and patted her back until her body was no longer shaking, then picked her up, depositing her into my waiting arms. "It's not like Joanne, Kingston. Teeka's going to be fine. She's alive," he said, his voice raspy from the saltwater. "It's Teeka. Not Joanne. Teeka." He repeated her name until the haze that surrounded me, cleared.

Finally, I was able to breathe.

And as I stroked the soft slope of Teeka's face, the rest of the world faded away. I smoothed the hair that had unraveled from her barrettes and kissed her forehead, tasting the ocean on my lips. As the sirens of the ambulance wailed closer, her eyes fluttered open and she jerked again. "It's okay, sweetie. I've got you. I've got you." I placed kisses all over her face until a barely visible smile lifted the corners of her mouth. When I bent down and put my lips against her ear, my words were merely a whisper, "See, Teeka, I told you I wouldn't let anything happen to you."

As her heart beat against mine, a white bird swooped low, wings casting long shadows on the beach. The small echo of Joanne's voice—bringing messages of friendship that endured despite death—carried over the rush of the waves.

"I love you, too," I replied.

Chapter 33

It was garbage day and the thick smell of decaying trash saturated the entire block.

"Kingston, just go pee on the stick, already." Keela sighed with exasperation. "There's no sense in stressing out about it if we don't know for sure. Now go pee. I'll hold."

"Okay, okay. I'll be right back." I laid down the receiver and trudged to the bathroom to do something I never thought I'd do as a single woman—take a pregnancy test. I squatted over the toilet and tried to pee in a straight stream. It would only take three minutes for the dot to show up pink or not at all. It was quite possibly three of the longest minutes of my life.

At least everyone was gone. I needed peace and quiet. Queenie had gone to the store to pick up ground beef for dinner, and Bianca had taken Teeka to get her hair done, then to get ice cream. I figured I had a good hour or so before they returned—an hour that promised to be full of anxiety or prayer of thanksgiving.

The month had passed quickly. Work consumed much of my time, with the rest being claimed by Teeka. She was thriving under the diligent care of Queenie, Bianca, and myself and I was thriving under her unconditional love.

The turning point had been that fateful day at the beach.

Teeka's near drowning had stirred up feelings that I hadn't bothered to explore since Joanne's death. After that day, the questions about her mother had dwindled from daily to every-so often and it didn't seem to bother Teeka anymore that I didn't have an answer as to when Sharneesha would be joining us. She sometimes even called me Mommy if she was hurt, sleepy, or just wanted to be, which was more than fine with me. Every day with her seemed like sunshine and I was feeling more and more like her real mother.

"I'm back," I said and sat down at the desk, laying the indicator on a paper towel.

"How long does it take?" Keela asked.

"The package says three minutes."

"We'll start timing now just to be sure."

"So what do we do for the next three minutes?"

"Everything's going to be fine, Kingston. Don't worry."

"I'm a worrier. You know that."

We sat in silence for a few seconds before Keela chimed in again. "Anything yet?"

I rubbed my forehead in frustration. "You're only making it worse, Keela."

"Sorry." She cleared her throat. "Did I tell you that they're planning a baby shower for me at work?"

"Yes, you told me."

"Did I tell you that it's going to be at Bogart's?"

"Yes, you told me that, too. Can't you think of anything else to talk about besides babies?"

"My, my, my! Aren't we crotchety this morning? Seems to me like those hormones are kicking in already."

I looked down at the pregnancy test and my whole body felt like it was cemented to the chair. "I guess they are," I said, as a pink dot winked back at me. I blinked and looked again, but the color remained the same.

The wrought iron gate squeaked open, so I quickly wrapped the indicator in the paper towel, and tossed it in the waste paper basket.

"They are?" Keela asked, shock seeping through the phone.

"They most certainly are." I waved at Queenie as she passed through on her way to the back of the house.

"What exactly are you saying?"

I covered the phone and whispered, "Dammit, Keela, you know what I'm saying. I'm pregnant!"

Chapter 34

Two days later, when I walked down to Damon's house, it was all business. I didn't harbor any expectations or high hopes. Far from it. I just wanted to tell Damon that he was going to be a father and that I really did love and want to be with him after all. Then the ball would be in his court.

He'd been in Hope Bay for the past few weeks helping to build a community clinic. It had felt like a year.

Tiny opened the door with a smile and curtsey before ushering me back to his office. Damon was bent over his desk studying a medical chart, his finger saving his place in a thick textbook, a frown furrowing his brow. I cleared my throat to announce my presence and he jumped, startled. He didn't say anything as I closed the door and leaned up against it. A smile flirted with the corners of my lips as he sized me up. I had taken particular care with my dress; a casual fitted shirt and denim skirt hugged and showcased my assets just the way I wanted them to.

He nodded formally, then stood and indicated the chair next to him with a wave of his hand. "Would you like to sit down?"

I shook my head. "I won't be staying long. I can see you're in the middle of something." That was the excuse I gave, but in reality I didn't want to get too close. I was too busy gazing at his lips and imagining how sweet they would taste and looking at his hands and imagining them all over my body.

"Ms. Gladys was down this morning with a list of symptoms and I'm trying to come up with a diagnosis, but can't find anything. I think it's just loneliness. She's been sick almost once a week since her husband died. She's coming back in about an hour so I have some time." Damon shrugged. "But suit yourself. How's everything going with the estate?"

"It's going very well. Better than I could have expected. The community has been very responsive. Bianca has stayed to help. We're organizing workshops on etiquette, interviewing, and setting up tutoring sessions." Walking over, I dropped a check on his desk.

"Speaking of that, this is your first installment from the estate. Hopefully, we can sponsor a free clinic one day soon." Damon picked up the embossed envelope, but didn't open it. He turned it over once before stashing it in his top desk drawer. "How's Teeka?"

"She's good. She's been asking about you."

"I was going to come down this afternoon. I wish I could have come down sooner, but it's been busy since my return from Hope Bay," he explained, his eyes holding mine. "She's okay, isn't she?"

I nodded. "She's fine. I think her near-drowning has shaken me up more than her. And it made me more determined to make sure she's always taken care of. I've talked to the lawyer about filing for legal adoption."

"If her mother could just abandon her own flesh like that, then she's better off with you." Damon locked his fingers together behind his head.

"I feel the same way. It's going to take a minute to get used to this motherhood thing. It's a lot harder than it looks, but luckily I've had Bianca and Queenie to help me. At the rate we're going, Teeka's going to be spoiled rotten."

"A little spoiling never hurt nobody," Damon said with an amused grin on his face. "I always thought you'd make a great mother, but I'm sure you didn't walk all the way down here to talk about that. Something must be on your mind. So, what can I do for you?"

"You get right to the point, huh?" I shifted weight and took a deep breath. He was right, no use in beating around the bush. "Listen, Damon, I've been doing a lot of thinking about things you said before you left Chicago—about me thinking with my head and not my heart. Well, you're right. Pride can be an ugly thing and I've let it rule my life for too long. In your note you said that you didn't want to pressure me and that if I ever wanted something to happen between us, then it would be my move." I smiled. "Well, consider this my move."

"I'm sorry?" Damon asked, cupping his hand to his ear and leaning toward me.

"You heard me." I crossed my arms in front of me, each second feeling more and more unsure.

"No, I don't think I did," Damon answered as the corners of his mouth pulled back into a big cheesy grin.

"See, that's why I wasn't going to come over here." I pointed my finger at him. "You always make things so damn difficult."

"What are you talking about, Kingston?"

"You know good and damn well what I'm talking about."

"I'm not quite sure I do, so show me," Damon said and leaned back in his chair, the dare shining in his eyes.

Accepting the challenge, I walked over to him and ran my hands over his shoulders and up his neck until they were cupping his face. If he needed me to prove that I was ready, then that was what I would damn well do.

I leaned down until my lips were touching his. "I love you, Damon. I never thought I could ever love anyone as much as I love you. I love you more now than I did ten years ago, and I will love you more tomorrow than I do today. You complete me. Forever would not be enough time to spend with you." Then I kissed him with all the feelings that had been penned up for so long, the feelings that I was no longer ashamed to show.

Damon ended the kiss with a gentle push and stood. "Sounds good to finally hear that, Kingston, but you've made me wait a long time. I think I may need a few days to think about this."

His words came as a slap in the face. I felt as if he had just poured a pitcher of ice-cold water over my head and I struggled to keep my composure.

"That's fair," I said despite the war that was raging in my head. "You know where to find me. Let me know what you decide." I turned to leave, determined to get home before the sobs that were building forced their way out. But before I could reach the door, Damon grabbed my hand and spun me around.

"I was just joking." His eyes danced with merriment.

"Well it wasn't funny, Damon." I started crying, purely out of anger and embarrassment.

"I'm sorry. I couldn't resist. You know I love you. How could you not know that?" He sat down and pulled me onto his lap. "I just want you to be sure."

"No, I want you to be sure because it's no longer just me. Teeka is a part of my life now, so we come as a package deal."

"Then, I accept."

"Wait, not so fast. There's something else I need to tell you."

"I'm listening," Damon said, as he nuzzled my ear.

"I'm pregnant."

His lips paused in midair. "Come again."

"I'm pregnant," I repeated slowly, but Damon's face remained blank. "Don't look at me like you're about to ask me who the father is."

Damon frowned. "I wasn't going to ask you that. I know it's my baby. You were born to be the mother of my child. I'm just trying to figure out how you feel about it."

"I'm happy about it; a little surprised that I'm now the mother of two or about to be."

"How far along are you?"

"Just a few weeks. I used one of those early pregnancy tests."

"So Christmas?"

"That's what I figure. I need you to recommend a doctor so I can get formally examined." When he grinned, I added, "And no, it's not going to be you."

"There are a lot of qualified gynecologists in Kingston."

"Good. And Keela's gonna come for awhile after the baby is born."

"Keela knows?" Damon asked, a hurt look on his face. "Why didn't you just come and tell me?"

"I needed time to think about all of this. I wanted to know what I was going to do before I came to talk to you."

"And what do you want to do?"

"I want to be with the father of my child."

"Then the only question left is do you want to be married to the father of your child?"

I tried not to swoon. "Are you asking me to marry you?"

"I guess I am."

"Good, because if you hadn't asked me, then I would have asked you. When?" I asked as if this were a business meeting and we were in the middle of negotiations.

"As soon as possible." He smiled before burying his face in my stomach and rubbing his head back and forth slowly. "I can't believe my baby is in here." He kissed my tummy. "You're not showing at all."

"I'm only a few weeks," I said as I pulled the necklace that Damon had given me for Christmas out of the pocket of my miniskirt. I passed it to him and he clasped it around my neck. He ran his hands up the back of my thighs and traced the outline of my lace bikini while I pressed my lips to the top of his head. Then, I came to my senses.

Fighting against the tingle in my stomach, I swatted his hands away. "Don't even try it, Damon. We're gonna do it right this time. Pregnant or not, we don't make love again until we're husband and wife."

"Not at all? You mean you're completely shutting down the sugar factory?"

"Yep. So don't even think about trying to open the door. It's locked and I have the only key."

"So I can't do something like this?" Damon ran his tongue along the waistband of my denim mini-skirt.

"Definitely not something like that," I said, but didn't pull away; just the opposite, I leaned in a little bit closer.

"Then this wouldn't be allowed." He slowly slipped a finger inside of me.

"You damn right it wouldn't be." I wiggled my hips, tried to escape, but he would not be dissuaded.

"So then tell me, Kingston. What about something like this?" In went another finger.

"Damon," I breathed, feeling as if I were going to burn from the inside out.

"Wait, I have another question. Is this on the list, too?" And suddenly my mini skirt was pushed all the way up and his tongue had made it to the sugar factory. I tossed my head back and prepared myself for an out-of-body experience; but just as the factory was about to explode, there was a short rap on the door.

"Doctor," Tiny's voice squeaked. "Your next patient is here."

Damon swore viciously under his breath as I fought to control the tidal wave that was crashing inside.

"Give me five minutes to finish up and then bring her back."

"Yes, sir," Tiny said, her heels clicking all the way to the front room.

"Just five minutes?" I teased.

"I'm sorry, sweetheart. Ms. Gladys is here for her diagnosis," Damon said as I straightened my skirt over my hips, pushed my hair back into place. "Are you ready?" Damon kissed me tenderly on the lips, still tasting of me, then touched the chain that lay against my chest. It was now a symbol of our love.

I nodded.

"Ready for everything?" Damon asked and I smiled, full of the knowledge that I really was ready for all that God had chosen to give me. Damon returned the smile and opened the door just as Tiny's fist was raised in the air, prepared to knock again; an older woman right behind her stared at us over horn rimmed glasses.

"Tiny, Ms. Gladys, I'd like to introduce you to my fiancée, Kingston."

Tiny fluttered, while Ms. Gladys offered her congratulations.

"I'll be down for dinner," he said with a quick kiss on the cheek, already claiming his territory. I nodded and kissed Damon one more time, leaving Ms. Gladys and Tiny with more than a little to gossip about before heading home and trying to come up with the words on how to break the news to Bianca and Teeka.

Chapter 35

"Mommy, mommy!"

I swung away from the full-length mirror, scooping up the cascading ivory satin train just in time to save it from being trampled. "Hi, sweetie," I said and kneeled down so Teeka could wrap her arms around my neck, kissing her loudly on the forehead before pulling back, and giving her the once over. "My, don't you look pretty in your new dress!"

The purple lilacs on her dress danced as she spun around the room like a ballerina, beaming at the compliment.

"And you look absolutely stunning, Kingston," Bianca commented as she walked into the Church's choir room that doubled today as my dressing room. She was wearing an adult version of Teeka's dress and would stand beside me as my maid of honor. Her hair was twisted in a French bun sprinkled with small lilacs. With a smile, I rose carefully, not wanting to step on the hem of my dress.

"I can't believe you're getting married." Her voice broke and I grasped her hand. "Please, don't start crying. You'll make me start crying and then I'll ruin my makeup."

"I'm sorry. I'm just so happy for you," she said sincerely.

"Thanks, Bianca."

Bianca turned to Teeka. "Want to go with me?" Teeka answered by grabbing her hand. "I'm gonna go check on things out there again. Give you a few minutes by yourself."

I watched them leave, hands clasped and their arms swinging between them. I couldn't ask for more; Damon, Keela and Bianca had accepted Teeka into the family without question and I was about to marry the man of my dreams and have his child.

Standing in front of the mirror, I turned from side to side. Small, iridescent pearls decorated the bodice of my wedding dress that tapered to a cinched waist and form-fitted skirt. I had elected to leave my hair down, but did agree to let the beautician straighten it at Bianca's insistence. It was parted and fell gracefully to the middle of my back. Mama Grace's simple pearl drop earrings dotted my ears and her pearl necklace was clasped around my neck.

"You don't even need make-up today. That 'pregnant and I'm about to be a married woman' glow is more than enough—you could light the whole church up," Keela said just as her face appeared in the mirror. Our eyes caught and we smiled.

"I'm so glad you could make it, Keela. I thought I was going to have to get married without you."

"Never that. You just have to repay me the money I used to bribe the doctor to release me to travel this far in my pregnancy."

"I would have gone to Chicago and kicked that doctor's ass if he hadn't agreed to let you come."

"Yeah, well, now I might deliver this baby at the reception." She rubbed her protruding belly, a hand pressed in the small of her back. "Just wait, you'll understand soon enough." Her maternity bridesmaid's dress made for extra room just a month ago was stretched tightly against her stomach.

"Damon's a good doctor. You'll be all right."

Keela laughed. "Does he have any of the good drugs hidden in that tuxedo? 'Cause I don't want to wake up until it's over." Keela rubbed her tummy. "But today's not about me, it's about you."

Bianca and Teeka walked back in the room. "Looks like things are actually going to get started on time. Are we ready?"

"I'm ready!" Teeka squealed, her hand shooting in the air.

"Well, if you're ready, Teeka, then I guess I am, too," I teased, rubbing my hands together. "Let's get this show on the road."

"I'll let the organist know. And we should take our places." She nodded to Keela.

I took one last look in the mirror before turning to face them—there wasn't a dry eye amongst us.

"I'm so glad my best friends are here with me today." I clasped their hands with mine. "I couldn't imagine doing it without you guys. I love both of you."

"And we love you, too," Keela said, pulling us into a group hug. Teeka struggled her way into the middle and wrapped her arms around my legs.

"Me, too, me too!" she yelled.

"Yes, you too, Teeka!" I smiled down at her and gave her a special hug. "Now let's get out there and marry Daddy."

We walked from the choir room to the foyer of Coke Methodist Church and lined up behind the oak double doors that led to the sanctuary.

This was the church where my grandparents had been married, I had been christened, and we said goodbye to Mama Grace. My union to Damon would start the cycle of life once again.

The doors flung open and the organ started playing Teddy P's song, "Greatest Inspiration."

I hummed as Teeka walked in first, tossing roses to the left and to the right, only stopping when she reached Damon's side.

"You're my latest, my greatest inspiration," crooned Teddy.

Damon stood alone, handsomely dressed in his tuxedo. Two of his cousins that I'd just met the night before stood with him, a little off to the side. Reverend Pegue loomed over the proceedings from the pulpit.

Bianca looked back one last time before walking down the aisle, followed by Keela. I would tease her later about waddling at the reception.

Finally, it was just me. When the organist segued into the traditional wedding march, I clasped my bouquet closer to my breast and looked at my prize. The church fell silent and eventually the well-wishers that packed the pews disappeared.

It was just Damon and me. And as I stood looking into his sugar brown eyes—I saw that what was imprinted on my soul was imprinted on his, too.

In that moment, I knew that I had everything that I'd ever need right here in this church.

Nikki Woods

Nikki Woods, the author of Easier Said Than Done, is a Multi-media personality, Social Media and Personal Branding Coach, Motivational Speaker and Voice-over artist, and the CEO of Nikki Woods Media. She is also the senior producer of the acclaimed, nationally-syndicated Tom Joyner Morning Show (TJMS), the most successful syndicated urban radio show in history reaching more than 8 million people on a daily basis. She is responsible for the engaging on-air content heard each morning on the over-100 affiliate radio stations that air the award-winning program.

Woods is also a "TJMS" contributor, dishing out her own brand of info-tainment on weekend events and activities in the segment; she created and produces, "What in the Weekend with Nikki Woods." She can also be seen and heard on a variety of programs, including "The TJMS Community Watch" on WSRB Soul 106.3, their Chicago affiliate; and "Beyond the Studio" celebrity interviews on BlackAmericaWeb.com. Her "Mamas Gone Wild" website and weekly blog entries on BlackAmericaWeb.com highlight—with insight and hilarity—the ups and downs of being a hard-working radio producer by morning, an ever-patient classroom mom by afternoon and adventurous mother of two by night.

As a highly sought after keynote speaker, who serves as both an OWN ambassador for Pretty Brown Girl Inc., Nikki has earned the title of Global Visibility Expert and continues to reach millions and growing using multi-media to empower and train audiences with messages and methods for excelling in business, marketing and personal growth.

Find her on the web: www.nikkiwoodsmedia.com

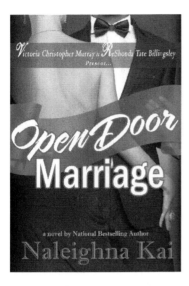
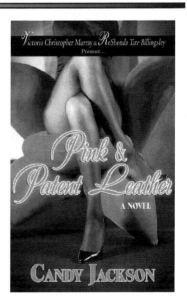

Printed in Great Britain
by Amazon